RED STATION

RED STATION

Adrian Magson

This first world edition published 2010
in Great Britain and in the USA by
SEVERN HOUSE PUBLISHERS LTD of
9–15 High Street, Sutton, Surrey, England, SM1 1DF.
Trade paperback edition first published
in Great Britain and the USA 2011 by
SEVERN HOUSE PUBLISHERS LTD.

Magson

British Library Cataloguing in Publication Data

Magson, Adrian.
   Red Station. – (A Harry Tate thriller)
   1. Great Britain. MI5 – Fiction. 2. South Ossetia War,
   2008 – Fiction. 3. Conspiracies – Fiction. 4. Suspense
   fiction.
   I. Title II. Series
   823.9'2-dc22

ISBN-13: 978-0-7278-6939-5   (cased)
ISBN-13: 978-1-84751-277-2   (trade paper)

Severn House Publishers support The Forest Stewardship Council [FSC],
the leading international forest certification organisation. All our titles that
are printed on Greenpeace-approved FSC-certified paper carry the FSC logo.

 **Mixed Sources**
Product group from well-managed
forests and other controlled sources
www.fsc.org Cert no. SA-COC-1565
FSC   © 1996 Forest Stewardship Council

Typeset by Palimpsest Book Production Ltd.,
Falkirk, Stirlingshire.
Printed and bound in Great Britain by the
MPG Books Group, Bodmin, Cornwall.

For Ann,
who always believed Harry would make it home.

ACKNOWLEDGEMENTS

Self-belief is one thing. But the support of the following friends has been enormous: Matt Hilton and Sheila Quigley, who know just what it's like; Mike Stotter and Ali Karim of *Shots Magazine*, who were so quick to welcome me into the crime/mystery community; Adrian Muller for spreading the buzz; Lizzie Hayes and Sue Lord for their absolute belief; James Nightingale, eagle-eyed editor; and last but certainly not least, super-agent David Headley, for his energy, friendship and absolute commitment to *Red Station* and beyond.

Thank you, all.

ONE

Autumn 2008

Death came in at three minutes to four on a sluggish morning tide, and changed Harry Tate's life forever. It edged up a shrouded Essex inlet, a scrubby white fifty-foot motor launch with a fly bridge, its engine puttering softly against the slow current. The exhaust sounds were muffled by a heavy, early mist rolling along the banks, blanketing the dark marshland like cold candyfloss.

Three figures stood outlined by a flush of refracted light from the open cockpit. One was on the forward deck, a swirl of dreadlocks framing his head like a war helmet. He was holding a thick pole balanced on one shoulder. Number two, the helmsman, was a bulky shape up on the fly bridge, head turning constantly between the instrument panel and the banks on either side.

The third man stood on a swimming platform at the stern, inches above the murky wake. Skeletal, with long, straggly hair under a baseball cap, he had one hand down by his side, the other bracing himself on the rear rail.

'It's Pirates of the frigging Caribbean!' The whisper drilled softly into Harry's earpiece, gently mocking, forcing a smile in spite of the tension in his chest. The voice belonged to Bill Maloney, his MI5 colleague, in cover fifty yards along the bank to his right.

A light breeze lifted off the water, brushing past Harry's position behind a hummock of coarse grass, fanning his face with the sour smell of mud and decay. The sickly tang of diesel oil seemed to ooze out of the ground everywhere, and something was seeping through his trousers. He tried not to think about the kinds of toxic waste festering beneath him from decades of commerce, skulduggery and neglect.

He toggled his radio. 'Where the *hell* are you, Blue Team?' The query was strained with urgency. As Ground Controller, he'd been chasing the back-up police unit for fifteen minutes with no response.

Still nothing. Accident or a comms malfunction? Either way, they weren't here. He swore softly. Having been slashed at the last minute – economic demands, was the vague explanation – and now with the support van lost somewhere in the darkness, they were down to three men. With what was rumoured to be concealed in the boat's bilges, from bales of hash to 'bricks' of heroin, each containing up to fifty individual pay-and-go bags, and enough methamphetamine crystals to send half the kids in London off their heads for a month, the prize was too valuable. They needed all the help they could get.

But it wasn't there.

He leaned to his right and peeled aside some strands of grass, eyeing the misty darkness where Blue Team should have been in position. Nothing. Instead, he heard a click in his ear, then a hiss of static.

'That's a negative, Red One . . . repeat negative. We're up to our axles in mud, five hundred yards from your O.P. The fucking ground's like molasses. Blue Team out.'

Harry's gut turned to water, the urgency now the bitter pre-taste of panic.

With a narrow window the previous day to reconnoitre the area where the shipment was coming in, he and Maloney had ambled in on foot, posing as sometime fishermen on an idle day out. The inlet, bordered by a muddy track, was mostly used by working boats, weekend sailors and jet-skiers. The going, while reasonably solid underfoot, showed some evidence of a spongy sub-layer.

They'd spent an hour in the area, fishing, sipping beer and competitively skimming stones on the water, all the while scouting for cover in hollows, bushes and overturned or rotting boats. Other than a woman walking her dog and a couple of dinghies making laboured trips to boats further along, they had seen no-one who shouldn't be there.

As they were leaving, it had started to rain; hard, slashing drops like liquid gobstoppers, pounding the softer patches into mud holes and blanketing the harder ground with a layer of filthy water. They had highlighted these areas on a laminated map for special attention.

Blue Team clearly hadn't read the signs.

Harry closed his eyes against a rising nausea. Of all the

luck. He could be at Jean's place right now, replete and warmed by her infectious humour, enjoying her company. Instead, he was stuffed with a growing disaster of Titanic proportions.

Except that he knew deep down that this was as much a drug for him as the narcotics on the boat were for others.

'Stand by.' He toggled the switch to warn the other two men and watched the boat slide by thirty yards away. It was too late to abort, too risky to do nothing; within hours the stuff on board would be hitting the streets, flooding veins with its false promise and sending the weak and vulnerable to an early, hazy oblivion.

It was now or never.

He was clutching a handful of grass with his right hand. He forced himself to let go and slid his fingers into his jacket, to the reassuring touch of a semi-automatic.

'Is it a go or not?' Parrish, the third man. A firearms officer on loan from the local force, he was to Harry's right, close by the water's edge, positioned to cut off the boat's retreat. A last-minute replacement for an MI5 officer off sick, he was nervy, impatient and looking to prove himself.

'Wait!' Tate breathed, and hoped the idiot wasn't about to leap from cover and do a Rambo along the bank. As he spoke, the helmsman on the boat called a soft warning to his companions and cut the engine, steering the nose towards a short wooden jetty jutting out from the near bank.

'Blue Team . . . you out yet?' It was a wasted call, but gave him a few more seconds before having to make a final, no-going-back decision.

'Negative, Red One. We're not going anywhere. Sorry.'

'You forgotten how to fucking *run*?' he blasted back, and instantly regretted it. Five hundred yards in full gear, stumbling through the dark; even with night-vision kit they'd be like a pack of elephants.

He decided to give it another two minutes, to allow the boat's crew to split up and come ashore. Divide and conquer. Maybe, he thought wryly, when they saw they were surrounded by just three men stranded on a muddy bank in the dark, they'd give up without a fight.

Then bad luck and timing chose that moment to join the party.

From Harry's left, the opposite end of the approach track

from Blue Team's last position, the familiar harsh roar of a
Land Rover engine pierced the night, and a dark, square shape
burst into view. Its lights were on low, but were sufficient to
burn through the mist and highlight the surrounding bank . . .
and the white hull of the docking vessel.

TWO

'*F uck!*' Maloney's curse registered deep shock. 'Where
the hell did *he* spring from?' All approaches to the area
were supposed to have been shut off one hour ago. Any
sooner would have alerted the traffickers that their plans were
blown.

'What's happening?' Parrish again, and by the catch in his
voice, Harry knew that the firearms officer was about to make
a move.

'Hold your position!' He turned to focus on the approaching
car, gripping the hard outline of the gun and gathering his
legs beneath him. Either someone had stuffed up the security
cordon or the informant had lied about the smugglers' plans.

He used his radio. 'Red Three, this is Red One. A vehicle
just arrived. What the hell's going on out there?' Red Three
was another MI5 officer – a floater – operating the outer
cordon with the local police. He should have warned them
about the car's approach.

'Red Three?'

Silence.

'*Shit!*' He pounded his fist into the soft ground. What else
could go wrong?

The Land Rover slid to an untidy stop ten yards short of
the jetty, throwing up a spray of ground water. Both doors
opened and a man sprang from behind the wheel and ran
round to the passenger side. He appeared to be urging the
passenger – a young woman in a floaty dress – to stay inside,
but she had already slid from the car's high seat, followed by
the heavy beat of hip-hop music.

Christ, no, Harry thought, hardly able to believe his eyes.
This is all we fucking need . . .

As the driver tried to turn the girl back inside the car, he glanced at the boat ghosting into the jetty, its crew of three illuminated by the car's lights, and lifted a hand towards them.

But the girl didn't seem to understand.

'Hey, baby,' she cried plaintively, her voice slurred. 'Whassup? What're you doing?' She ducked past him and peered at the incoming vessel. 'Who're they?

As the boat brushed the jetty, the man with the dreadlocks moved forward on the deck, bouncing the pole up and down on his shoulder. Behind him, the figure on the rear platform got ready to jump ashore, a glint of something stubby and metallic in his free hand.

Harry Tate felt a kick of anguish deep in his gut.

'*Don't . . .!*'

Afterwards, he never was sure what he'd intended to say – something more definite, for certain – and nothing like the single, useless utterance which came out of his mouth. He pushed himself to his feet, muscles cramped after too long in the same position, and brought up his gun. It was a long shot for a handgun but doable; he'd managed under worse conditions before now. His instincts told him Maloney was still somewhere to his right, also ready and willing to mix it if he had to.

'Stop! Police! Don't move!'

It was Parrish. Shouting and running forward along the bank, faint in the reach of the car's headlights, he was swinging his Heckler & Koch in the air, the barrel aimed at the night sky. Harry couldn't tell if it was bravado or stupidity, but the gun was pointless if he wasn't going to use it.

And he was running across his colleagues' direct line of fire.

'Get down, you prick!' yelled Maloney.

Too late.

The man with the dreadlocks looked at Parrish, then turned back to the Land Rover and screamed in defiance. He swung the pole down from his shoulder, catching it with a solid smack in his other hand. The car headlights glinted off dark metal.

Shotgun.

The muzzle-blast ripped the night apart, and the driver of the Land Rover was punched off his feet. The girl screamed as he was torn from her grasp, and her legs sagged. She whirled round to see what was happening, incomprehension on her face. Then a stutter of automatic fire came from the man at the rear of the boat. It ripped into her, shredding the floaty dress and sent her spinning to join her companion.

Without pause, Dreadlocks swung his gun and pulled the trigger again. The heavy charge knocked Parrish over backwards. The helmsman shouted a warning and hauled on the wheel, surging away from the bank with a howl of engines. Taken by surprise, Dreadlocks grabbed for the side rail but missed. He sprawled headlong on the deck, while the man on the stern platform danced off-balance for a moment before grabbing the side bar and holding on tight.

Harry cursed. Whatever was housed below decks wasn't a standard engine, but something bigger – possibly twin diesels. The boat was already on its way out and would soon be gone for good if it wasn't stopped.

He took aim and squeezed the trigger, a controlled double-tap followed by another, then a third. He was aiming at the helmsman; stop the driver and the boat would go nowhere. The volley of shots was lost among the roar of the engines, and puny in contrast to the stunning blast of the shotgun. But a section of glass windshield exploded and the helmsman ducked as a chunk of moulding blew apart alongside the wheel.

Maloney was up and running, tracking the boat along the bank. He began firing steadily at the charging vessel, now nose-up as it increased speed, the wash flashing white against the sloping mud walls on either side.

At the stern, the man with the machine gun was trying to bring his weapon to bear, but was thrown off balance as the boat bounced and swayed in the narrow inlet. Dreadlocks, however, had regained his feet. Gripping the rail with one hand, he raised his shotgun and lined up on Maloney, barely thirty feet away and with nowhere to hide.

'Bill, down!' Harry bellowed, and as Maloney threw himself to the ground, still firing, he emptied his clip at the gunman.

Shots from both guns caught the man high in the body, flipping him overboard.

Seconds later, the boat had gone, leaving in its wake three bodies on the shore and a fourth bobbing in the cold, black water.

THREE

'**W**e're sending you out of the country. Pro tem.'
The speaker was George Paulton, Harry Tate's
superior and Operations Director for MI5. His
office in Thames House had a fine view of the river below,
but the scenery was lost on the three men facing each other.

'Why?' Harry stared at his superior, then flicked a glance at
a heavy figure standing in one corner. The man, nameless and
grey as battleship paint, had said nothing when Harry had entered
the room, and there had been no introductions.

Two days after the shooting, and a raft of internal MI5 and
Metropolitan Police enquiries had been kicked off with star-
tling speed, engineered to analyse failure and avoid blame.
Still numbed with feelings of guilt and remorse about the
deaths of the young couple and Parrish, Harry had been called
to Paulton's office to face what he was sure would be intensive questioning, yet maybe a reassurance that all would be
well in the end.

Now he wasn't so sure.

'Needs must, I'm afraid,' Paulton explained smoothly. 'The
press will be all over this like a rash, especially after Stockwell.
The de Menezes affair,' he added unnecessarily, and adjusted
a buff folder on his desk.

'That wasn't the same thing,' Harry protested. 'We didn't
have enough men—'

'Maybe not. But we have to view things in a broader context.
There are . . . gaps in the sequence of events. Gaps we need to
deal with. We can't do that while there's a danger you might be
compromised by the press discovering your name.'

'How could they?' Harry looked from Paulton to the other
man. He didn't like the way the conversation was going.
'There's no way they can find out, unless someone talks. And
what gaps?'

'You're right: on balance, they shouldn't find out. But we
can't take that chance.' He waved at the folder, which Harry
guessed contained his and Maloney's debriefing notes. 'As to

gaps . . . there's the question of why the secure perimeter around the site allowed two civilians to pass through. And why the police officer on assignment wasn't managed correctly. It doesn't look good.'

'I've already been over this.' Harry had faced a three-person committee earlier that morning. A woman from Legal and two men, one from Human Resources and the other a limp-wristed individual from Operations. All faceless, all void of any emotion, they had absorbed detail like sponges but offered no help or empathy. It was as if his career so far counted for nothing.

It had been like facing a death tribunal.

'We're trying to safeguard your situation,' Paulton purred.

'Is that what it is?' Harry felt an uncommon rebellion building. His dealings so far with Paulton had been relatively few and at best remote. But he had always seemed to be on the side of his officers. Now something different seemed to be hovering in the air. 'Why do I get the feeling that the fault for what happened is being shifted my way?'

'There were failings, you can't deny that.' There was a hint of steely reproof in Paulton's voice.

'Damn right there were. Like the last-minute reduction in team numbers. Economics, I was told. What kind of economics?' Harry continued, before the other could interrupt, 'We were in the middle of an operation!'

'You could have vetoed it.' Paulton tapped the folder, his cheeks flushing. 'If you felt there were insufficient resources at your disposal, you could have said . . . *should* have said. It's every officer's right . . . every officer's judgement.'

'And let those drugs out on the streets? We'd have been crucified and you know it.' Harry felt himself beginning to boil over. He breathed deeply. Losing it here and now wouldn't do any good. But after the meaningless debriefing with the three Stooges earlier, he could sense the drawbridges going up all around him. He wondered if this was how establishment stitch-ups began.

'It was still your call.' The dig came from the man in the corner; pointed, cold, unfriendly. Silent until now, he had clearly decided to wade in on Paulton's side.

'Really?' Harry turned, the heat rushing to his face. 'And who the hell are you? When did you last go out on an op?' He glared at the man, saw only empty, hooded eyes staring back from a well-fed face. 'When did you last lie in shit and sewage for hours at a time, waiting to face men armed with automatic weapons – men who don't give a flying fuck about law and order because of what they're bringing in? You think they give a pig's tit about "stop, police" or us waving our ID? They don't.'

'The planning—' Paulton tried to interject, but Harry was on a roll, sensing his future going up in a fireball.

'The planning was done by the book, with all the assessment boxes ticked, just the way the suits like it. But guess what – someone was too concerned with budgets, targets and key performance indicators!'

'Tate—' The unnamed man lifted a pudgy hand, his eyes as cold as granite.

'It's *Mister* Tate to you,' Harry growled. 'Those two civilians died because they were allowed to penetrate a compromised security cordon and ended up in the wrong place at the wrong time. As for not 'managing' the dead officer, that's bullshit. He ran across the firing line. He was brave, certainly, but stupid; he should have done as he was told and kept his bloody head down.' He could have added that in running out from cover, Parrish had probably exacerbated the situation and drawn fire on to the couple while using their arrival as a distraction. But he didn't say it; the man was dead. 'Ask Maloney – he'll tell you.'

'Maloney has made his report. He has been taken off operational duties pending an enquiry.' Paulton fixed him with a glare. 'As of now, you are not to have any contact with him. Understood?'

'Why? That's ridiculous. He's my number two—'

'*Was* your number two. As of this minute, we're offering you a new posting. Overseas. It's a career position, with additional benefits at an enhanced grade.' He gave a thin smile. 'Should help your pension entitlements, I'd have thought.'

'Jesus, the *pension*!' Harry wanted to spit, he was so mad. 'For how long? Doing what?'

Paulton shrugged. 'For as long as necessary. Until things calm down, at least. You'll be briefed on arrival by your head of station. I recommend you take the post.' He studied his fingernails. 'Right now, I don't see any alternatives.'

They were protecting themselves, Harry knew. They wanted

him out of the way while all the official wailing and gnashing
of teeth went on and they could build a credible explanation.
But what were his options? Stay and face a public enquiry,
the token guilt figure? Resign and be hounded by the press?
Or take their dubious offer and work his way back?

'How long do I have to think about it?'

'You don't. You leave today.'

Against all his instincts, Harry took the offer.

After leaving Paulton's office, Harry went home to pack a single
bag and make a few phone calls. To friends to say he would be
away for a while; to Jean, a slim red-head in her forties who
referred to herself with dry wit as the OD – Occasional Date.

Instead of Jean, he got Felicity, her Sloaney business partner
in a west end flower business.

'Off again? She'll be sorry she missed you.'

'Really?' Harry wasn't so sure. Jean knew what he did but
had never asked questions. Until now, he'd taken it for a judi-
cious lack of interest.

'Obtuse man.' Felicity's voice was friendly, gently reproachful.
'Don't you know you're the only person who makes her smile?
Come back soon.'

He put down the phone amid conflicting emotions; resumed
packing to get his mind in gear. The department would deal
with the letting of his flat while he was gone, so he boxed up
his personal things and left them in the middle of the floor
for removal and storage.

A short taxi drive took him west to RAF Northolt, where he
was shunted aboard a military plane and handed a flask of
coffee, a bottle of chilled water and a tuna sandwich. He took
his seat and found he had two escorts sitting nearby. Military
policemen by the look of them, hard and capable. They ignored
him completely. He knew that if he tried to get off, they'd
have him face down on the cabin floor before he reached the
door.

He ignored them in return. Drank his coffee, ate half his
sandwich, saved the rest for later. Not that he liked tuna especially. But better than nothing. He fell asleep thinking of Jean.

They prodded him awake at Frankfurt. Gummy-eyed, he
stared through the window. The plane had stopped behind a

military hangar, shrouded in shadow, distant arc lights casting an eerie glow. He was urged down the steps and into a plain, white van reeking of oil and stale sweat. Three minutes later he was in the civilian terminal, where he was told where to collect his tickets for his onward flight. He signed a docket at the desk and turned to see if his escorts were coming, too.

They had disappeared.

FOUR

'In hindsight, Tate should have had more back-up and support.' Paulton tossed his listeners an early *mea culpa* to be going on with. It was chicken bones at best, probably pointless, but might keep them at bay for a while and sit well on the record should a board of enquiry be convened.

'Is that all you can say? After all that work and preparation?' Gareth Nolan, Deputy Commissioner for Operations in the Metropolitan Police, scowled across the table. He was clearly intent on levelling blame towards MI5 for the failures. 'You're defending the man?'

They were in an anonymous, polished room in the bowels of a building off Horse Guards Avenue. The flak from the failed operation was beginning to settle around everyone's ears as the story gradually became public knowledge, and this was not the only meeting Paulton had been called to.

'It's not a matter of defence,' he said curtly. 'It's the facts I'm interested in.'

The senior policeman shrugged it off. 'It was a bloody cock-up, right from the start! It cost one of my men his life, *and* two innocent civilians. Your man – Tate, is it? – should be charged with incompetence at the very least! What is he – a trainee, fresh out of university?'

'*He* is a former army officer,' Paulton said calmly, a defensive stance for the record rather than loyalty to his man. 'He served with distinction in Kosovo and Iraq, among others, but he isn't Superman. Circumstances went against him . . . against the team. It happens.' He smiled coldly, adding, 'Besides, if I understand the facts, it was your officer who put himself at risk; your team who got stuck driving their van into a mud-wallow. Don't you teach them ground-reading skills anymore?'

'*Gentlemen.*' The voice of the third person in the room cut off Nolan's intended retort, leaving him fuming impotently. 'Let's press on, shall we?' Marcella Rudmann, chair of a Joint Intelligence Subcommittee overseeing security operations, flipped open a folder in front of her. 'This business is appalling by anybody's standards. Which is why this meeting involves just the three of us . . . so far.'

The subtle warning did not go unnoticed by the two men. They were in session with one of the most powerful women in Whitehall, against whom arguments were like light rain on a metal roof. She had the Prime Minister's confidence and the support of senior cabinet members.

'Two civilians dead – one the daughter of a local VIP, we believe – a courageous firearms officer killed and one dead drug-runner. I couldn't care less about the last one, but the other three are going to keep the press on our collective necks for months to come. What are you doing about it?'

'Doing?' Paulton raised an eyebrow, although he knew perfectly well what Marcella Rudmann was alluding to. A head had to roll and, more importantly, had to be seen to roll. More than that, any source of embarrassment had to vanish quietly, beyond the reach of the press. He felt for a moment the spectre of blame settling around his neck like an icy collar. If anyone had to take the fall, it should be the weasel in uniform across the table from him; it had been his men who had thrown the drugs bust into disarray after many months of work, leaving the MI5 operators and the on-loan firearms officer to deal with the ensuing firefight. There was also the manpower cuts forced on them at the last minute by the Home Office; cuts meaning that resources were tailored to the threat level involved. Intelligence reports had advised that the threat level of the operation in Essex was likely to be low, and therefore required minimum personnel on the ground.

It had been a bad decision, but one Paulton himself had reluctantly agreed to. Outgunned and on foot, Tate and the others hadn't stood a chance. He wondered idly whether senior police officers were issued with swords on which they could fall. Probably not; their health and safety department wouldn't allow them near anything sharp.

'About Tate.' Rudmann was in her fifties, attractive and poised, but possessed of an aggressive approach which belied her looks. She had a reputation for caring little about individual sensibilities or rank, evidenced by several big-gun civil service carcasses littering the ground behind her.

Paulton forced himself to remain calm. Was it really going to be this simple? Had she just given him a clear, unambiguous signal that the man on the ground was to take *all* the blame? He sighed; he'd be stupid to toss it back in her face. Tough on Tate, especially at his time of life. Forty-something, he seemed to recall.

Better for himself, though. If he was careful.

Nolan wasn't slow to pick up the inference, and snickered in triumph. 'Tell me, Paulton, what *do* you do with security types you want rid of? You can hardly send them down to the local job centre, can you? Or have them spilling their guts by writing their memoirs.'

Paulton shot him a look of genuine loathing and resisted the instinct to mention the Stockwell tube shooting in 2005, by a police marksman. Instead, he replied, 'Actually, we execute them. Saves time and paperwork. We could always extend the practice to your lot, if you like. Care to be the first candidate?'

Nolan's face paled and he began to protest. But Rudmann's hand came down flat on the table, the rings on her fingers giving the sharp, flat echo of a gunshot.

'Your solution, George.' It wasn't a question.

'You mean here and now?' He was damned if he was going to give her an answer in front of this jumped-up traffic cop – not when it meant admitting he was surrendering the head of one of his officers. It would be tantamount to admitting that he had the guts of a slug. He slid a glance at his watch.

Tate's flight should be taking off anytime now. A few hours and he'd be beyond reach. For good.

Rudmann's hand drifted ominously towards a phone at her side. 'Make it quick, George. Time's running out.'

He gave in, convincing himself he was fighting his corner but battening down on the tiny worm of self-contempt seeping into his bones.

'It's taken care of,' he said with feigned reluctance, aware that Nolan would practically soil his pants hearing what he was about to say. 'We have a place . . . a posting. It's a recent innovation. It will put Tate beyond the reach of the press, or . . .' he hesitated, eyeing Nolan, '. . . anyone else who goes looking for him.'

'What sort of place?' Rudmann had been fingering her watch, no doubt late for another meeting. But she stopped at this latest revelation.

'A branch office. I don't want to disclose the precise location, but it's not in this country.'

Nolan's eyebrows shot up to join his receding hairline. 'How? Five doesn't have jurisdiction out of the country.' He looked at Rudmann for support.

'Actually, you'd be surprised where we have jurisdiction.' Paulton gave him his nastiest smile, pleased to have taken the policeman by surprise. 'But that's all I'm saying.' He waited for Rudmann to insist. This one should be a definite no-go area, even for her.

She nodded. 'Very well.' She closed the folder before her and stood up. 'That's all, gentlemen.'

Nolan looked crestfallen at being frozen out, but hurried away, no doubt eager to begin spreading tales. Paulton watched him go, determined not to share even the same corridor space with the man in case he was tempted to do something physical.

He turned and faced Rudmann. Her expression was a mask.

FIVE

'I wasn't going to insist,' Rudmann said quietly after Nolan had gone. 'Especially in front of that odious little creature. But there are others who will. Is it wise sending Tate to this . . . posting?'

It suddenly occurred to Paulton that she might already know about the place he was referring to. He couldn't think how, but she undoubtedly had contacts he wasn't aware of; resources he didn't know about. It was an unsettling thought. 'The PM, you mean?' He caught a hint of perfume and wondered vaguely what it was. And where she daubed it.

'Probably not. But his office. They will want to be sure

Tate isn't going to pop up somewhere foreign and start talking. That really would be a disaster – for everyone.'

'He won't.' Paulton mentally gagged at the idea; it would be a career killer. The decision to tell her something – anything – was easily made. It might keep her off his back and satisfy others that a head had rolled; that all was well in the world. Most would see it as a classic display of self-defence – a civil service skill customarily absorbed on the first day in the job. Not that Tate would appreciate the subtlety. 'He's been assigned to the modern equivalent of Fort Zinderneuf. It's remote, unpleasant, and he'll be monitored to ensure he doesn't go AWOL. It should suffice.'

'I see.' She gave him a sharp look. 'You'd planned this already.'

'I thought it might be on the cards, yes, after . . . previous incidents. It's a precautionary measure.'

'How astute. But why? What's so special about Tate?'

He paused for several beats, wondering how much to tell her. Thrown a small bone, it might be enough to put her off-track for the time being.

'Nothing, as such,' he said finally, choosing his words with care. This could come back and bite him on the arse if he said the wrong thing. 'Tate's old school; knows things we'd rather he didn't get prised out of him by a clever hack. He's one of those intelligence officers who crept up on the outside rails without being noticed; diligent, solid, good at his job, does what he's told most of the time.'

'But?'

'He can be bolshie when he thinks he's right. It's best we keep him out of the way.' He could have added that Harry Tate had refused to play the game of musical chairs which passed for a career path around here, but he'd been around long enough and deep enough to know where several skeletons were buried. Even if he didn't know that he knew. It might be a good time to ensure it stayed that way.

The main fact was that Tate, good and obedient servant that he was, was feeling justifiably annoyed at being left dangling out in the Essex marshland. Reason enough to move him out of anyone's sight and hearing before he exploded.

Rudmann seemed satisfied. 'How long will he be there?'

'For as long as we think fit. He'll be allowed back eventually – subject to safeguards, of course. No contact with home and hearth, all communications with Thames House to come via his head of station. Even his family won't know where he is.' Not that Tate had any, he recalled. Divorced and likely to stay that way. An odd fish. Probably a drinker, on the quiet. With a shudder, he realized the man actually had the potential to be the worst kind of spook to have on your hands when the shit hit the fan.

'Who else knows about this place?' Rudmann dragged him back.

'Six. But nobody else.' He held his breath, aware that he was on thin ice. What if she asked why this had not come up before?

'I see. How often do you . . . use it?'

'Rarely, so far. As I said, it's fairly new. Experimental, you might say.' He forestalled further questions by asking, 'Is there anything else?'

Rudmann shook her head. There was something of the prude in her expression, as if finding something about him and his world which she did not like. Even so, it was evident that she was fascinated by what he had just told her.

'What on earth do you call this place?'

'There is no official designation.'

'Why not?'

He shrugged. 'If nobody has logged it, nobody will find it.'

There was a lengthy silence, then, 'But you must have a name for it.'

'Yes. We call it Red Station.'

SIX

Harry Tate celebrated his birthday with a miniature of Bell's whisky while waiting for his bag to come off the plane. Between sips, he was trying to convince himself he'd been born lucky.

There was little talk in the drab terminal; most of his fellow passengers were in deep shock after an aborted first landing. About to drop on to the runway, the pilot of the Antonov AN

24 had suddenly hauled the nose up without warning, the
ageing engines screaming under full power as they fought to
claw the aircraft back into the thin air above Mukhrani airport,
Georgia. Cries of alarm in several languages had joined the
sounds of tumbling crockery in the galley. But the near-stall
manoeuvre had paid off, dragging them in a juddering curve
away from the airport and out over the open countryside,
vibration shaking every rivet and leaving behind a heavy flow
of muddy exhaust fumes like a giant crop-duster.

As they had circled for another try, the reason for the go-
around became clear: a green armoured personnel carrier was
sitting squarely in the middle of the single runway. A volley
of swearing had echoed from the flight deck, followed by a
burst of radio chatter. Then silence. Nobody in the cabin spoke,
the atmosphere changed instantly from dulled relief at
journey's end to one loaded with tension at the implications
of what might be happening on the ground.

Whatever the outcome of the radio exchange, the aircraft
circled and lined up again. With minimum fuss, it sank on to
its landing path and touched down with a heavy thump, causing
several overhead lockers to open and cascade a variety of
hand-luggage on to the heads below.

As they flashed past the APC, which had pulled back on
to the grass, Harry recognised it as a Cobra, an image dredged
up from a distant weapons-recognition class. Perhaps the
local tourist board had decided that meeting incoming aircraft
with light armoured vehicles was the latest way to impress
visitors.

After the air-conditioned cabin, the atmosphere outside the
plane was muggy, and the walk across the oily tarmac to the
terminal was like stepping through a steam room. Beyond
the single-storey structure, the distant line of the Caucasus
Mountains rose to the north, their jagged peaks hazy against a
dirty sky. Elsewhere, the view was of shabby hangars and smaller,
unnamed buildings set back from the runway, surrounded by
scrubby grass. The tang of aviation fuel hanging in the air mixed
disturbingly with the acrid fog of cheap cigarettes.

The combined aroma made Harry feel nauseous. It
wasn't just the landing though; he'd been cheated of
sleep by a fat journalist from Ohio named Carl Higgins,
who had insisted on talking non-stop about his family.

Passport control consisted of a pair of plywood booths with edgy-looking uniformed men inside and soldiers in camouflage outside. To add to the lack of welcome, none of the video screens around the walls appeared to be working and there was no air-conditioning to combat the oppressive humidity. Throughout, the overhead lights were a dull yellow, adding to an atmosphere of heavy gloom.

After nearly an hour, during which his passport was scoured twice at length from front to back, Harry arrived at the baggage reclaim hall, another shed tacked on to the arrivals hall. He crossed to the window overlooking the landing area, where a team of baggage handlers was abusing luggage off his flight. His own bag was in there somewhere, but he'd long ago given up taking anything of value on foreign trips. Experience had shown that it was better to move lean and light, unencumbered by unnecessary weight.

Another APC lumbered into view on the far side of the airport. The rear hatch swung open and several armed men in camouflage uniform dropped out and scurried away into a row of bushes. Practice or reaction? The sight made him uneasy.

He caught sight of his reflection in the glass. Solid and squalid, his father would have said, in need of some exercise, rest and healthy food. He wondered what it was about him that made Jean smile. He knew he looked pasty, with red-shot eyes under a brush-cut of dark hair peppered with hints of grey. Where he was going, the exercise might be guaranteed, but the rest and healthy food might have to wait.

One of the baggage handlers pulled a black holdall out of the aircraft and drop-kicked it into a wire cage, then held up his arms to acknowledge applause from his co-workers. When he saw Harry watching, he made a short, one-handed gesture. It might have been obscene, might not. Harry responded with a genial tilt of his whisky miniature and went back to waiting for the carousel to start up. At least his bag would be easy to spot, as it now had a large dusty boot-print embedded in one side.

He yawned and felt his jaw click, and tried not to think about the unseemly haste with which he'd been bundled out of the madness of London. It must have broken civil service records for speed and efficiency, especially in Human

Resources and Travel. He hadn't even been asked to surrender his weapon, but told they would send it on in a secure bag.

They were clearing the decks before the press got to him. It was the MI5 way. Move the man, move everything associated with him. Sanitize and deny. Avoid awkward questions and embarrassing answers.

It may have been dressed up as a new posting, but he was beginning to regret his decision already. He had followed orders, the same as always.

He felt hungry. Remembering the sandwich they'd given him at Northolt, he took out the other half and bit into it with dull enthusiasm. It prompted a reminder of his escorts from London. They may have disappeared from sight, but he didn't believe he was being allowed to move without being observed.

To test the theory, he kept his head down, blanking out the activity around him and recapping who he had seen so far. He discounted the obvious ones – hard-nosed, copper or army types – because they were usually innocent. His money was on a young bloke with a buzz-cut lounging around near the main doors, pretending to be waiting for an incoming passenger.

Thirty minutes later, as Harry carried his bag towards the main exit, the man with the buzz-cut was using a mobile phone on the far side of the arrivals area.

'He's just leaving,' he said quietly. 'Heading for the cab rank.'

'Has he talked with anyone?' The voice on the other end was calm but clipped, establishment English. No background noise. A quiet office close by the Thames.

'No.'

'Good. Did he see you?'

'No way. He was busy sucking on a miniature of whisky. He hadn't got a clue.'

'If you believe that,' the voice said with cold contempt, 'you're an idiot. The only way Harry Tate would have missed spotting a tail was if he was unconscious and blindfolded.'

SEVEN

There were more military personnel outside the terminal building. All armed, looking alert or bored depending on rank, and most looked as if they had been dressed and assembled in a rush.

There were no takers for cabs at the rank, and only a single vehicle waiting; a dusty Mercedes with a crumpled wing. The driver was a young man with spiky hair, oval spectacles and a faded Def Leppard T-shirt. He lifted his chin as Harry caught his eye, and popped the boot. Harry handed him a slip of paper with the office address, and the man pursed his lips and nodded. He seemed about to say something when a large shadow loomed over them.

'Hey, Tate – you got the only ride left! Care to split the fare?' It was Higgins, the American journalist. He was sweating profusely and clutching a large overnight case and a plastic duty-free bag. His suit looked as if it had been used to bed down a donkey.

'Sure. Climb in.' Harry could have done without the company, but refusing the suggestion would have made him stand out.

'Jesus, what a shit-heap!' was Higgins' opening comment as they left the small airport and headed out along a narrow perimeter road. He banged on the back of the driver's seat. 'Hey – does this thing have air-con? Stinks like a dead beaver in here.'

The driver tapped a button on the centre console, and a fan stirred lazily but with little effect.

As they turned on to the main road, Harry looked back. There were no other vehicles in sight. If his watcher from the airport was still there, he must have borrowed Harry Potter's invisibility cloak.

During the journey, which changed from a scattering of commercial units and residential blocks around the airport, to occasional farms and clusters of low houses in open, gently-climbing countryside, Higgins complained at length about the trip, the flight, the landing and the lack of facilities. The only thing he appeared not to have an opinion on was the over-abundant display of military personnel and vehicles in the area. Stationed at crossroads and junctions, they were watchful but unthreatening.

As they cruised into the drab outskirts of a medium sized town, Higgins took up a running commentary about the country and the people, little of it complimentary. Harry wondered if the driver spoke English. He occasionally found the man's eyes flicking up to the mirror and meeting his with a quizzical expression, although he remained silent.

The town, set in the cooler air among low foothills, was un-sophisticated and raw, and reminded Harry of a western frontier town from a Sergio Leone film. A maze of narrow streets inter-sected by several empty, tree-lined boulevards, it boasted a bare handful of four-storey buildings which would have been con-sidered for demolition anywhere else. Some of the streets were bordered by large, rubbish-strewn gutters on either side, with planks laid across the gap for pedestrians, who seemed to use the street like a walkway and paid little attention to surrounding traffic. Overhead, electric wires sagged between the buildings, barely high enough to avoid the radio aerials of the large trucks pounding through and dousing everything in heavy exhaust fumes. The people looked grey, shuffling along with little signs of conversation, moving between the shops which ranged from garish to utilitarian and shabby.

Two hours after leaving the airport, the driver turned on to one of the boulevards and stopped outside a hotel boasting an awning and a cluster of tables with parasols on the pave-ment outside.

Higgins looked at the driver and shifted his bulk forward to pound on the back of his seat. 'Hey, Spikey – how did you know where I was staying?' He turned to Harry without waiting for a reply. 'Did I say where I was staying?'

Harry shrugged. The driver merely smiled in the mirror.

Higgins swore at the lack of reaction and nudged Harry with a beefy elbow. 'See this dump? It's called the Palace. My bath-room at home is bigger than this. Say, where are you staying, Tate? You here, too?' It obviously hadn't occurred to him that the hotel might have guests other than himself.

'No,' said Harry with quiet relief. 'My firm made other arrangements.'

'Your firm? Oh, you in oil or something? You never said.'

'You never asked.' Harry wanted the man out of the car.

Higgins appeared not to hear him. 'I know a lot of guys in the oil business. Mostly engineers. They work on the pipeline going from Baku on the Caspian all the way through to the Med. Anyway, I gotta go. See you around, Tate. Maybe we'll have a drink sometime. Watch out for bed-bugs – they're built like fuckin' raccoons.'

He levered himself out of the car and tramped heavily into the hotel, his jacket tails flapping like a tent. He had made no offer to share the fare. Harry let him go. The peace and quiet was worth it. He made a mental note to avoid the Palace Hotel and signalled the driver to move on.

Three minutes later, the Mercedes stopped outside a plain-fronted, three-storey building rendered in a sickly cream coating speckled with dust. There were few vehicles or pedestrians about, but two soldiers were standing on the nearest corner.

As Harry pulled out some notes, the driver turned and draped one arm over the back of his seat.

'And they have the fucking cheek to wonder why everyone hates them.' His voice was heavy with disgust, his accent was from somewhere south of Birmingham. He smiled at Harry and held out a hand. 'Rik Ferris. Comms, IT support, research and general jobsworth. The boss said to come get you in case you got kidnapped.'

The spiked hair and pop T-shirt seemed almost homely. Harry smiled and took the offered hand. 'Nice of you. Is kidnapping a likelihood?'

'It happens, yeah. Usually oil engineers; the local bandits know they've got plenty of cash and their companies need their expertise.'

'They wouldn't get much for me, then. But thanks for the warning.'

'No problem. Welcome to the lower rectum of British Intelligence, Central Europe. If you've any taste, you'll hate the place. I'll get your case.' He jumped out and went to the boot.

Harry followed him across the pavement into the building, his skin reacting instantly to the cooler climate after the airport. As the door closed behind them, Rik held a finger to his lips and flapped his hand over one ear.

The message was clear: the walls have ears.

On the second floor, he fed a code number into a worn keypad and threw open a heavy wooden door, ushering Harry ahead of him. They were in a large open office with high windows overlooking the street on one side and a jungle of a garden on the other. A through-breeze stirred sheets of A4 paper pinned to bulletin boards around the walls, while the hum of electronic machinery filled the background. Papers and cardboard folders were stacked in trays, with spare boxes of stationery and brochures piled under desks and in between cupboards and side tables, and a tangle of cables criss-crossed the scuffed wooden floor. It could have been any commercial office anywhere in the world.

The door closed behind them with a click of security dead-bolts, and Rik came and stood beside him.

'You can say anything you like in here; sing the Red Flag, tell dirty stories about Putin, but don't be rude about our lords and masters, because they're probably listening, the cheap, chuckle-starved sons of gits.' He grinned and pointed to a woman in her thirties sitting at a PC near the back window. She had long dark hair scraped back into a ponytail, brown eyes and what might have been a broken nose. She was devoid of make-up. It made her look drawn. 'Clare Jardine, Harry Tate; Harry Tate . . . well, you know the rest.'

Harry nodded. She returned it without expression, then went back to her work.

A door opened on the far side of the room and a heavyset man entered. He had greying, stubby hair, neatly brushed, and wore well-pressed dark blue trousers and a blue shirt with black shoes. Almost a uniform, thought Tate. The man gave Harry a wary look.

'Keith Fitzgerald, our security hound and resident heavy,' said Rik.

Ex-army, Harry decided as they shook hands. Strong grip. Probably came out with three stripes and a pension, kids and wife gone, no family, a host of war stories and looking for a job to call home. And this was it.

'Keith,' he murmured. He dropped his bag on a chair and said to no-one in particular, 'I was expecting to see Stuart Mace.'

'He said he'd meet you for coffee,' Jardine said without

looking round. Her voice was cool, matter-of-fact, the accent neutral. She pointed over her shoulder. 'Back out, turn left, right at the top and fifty yards along. The Odeon.'

Fitzgerald coughed. 'We'll need to go through your induction,' he said. 'Security procedures and protocols, who's who, routes in and out, basic travel details, that kind of thing.' He waited, eyes carefully assessing.

'After coffee do you?' There was no sense in trying to avoid it, and the security man was only doing his job.

Fitzgerald nodded, positions agreed, and Harry turned and left them to it. They would probably dissect him the moment he was gone, anyway, the way people do in these situations. He wondered how much they knew.

Outside, the earlier mugginess had cooled, and he walked down the street trying to relax and shake off a growing feeling of despondency. He passed three men in combat uniforms, and saw the ugly snout of an APC parked at the intersection. Another soldier was standing nearby. The men were unshaven and heavily-built, their uniforms crumpled and greasy. His former RSM would have gone ballistic.

As he approached the end of the street, he heard footsteps and realized the three men in combats had turned and followed him. Then the man by the APC stepped out and blocked his way, one hand on the holster at his side. The other three stopped behind him, blocking the way back.

Across the street, two women with shopping bags turned the corner, took one look at the situation and scuttled back the way they had come.

'*Pass*,' said the soldier, and tapped his breast pocket.

EIGHT

'GeORGE?' It was Marcella Rudmann, in a neat grey business suit and glossy shoes. Her hair was coiffed and shiny under the lights of the main hallway of the Ministry of Defence, and she was carrying a smart document case and a mobile, traditional armaments for a meeting. She seemed surprised to see Paulton.

Stuff her, he thought rebelliously. She doesn't know everything.

'Good morning.' He almost called her Marcella but decided against it. Familiarity paid off only with those innocent or pompous enough to be fooled by it.

'How did the . . . posting business go?' She was referring to Harry Tate.

'Very well, actually. He should already be in place by now. Why?' Paulton didn't like the idea of being checked on; watching people was his job, not hers.

'Oh, no reason. The Deputy Prime Minister was asking if the press were likely to get hold of Tate's name. There are questions being asked which come uncomfortably close to the truth.'

'Questions? By whom?'

'Shaun Whelan – who else?'

Paulton puffed out some air. He wasn't surprised. Whelan was a poisonous little hack who'd been booted out of RTE, the Irish broadcasting network, for disclosing private information about government officials in Dublin. He now worked as a freelance, nosing around the corridors of Whitehall like a bitch on heat. Thankfully, few took him too seriously, but his clumsy probing had a habit of causing unwelcome ripples.

'Doesn't it bother you?' Rudmann's voice was insistent, her eyes digging into his. 'You know his reputation.'

'He'll keep.' Paulton wondered how much power this woman really had. The fact that she was being so blatant in her interest over the shooting was becoming a worry. Maybe she had discovered a way of consolidating her career by riding on the back of a potential scandal.

'I hope you're right. I told the DPM you had the situation in hand.'

Paulton felt a further pinprick of annoyance. It was the lack of subtlety as much as the superior attitude; that they felt no hesitation about letting him know they didn't entirely trust him to do what was required. Had the boot been on the other foot, he knew they'd have been outraged at the suggestion that *they* couldn't cope. But he couldn't help feeling a touch of alarm. Had someone been pointing a finger? Was that it?

'It's all in hand,' he confirmed, with a cool undertone. 'Perhaps the DPM would like proof? We have a satellite going

over shortly; I'm sure we could get Tate to look up and wave
if you like.'

Her face stiffened but he was beyond caring. Time was,
he'd have been left alone to get on with the trickier elements
of his job without interference. Now, politicians were all
damage-control experts – especially when they thought their
own careers were at risk.

'I don't think there's any need for that,' she muttered, the
ice in her voice a clear warning. She began to walk away,
then turned and said carefully, 'Just see that none of this ever
goes public, that's all. Do you understand?'

'How could it?' he said coldly. 'Whelan doesn't know where
Tate is.'

As he left the building, he had a sudden, uncomfortable
thought. What did Rudmann mean when she said that none
of this affair should 'go public'?

Was she referring to Harry Tate . . . or Shaun Whelan?

Later that day, Marcella Rudmann returned to her office and
opened a folder sitting in the middle of her desk. It was a
summary file on the life and work of Harry Tate. She skimmed
through it, noting a few high points in his army and intelligence career, but nothing to suggest he was or ever had been
a star. A plodder, by all accounts; solid, unremarkable, a good
and loyal servant who did his job and caused no ripples. In
many ways an ideal intelligence officer. There were a couple
of blips, though, she noted; one minor, the other surprising.

The minor one was a report on Captain Harry Tate disarming
a drunken member of 2 Para who'd gone on the rampage in
a bar in Wiesbaden, Germany, in 1995. It wasn't the fact that
he'd done it that was noteworthy, but that he'd broken the
other man's arm in three places, and none of the man's Para
colleagues had intervened.

The second notation was very different. In August 1999,
Tate had been assigned to a United Nations KFOR unit in
Kosovo, looking for signs of ethnic cleansing. Serb forces were
suspected of systematically rounding up and 'disappearing'
numbers of Kosovar Albanians, and the UN desperately needed
proof. On a reconnaissance mission in the hills ten miles from
Motrovica, they had stumbled on a group of heavily-armed
Serb paramilitaries. An armoured personnel carrier stood at the

side of the road, its 20mm machine gun cocked and ready to fire.

The UN convoy was faced with an unenviable choice: back down or make a fight of it to prove their credentials. The senior officer had urged caution, ordering his men to turn back. The alternative route would add hours to their journey, but it was better than a fire-fight and serious casualties.

But Tate had seen something none of the others had noticed: three small Albanian girls were huddled behind the APC, their clothes torn and dirty. It was clear they didn't want to be there but were too traumatized to ask for help.

Tate had argued that the men had taken the girls prisoner, and that they should investigate further. The senior officer – a Dutch Major – had declined, fearing escalation, whereupon Tate had jumped down from his vehicle and walked over to the APC. Ignoring the Serb soldiers, he had clambered up the side, knocked the gunner cold and turned the gun towards the watching Serbs.

They had handed over the three girls without argument.

Rudmann pursed her lips. So, she reflected, a good and loyal servant with an occasional spark about him. But that had been years ago.

Pray God he kept it bottled up.

She sat back and stared at the ceiling. Part of her brief was to make sure that there were no 'own goals' in security operations which could come back to haunt the government later. Like the Essex operation. Getting him out of the way had been an instinctive move, and Paulton had obviously foreseen the need. But her brief gave her considerable power and responsibility – far more than men like George Paulton were even aware of – and she took the work seriously. For that reason, she had sent for Harry Tate's personnel file, just to be sure he wasn't a rogue male who might bring disaster on them, no matter what Paulton's opinion of the man might be.

She closed the file and summoned her secretary to return it. Harry Tate had once shown a spark of something, but that was all. Sparks didn't always translate to flame. Even so, he was better off out of the way. For all their sakes.

'Get this back without fuss,' she told the young woman who entered the room. 'Remember, no signatures and no record.'

NINE

The inside of the Odeon Restaurant was dark and cluttered, a sombre cavern with lots of rough-sawn wood, wall-hangings of indeterminate origin or purpose and smoke-stained varnish. Ethnic, Harry decided, and more bar than restaurant. Maybe it said something about Stuart Mace, the Head of Station, if this was his local watering hole.

A single figure was sitting at the rear of the room, facing the door and reading a newspaper. A cup of coffee sat by his elbow. He looked up as Harry approached, studied him for a moment, then shouted towards a doorway in the back wall.

'Found us, then.' Stuart Mace was in his late fifties, with a fleshy face and the tired eyes of a bureaucrat. His hair was silvery grey and swept back in elegant wings. Had it not been for his present location, he could have been a prosperous, if worn-down GP, looking towards retirement and some time on the golf course.

'Thanks to Rik Ferris.' Harry sat down just as a cup of thick coffee was set before him by an elderly woman in a black apron and a dress covered in small, blue flowers. She left without making eye contact.

Mace nudged a small jug of cream towards him. 'Help yourself. Stuff'll melt your teeth, otherwise. No trouble getting here?' Mace spoke in economical bursts, as though unnecessary words might spin off and be overheard. Harry had met others with the same habit. Spooks and career criminals, mostly.

'The landing was interesting. And I just got stopped in the street by the military.'

Mace nodded. He didn't seem unduly concerned. 'What did they want?'

'Money. Is that normal?'

'Nothing's normal around here. They've got lots on their minds at the moment – separatist stuff to the north, mostly. They think anyone new in town is out to get them. They're probably not wrong. You met any of the crew apart from young Rik?'

Harry poured cream and tasted his coffee. It was muddy and strong enough to float a brick. Sugar made no noticeable difference. He debated mentioning meeting Higgins, but decided to leave it for later. 'Jardine and Fitzgerald. Unless the watcher at the airport was yours.'

Mace lifted an eyebrow. 'Seriously?'

'Yes.'

'Probably security police. Never mind; gives 'em something to do, watching new arrivals. There are four of us puppies here, now you make five. Enid Blyton would be ecstatic.' He toyed with a teaspoon for a moment, drumming on the tabletop, then said, 'I heard about your trouble. Sorry business. Sounds like over-reaction, shoving you out here.'

'You could say that.' Harry couldn't help a touch of bitterness; he was still trying to get to grips with what had happened and the speed with which he'd been shuffled out of London.

'Or was it that you didn't play the game and relied on the wrong people?'

'Say again?' He was only half listening, trying to work out whether sitting here with this man was part of his punishment. He was also surprised to hear Mace talking so openly about who they were. There might not be any other customers but it was sloppy tradecraft for a man of his seniority.

Mace read his mind. He flapped a hand to indicate the four walls around them. 'You gonna tell me this is breaching rules and regulations? Walls have ears and all that bollocks?' He sniffed. 'One, the walls don't speak English; two the old woman's as deaf as a dead dog – she relies on picking up vibrations like a bat. Anyway, Fitzgerald regularly gives the place a going-over with his electronic sweepers. It's clean.'

Harry shrugged. 'If you say so.'

'I do. As I was saying, you telling me you never got dumped on in the army? That they don't have self-serving shits in uniform who'll shaft you soon as look at you?'

'I suppose so.'

'Bloody right. I'm surprised a man your age hasn't learned life's most valuable lesson: make sure you've always got an exit strategy – even if that means dumping on someone else before they do it to you. Never mind, you'll get over it.'

Harry nodded. Mace was right. It didn't make him feel any better – or bring him any closer to what his purpose was in being sent here, other than getting him out of the way. But placing him on garden leave in Brighton or Harrogate could have done that. Unless they knew something he didn't.

'So what exactly am I here for?'

Mace blinked. 'You don't know?'

'I know why . . . I just don't know what I'm supposed to do.'

'You're here because you screwed up. Same as the rest of the security services' fuckwits out here.' He flapped a hand. 'I mean, look at the place. Who'd volunteer for this?'

'Nice to be appreciated.'

'No need to get touchy; I'm the biggest fuck-up of all. Difference is, they don't want me back in London and I don't want to be there. Place is a snake pit. You'd think they might forgive once the dust has settled. It's not as though officers with your kind of experience are thick on the ground.'

Harry let that go, but his curiosity was aroused. So Mace had tripped up, too, along with the others. Christ, what was this place – a penal colony for spooks?

'How long will I be here?'

'Didn't you ask – what's his name . . . that self-serving little shite, Paulton? He's the one sent you.'

'I would have, but considering the speed I got bounced with, we weren't really on normal speaking terms.'

Mace chuckled. 'Not too surprised, are you? They don't want to get tainted, see. Better to get you out of the way where you can't do their pension entitlement any harm. Bastards. A few years ago, a couple of incidental deaths wouldn't have raised an eyebrow, not in the grand scheme of things. Things're different now, though; risk assessments, health and safety, rules of engagement – we're all accountable. It's like working in a glass case. Still, at least you got a travel slip to foreign climes, such as they are.'

'So how long?'

'Easy. You stay here until they decide you can go home . . . or a public enquiry is convened and you get dragged in front of the cameras as the sacrificial idiot.'

'Is that likely?' Right now he was dust under the carpet. The only question was, how long could he stay that way?

'Who knows? Until then, you pretend you're attached to the British Council and promote British interests, culture, language and way of life and generally act like a boring and bored administrative wonk. In actual fact, you'll do what you've been trained to do: keep your eyes open, your ears pinned back and report back on whatever looks interesting.'

'So suddenly I'm a spy? I thought that was Six's job.'

'Don't get precious; you know the score. We're all in this together. It's called multitasking.' He paused, then said, 'They mention the no-communications rule?'

'Yes.' Paulton had made it clear that where Harry was going would be a dead zone. No communication in or out except via his head of station, which was Mace. It included everyone: friends, family, past loves, present colleagues, the press . . . most especially the press. For the foreseeable future, Harry Tate would be deemed to have dropped off the face of the earth.

'Make sure you stick to it. Any breach and you'll be hauled out of here fast.'

'You man there's a worse posting than this?'

'Better believe it. I suggest you take a few days to get acquainted with the town. There's not a lot on at the moment, so we can spare you for that. The others'll help.'

'So what's special about this place?' Harry had been trying to think why *here*, so far from just about everywhere and every conceivable operation MI5 might be involved in. His colleagues were constantly working the drug routes across Europe in their attempt to monitor and identify the traffickers who used various points of entry and arranged staging-posts for their illegal trade. But this seemed an odd place to be watching.

Mace pushed out his chin. 'There's nothing *special* about it. Last bloody thing you could call it. Even the flies feel underprivileged. There's a saying among the locals that this place was made up of God's leftovers. Not far wrong, either, although I've seen worse.'

'That still doesn't tell me what I'm supposed to be looking for.'

Mace grinned. 'They said you could be a bit churlish.' He placed his hand flat on the table. 'There are rumours going around town – well, all over, really – that are causing a bit of bother in political circles. If they're correct, then we're all about to be dumped in the kaka.'

Harry resisted the desire to reach across and yank Mace's shirt collar tightly around his throat. 'What rumours?'

'The Russians are coming.'

TEN

Mace refused to elaborate further. 'It's early days yet,' was all he would say. 'No point in going off half-cocked. Let's just keep our ears and eyes open, shall we?'

Harry left him to his newspaper and walked back to the office. Whatever the rumours, Russian involvement was no surprise – not this close to Moscow's ragged borders. But he was shocked that London hadn't briefed him before he came out here.

Unless they hadn't known.

He was greeted in the office by Fitzgerald. The briefing began with a demonstration of the layout of the building from ground to top floor, using a coloured map showing exits, stairways and a schematic of the alarm system, and the codes to use for out-of-hours working. Before they left the main office, he looked at Harry with a serious expression.

'Outside of this room, we only talk British Council business. Nothing else. I run regular sweeps, and so far we've never found anything. But that doesn't mean they won't find a way in. Right?'

'Sure.' Harry was accustomed to the paranoia of security people in foreign postings. They had learnt from others' mistakes over the decades, and nobody took the matter lightly.

Fitzgerald led the way downstairs, talking mundane matters and showing Harry a selection of rooms in the basement for odds and ends of furniture, stacks of leaflets and boxes of promotional literature in several languages. The air smelled of dust and printing ink, and damp cardboard.

'Our main job here,' he continued aloud, 'is to field cultural and educational enquiries, and send out leaflets to interested parties so they can locate contacts and partners. We encourage them to go through their trade delegates in London or the appropriate section of our embassy. There's a list upstairs of addresses you can give them.' He beckoned for Harry to follow and moved to a room at the rear, where the walls were lined with metal racks holding more boxes and a selection of conference and exhibition equipment.

He lifted a square of carpet to one side. Underneath was a small metal trapdoor.

Fitzgerald took a metal hook from a nearby rack and inserted it in a slot. He pulled hard and the trapdoor came up revealing a recess dug into the foundations. Reaching down, he tugged hard on something out of Tate's line of sight. A wooden box slid into view.

Inside, nestling in foam packing, were three handguns, the light gleaming off the oiled metal, and spare clips of ammunition.

He replaced the trapdoor and carpet, then led the way back upstairs. As soon as they were in the main office with the door closed, Harry turned to him.

'What the hell are they for?' he demanded. He was aware of Jardine and Ferris watching in the background. They said nothing.

'They've been here from the beginning,' Fitzgerald replied calmly. 'The boss said you should know they were there, just in case.' He turned and beckoned Harry to follow. This room was divided into two offices with glass panelling down the middle. Stuart Mace was sitting on the other side of the glass, talking on the phone. It looked like any bureaucrat's den, with book-lined walls and filing cabinets, and family photos on the shelves.

'I'll take you through our security procedure and protocols,' said Fitzgerald, moving behind a cluttered desk. 'Then Rik or Clare will give you a quick tour and drop you off at your digs. You might as well get to know the place.'

'Just in case?' said Harry.

'You got it.'

For the next forty minutes, he listened as he was shown through a succession of procedures, including basic personal safety, building security and local maps. One town map showed buildings marked in red. Most were in the narrow streets on the edge of town to the north, where Harry hadn't yet been.

'What are those?'

'Hostile or possibly hostile locations. My advice is, don't go there.'

'Hostiles.'

'Yeah. This and this,' he pointed to two buildings closer to the centre, 'are local security police. They leave us alone most of the time. The others are bandits. Local clans. Don't mess with them; they have a habit of not returning people who stray into their territory. The cops leave them alone because they've got their own private militias.' He sniffed. 'It's the militias in this neck of the woods that control most of what goes on.'

'What about this place?' Harry indicated a large red building on the map not far from where they were standing. It was the Palace Hotel.

'We call it spook central. It's the only decent hotel in town. The Yanks kip down there along with journos and a few other interested groups like the French, Germans and Russians.'

'You know any of them – Americans, I mean?'

'Sure. A couple. Engineers, so they say, although I doubt it. Why?'

'A man named Higgins was on the flight in. Said he was a journalist.'

'He isn't,' Fitzgerald said shortly. 'Fat, loud, self-opinionated and sweats a lot?'

'That's him.'

'Yeah. Rik said he'd cadged a lift. He comes and goes, makes a lot of noise about the hard life of a news reporter. Not sure who he's with, but it's either CIA or National Security Agency. He might have tagged you but I wouldn't worry about it.' He paused. 'You see anyone else like him?'

Harry thought about the young man at the airport. 'Not yet.'

Fitzgerald smiled without humour. 'Don't worry – you will.'

ELEVEN

Next morning, Harry walked to the office to get a feel for the town. The air was colder, with a heavy layer of cloud hanging over the buildings and reducing the sparse colouring to shades of grey. The atmosphere bore a taste of burnt fuel, which he guessed was cheap heating oil or badly maintained vehicle engines.

He passed few people on the way. A group of soldiers standing around a makeshift brazier eyed him suspiciously but didn't stop him. Other pedestrians steered clear of the military as if by instinct, crossing the streets with eyes down, intent on being invisible.

After leaving Fitzgerald, he'd been taken by Rik Ferris on a whistle-stop tour of the town, with the communications man pointing out local landmarks. These had been few and far between, mostly given to the town hall, the museum, the railway station . . . and the so-called hostile buildings referred to by Fitzgerald. Detached houses in the main, these were sheltered behind walls or railings, with security cameras trained on all sides. There had been nothing overt about them to suggest any dangerous presence, such as armed guards, but the metal shutters on the windows, the fresher paint compared with their neighbours and the heavy four-by-four vehicles parked in the alleyways alongside, indicated they were not your average residential premises.

The last stop was outside a three-storey building in a quiet back street.

'Home sweet home,' Rik said cheerfully. He handed Harry a key on a plastic tag. 'Top floor, so you can make as much noise as you like, hold wild parties and stuff like that. Make sure you invite me, though. The only other tenant is a press photographer on the ground floor, named Mario. Comes from Rome. Nice bloke.' He frowned. 'Actually, I haven't seen him around for a couple of days. Must have found a story to cover. I've stocked up your kitchen with the basics, so you won't need to shop for a few days. Not,' he added, 'that you'll find shopping much fun around here.'

'Thanks. Where do you call home?' asked Harry. He hadn't had much opportunity to talk to the younger man yet. If he was a communications specialist, he couldn't exactly be rushed off his feet, and Harry hadn't seen much in the way of communications hardware in the office.

'About quarter of a mile away.' Rik pointed out to the suburbs. 'It's on Novroni. Number twenty-four. Old and scabby, but I'm doing it up to keep myself from going stir-crazy. Clare lives a few blocks that way.' He indicated north. 'The other two live on the outskirts.' He hesitated. 'Did Mace tell you about the no-comms rule?'

'Yes. Everything goes through him. Is it set in stone?'

'You bet. I have access to a server in London, but that's
purely for messages. It's monitored closely and as bomb-
proof as my granny's knickers. Mace has a secure terminal
in his office, but nobody else gets to touch it. It's level-Alpha
password-protected.'

'I'll pretend I know what that means. What about my
mobile?'

Rik held out his hand. 'Here – I'll show you.'

Harry passed him his Nokia, which he hadn't used since
leaving London. Rik switched it on. He held it up so Harry
could see the screen. It was blank.

'They wiped it before you left. It won't pick up a signal
here, so you might as well dump it. I'll give you a new one
in the morning. It'll be OK for the local network, but no
further.' He handed the phone back and put the car in gear.
'It's not too bad here. You'll get used to it.'

'That's what Mace said.' Harry wondered when they'd
managed to wipe his mobile. At the time of the debriefing,
probably, when he'd handed it in at security.

'He's right. Welcome to paradise.'

Harry watched him drive away before making his way inside
and up three flights of narrow, concrete stairs inlaid with coarse
tiles. They were worn down in the middle from the passage of
feet over the years, and crackled with grit underfoot. The air
was cold and damp, a depressing contrast to the conditions at
the airport.

He shivered, wondering if this was a taste of the winter to
come.

The interior of the flat was spacious but minimally furnished,
like a student's lodging circa 1968. Most of the items looked
as if they had been sourced from a bric-a-brac salesroom. The
living room, bedroom and kitchen held the basics, and carried
a faint aroma of mildew and cleaning fluid. A wood-burner
stood in the living room, black and cold and squat as a beetle,
and the bathroom was ancient and damp, echoing to the plunk
of water dripping from a furred-up shower-head the size of a
soup tureen.

He sat down on the bed and contemplated his future. So
far, he'd been a man in motion, one foot in front of the other
like an automaton, following orders. Now he was here, he

couldn't see beyond the bleak surrounds of these four walls and the grubby little cowpat of a town outside.

Even Jean seemed too far away to be more than a vague memory.

He leaned back, depressed, suddenly too tired to care, and fell asleep dreaming about the young couple in the Land Rover and a tall gunman with dreadlocks and a pole belching fire.

TWELVE

Mace was in his office by the time Harry got in, feeling worn out from a restless night's sleep. He tapped on the glass door and walked in, and was surprised to smell alcohol in the air. A half-full glass of amber liquid sat in the centre of the Station Chief's desk.

'Come in,' said Mace, his words heavily precise. 'Set yourself down and pull up a coffee.' He waved vaguely in the direction of a filter machine in the corner.

Harry decided against it. The rim of the glass bowl looked toxic.

'Your digs all right?' Mace asked.

'Magnificent. I'll soon have it looking just like home.' Harry didn't bother pretending; he was sure the last thing Mace was concerned with was the well-being of his staff.

'Good. Good.' Mace ignored the sarcasm and sat back in his chair, nursing his glass.

'Is there something you want me to do?' Harry hoped this wasn't chancing providence. He felt washed out, his eyes gritty, and wanted nothing more than to get through the day, have a decent meal and get to bed – preferably alone, although he'd have felt a lot happier if Jean was here.

'Not really. Thought it was about time I let you in on all the gossip.'

'How do you mean?'

'Well, let's say you're not unique, all right?' Mace held up a finger. 'Take young Ferris. MI5 computer bod. Something of a wiz, recruited from university and put to work for the greater good minding other people's business. Trouble is, he got bored

ferreting about in websites and computers belonging to terrorists, trouble-makers and general malcontents, and began using
his skills closer to home; people in the government, people in
power. One or two of 'em in the security services.'

'Christ.'

'Yeah. He'd have hacked Him too if he could have found
His website. He wasn't all that clever, though. He talked about
what he'd done after hours. Silly boy. Should have known
he'd get dobbed in by some back-stabber with ambition. Lots
of that in this business.'

'What happened?' Harry was surprised Ferris wasn't
languishing in a cell somewhere. Hacking any computer was
an offence; taking on the security services at their own game
was tantamount to suicide.

'He got tabbed. That's a fancy name for having your legs
taken from under you and sent out here, which is what happened
to you. Your file gets tabbed, you're due for a nasty surprise.'
He showed his teeth in another grin. 'The people he took a
sneaky look at didn't want him loose on the labour market, so
they decided to put him somewhere where they could keep an
eye on him. Lucky for him.'

'Why?'

'He might have been propping up a patio in SW16, otherwise. They sent him here instead. Some might say there's not
much difference.'

'Why are you telling me this?' Harry felt uncomfortable
hearing about the transgressions of his colleagues. He had
second thoughts about the coffee and poured a cup. Even
loaded with sugar it tasted like sump oil.

'Why not? Clean sheets makes for untroubled sleep, so my
dear old mother used to say. Course, they wouldn't agree back
at HQ, but that's why we're all here, isn't it?'

'If you say so.'

'I do. Where was I? Oh, yes: Clare Jardine. Nice girl, but
don't get on her bad side. She comes from Six, along with
all sorts of vile habits. She doesn't do fluffy.'

'Six?' Harry was surprised. 'I thought this was strictly a
Five set-up.'

'It started out that way. Then Vauxhall Cross asked to join
the party in case they needed to export one or two of their
own clandestine miscreants.'

'I'm surprised they have enough to warrant it.'

'You kidding? With over five thousand employees between 'em, it'd be a bloody miracle not to have some lame ducks. You any idea how many Fivers and Sixers get quietly canned every year?'

'No.'

'About two dozen at the last estimate, although they're mostly minor. Some end up behind bars, others get the order of the boot and a rap over the head with the Official Secrets Act.' He broke off and took a sip of his drink. 'Then there's the ones they can't afford to kick off the end of the plank. Which is where this place comes in.'

'Go on.'

'Take young Clare, for instance. Passed all the courses with flying colours, didn't put a foot wrong in the assessments and practical tests and left everyone else on her intake streets behind. She was only in Six for a year before she got spotted and chucked in at the deep end. Too deep, as it happened.'

Harry stirred his coffee and tried to match the woman he'd met with the kind of officers MI6 trained and ran. He'd got to know a few but they'd mostly been men.

'How do you mean?'

'You know what a honey trap is?' Mace's voice was low.

'I know the theory.'

'Right. It needs two willing parties. Well, one willing, the other as gullible as buggery. The trapper and the trappee. Jardine got badly stung.'

'She was the target?' It made him wonder why – and what she knew of value.

'Knew you'd think that.' Mace shook his head. 'Our Clare was the honey pot.'

'Oh.' Harry revised his opinion. She clearly had hidden depths.

'Trouble was, she got too close, too friendly.' Mace shrugged. 'Big no-no, that. Scale ten on the rectum-quivering chart. She should have made her excuses and pulled out, as the old-time *News of the World* journos used to say. But she didn't. She stayed and tried to work the situation . . . and got burned. Turned out the target was setting her up, not the other way round.'

'So why is she here?'

'Like I said, she's good. And hard-nosed. Don't let the fact that she's a woman fool you. She got snitty with her controller when he hauled her in, and threatened to tell what she knew. Seems in between the door and the target's boudoir, she stumbled on some sensitive information. Nobody's saying what, but it was enough to get her tabbed and sent her out here to lose her memory.'

'Is it working?'

'It's fading.'

'And Fitzgerald?'

'He's just unlucky. Ex-para, one of Five's heavies for a few years – the kind used to lift someone off the street when they needed it. Then his wife ran off with the milkman, turned his kids against him and he lost the plot. Smacked a colleague who said the wrong thing. They were going to pay him off but he asked for a hard posting instead. This was it. Should have known better, being ex-army. Never volunteer for nothing.'

Harry looked at him and said, 'What about you?'

Mace's face remained blank. 'You don't have clearance for that information, son.' He shifted in his seat. 'Anything else you want to know?

'Yes. What you said about the Russians coming; is that what all the local military activity is about?'

Mace eyed him for a few moments, then grunted. 'They didn't let you in on much before sending you out here, did they? Christ, what a bunch.' He finished his drink and pushed the glass away. 'Right, quick briefing. Thirty miles south of here is the Baku–Tbilisi–Ceyhan oil pipeline. It runs oil from the Caspian all the way through to the Med. It's what some folk call strategic . . . turn off the pipeline and there's no oil for the motoring masses in Europe to drive their four-by-fours. Amazingly, our lords and masters have only just woken up to the fact. To the north is a breakaway region called South Ossetia, which sits up against the border with Mother Russia. And this is where things get interesting: the Ossetians have decided they want to be Russian rather than Georgian, which isn't going down too well with President Saakashvili and his mates. It's a source of tension.'

'I heard.' Like much of what passed for news, it had gone in one ear and out the other. But Harry wasn't entirely ignorant of what was going on in this part of the world.

'Good. What you probably won't have heard is that things have been hotting up in this region. The separatists are pushing the envelope 'til it bursts and the Georgians are getting pissed and rattling their sabres. Can't say I blame them, really.'

'How seriously?'

'Enough for some ordnance to have been lobbed back and forth over the border. Homemade, a lot of it, but it still goes bang when someone gets too close. Serious enough –' he paused and scratched his face with a bitten fingernail – 'to have attracted the attention of Moscow. And we all know how that could pan out.'

Harry tried to work out what might happen, but gave up. It was a tortuous trap of a puzzle with no predictable outcome. 'What are the odds?'

Mace pulled a face. 'Putin doesn't take any pushing around. If he gets in the mood, he'll do something. It doesn't have to make sense to us, just his own people. Still,' he smiled, revealing coffee-stained teeth, 'that's above our pay grade. All we can do is monitor the situation and hold on to our hats.'

'And if it blows?'

'If it goes tits up, just hope for a clear road to the airport and a full tank of petrol.'

THIRTEEN

Clare Jardine was waiting for him when he left Mace's office. She was dressed in black cargo pants and walking boots, with a dark fleece top. Her hair was tied in a severe bun. She clearly wasn't dressing to impress.

She tossed him a set of car keys. 'I'm going out. Mace says I have to take you with me, God help me. I'll let you drive; it'll be your first taster of life out here.' She indicated a kettle on a side table, with a couple of flasks standing next to it. 'Make yourself some coffee; we'll be operating in a Starbucks'-free zone.'

I love you, too, thought Harry, and picked up a flask while she paraded impatiently back and forth. 'Where are we going?' he asked, pouring in boiling water.

'I'm meeting a contact at a truck stop twenty miles north of here. He says he's got some figures on military truck movements which he thinks might be of interest.' She rubbed her thumb and fingers together to indicate that money was involved.

Harry shook the flask and screwed on the top. He'd made it black and strong, to keep him awake. It seemed to be what everyone drank around here, with the possible exception of Mace. Maybe it explained Jardine's spikiness; she certainly seemed wired up.

'So why would exposing me be a good idea?' he said.

Jardine stopped pacing and stared at him. Rik Ferris, working at a PC monitor, looked up with interest. 'Why wouldn't it?' she replied coolly. 'You saying you don't want to come?'

'I'm saying your contact might know you, but he won't know me from a fence post. Seeing me will either scare him off or give him another face to identify if he gets compromised.' He shrugged. 'Just thought I'd mention it.'

Jardine's jaw worked hard as she processed the inference. 'Are you an expert?' she said, her cheeks colouring, 'or is this just superior alpha male bullshit?'

Harry sighed. She'd taken his response as a challenge, but he really didn't give a rats. He had no idea how solid her contact was, nor how long she had been working him, but he wasn't about to follow her blindly without question, no matter how well she knew the ground. It was his neck at risk, too.

'Think what you like. But I'm entitled to ask when a risk is worth taking. Besides, can't satellite tracking give us troop movements?'

'You're right, it can.' Mace was standing just inside the doorway. 'But we need more details than satellite images can supply. A lot of these buggers aren't big on badges and we need to know who and what they are. Up close and personal is the only way.' He nodded and went back to his office.

Harry shrugged. It sounded reasonable, but he still didn't like it. When Clare Jardine turned and walked out, he followed. As he passed Rik's desk, the young man lobbed him a small black mobile and said, 'Remember, no calls to Australia and no online gambling.'

By the time he got downstairs, Jardine was standing next to a battered grey Toyota Land Cruiser. Harry pressed the remote and they climbed aboard. The engine sounded smooth, although the car looked as if it was a survivor of a demolition derby.

He soon discovered why.

Jardine told him to head north and pointed the way. He took the vehicle out through the town, and they were soon in open country, on a road which might have been a major route here, but would have been downgraded as a track elsewhere. The surface was pitted with holes and the edges were crumbling, with deep gullies waiting to catch unwary drivers. The locals held the centre of the road with suicidal aggression, their victories marked by a regular scattering of broken car and lorry parts along the verges.

Ten minutes out of town, they passed a convoy of military trucks filled with men in drab uniform and helmets. They looked heavily-armed and wary. Harry saw no obvious regimental or unit insignia save for a small lightning bolt on one sleeve.

'Local militia,' Jardine explained. She sounded cool but professional.

'Whose side are they on?'

'Their own. They follow orders from their regional commander – a sort of warlord.'

'Won't that conflict with the regular army?'

She gave a ghost of a smile. 'If it does, they'll probably kick the army's arse. They're better equipped, better motivated and get paid more. Until then, they flex their muscles and train a lot just to remind everyone who really runs the place.'

'Let's hope they don't get tested by someone with bigger muscles.' He was thinking of what Mace had said about the Russians.

She looked at him, probably wondering how much he knew of the local situation. 'It depends who they decide to back. If they fall back on old loyalties, they could jump either way.' She pointed to a fork in the road, and he followed her directions to take the left one. 'Let's hope it never comes to that.'

The road they were now on became wider, but not much better. There was almost no southbound traffic, and Harry was able to pull out and overtake whenever conditions allowed. They passed several huge haulage or military trucks, belching fumes and hogging the centre line, and more than once Harry found himself holding his breath as the Land Cruiser was nearly brushed off the road by one of the lumbering vehicles.

To have squeezed over too far would have invited disaster, but the alternative – to be wiped out by a clash against one of the huge wheels – would have been terminal.

A flash in his mirror and a blast of air horns alerted Harry to someone else heading north. He pulled over as a big four-by-four shot by, nearly taking off their wing mirror. Clare Jardine grabbed for a handle, but seemed unfazed by the manoeuvre. The vehicle disappeared, leaving Harry with a vague impression of two men inside and a smiley face sticker on the rear window.

Forty minutes after leaving town they came to a large, low building ahead, plastered with signs and posters and surrounded by trucks. Jardine signalled for Harry to pull in. He did so, parking close to the building. There were no other cars that he could see, and he guessed this was the area's one and only truck stop.

They climbed out and stretched, studying the building. The windows were heavily steamed up, and although it was morning, the neon lights advertising vodka and beer were ablaze.

'Follow my lead,' said Jardine. 'Try and pretend you belong.'

Harry glanced at her. In spite of the tough act, he guessed she was nervous. He nodded, and she walked ahead of him and pushed through a pair of heavy swing doors. They were hit by a hot, smoke-filled rush of air from inside and the blast of loud conversation. There was no music, Harry noted.

There must have been over a hundred men in the room, seated at rough tables or standing against a bar running from front to back. They looked like truckers everywhere, most of them big and flushed. The clink of glasses and the clatter of crockery vied with the background sounds of steam machines and shouts from the kitchen.

Conversation dropped appreciably as Harry and Clare moved into the room. Harry wondered whether it was because they were strangers or because Clare was one of the few women in the place. He now saw why she had come without make-up; a trace of lipstick and there would have been a riot.

They took a table near the front window and were approached by a waitress dressed in jeans and a shapeless jacket streaked with food stains. Clare ordered two beers and looked out of the window, ignoring the stares. Eventually, the conversation returned to its original level as the truckers resumed the business they were here for, which was food, refreshment and gossip.

Harry was halfway down his beer when the doors opened and three men in military uniform stepped inside. The first was an officer, the other two without rank. They stood and surveyed the room, unaffected by the unfriendly faces turned their way.

This time, all conversation ceased.

The officer walked slowly along the bar, hands behind his back. He was followed by one of his men. The other remained by the door.

They began checking papers. A rumble of protest went through the room but nobody argued. Gradually, the officer and his colleague worked their way through the crowd. Many of the drivers began to leave, their drinks unfinished. They went unchallenged by the man at the door.

'Is this normal?' asked Harry. He watched as the officer approached a large man at the bar dressed in jeans and a heavy jacket, a woollen cap pulled down over his ears. There was a burst of muttered conversation but the man eventually slid something along the bar and shook his head.

Clare shook her head. 'It's a random check; vehicles and papers – mostly vehicles. The ones leaving are drivers without papers or those with dodgy loads.'

'Why aren't they being stopped?'

'They are. Take a look outside.'

He checked through the window, brushing aside the heavy condensation. The parking area was dotted with soldiers, pouncing on the truckers as they left and accompanying them to their vehicles. Nobody was exempt.

Harry watched as the officer worked his way towards their table, gradually clearing the room. Then he realised: the truckers weren't the ones he was after.

'Don't.' Clare gave him a warning look. 'If he speaks to you, shake your head and play dumb. Hand over your passport only if he asks.'

Then the officer was at their table and looking down at them. Up close, Harry could see he was freshly-shaven, and smelled of soap and leather. He was in his forties, with clear, dark eyes and a blunt nose, and held an unmistakable air of authority. He held out his hand and Clare handed him her

passport. Without returning it, he held out his hand for
Harry's.

He took a long time studying the documents, flicking pages
back and forth while the soldier waited nearby. The few remaining
patrons in the place took no notice, turning their backs and
pretending the soldiers weren't there. What happened to two
foreigners was of no concern; they had problems enough of their
own. Behind the bar, the owner, a short, squat figure with a
balding head, glared sourly at the loss of business.

'Thank you,' the officer said in English, then dropped the
two passports on the table. With a brief nod, he turned and
marched outside, followed by his men.

Harry picked up his passport and began to stand up, but
Clare reached out and touched his hand.

'Wait. Give it a while.'

Five minutes later, they heard a shout and the soldiers began
clambering aboard their trucks. Moments later, they were gone,
leaving the air over the lorry park thick with exhaust fumes.

'Time to go.' Clare stood up and paid the waitress, then led
the way back outside. Over half the trucks had disappeared,
but several drivers were making their way back to the building,
laughing or muttering, depending on their luck with the vehicle
check.

'What now?' said Harry, as they got back in the Land Cruiser.
'Looks like your contact was scared off.'

'No, he wasn't.' She took out her passport and opened it
below the level of the window. A slip of paper fluttered out
and fell on her knee. Harry caught a glimpse of some numbers
and scribbled words before she folded it and put it away.
'See?'

'Neat,' said Harry. It was, too. To have a contact here at all
took some doing. To have a contact who was an army officer
was nearly miraculous. He wondered if London knew . . . or
cared. 'What is it?'

'Not sure yet. Map co-ordinates, I think.' If she knew more,
she clearly wasn't going to share anything with him.

He shrugged. Silly games. Let her get on with it. Then his
attention was drawn to another vehicle starting up nearby. It
was thirty yards away, and had been hidden by other vehicles
when he and Clare had arrived. It was a large four-by-four, with
two men inside and a smiley face on the rear window.

The road hog who'd nearly taken them off the road on their way here.

It charged away with a roar of the exhausts, and Harry watched it go, eyes on the man behind the wheel. It was the big man in the woollen cap.

It was only when they were back on the road that he suddenly realized that he knew who the man was.

Carl Higgins.

FOURTEEN

T hat evening, Harry unscrewed the ancient shower-head and idled time away digging limescale out of the holes with a needle. He found it oddly therapeutic and rewarded himself with a hot shower and a glass of whisky, courtesy of another two miniatures from the flight in.

It did little to deaden his underlying feelings of dismay, but helped him relax to a point where he could begin to worry about it less.

He was sinking slowly into a welcoming sleep when he heard a noise outside his door. He wasn't yet accustomed to the building and all its various clicks and creaks, and whatever had alerted him might be one of those. He lay for a while, analysing the sounds: the wind, a shutter flapping, a passing vehicle, someone shouting in the distance, the creak of a shutter. Normal stuff. He relaxed, eyes growing heavy.

Then it came again. The scuff of a footstep on the stairs.

Somebody had moved along the landing.

He slid out of bed and padded through to the door. At first he couldn't hear anything. Then he detected a slight murmur, lifting out from somewhere below and carrying up the stairway. Voices.

Mario the Roman photographer back from his assignment? Or visitors?

He went to the window and peered down. A dark car stood at the kerb. No sign of exhaust smoke, but a man was standing by the driver's door, hip against the bodywork. He wore a uniform jacket and had a holster strapped to his side. A curl

of cigarette smoke rose in the air, ghostly under the street
lights.

Not Mario, then.

A crash of something breaking echoed in the night. It was
enough to make the man by the car turn his head, but lazily,
unconcerned.

Harry scrubbed at his eyes. He was tired and his mouth
tasted gummy with too much coffee, but going back to sleep
was out of the question. He put on his trousers and shoes,
went to the front door. Easing it open, he looked through the
crack towards the stairs. If anyone was waiting out there, they
were on a lower flight, out of sight. He opened the door wider
and stepped on to the landing. The murmuring was louder out
here, punctuated by a low huff of laughter.

He leaned over the stairway and looked down. A man was
standing in the middle of the small foyer. He looked up and
Harry jerked his head back. Waited for the sound of footsteps
moving up. But there was silence.

More voices and footsteps moved across the foyer and out
the door. Silence.

Kicking off his shoes, Harry went downstairs, keeping to
the inside wall. He reached the last step and checked the front
entrance. The door was closed.

But the door to the ground-floor flat wasn't.

A car engine clattered, fading quickly into the night. He
counted to twenty before moving to the door of Mario's flat.
He pushed it back and stepped inside.

His first impression was of stale cooking and something
faintly chemical. Developing fluids? He wasn't certain. Surely
they'd all gone digital now.

He prowled through the flat, feeling like an invader. It had
been neat once. Basic, like his own place, but with personal
touches here and there. A photo frame on a sideboard, showing
two older people and a younger man – a family shot; some
books, magazines, even a small television. Items of clothing
lay on the back of an armchair, crumpled as if ready for
ironing. Home from home. He knew the process well; a minute
reflection of the place the man had come from, a memory of
somewhere familiar.

The place had been tossed with little care. Moving furniture and not bothering to replace it; opening books and leaving

them up-ended like dead birds, the pages bent and creased; cushions opened by a sharp blade, the stuffing emptied on to the floor; and a wastebasket up-ended with scraps of paper and cardboard wrapping from a camera store lying nearby. A vase lay broken on the thin rug in the centre of the room.

The sound of breaking he'd heard earlier.

He went back upstairs, leaving the door the way he'd found it. If the visitors came back and thought someone else had been inside, they'd be calling on him next.

Harry closed his front door and dropped his shoes on the floor. He took a small rubber wedge out of his bag and jammed it under the door. It wouldn't stop a tank or even someone mildly determined to get in, but it would give him a few moments' warning. Enough to start throwing furniture.

He climbed back into bed and waited for sleep, wondering what the Roman photographer, Mario, had been up to. And where he was now.

FIFTEEN

'Who were they?' Rik's face next morning went pale on hearing the news. 'Security police?'

Harry wasn't sure what the local security cops looked like, but the men he'd seen last night had conformed to a type.

'Them or army intelligence.' He described the driver's uniform.

'Shit,' Rik breathed. 'That's not good.' He blinked quickly and looked around as if unsure what to do.

'How well did you know him?' Harry asked.

'How do you mean?' Rik looked defensive.

'I mean, how well did you know him? Like, were you drinking buddies, nodding acquaintances, were you about to be engaged, what?' He waited but Rik looked blank, so he said heavily, 'They searched his flat – they even sliced open the cushions. Are they likely to find anything that might bring them here, to you?'

'No. *No*.' Rik looked shaken but defiant. 'Of course not.

I met him a few times around town, that's all. It's standing orders, to chum up with other foreigners, so I did.' He explained, 'I've always been interested in photography. He was happy to talk.' He gave Harry a wary look, as if he might have made a grave error, then said, 'These blokes . . . what did they look like?'

'It was dark. I didn't see much, apart from the one in uniform.' He thought back to when he'd looked out of his window. He hadn't got a clear view of the man, and the street lights weren't good. 'Short hair, thin face . . .' he shrugged. 'The others, I only saw the tops of their heads. Why?'

But Rik wasn't listening. 'Jesus, I was right!' His face had gone even paler, and his eyes were gleaming as he stared round the room. 'I knew it . . .'

'What's going on?' Mace had entered the office with Clare Jardine in tow. 'You two not falling out, I hope.' He hadn't heard Rik's last words, but had picked up on the tension in the air.

'No.' Rik jumped in before Harry could say anything. 'Harry was saying some blokes went through Mario's flat last night. One of them was in uniform. Security cops.'

Mace looked at Harry. 'That so? Well, well. Wonder what our Latin snapper's been doing. You take a look?'

'Yes. Nothing I could see, but they'd tossed it fairly comprehensively.' He paused, wondering what was bothering Rik Ferris. But there was also something from last night coming back to him. Something about the contents of Mario's flat. Or, more accurately, the lack of.

'What?' Clare Jardine was watching him, had spotted something.

'He's a press photographer, you said.' Harry looked at Rik.

'That's right. A freelance. Why?'

'There was some wrapping from a camera shop near the wastebasket. They'd kicked it over. I didn't think anything of it at the time. I think it was for a camera.'

'So? Maybe he needed a new one.'

'Maybe,' Harry agreed. 'But how many press photographers leave it until they get somewhere remote before buying a camera? Most photographers have a ton of photographic equipment lying around.'

'The cops could have taken it,' Mace suggested. 'If he's been a naughty boy, they'd collect it as evidence. Or to sell.'

Harry shook his head. Mace was being obtuse. 'They were empty-handed. And there was nothing inside the flat; no cases, no lights, no lenses – nothing.'

Mace shrugged, anxious to move on. 'I don't see there's anything we can do. Best keep out of it.' He looked at Rik. 'Any chance he was Italian intelligence?'

'I don't know.' Rik looked shell-shocked. 'Maybe. Probably.'

'Bloody right, probably. You'd best hope he doesn't give 'em your name just to wriggle out of whatever mess he's in, otherwise you'll be next.' He turned to Harry. 'You'd better come in – you, too, Rik. Something to show you.' They followed him into his office, where a PC monitor was humming on the desk.

'The details Clare picked up yesterday from her contact,' he said, moving behind his desk, 'were map co-ordinates.' He flipped a hand towards a large map of the country on the wall behind him. A red marker was positioned up near the top edge, north of a dark, jagged mass representing the Caucasus Mountains flowing from left to right. 'We sent them to London yesterday afternoon, and they've come back with this.' He spun the monitor on its base so they could all see the screen.

It was a high-altitude photo, grainy and sombre in a mix of dark greens and greys, with a darker shape like a thin tadpole, the narrow end of the tail pointing north.

'What's that?' said Harry. He recalled what Mace had said about the Russians coming, and his mouth went dry. *Surely, bloody not . . .*

'We think it's a military convoy: trucks, APCs, troop carriers . . . maybe even tanks. London's waiting for another sweep to get more detail.' Mace pointed further south, where a line me-andered through the hills. 'This is a road through the moun-tains called the Kazek Pass. It's narrow but negotiable, and spills out on to a plain about thirty miles wide. South of there,' his finger moved down, 'is open country all the way.' He sat back and looked at them. 'And by all the way, I mean all the way here.'

'Why would they do that?' Rik asked.

'They want to keep what's theirs.' It was Clare Jardine,

speaking from near the door. She had evidently seen the photo already. 'There's been trouble brewing for months over the gradual erosion – as Moscow sees it – of land with emerging states calling for independence. Each one opting out chips away at the Russian map, especially with the new states looking towards the European Union. Moscow doesn't like that. They've begun to fight back.'

'Let's hope not literally,' said Mace. He swept an arm across the map, right down to the borders with Iran. 'Because if they do, and that lot comes through the Kazek Pass, they could end up rolling right over our heads.'

SIXTEEN

'Something bugging you?' Harry dumped coffee powder in a mug. Rik was poking about in the back of a computer monitor.

Rik shook his head. 'Just . . . stuff.'

Harry looked round. Clare Jardine had gone out and Fitzgerald was with Mace in his office, going over a destruction plan if the Russians did arrive. 'It sounded more than stuff.' He poured water and stirred the mix, waiting.

Rik dropped the screwdriver he was using and stood up, flicking a glance at the door to the connecting office. He came over and made himself some tea, jabbing at a teabag as if stabbing it to death.

'We're being watched, you know that?' His voice was tight.

'Who by?' It wouldn't have surprised Harry, not after the last few days.

'I call them the Clones.' Rik looked at him, eyes bright. 'There's a team of four. Fitz said he might have seen them . . . Clare thinks she did, although I reckon she was taking the piss. Nobody wants to talk about it. Mace thinks I'm delusional.'

Harry held up his hand to halt the rush of words. 'Whoa, slow down. Who are these . . . Clones?'

'Local security police, I guess. All I know is, they're watching us. Christ, that makes me sound paranoid.' He laughed nervously and Harry realised he must have been itching to talk about this for some time.

'Go on.'

'There's four, right? Never more, sometimes less . . . but I reckon it's because they're on a rota system . . . two on, two off kind of thing.'

'Thanks,' said Harry dryly. 'I get the concept.'

'Sorry. Forgot. Anyway, they're always hanging about, sometimes on foot, sometimes in a car down the street.' He sipped his tea and winced at the heat. '*Shit*. I've even had them show up outside my place.'

'What do they look like?' Harry decided to keep it as calm as possible. If he really had spotted a team of watchers, it meant they'd undoubtedly now added his face to the collection of spooks in this building. Interesting, but not unusual. The Russians had already accused British Council staff of fomenting trouble among local minority groups. Other local intelligence organizations probably held similar views.

'Youngish, about thirty . . . fit-looking, jeans and street clothes – and shaven heads, although that's pretty much par for the course around here.' He grinned quickly. 'A short back and sides in this town is short all over.'

The description fitted half the men Harry had seen so far. Including the watcher at the airport.

'No special characteristics?'

'Not that I've noticed. Sorry.' He looked at Harry as if weighing up whether he'd been believed or not.

Harry put down his mug. 'Come on. Time for a cup of real coffee.'

'What?'

'We're going walkabout, see if we can spot one of these Clones.' He wasn't sure why he should care, but it was better than doing nothing.

He led the way downstairs. On the way out, he picked up a large brown envelope and handed it to Rik, with instructions to make his way to the railway station. 'Walk normally. If you clock one, don't do anything, just keep going as if you're on a boring errand. I'll see you there.'

'Where will you be?'

'Closer than you think.'

He waited for Rik to clear the end of the street, then slipped outside and followed at a discreet distance.

He picked up the first watcher a hundred yards out.

Heavy rain clouds had closed in on the town overnight, dumping a blanket of cold drizzle on the streets and filling the paper-choked gullies. Potholes were invisible under a covering of water, and Harry hugged the buildings to avoid a drenching from passing trucks.

The first man he saw fitted Rik's description to the letter: young, lean, anonymous, bristle-cut hair and nothing to mark him out. He wore a scruffy denim jacket, patched jeans and trainers, and hunched against the cold rain; he would have been invisible in any crowd.

He was also good at following a target.

Five minutes later Harry spotted another likely contender. This one appeared out of a shop doorway across the street. He sloped along, keeping Rik in his sights without losing pace. If there were any signals exchanged between him and his colleague, they kept them discreet.

The railway station was a heavy concrete structure with no pretensions of style, a plain, arched entrance and few windows. Like a brick shithouse with trains, thought Harry. He walked on by, allowing the first Clone to follow Rik inside. The other man had disappeared, and Harry guessed he had gone to cover the other exits. If there were any more on the job, they were keeping well back.

Once out of sight of the station entrance, Harry stopped and counted to fifty before doubling back. He passed a cheap clothes shop on a corner and ducked inside. When he came out he was wearing a waterproof ski hat pulled down over his ears.

The inside of the station was noisy, damp and unwelcoming, with a cold wind cutting through the concourse and tugging at a row of pennants strung across the front of the ticket office. Stalls selling hot drinks and snacks were doing a good trade, and he stopped at the nearest to buy a coffee and get his bearings.

He spotted Rik hovering by a stall selling nuts and dried fruit. He was holding the envelope and digging in his pocket for some coins. He looked at ease, a man on a minor errand, and Harry was impressed; from his earlier display of nerves, Rik was coping well with being thrown into the role of a decoy.

Clone One was loitering nearby, nibbling on an apple while reading the timetables, but rarely taking his eyes off Rik for more than a few moments. It was a few seconds before Harry realized that the man was speaking into a thumb-microphone.

Clone Two must be close.

Harry stayed where he was, using the other customers as cover. He had no chance of blending into the background; his clothes, although fairly nondescript, were still sufficiently different in cut and style to make him stand out if anyone looked at him carefully enough. And if he went walkabout in such a confined area, he'd be spotted immediately.

It wasn't long before he realized that the other Clone hadn't put in an appearance. He soon saw why: the man was behind him, in the shelter of a doorway. He could feel his eyes on the back of his neck.

Harry finished his coffee and dumped the mug in a rubbish bin. He'd slipped up; the man had spotted him as a newcomer, and therefore an oddity. Or maybe they had pictures and had picked him out the moment he showed up.

He nodded a thank you to the stallholder and walked away, taking him on a course which would pass close by Rik's position. As he drew level, he raised his hand close to his chest and pointed towards the exit.

Rik blinked once to show he understood.

Twenty minutes later, after taking a circuitous route through the town, Harry arrived back at the office to find Rik already there nursing a cup of coffee. He looked unsettled, and Harry guessed he probably hadn't done this kind of thing since basic training.

'Did I do OK?' asked Rik nervously. 'I don't think they clocked you, did they?'

'You did fine.' Harry wasn't about to tell him that he had been made, or that identifying two of the Clones wasn't bad. But it wasn't great. Somewhere in the background, unless they were resting, the other Clones had been operating unseen. If so, they would have identified him, but he had no idea what they looked like.

For now, though, he had other things to think about. On the way back, he had passed an alleyway with an army truck

parked in the entrance. Near the rear of the truck stood three
men. Two were in uniform, although he couldn't see any
insignia. The other man was in civilian clothes, and handing
out cigarettes, chatting amiably. It was an everyday scene,
even given the military presence.

The only anomaly was the civilian.

Harry wondered how Carl Higgins of Ohio had become so
fluent in the local language.

SEVENTEEN

Harry spent several days getting to know the town, its
layout, the road network, the general infrastructure
and its people. While what he could see was simple
enough to commit to memory, the people, although genial
enough when faced with a foreigner who didn't speak their
language, proved an odd nut to crack. Some were immediately friendly, in spite of the language problem, while others
showed open distrust, as if he had 'MI5 Officer' emblazoned
across his chest.

The town itself was an odd hotchpotch of tired, shabby buildings interspersed with newly constructed offices and shops. In
among the clearly care-worn structures of the older shops, with
tin roofs and crumbling brickwork, were occasional signs of
coming prosperity, international brand names jostling for space
with local products.

By way of contrast, each intersection had its huddle of
traders dealing in everything from cheap watches, jeans and
mobile phones, to vodka and even petrol. In between, men
argued and smoked with zeal, while elsewhere, rounded
women swathed in heavy coats and headscarves carried giant
sports bags or cloth bundles tied with string, on a never-ending
journey from one part of town to another.

The outer boulevards were wide yet deserted, mainly residential, while the inner streets were narrow and congested
with vehicles and pedestrians, their surfaces deeply potted and
crumbling. It was as if the inhabitants found it safer or even
comforting to stick to this tight, worn network of thorough-

fares rather than the open spaces. Yet there was something else; and the more he moved around, the more he began to feel that something in the air. He wondered if it had anything to do with the growing numbers of soldiers in the town, and the accompanying aura of threat hovering around them, even when they were not on duty and unarmed. They were everywhere, yet somehow disconnected from the hustle and bustle around them, like onlookers who had no place being there.

Two days after his first sighting of the Clones, Harry spotted another watcher.

Coming out of a small fruit store, where he had bought some apples, he saw a man across the street. He was checking his watch as if waiting for a lift.

It was the watcher from the airport.

Twenty minutes later, he saw him again. This time he was getting out of a car, which pulled away and sped out of sight.

Harry ignored him; if he was local security police, he'd have to make sure he did nothing they could pick him up for. But the idea that he might be another MI5 watcher made him feel increasingly edgy.

Each time he was in the office, Harry checked out the news channels on one of the PCs for news about the shooting in Essex. Paulton had made it clear that the last thing they could afford was for his name to come out. If that happened, it could compromise other ongoing operations. And if the press were able to identify one member of MI5 to the public, others might follow. The chain-reaction, aided by disaffected former officers or whistleblowers, could be devastating.

Harry soon began to feel he was being observed too closely, and on one of his forays through the town, he mapped out a number of internet cafes. Most were little more than a basement bar with a couple of computers on rickety tables. But they might prove his only alternative link with the outside world. And keeping an eye on the news which might affect him and his future was uppermost in his mind.

The first time he used one of the internet bars, he took a random route around town, stopping occasionally and doubling back. Twice he saw faces which didn't seem right, and he concluded that there was more than one man on him. Coming out of a store, he deliberately fumbled with change, and while stooping to pick up a fallen coin, checked his surroundings. Two more faces, although too distant to be sure if they were the Clones he'd seen before.

The bar he had selected was close by the town's market. The streets here were jumbled together like a child's toy-town, and the shops, although drab and unsophisticated, were small and busy. The bar was called ZOLA and located under a shoe mender, accessed by a short flight of stone steps.

Harry walked in and waved to the barman, then pointed to one of the two vacant computers at the back of the room. The barman nodded and said something in return, by which Harry presumed he was giving him the rate it would cost. When he looked blank, the man pointed to a blackboard over the bar with the minutes and hourly rates, then held up a glass.

Harry pointed to the nearest beer pump. When the glass was full, he took it and sat down at the computer.

The shooting was still in the news. As he scrolled down the BBC's main news page, his spirits sank. He checked the commercial television channels, which told him nothing more, then flicked through the websites of the British nationals. Some of the speculation was wildly off-target, but the guesswork contained a disturbing amount of accurate detail. One report even spoke with relish of an official cover-up, claiming in knowing tones that 'according to unnamed sources within the police, the name of an unknown security agent who was present at the shooting has been withheld by the Home Office pending internal enquiries.' The report went on to say that the name of this 'agent' would soon be a matter of public record, and that the Home Secretary, who was facing calls to bring in an outside senior police officer to take over, could not delay in replying for much longer.

As he read this, Harry wondered how much of the speculation was a result of unofficial briefings carefully leaked to keep the public temporarily satisfied until a coherent strategy could be decided on. He noted the name of the report's author, and hoped sourly that Shaun Whelan, whoever he was, would trip over and break his neck.

Tired of staring at the screen, he switched off the machine and paid the barman. He'd check again tomorrow. Maybe London would flood and they'd forget all about it.

Half an hour later, he turned a corner and stopped. He'd managed to lose his bearings, and instead of arriving back at the office, he'd somehow veered off course and arrived across from the Palace Hotel.

He entered the main doors and crossed a large, tiled foyer scattered with potted palms and comfortable chairs. A sign pointed to a bar, from where he could hear the sound of laughter and the clink of glasses.

He checked the room before walking in. Four men and a woman, all westerners, were gathered around a table. Two of the men were working at laptops, while the others had their heads together in discussion. They did not spare Harry more than a cursory glance.

There was no sign of Higgins. Harry went to the bar and ordered a beer, then found a comfortable chair in one corner, in line-of-sight of the door, but set back from anyone walking by.

The other customers were a mix of German and Swedish, and appeared to be part of a news team gearing up to head north. There was talk of local guides, 'road' rations and where to stay if they got bogged down anywhere remote.

Ten minutes later, Carl Higgins walked in.

He gave the group a friendly wave, then bellied up to the bar, flicking a finger at a lager pump. Moments later, he was joined by one of the newsmen. They spoke in soft tones for five minutes. The other journalists ignored them.

When three more men walked in, the journalist with Higgins returned to the table and the talk continued as if he had never left.

The three newcomers, all dressed in suits, scanned the bar, eyes passing over Harry without a flicker. They were all in their late thirties or early forties, with smooth shaves and the well-fed look of diplomats who believe in keeping trim. They joined Higgins at the bar, and the man from Ohio ordered more drinks, then led them through a glass-panelled doorway into a restaurant. The last man in dragged a heavy CLOSED sign across the floor and shut the door behind him.

Harry felt the beer turn sour in his mouth. Could they be any more bloody obvious? He got up and left. He had seen enough.

Higgins was a spook.

EIGHTEEN

Journalist Shaun Whelan was feeling his age, if not his weaknesses. He stepped out of the lights and echoes of Clapham South underground station, and headed towards a nearby stretch of open parkland. It was just before ten at night and a chill was in the air. But in spite of the temptation to turn for home and curl up with a glass of Chablis, he was feeling the pull of another, far stronger temptation; one which he knew would not easily fade.

A thin-faced wisp of a man with fair hair and soft skin, he had long ago become accustomed to the twin attractions in his life: the pursuit of a good story on one hand, with all the stresses, frustrations and disappointments that brought, and on the other, the desire for something he thought of as affection . . . even love. Which, he conceded with a nod to irony, was as stressful and disappointing as the day job . . . and just as frustrating on a different level.

He pushed the thought away and pulled up his collar, distancing himself from a group of youths loitering on the pavement. He was hoping the brief eye contact and the slip of paper exchanged in the pub near Westminster at lunchtime had not been an elaborately cruel tease. Some of the young set were like that, building up older men for a fall, mindless of the damage they were doing to frail egos and frailer bodies. As if it were not wounding enough to be getting on in years, having the salt of unkindness rubbed in was an injury he could do without. And after losing Jamie, his companion of the past decade, he needed all the warmth – however fleeting – he could find.

He tried to take his mind off the darkness and its potential perils by focussing on the story he was currently chasing around the cubby-holes of Whitehall. It remained tantalizingly short on detail and would probably stay that way unless he got spectacularly lucky, but what was certain was that a combined security services and Met police drugs snatch had gone disastrously wrong, leaving four dead in a hail of gunfire. Two were rumoured to be a courting couple, while a third had been a policeman from an armed response unit. The fourth was unknown, but possibly one of the drugs gang.

During his digging, Whelan had heard a name mentioned by one of his police contacts, although it was still unconfirmed. All he had been able to ascertain was that an MI5 officer named Tate had been transferred to 'other' operations shortly after the shooting. He felt certain it was no coincidence.

His initial research had revealed that a Harry Tate had started out in the army, transferring to the Intelligence Corps with service in Central Europe, before subsequently dis-appearing off the map. He knew what that signified: the man had most likely been scooped up by one of the security agen-cies, possibly MI5 or SIS (MI6), and his whereabouts and current role had been sanitized. The two agencies were always on the trawl for good people with useful backgrounds. Candidacy as a spy or counter-spy wasn't always judged by possession of a good degree and being 'spotted' by a friendly Oxford or Cambridge don; they needed their fair share of older people with solid experience in place of a creative CV – especially with the current focus on the war against terror. And Tate sounded just the right type.

If Whelan's sources were correct, Tate had been the man running the operation. He didn't have all the details yet, but the story was out there, waiting. The very idea was nearly enough to make him turn and go home, where he could continue trawling through the files for more sources.

But not quite. As he crossed the pavement and on to a path stretching across the park, he saw a figure ahead of him in the gloom. The build looked familiar and he felt a knot of excitement in his chest.

Whelan hopped over a short fence and entered the shadows close to a public convenience. The air was heavy with the aroma of damp earth, rotten vegetation . . . and toilets. His nose twitched, the Whitehall story suddenly pushed into the background. No way was he going in there; it was a death-trap waiting to happen. Instead, he veered towards a line of

trees on the far side, where the back-glow of street lights cast
at least an element of warmth and normalcy.

He increased his pace, eyeing the bushes to one side. The
figure he'd seen earlier had disappeared. The darkness here
was virtually impenetrable, but he saw something out of the
corner of his eye, a flash of movement against a lighter background. Friend or foe? Warmth or chill? His breathing increased
and his blood began to race, buoyed by the thrill of the chase.

He forced himself to slow down. No sense in making himself
look too desperate; a quick way of turning the boy off, if
anything.

As he followed the path around the darker morass of a
pond, picking up the metallic, muddy tang of standing water,
he saw the figure more clearly, standing beneath a tree, backlit
by distant lights. Medium height, slim, dressed in the loose
clothing of the street, easy to slip out of.

Easy to slip into.

His excitement began to build, and he jammed a hand into
his trouser pocket. Anxiety and anticipation were the twin
fuels which kept him going at times like this, but they could
easily become all-controlling. *Christ, he was like a sixteen-
year-old on his first time! Cool it, Whelan, or you'll blow it.*
Although, come to think of it, he reflected with a dizzy chuckle,
wasn't that rather the point?

'You made it,' he called. His voice was shaky, breathless,
and sounded inane. Like a line from an old movie. Yet what
else could he say?

'I said I would.' It was the voice from the pub. It had been
competing with the din of music and laughter, but he recalled
the tight build, the young, handsome face and the strong hands.

Especially the hands.

Not the eyes, though. He felt a touch of unease. The eyes
looked . . . different. Not like the voice and the body language.
Yet there had been so much more . . .

Then it was too late to change his mind, even if he'd wanted
to. *Sorry, Jamie,* he thought briefly, and stepped up close to the
youth, his heart pounding. This was too good to waste. Too rare.

The youth responded, moving in close. Whelan took in the
scent of aftershave, something lemony and subtle, and the heat
of sweet breath on his cheek. He abandoned himself to the
feeling of being cherished, of being warmed.

The feeling lasted just three seconds.

Then Whelan felt an ice-cold burning deep in his gut. His legs began to fold, their strength suddenly ebbing away. He felt his bladder loosen, humiliating and hotly wet down his legs. He struggled to hold himself upright, to lock his knees against the downward pressure, but the muscles and sinews wouldn't obey. Nothing would.

He coughed, but couldn't understand why.

The youth stepped back. In his hand, a flicker of steel, and on his face, total blankness.

Whelan turned his head away, his last voluntary action. In the sudden, bitter knowledge of disappointment, he was sure he saw Jamie standing off to one side, pale and translucent in the night. Waiting.

Then everything went black.

NINETEEN

The Odeon restaurant was empty again, save for Mace. The station chief was sitting near the back wall, at his usual table. He had left instructions at the office for Harry to join him. There had been no reason to refuse, and Harry had seen enough of the town for a while and wanted to see what information Mace might have other than gossip about his colleagues.

As he sat down, Mace called for the old woman. She shuffled out bearing a tray loaded with bowls of food, and placed it on the table.

He stared in surprise. He saw green chicken, egg-fried rice, onions, bean shoots and a mix of what could have been pork and beef.

'Christ, where did this come from?'

Mace's eyes gleamed. 'Best Thai for miles. Actually, the only Thai for miles. Beats me how or why; she must have travelled a bit in a former life. Served it up one day without asking. Never seen anyone else get it, so maybe she fancies me. Tuck in.' He picked up a spoon and scooped up chicken, bean shoots and rice, humming cheerfully.

Harry wanted to refuse; to tell Mace to stuff his fancy food and get lost, that he wanted to go home. But Mace had his orders, and sending a member of the awkward squad back to London wasn't part of the agenda. Besides, Harry's professional side was intrigued to want to find out what was going on here. He sat down and reached for a spoon and plate.

They ate in silence, and Harry was grateful for the first decent meal he'd had in what seemed like days. Airline food and greasy takeaways were beginning to take their toll on his system.

'You been taking a snoot at the Clones, I see,' Mace muttered eventually. His eyes twinkled with amusement. 'Young Rik's seeing shadows.'

'You don't believe him?' Harry wondered about Mace's scepticism. Did he know more than he was letting on?

'Never said that. Just said he shouldn't let it get to him.' He dabbed his lips with a paper napkin. 'Bound to be under scrutiny, aren't we? Stands to reason; we're the enemy. Anyone who thinks our British Council cover fools anyone needs their bumps felt. Same in London with their trade delegates. We stand out like spare dicks at a wedding.' He hoovered up more rice. 'How many did you spot?'

'Two. Rik says there are four.'

'That would be about it. They probably hang on the Americans and French tails, too, with regular changeovers to keep 'em fresh. I wouldn't worry about it.'

'They both have intelligence teams here?'

'Course they do. This close to Mother Russia and the Caspian, they'd be negligent not to. Most of them are so-called oil engineers and the like, but their cover's paper thin.'

Like Higgins, thought Harry. Different skin but the same animal underneath.

'So we ignore them?'

'Ignore them, forget them, stay well away, is my suggestion.' His eyes locked on to Harry's. 'That's not bad advice, either.'

Before Harry could reply, the restaurant door opened and two men stepped in off the street.

The first was large, like a bear, unshaven and with lank, black hair, but dressed in a smart suit, white shirt and buffed shoes. His shadow filled the doorway. The other man was shorter, slim like a dancer, and dressed in black. He moved round the bigger man, light on his feet, and stood to one side, waiting.

The big man approached their table.

'Mr Mace,' he said genially. His eyes slid over Harry in a rapid assessment. 'I see you are enjoying our excellent native cuisine.' He chuckled at his wit and smoothed the front of his suit.

'Mr Mayor,' Mace greeted him, and sucked in a bean shoot with relish. 'Care to join us? There's plenty.'

'Thank you. Not today.' The man looked at Harry again and Mace shifted in his seat.

'Oh, sorry – rude of me. Geordi Kostova . . . Harry Tate.' He looked at Harry and explained, 'Geordi's the local mayor. Very important man, hereabouts.' He turned to the mayor. 'Harry's on assignment from England, come to join our little crew.'

'So? A replacement for Jimmy Gulliver, yes?'

Mace's smile slipped for a second, but he hoisted it back quickly. 'Sort of. Head Office likes to rotate new employees. Field experience, you could call it.'

'I understand. Such a pity Jimmy had to return home. I enjoyed his company. Well, Mr Tate – Harry,' Geordi smiled and bowed courteously, 'welcome to our humble town. I hope you will find much to enjoy here.'

'I'm sure I will. The countryside looks beautiful.'

'Yes. Very true. But be careful where you go.' Kostova put a large finger against his nose. 'Such beauty holds many dangers and our roads are not for the faint of heart.'

Tell me about it, thought Harry. Ploughed bloody fields spring to mind.

Kostova glanced at his watch, a Rolex. 'Please excuse me, but as mayor, there are many duties I must attend to in these troubled times.'

'Troubled?' Harry detected a warning look from Mace but ignored him.

Kostova shrugged, a heft of huge shoulders. 'Some local land matters,' he explained in a bored tone. 'Nothing for you to worry about. Enjoy your stay.'

He turned and walked out, the slim man falling in behind him like a shadow.

'He just told us to mind our own business,' said Harry. 'Nice.'

'Not surprised. You notice the other fella?' Mace scooped up more rice. 'Geordi's wingman, goes by the name of Nikolai. Watch out for him. He's a cutter if ever I saw one.'

'Why would a small-town mayor need a bodyguard?'

'Well, apart from status, this area's full of tribal conflict, that's why. They'd never think twice about popping off someone like Geordi if he didn't play fair. Bodyguard, chauffeur, fixer – Nikolai's always there. See the mayor and Nikolai won't be more than six feet away.' He took a swig of water. 'Geordi has lots of interests, see, outside of being His Worship.' He smiled sourly. 'Well, he'd have to, wouldn't he? Can't make a living being mayor of a dump like this.'

'What sort of interests?' The suit and Rolex hadn't been picked up at the local market. And there was something about the man that reminded him of other local politicians he'd come across in the Balkans. Usually well-fed, mostly highly intelligent and never less than devious.

'Trade, mostly. Anyone wants it, Geordi can get it – for a price. Got lots of contacts all over the region. Some of 'em up north.' He left the meaning hanging, and concentrated on clearing his plate.

'How far north?' Harry prompted. Mace's abbreviated talk and his oblique references were getting on his nerves.

'What?'

'You said contacts up north.'

'Oh, right. Well, all the way to Moscow, as it happens.' He tapped a finger on the table. 'A lot of 'em do around here, if they know what's good for them.'

'Official, you mean? Or not?'

'Official. If they've got other friends, they probably keep it very quiet, if they've any sense.'

'So what was that just now – a chance visit?' He didn't believe it for a moment.

Mace confirmed it. 'Geordi doesn't do things by chance. He's a planner – a strategist. He wanted to see who you are. He likes to keep close tabs on everyone who drops by his little bailiwick.' He grinned sourly. 'He'll soon have more than he can deal with, I reckon.'

'Would that include keeping tabs on Carl Higgins?' He explained about his sightings of the journalist around town.

Mace nodded. 'He's another busy bee. The Americans are keeping a watching eye on the situation, like us. Steer clear, is my advice.'

Harry pushed his plate away, appetite gone. He had a feeling

Mace still wasn't telling him everything. 'So Kostova's not just the mayor.'

'No. On the surface, he's a political appointee. He just put more money into the regional government's pot than the next man, that's all. And he's got mates. Prick any mayor in this neck of the woods and you'll find their veins running with greed. And deep, deep loyalties.'

'He dresses very well.'

'Yeah, he's a real dandy, is Geordi. Likes to travel, too.' He stood up, brushing at the front of his jacket. 'You done?'

Harry nodded. 'Who was Jimmy Gulliver?'

Mace's eyes were cool. 'He was here for a while, same as you. Then he went home. End of story.' He turned and walked out, leaving Harry staring after him.

TWENTY

George Paulton eyed the bodies assembled in the large room and sensed his spirits stirring. An emergency meeting had been called and the air of excitement was palpable. He noticed a number of eyes normally dulled by the mundane, gleaming with an inner fire.

Of the men and women here, at least six were involved in the Middle Eastern and Central European desks of their various agencies, while others were co-optees, on standby for whatever specialist information they might harbour in their little grey cells and black portfolios. He noticed the Deputy Director of Special Forces, Lieutenant-Colonel Spake, tall, tanned and dangerous-looking, standing at the back of the room. Near him, another man in a dark suit who could only be American, and further along, a face he seemed to recall from a GCHQ meeting a few months back. There were also people from the Foreign Office and the MOD, and the heavy figure of Sir Anthony Bellingham of MI6.

Marcella Rudmann rapped on the table and everyone found a seat and settled down. Bottles of water were uncapped and glasses rattled, but it was clear that everyone – like Paulton – was intrigued.

Almost everyone, anyway, he reflected, staring at Spake.
The officer seemed slightly bored, a sure sign that he knew
more than anyone else. Interesting.

Rudmann cleared her throat, waiting for silence. For a brief
moment, she caught Paulton's eye. He looked away, prefer-
ring not to face her. News of Shaun Whelan's sordid demise
had filtered quickly into the wasp-nest of Westminster, and
he realized he might have moved just a shade too fast in
dealing with that particular problem. Not that anyone could
prove anything; another stabbing was hardly news. But a gay
older man knifed while cruising on Clapham Common might
be sufficient to rattle a few cages among the moral majority.
Especially as that man was a well-known journalist.

'Just over eighteen hours ago,' Rudmann began, 'we received
information that Georgian Forces were moving north into the
breakaway region of South Ossetia.' She indicated a stack of
folders on a side table. 'Full details are contained in the
briefing notes, so please refer to them later. Due to circumstances, this briefing is exactly that – brief. We'll call further
meetings as and when the situation develops.' She glanced at
Spake and added, 'I'll ask the Deputy Director of Special
Forces to take up the briefing.' She nodded at the army officer
with a faint flush of her cheeks, and sat down.

Paulton smiled to himself. Jesus, the bloody woman was
almost salivating. He stored the thought away for future
reference.

Spake climbed languidly to his feet and stepped over to a
large interactive map on the back wall. It showed the entirety
of Europe stretching right across to the border between
Pakistan and Afghanistan, and Paulton felt his spirits sink.
God, don't let it be another briefing on some shitty rock-pile
where they think they've found Osama Bin Laden playing
backgammon and drinking coffee. It would be like all the
other 'sightings': totally bloody useless and time-wasting.

But Spake soon put paid to that theory. He tapped the map
with a tanned finger, on an area to the west of Afghanistan,
near the Caspian Sea.

'As Ms Rudmann just said, Georgian army units including
battle tanks, APCs and troop transport have moved north into
the separatist area of South Ossetia. They're backed up by
helicopters and fighters, but we have no news yet of how

active any air units have been. As some of you may know,
there have been tensions between the two for some time, with
clashes at numerous points along the disputed border. So far,
though, it hasn't broken out into outright war, and it could be
that some mediation by the US government has been a
restraining factor.' He glanced at the man in the dark suit, who
nodded slightly. 'However, that looks like changing as the
Georgian government sees itself being challenged by this –
and other – separatist areas. If Georgian forces go in hard,
and ignore international appeals, then it doesn't take much to
realize what might happen.' He moved his hand and tapped a
dark area on the map representing a stretch of mountains.
'The Caucasus Mountains; the dividing line between Georgia,
South and North Ossetia . . . and Russia.' He turned and faced
the audience. 'Our information is that heavy troop numbers
have been building up, and that a surge of movement can be
expected any day.'

'Are you saying?' A florid-faced man in a sharp grey suit
posed the inevitable question, 'that the Georgians might push
right through to Russia? That's madness.'

'No. I'm saying the opposite,' Spake replied shortly. 'The
people in Ossetia now have Russians citizenship. If Moscow
chooses to exert its right to protect those people, there's only
one way to do it.'

There was a lengthy silence as the words sank in, punctuated by a pigeon flapping on a windowsill outside. If there was
a collective thought among the listeners, it was one of alarm.

'I don't believe it,' a voice muttered. But nobody hurried
to agree.

'What about the Americans? They've been supporting
Georgia. What are they doing?' The first speaker looked at
the American as if he alone were responsible. The American
ignored him.

'That's why we're monitoring the situation.' Spake tapped
the map. 'As of forty-eight hours ago, two teams – one from
the US Delta Force and the other from our own Special
Reconnaissance Regiment – were inserted to watch the possible
approach routes from the north.'

'Inserted? How?'

'The usual way. Quietly.'

'It's leaving it a bit late, isn't it?' said another man. 'By the time the teams spot anyone, they'll already be over the border and heading south.'

'You're right. But dropping men to the north of the mountains, where they could spot any movement earlier, would be too hazardous. The Russians have already been increasing their monitoring operations in the area for some time.'

The voices died again as they digested these implications, and Paulton reflected that if it hadn't been the Deputy Director Special Forces delivering the sobering facts, the place would have been in an uproar of doubt and sheer incredulity. As it was, their belief was total. He glanced at his watch and wondered how soon he would be able to get out of here. His involvement was going to be minimal from here on in.

The next question killed any such notion.

'What if they do move south?' Marcella Rudmann queried. 'How far might they go?'

Spake studied her face for a moment, and she blushed again under the scrutiny.

He shook his head. 'We don't know. Nobody does . . . except possibly Mr Putin.' It did not go unnoticed that he made no mention of President Medvedev.

'But your best guess?'

He studied the map and reached out his hand. It hovered for a moment on the mountain region of South Ossetia . . . then stabbed down further south.

Much further.

'Best guess? At least Gori . . . but possibly the capital, Tbilisi. And anywhere in between. God help anyone who shouldn't be there.'

And George Paulton, watching where the finger finally came to rest, felt his guts turn to ice.

TWENTY-ONE

Sixty miles to the north of Tbilisi, in the foothills of the Caucasus, a late breeze was sliding off the mountains, bringing a cold snap from the peaks. It was a welcome relief from the unusually warm lull that had been hanging around the lower plains during the day, and the man on watch shivered slightly under his camouflage smock. Winter was making its first move, far to the north and east.

He moved with care, scanning the lake three hundred metres away. The lightweight thermal infrared monocular was good to go in any light, and the long range optics could pick up any heat source or movement.

At any other time and place, he reflected, such as his native Michigan, it would have been a joy to sit and drink in the utter stillness and beauty of nature. A few birds were swinging slowly over the water, occasionally dipping to gather insects or some drops of moisture, then soaring upwards like elegant kites, feeding off the remaining thermals. A bunch of crows called among a stretch of conifers over to the right, their haunting sounds echoing across the lake, and a fox poked its nose out of the bushes and made its way down to the water's edge, where it drank in brief bursts, before slinking back into the shadows.

The watcher, whose name was Jordan Conway, glanced at his watch. The dulled case and face reflected nothing, both treated with light-absorbing film. For out here, even the smallest movement, the tiniest glimmer, could betray a man's position in an instant. As if to test the theory, he stared beyond the trees to the right of the lake, where he knew Bronson and Capel were dug in, watching their flank. There was no sign that they were there. He hoped it stayed that way.

'How's it going?' The whisper came from a few feet to his rear. The speaker was Doug Rausing, the leader and fourth member of the Delta team and a ten-year veteran of covert operations on behalf of the Pentagon and the White House. He came from Tennessee, although none of his colleagues held that against him. Surfacing from a brief sleep, he was inching forward to take over from Conway as soon as the light dropped.

'No signs,' said Conway. 'Just the birds.' He wished he could move and scratch the itch on his upper right arm, which was driving him crazy. He was sure he could feel the tiny electronic biscuit under his skin, although they'd told him he wouldn't; that it was buried too deep. But they'd also said the alien object wouldn't trouble him after the first couple of days. Darned fool scientists, what the hell did they know? Did they ever come out here in the field and test this stuff for themselves?

Behind him, Rausing was also fingering his upper arm and wondering how the others were coping.

Two hundred miles west of Conway's position, three members of the British Special Reconnaissance Regiment were in their initial observation post, rotating to watch the northern approaches. Shrouded in a makeshift basha, they had eaten their rations and were waiting for the light to fall before moving forward to take up a better position on the lower slopes. This would place them at the neck of a narrow pass leading through the foothills. It was a two-mile hike, but would be easy meat, and a necessary move. Intelligence briefs had told them this was a likely line of approach by motorised forces. Such was the lie of the land, even a squirrel would find it difficult to move without being seen.

The leader of the three-man team, a stocky Para Regiment veteran named Mike Wilson, lowered his binoculars and rubbed his eyes. Then he eased himself backwards a few inches off the brow of the hollow towards Jocko Wardle and 'Hunt' Wallis, his two colleagues, who were asleep. He nudged them awake with his foot without taking his eyes off the landscape before him, and waited while they stirred and opened their eyes, moving only to reach for their weapons.

'Ten minutes to go,' he told them quietly. 'Clean up.' It was something none of them needed telling, to check the ground where they had been lying, but repeated procedure was the way to do things right. Even the tiniest scrap of personal litter – a wrapping, a piece of foil, a button – would reveal their passage and tell anyone looking that they had been here. And in this relatively barren landscape, if that happened, they would be unlikely to survive for long.

Wilson checked his own kit. When he was satisfied everything was in its place and tied down tight, he slid to the front of the O.P. and began scanning the terrain in front of him for signs of movement.

There was nothing. But he felt uneasy all the same. It was too quiet.

He paused only to scratch at an itch in the top of his arm.

TWENTY-TWO

'We've got another job.' Clare Jardine was waiting in the office next morning, nursing a cup of tea. She was dressed in what Harry thought of as her Lara Croft look, and looked as friendly as a pit-bull.

'Oh, goody,' he said dryly. 'Another pick-up?'

She ignored his sarcasm. 'We're going to eyeball a convoy moving north. It looks like part of a much larger force. The satellite images are inconclusive, and London wants us to ID the unit and report back on numbers and density.' Jardine meant seeing if the vehicles in the convoy were full or empty. Unless the convoy was obliging enough to reveal its load just as the satellite passed overhead, there was no way of telling, save for sending in someone on the ground to take a look.

Harry was surprised Mace hadn't mentioned it, or that he hadn't been brought in on the transmission from London. In a place this small, all hands should be aware of the general nature of things, in case someone dropped out through illness or accident. He wondered what else he wasn't being told about.

They took the same Land Cruiser as before, this time with Jardine at the wheel. She drove with skill, using the right amount of aggression to compete with the local trucks and cars, and said nothing for twenty minutes until they were clear of the town. When they reached the fork in the road, she took the right one this time, the suspension protesting at the rougher surface. Harry noticed that theirs was the only vehicle.

'This leads north into the hills,' she explained. 'Nothing much to see up here, so why bother with a decent road?'

Harry nodded. It was clearly not her first time on this road, so he sank back against the door pillar and closed his eyes. He'd had another restless night, haunted by images of Parrish charging along the bank of the inlet and the man in dreadlocks calmly shooting him with a wooden pole. The young couple had been standing in the glare of the Land Rover's headlights, clothes torn and bloodied by gunshots, applauding the outcome. He had woken in a confusion of sweat and shivering, trying to figure out how the couple had penetrated the secure cordon without being seen.

'Mace told you about me,' Jardine interrupted his thoughts. It wasn't a question.

Harry shook off the images from his dreams and shrugged. 'Only that you're with Six.'

'Liar. Mace couldn't keep a secret if his balls were on fire.' There was no heat to her words, which made him even more certain that Mace had told her and the others why he was here.

'You know him better than I do.'

'Damn right.'

'OK, so what brought you to this lovely spot?'

'That's none of your business. I didn't stick to their stupid rulebook; let's leave it at that.'

'But you know all about me.'

'Jesus, everyone knows about you.' She touched the brakes, skimming uncomfortably close to a tractor parked on the side of the road. 'Not many Fivers get tabbed for allowing two civilians and a cop to get killed.'

Harry stared, surprised by the brutality of her words. He wasn't sure whether to be angry or not.

'I didn't—' He stopped. She might not know all the grubby details, and he'd almost been lured into telling her. It was a reminder of her job prior to being sent here.

She looked disappointed. 'Never mind; if you don't want to tell, don't. We hear rumours – and we get the newspapers here, and the internet, just like they do in SW1. You'd be famous, if only the public knew who you were.' She glanced across. 'I suppose there's more to it than meets the eye?'

'A lot more.' He wondered how much to tell. But what could she do to him that hadn't been done already? 'It was a combined drugs bust. Five and the police. We had strong intel about a shipment of mixed narcotics. We were all ready to go, then the team was cut back hours before the operation on economic grounds. I decided it was too late to call it off, that the shipment was a big one and worth stopping.'

'What happened?'

'We were outgunned. Two civilians got in the way. I still

don't know how. They popped up out of nowhere.' He didn't elaborate; there was no need.

She drove in silence for a mile, then said, 'So what made you come here? You could have refused.'

He shrugged. 'I've always gone where they sent me. It seemed a good idea.'

'And now?'

'It was a mistake.' It sounded resentful, even weak. Maybe that was the trouble; he had meekly done what Paulton had told him, rather than risk facing exposure and possible humiliation, even though both would have been inherently unfair.

It still didn't answer the mystery of the young couple who had died. The other question bugging him was, why a Land Rover? It was hardly the best transport for a bloke on the pull. And why had the man held up his hand the way he did just before he was shot? Was he trying to be cool? Did he think that would be enough to protect him?

Or was it a signal?

Later, as they passed through a huddle of small houses and began a steady climb into the foothills, Jardine asked him to pass her a cigarette from the glove box. He hadn't seen her smoke before. She opened the side window and turned up the air-blower, and when she had the cigarette going, said, 'Sorry. Nasty habit I picked up recently. It keeps me sane. I'll pull over and have a quick drag outside if you'd prefer.'

Harry shook his head, wondering what other surprises were waiting for him.

'I was tabbed for letting the game get away from me,' she announced suddenly. She sounded angry. 'I overstepped the mark and broke the golden rule of the Whitehall gentlemen's club: I screwed the enemy.'

Harry remained silent, which seemed to annoy her even more.

'Christ, you men are so bloody two-faced! How many of you,' she demanded hotly, 'if you had to get close to a target, and found her to be – I don't know, a twenty-three-year-old with a body to die for and who wanted you – would say no? Tell me that.'

'Beats me,' said Harry honestly. 'I've never been in that

position.' She had a point. Would he be able to resist, given those circumstances? He didn't know. Not that he was expecting it to happen anytime soon – not unless the enemy started fielding older Mata Haris with a weakness for out-of-condition British men on the downward slope of manhood. Anyway, playing down and dirty in the street was one thing – he'd done it for years and was good at it. Boudoir games weren't part of his armoury. 'Did you know Jimmy Gulliver?'

She changed down and swerved past a donkey and cart loaded with cut grass. An old man watched them go, flicking a makeshift whip over the animal's flanks.

'What about him?' She hadn't answered the question, he noticed.

He told her about meeting Geordi Kostova and his wingman, Nikolai.

Clare nodded and said, 'If you shook hands with Kostova, don't bother counting your fingers – he'll have kept one. He's a wheeler-dealer. The only difference between him and a Mafioso is that he actually made mayor without sticking a gun to anyone's head.'

'You mean he paid for it.'

'Did Mace tell you that?' She shrugged. 'It's possible, I suppose. Mace knows more about him than I do. He's welcome. I had Kostova grease up to me once. He's a toucher, he can't help it; but he soon pulled in his horns.'

Harry recalled what Mace had said about her being hard-nosed. 'What did you do?'

'I showed him my little toy.' She threw her cigarette out of the window and took a shiny black object out of her pocket. It was crescent-shaped, the width of her hand and carried a trace of powder residue on one edge. Clare rubbed it across her thigh to clean it, then gave a flick of her wrist. The compact opened into a razor-sharp knife with a three-inch curved blade. 'It seemed to convince him.'

'Nice.' Harry's belly contracted at the sight of the cold steel. He'd seen something like it once before, in the hands of a Dutch prostitute who believed in affirmative action. It was called a drop-point blade and for cutting rather than stabbing. He decided that Mace's description of Clare Jardine had been much too generous.

'I spent some time in Miami,' she explained. 'Got close to a girl who ran with a Cuban street gang. She got raped once and vowed never again. She showed me how to use it.' She closed the blade with a click and put it away. 'You say Kostova mentioned Jimmy Gulliver?'

'Yes.'

She was silent for a mile or so, then said, 'Jimmy was already here when I arrived. He stayed about a month. He was one of the first postings after Mace. He was nice. Sorry if I sounded cagey, but I wasn't sure if you were just fishing.'

'I was. Mace acted as if the name meant something.'

She threw him a glance. 'It would. Jimmy never told us why he'd been sent here, and if Mace knew, he didn't let on.'

'He played dumb with me, too. What did you know about him?'

'Only that he was part of a fast-track intake and marked out for higher things. Then something happened. He was pretty deep into the organization, considering his age. He was thirty-two. He hated being here – he thought it was a dead-end.'

'Isn't it?'

'I suppose so, for some. Anyway, one day he packed his bags and went home.' She grimaced. 'I'm surprised Kostova admitted to knowing him.'

'To me, you mean?'

'Yes.' She gave a sideways look. 'You're still an unknown quantity.'

'Kostova knows what we do?'

She nodded. 'Bound to. There isn't much goes on in this town that he doesn't know about. I doubt London will have been pleased to hear he and Jimmy knew each other – that's if Jimmy ever admitted it.'

'They'd have found out,' said Harry. Any debrief after a posting like this place, so close to the Russian border, would have been highly intensive. Add in the punishment element and Gulliver would have been under the spotlight for weeks, every fragment of information about his movements and contacts being wheedled out of him by the company shrinks until he was left dry.

Clare nodded. 'I guess. Still, nice to know – that he went back, I mean. It says there's a chance for the rest of us, doesn't it?'

'Have you heard from him since?'

'No. Not a word.' Her voice carried a frown, but she didn't elaborate. He wondered how close they had been. Then she added, 'No surprise, though; once they go, they stay gone.' She hesitated. 'It would have taken a while, though.'

'Why?'

'He was going overland. He'd got a fantastic rate on a car from a local rental place, and the arrangement was he could drop it off at the dealer's brother near Calais.' She shook her head. 'I said he was mad, because it's a hell of a trip. But he said he wasn't bothered because he hated flying. I think he just wanted a taste of freedom for a while. Who could blame him after this?'

'Did he have any family?'

'I don't think so. He had an aunt who brought him up, he once told me. Exeter, I believe.' She glanced across. 'What about you?'

The change of tack surprised him. 'No.'

'Wife . . . girlfriend?'

'That's private.' He definitely wasn't going to discuss Jean. Not with her.

'I'm Six,' said Clare. 'Nothing's private.'

He said nothing. After a mile or so, she said vaguely, 'I should tell you, the target I got burned by?'

'What about him?'

'It was a woman.'

'What's this?' he murmured, 'you show me yours and I show you mine?'

Before he could take it further, she was sitting forward, staring through the windscreen. 'What's this?'

They drew level with a khaki-coloured jeep with its nose buried in a bank at the side of the road. It looked abandoned. Later, they saw a military truck on jacks, with three soldiers struggling to change a shredded tyre. They stared as the Land Cruiser swept by, and Harry watched in his side mirror as one of the men leaned into the cab and backed out holding a radio. Calling home?

Two miles further on, he had his answer.

They were rounding a long, sweeping curve over a wooded gully, when Clare jammed on the brakes and called a warning. The tyres bit into the rough road, causing the vehicle to bounce, and she wrestled with the wheel as it threatened to tear itself out of her grip.

Harry had enough time to grab for his seat, when he noticed a line of soldiers scattering from the road right in front of them.

TWENTY-THREE

Stones hammered underneath the car like machine-gun fire and a dust cloud billowed up around them as they skidded to a halt. Amid a volley of shouting and the rattle of automatic weapons being cocked, the doors were wrenched open and soldiers motioned them to get out.

Harry moved slowly with his hands in clear sight. All it needed was a stumble and one trigger-happy soldier, and all hell would break loose. Some of the soldiers looked nervous, and he put their average age at little more than twenty. Then a large figure pushed through the men, waving away the dust cloud.

It was Geordi Kostova.

Behind him came Nikolai. They looked at ease among the troops, who moved aside without complaint to let them through. Kostova motioned Harry to stay where he was, and signalled for Clare to follow him. They walked away a few yards, with Nikolai close by, and the mayor made a display of studying Clare's passport. He rattled off a few questions, with gestures towards Harry, and although the words were indistinct, the bite in his voice was in distinct contrast to when he had spoken to Harry in the restaurant.

Harry concentrated on trying to stay calm and ignored the weapons pointed at him. Some of the men searched the inside of the vehicle and made a show of moving the seats and playing with the instruments.

An older man thrust his face forwards. 'You American?' He jabbed a grimy finger at the Land Cruiser, clearly seeing it as a badge of US wealth. 'CIA? NYPD?'

'Not me, mate.' Harry smiled, one eye on Kostova and Nikolai. They seemed at ease, but he wondered how friendly they really were. Would Kostova help them out if things got nasty? 'I work for the British Council. Education? Arts? Culture?'

The man scowled but fastened on one word.

'British? Ah, yes. British.' He looked towards Clare and asked, 'What she do?'

'She?' Harry rolled his eyes. 'She drives like a woman.'

The translation prompted an outbreak of laughter, and two of the men mimed jumping clear of the Land Cruiser at the last minute with slapstick grimaces and cries of alarm. Eventually, they lost interest and wandered away, lighting cigarettes.

When Clare returned to the car, she climbed behind the wheel and signalled for Harry to get in. Kostova and Nikolai stayed in the background, watching. When they were on their way back towards town, she asked Harry to pass her another cigarette.

'That was lucky,' she said, blowing out smoke. Her voice was shaky. 'He said if we'd been anyone else, we would have been shot.'

'Why?' Harry said. 'Is this a restricted road?'

'It is now. Military use only. They must have closed it after we took the fork back there.'

'Kostova must have clout, lording it over the military like that.'

'He has.' She glanced at him with a frown. 'What was all the laughter for?'

'I told them that back home you were a rally driver.'

She smiled. It transformed her face, an insight into how attractive she was under the cool exterior. A deliberate mask, he wondered, or a conscious desire to be as different as possible from the character she must have played in her deception role?

'Did Kostova say what all the military is for?'

'There's been a general mobilization. All leave has been cancelled, all units are on stand-by, and there's a push north towards the border.'

'That was open of him.'

'Perhaps because he knows they can't hide it any longer.' She pointed skywards, signifying the satellite overview of the planet from which very little could be hidden, then threw the cigarette out of the window with a grimace of distaste.

'He also confirmed the general talk gathering pace around town for a few days.'

'What's that?'

'The Russians are coming. Can you believe that?'

TWENTY-FOUR

'Y ou told me Jimmy Gulliver got back.' Harry pushed into Mace's office without knocking. Clare Jardine was in the outer office, typing up a report for London on what they had seen that morning.

Mace looked up from his desk, blinking like an owl. An empty glass stood by his elbow, a smear of colour across the bottom. Brandy or whisky, Harry guessed, and not the first. 'What?'

'You said Jimmy Gulliver returned to the UK. Where did he go?'

'I can't tell you that. Restricted information.'

'Crap. Who's going to know?'

Mace chewed on his lower lip. It was like watching a laborious series of checks and balances being considered before spewing out a response.

'You're pushing your luck, lad,' he muttered finally.

'Don't call me lad. I've been around the block nearly as many times as you.' Harry was ready for a fight. The idea of being here for months was already getting to him, but now something else was niggling away at him, disturbing his frame of mind.

'Why hasn't Gulliver been in touch?'

'Christ, what is it with you about Gulliver? Maybe he doesn't give a rat's backside. We're history to him – so what? He's hardly going to look back on this as his finest hour, is he?' Mace breathed deeply and shook his head. He sat back with a wave of his hand. 'OK . . . y'right. What difference does it make? No big secret any more.' He coughed and stared at the surface of his desk as if it might contain a script he could read from. 'Jimmy Gulliver. Good lad, he was . . . for a Sixer. Crying shame.'

'What did he do, to bring him here?'

'Jimmy? Not sure. I think he had a change of heart; expressed doubts about what he was doing. What MI6 was doing. Shouldn't have done that.'

'You mean we're not allowed doubts now?'

'Not at his level. I reckon he was too open about it. Shout too loud and they mark you down.' He blinked. 'Nice lad . . . but naïve.' He shrugged. 'That's my theory, anyway. Might be all bollocks, of course.'

'But you're Head of Station. You get copied on all our files.' He leaned over the desk, trying to keep the discussion on track.

Mace considered this seriously. 'Normally, I do. But not with Jimmy. His file was red-tagged.'

'What does that mean?'

'Means eyes-only, those at the top. Must have been into a lot of heavy stuff, know what I mean?'

'No. Tell me.'

'It means he was a high-level security risk. Someone they didn't want wandering around the planet with a story to sell.' He grinned lamely and waggled a finger. 'You're pushing it, askin' these questions. You'll get us both into trouble.'

'You think we're not already? Look around you.' Harry walked over to the window and back. 'Did Gulliver stay in the service?'

'No idea. Have to ask them, won't you? Wouldn't bet on a reply, though.'

'He's never contacted you?'

'Un-huh.' Mace shook his head. The movement made him wince. 'Why should he? Too bloody glad to be out of here, I should think. No sense looking back.'

'Odd, though, isn't it . . . for an ex-colleague?'

'Odd business we work in, that's why. Bloody odd world, in fact.'

'Tell me about it.' Harry turned to leave, then said, 'Were there any others who went back, apart from him?'

'Why do you want to know that?' Mace's voice took on a growl.

'Just asking. It's better than sitting here doing nothing. Does it matter?'

'Asking the wrong questions always matters – you know that.'

'Let's assume I don't give a rat's arse.'

Mace chewed his lip, then gave in. 'There was one before him. A Fiver named Gordon Brasher. Analyst by day, idiot plotter by night. He decided he didn't like the Official Secrets Act he'd signed and passed some data to a bunch of left-leaning loonies who wanted to blow up the planet. He was the first one sent out here after the place was established.'

'Why here? I'd have thought passing data was an automatic jail sentence.'

'Me too. But our lords and masters thought otherwise.' He stood up and picked up his glass. 'Like I said, you'll have to ask them.'

'What happened to him?'

'He went home, same as Gulliver. They did some psych tests on him and decided he was no longer a risk.' He picked up the empty glass, dropped it in a drawer, slammed it shut and gave Harry a hard look. The discussion seemed to have sobered him up. 'Now piss off and write up what you saw this morning. We got work to do.'

Harry waited for Mace to disappear on one of his regular 'breaks', then walked to the nearest basement internet bar. He signalled to the barman and got some time online along with a mug of coffee and a small jug of milk.

He checked out the news channels first. The usual items, from the twin conflicts in Afghanistan and Iraq, to the economic meltdown threatening the world. Nothing about the shooting. Had it finally run out of steam? He doubted it; maybe everyone was taking a breather.

He scrolled through the lists, discarding the stories as he went. He Googled 'Essex shooting'. It returned over a million hits, most of them involving gun clubs and clay pigeon shooting. He added the word 'police'. Fewer hits, mostly concerning firearms units and London-based criminals. And the death by stabbing of a reporter named Whelan. He clicked off the page, tired of following up leads that led nowhere. He was about to log off when he stopped.

Whelan.

He knew that name. But where from? He went back to the

link. It brought up a report from a south London newspaper's crime correspondent.

> A man found knifed to death on South Clapham Common after a suspected mugging has been named as Shaun Whelan, a freelance journalist. Police reports suggest his body may have been concealed for at least twenty-four hours in a small copse, and was only noticed by a park worker early this morning. Local residents say the area is a frequent haunt of gay men, and arguments are not uncommon. Whelan, 58, who had a reputation as a fierce campaigning journalist, began his career with RTE, the Irish radio and television broadcast service, before moving to London. At the time of his death, he was investigating the controversial shooting of a police officer and two innocent civilians during a drugs operation in Essex, which is currently the subject of an official enquiry. He was unmarried and lived alone.

Harry sat back, feeling guilty. Whelan was the man he'd wished a broken neck on.

What were the odds on a freelance reporter digging into a busted MI5 operation and getting himself knifed in a mugging? He believed in the realm of coincidence – even random occurrences. But some events stretched those laws beyond the point of believability.

And this was one of them.

As he left the café, a shiny silver BMW drew up alongside him, the tyres crunching over some discarded plastic in the gutter. Harry glanced sideways, expecting to give a shake of the head to a driver looking for directions.

It was Kostova, with Nikolai at the wheel.

'Get in,' Kostova invited him cheerfully, waving at the back seat.

'Why. Where are we going?' Harry checked the street for signs of lurking heavies. If he was being lifted, this was a civilized way of doing it.

'We go to my house for a drink.'

'OK,' he said. 'But we must stop meeting like this.' He climbed in the car and closed the door.

TWENTY-FIVE

Nikolai drove fast, hands light on the wheel. He caught Harry's eye in the rear-view mirror, nodded, then looked away.

Harry waited to see where he was being taken.

Kostova said nothing.

The interior of the car was beige leather and smelled of lemon freshener. It was a rich man's ride, with walnut panelling and thick carpets, and classical music easing smoothly out of twin speakers behind Harry's head.

They reached the suburbs, gliding at speed along one of the town's boulevards. Each side was lined with large villa-style houses set behind high fences. Some were inhabited, but many looked neglected and empty. They were almost at the end when Nikolai slowed and swung the wheel, taking the BMW between an impressive set of iron gates. They stopped in front of a two-storey house surrounded by thickly planted flower beds and bushes.

Kostova jumped out and stretched, openly savouring the fresh air. 'Come, Harry, come,' he said enthusiastically, and strode off towards the front door without waiting. A thickset man in a grey suit appeared in the entrance. He had the bearing of an army man, with a bristle of black hair across his scalp and no neck. He nodded to Kostova, but ignored Harry completely.

Once they were inside, he shut the door, then disappeared.

'Harry. You like a drink?' Kostova was standing in an oval hallway, checking through a pile of mail on a large antique table capable of seating ten people without overcrowding. The floor was richly tiled in grey and silver and the walls were hung with heavy, lined wallpaper dotted with pink cherubs blowing golden trumpets. The effect was one of money overwhelming style.

'Tea would be nice.' Harry decided that taking alcohol with Kostova might be a step too far. The mayor had the look and energy of a man who could take his drink and liked to prove it.

Kostova looked mildly disappointed but recovered with a

wide smile. 'Of course. Tea. Why not? Is good for the diges-
tion, anyway.' He clapped his hands and shouted, then walked
through a doorway to another room, beckoning for Harry to
follow.

The room was vast, with a scattering of heavy, deeply-
polished wooden furniture, comfortable armchairs and sofas,
and chandeliers hanging from the ceiling at each end. The
carpet was Persian over a wood-block floor, with heavy rugs
seemingly dropped at random, giving the impression of something between a de Rothschild manor and a carpet salesroom.

'Nice place,' said Harry.

'Thank you.' Kostova was standing by a window overlooking a side garden filled with rose bushes. He smiled
appreciatively. 'It is nice to come home to some comfort, I
think. Ah, tea.'

A youngish woman in a grey uniform dress and black shoes
had entered the room, followed by the large man in the grey
suit bearing a tray of fine china cups, saucers and a teapot.
The woman poured, then handed Harry a cup. It was Earl
Grey. She served Kostova, followed by Nikolai, who had
entered quietly and was standing by the door. Then she and
the heavy disappeared.

'So. How are you finding our little town?' Kostova slurped
his tea and beamed at Harry like a favourite uncle. 'I trust
you are comfortable?'

'Not bad,' said Harry. 'I haven't managed to explore everywhere just yet, but it's growing on me.'

'Good. Good. We are not London, of course – what you
are used to – but we have a very old culture and many pieces
of fine architecture and a very interesting museum.'

Harry buried his nose in his cup, and glanced at Nikolai.
The bodyguard was staring into his cup as if trying to decide
whether to drink it or toss it in the nearest available flow-
erpot.

'So, you knew Jimmy Gulliver?' Harry said. 'He was before
my time, so I didn't have the pleasure.'

Kostova looked surprised by the question. He glanced at
Nikolai before replying. 'Jimmy? I knew him . . . but not well.
He was a guest in our town, and I like to make our visitors
welcome.'

All visitors? Harry wanted to ask if that would extend to

visitors dropping in from the north. He doubted Kostova would want them tramping over his precious carpets.

'It was a pity,' continued the mayor, 'that he had to return to England. He was an interesting young man.'

Harry said nothing.

Kostova continued, 'He said he had orders to go back. A great shame. This town needs young people. We have too many old ones. Many who are not cultured.'

'You'll soon have lots more young ones popping by,' said Harry, 'if the rumours are correct.' It was impolite, given that he was drinking the mayor's Earl Grey. But this wasn't Eton Square and he doubted if he and Kostova would ever become bosom-buddies.

Kostova's eyes flashed. He said sombrely, 'We are not all masters of our own destinies, Harry. I think you know that more than anyone. For both of us,' he waved a vague hand, 'fate is decided a long way from this place.'

Harry was surprised. The mayor's English suddenly had taken a turn for the better. He wondered where he had received lessons. An institute outside Moscow, no doubt.

Before he could ask, Kostova drained his cup and called out. The woman in the grey dress appeared and took it from him.

Harry took the hint and also handed his cup to her.

'Thank you,' he said, and headed for the door.

'Enjoy your stay, Harry Tate,' Kostova murmured, and stayed where he was by the window. Nikolai was still studying his cup. There was no offer to drive Harry back into town.

He walked down the drive towards the gate, trying to work out what had just happened. An invitation for a drink had ended as abruptly as it had started. Had he actually managed to upset Kostova?

His mobile buzzed against his hip.

It was Mace.

'You having fun?' said the station chief. 'Dropping off the radar is not a good idea, know what I mean?'

'I didn't know I was on it,' Harry replied.

'Well, think again. You go missing, I want to know where you are.'

He wondered what was biting Mace's backside. He hadn't shown much interest in his movements thus far, so why now?

'I had an invitation to tea. It seemed churlish to refuse.'

'Tea? You taking the piss?'

'Kostova picked me up in his BMW,' Harry explained. 'Said he liked to meet new visitors. We drank Earl Grey served by two flunkies.' He wondered where this was leading. 'He made it sound like standard hospitality.'

'Standard? I'll bloody say not. When Geordi Kostova starts issuing personal invites to British Government personnel, it means he's up to something. You should have turned him down flat.'

'Why? He's the mayor, you said.'

'Use your head, son. How do you think he got that position? He's got the Moscow stamp of approval running through him like Blackpool rock. Why d'you think he's got all those fancy aerials at the back of his place – so he can download music off the internet?'

Harry turned and looked back. From his position in the back of Kostova's car, he'd missed the aerial array behind the main house, discreetly hidden by a clump of trees. He was no communications expert, but he guessed the array must have the ability to reach a long way. Like all the way to Moscow.

'London's not going to like this,' Mace continued, his tone lecturing. 'You've compromised yourself, lad.'

'London can go screw themselves. It was tea, not twenty questions.'

'They were just on the wire, asking where you were and what you were doing. Random check. I'll have to tell 'em.'

The phone clicked off and Harry swore. He'd been had. The invitation from Kostova had been deliberate, but had nothing to do with making friends or influencing people. And Mace must have known about it.

He'd been set up.

TWENTY-SIX

'I need a mobile. A throwaway, no contract.'

Harry collared Rik as soon as he got back to the office. The others were out of earshot and Mace was on the phone with his back turned. There was no way of knowing if

the young comms man would help him, or whether he'd simply
go straight to Mace. But there was only one way to find out.

'Why?' Rik grinned. 'ET not thinking of phoning home,
is he?'

'Don't ask. Someone I need to talk to.'

'Not wise, man. Not wise.' He pointed a finger towards the
atmosphere. 'They'll track it.'

'No, they won't. I won't be on long enough. You going to
help me or not?'

But Rik wasn't listening, too intent on showing his skills.
'Keywords, you see. You use any keywords, it won't matter how
long you're on. They'll have your footprint. Then you're toast.'

'OK, I promise I won't use any keywords,' Harry growled.
'Good enough?'

'Fine. It's your neck.' Rik sucked on his teeth like a plumber
giving an estimate. 'There's a place in town. A kiosk. Sells
bootleg cigarettes and *chacha*, among other things. He'll have
what you need. The guy's name is Rudi. But don't touch the
chacha – it's toxic.'

'What the hell is *chacha*?' He wasn't really interested but
it might be prudent to keep Rik onside.

'It's vodka, mostly made with grape juice, but they also
use fruit like oranges or mulberries. The best quality isn't bad,
but the rest is crap.' He checked to make sure they weren't
overheard. 'The good stuff is Mace's favourite tipple. He sticks
fruit juice in it to hide it but he's kidding himself.'

Harry stored away the information. Mace's drinking habits
were nothing more than an exploitable weakness. In his profes-
sion, such a chink in his armour might affect all of them.
'Where do I find this Rudi?'

Rik gave him directions to a street about ten minutes' walk
away. 'But seriously,' he added. 'They'll track you.'

'Yeah, I know. You said. Keywords.' Harry had a thought.
'What about Hotmail? That's not traceable, right?'

'Only like sticking a flag up a very tall pole.' Rik was scornful.
'If they're monitoring email traffic out of this area, they'd go
through the Hotmail first. They might not know who was sending
an individual message, but they'd soon find out.'

'How?'

Rik shrugged. 'By doing what they normally do: quoting
the war against terror. It's the modern "Open Sesame", isn't

it? They'd have instant access to whatever records they needed. It's too risky. You'd do better to stick with texting.' He smiled slyly. 'You do know what texting is, don't you?'

Harry knew. He'd been on a communications update course. He remembered the instructor saying that texting in code was almost impossible to spot unless a specific device was being monitored.

'Does this Rudi speak English?'

'Of course. He's a wheeler-dealer; he likes to score.' Rik scowled. 'I'd better come with you. He gets jumpy if he thinks the cops are around. Most of the stuff he handles isn't kosher, you know? That's why it's cheap. I'll check it out for you, so let me know when.' He gave Harry a steady look. 'You did this all by yourself, though. I don't want London giving me a load of crap for your misdemeanours – I'm trying to live down enough of my own.'

'Good luck with that.'

'What do you mean?'

'You seriously think they're going to let you back?' Harry gave him the benefit of a six-inch stare. 'I wouldn't count on it, sunshine. They've got long, nasty memories and they don't forgive easily.'

Rik swallowed. 'You think?'

'I know. Let's go.'

'What, now?' Rik glanced towards Mace's office. 'What'll I tell the boss? He doesn't like any of us going off without a reason.'

'Fuck him.' Harry was still mad at Mace over his visit to Kostova's house. Mace had contributed in putting another black mark on his record, for what purpose, he didn't know. Maybe it was part of his nature, to worm a bit of excitement out of working in this miserable place. It was bad enough getting carpeted as the man in charge of an operation that bombed; God alone knew how they'd react when they heard he'd enjoyed the hospitality of a political figure with known links to Moscow.

But he had to consider Rik. It would be unfair to drag him into it. 'Tell him I need your help in buying a coat. It's cold here and I don't want to die of hypothermia.'

From down the street, the kiosk looked rundown and colourless, slotted into a derelict space between two other shops. A stained canvas awning cast a shadow over the makeshift counter, covered with faded stickers advertising a variety of products, most of them unavailable on the open market.

After stopping to buy a plain padded coat from a general clothing store, Harry had followed Rik's lead and now stood fifty yards from the kiosk, watching the flow of customers – mostly men in rough working clothes and heavy boots – and eyeing the occasional vehicle passing by. None of the cars stopped and they saw no signs of watchers. Or, come to think of it, thought Harry, the Clones. Most of the customers accomplished their purchase with the minimum of chat, sliding money across the counter and retrieving their purchases before scurrying away.

'He trades in cigarettes, booze, fuel, electronics and perfumes,' Rik explained, anticipating Harry's question. 'And whatever toxic substances he can get.'

'You know that from experience, do you?'

Rik hissed briefly. 'Don't use it, never have. I get my kicks from a keyboard. If you ask Rudi, he'll get it. All it needs is the right money.'

'You said fuel. Is that what I can smell?'

'Yeah. It stinks, doesn't it? Worse than chip fat. Don't worry – you'll get used to it. The gangs siphon it from a spillage pipe at a refinery over to the east and sell it cheap on the streets. It smells so bad because they haven't finished the refining process, which is why anyone who uses it too much blows out their engines.'

'Regular little capitalist, isn't he?' Harry settled his shoulder against a wall, prepared to wait until Rik said it was safe to move.

'So,' said Rik, sensing a moment for casual chat, 'have you managed to get it on with our Clare yet or has she given you the moody like she does everyone?'

Harry stared at him. Rik obviously didn't know about her. 'You serious?'

'Just asking. You know why she's here, don't you?'

'Is it relevant?'

'Not really. Just gossiping. She overcooked a honey-trap and went all the way, according to chit-chat.' He fluttered his eyebrows. 'And we British don't do that, do we? Go all the way, I mean.'

'You reckon?' Harry watched as an army truck slowed near the kiosk. The driver was alone, probably checking out the place to see if he could make a buy without being seen.

'Anyway, it went sour and the suits didn't approve. She got tabbed out here.'

The lorry speeded up and disappeared at the end of the street, belching exhaust fumes.

'What about you?' Harry asked. He didn't need to hear Rik's story, but the more he learned about his colleagues, the less he might have to worry about.

'Me? That's no secret. I got my sticky fingers into a couple of restricted files and they decided I was better off somewhere far away.' He shrugged, smiling coyly. 'Stupid, really. They can't keep me here forever, can they?' He shifted his feet as the flow of shoppers across the street dwindled. 'Out of sight, out of the way, I suppose. It's the limit of their thinking.'

'Consider yourself lucky they didn't settle for a more permanent option,' said Harry. 'You don't find many computers in solitary.'

Rik scowled as if the idea had occurred to him before. 'I suppose. It's still like being locked up, though, being in this shithole. I mean, who thought of putting an office out here?'

'Nobody with a sense of humour.' It was the first time anyone had voiced an opinion about being here. Harry gave it a couple of beats. So far he'd tested the water with the phone; now was the time to push the envelope. He said, 'Did you know Jimmy Gulliver?'

TWENTY-SEVEN

'Gulliver? Not much. He wasn't here long enough to break the ice. Clare got on with him, though. He bunked off without warning.'

'I thought he was recalled.'

'No. He'd had enough. That's what Mace said, anyway.'

'What about Gordon Brasher?'

'Heard of him. Some sort of analyst. He was before my time.' He grinned. 'Another member of the escape committee. Why do you ask?'

'Just wondering.' Harry made a show of checking the street to break the trail of discussion. 'So what sort of files did you access?'

'The wrong sort. Some individuals . . . but mostly operational stuff. I heard about a couple of things on the grapevine . . . operations that had gone sour. I was intrigued about what goes on at the outer edges.' He looked at Harry. 'The areas you work in, I guess. I'm in support; we don't get to see the exciting stuff at first hand.'

'Think yourself lucky,' said Harry. 'Most of the time it's boring and repetitive. The rest is unpleasant.'

'Yeah, well it doesn't always go to plan, does it? I mean, there was one file I found . . . the original documents were all there, written up. So I had a trawl through. There was this amazing stuff about a long-term drugs op leading all the way from Kandahar to London. Five guys had been working the line for nearly a year. Then, just as it was going critical, they were pulled out without explanation. Most of the product ended up on the streets of London and Birmingham. It was coded like Blackpool rock, so they could track it all the way. Bloody criminal.'

Harry nodded. 'It happens. How did they find you out?'

'I talked to a mate and he blabbed. It was stupid of me. I said I'd been looking for hero stuff . . . you know – SAS missions, that kind of thing. They couldn't prove otherwise because I didn't leave any footprints.'

Harry thought Rik had been lucky. They'd shovelled him out of London because there was a chance he might have stumbled on something he shouldn't have. No matter how clean he'd wiped his trail, the suspicion would have remained. To have charged him would have risked exposing a serious lack of security, as well as revealing something they wanted kept quiet. Far better to send him somewhere isolated and keep him out of the way.

Like they had with himself.

'How do you keep your hand in?' he asked casually. It was unlikely that someone like Rik wouldn't be tempted to indulge whenever the opportunity arose. But it wouldn't be in office

hours; he'd be too easily seen entering screens he had no business using.

'When I can.' The reply was wary. He nodded down the
street, 'There's an internet café about a hundred yards down
there, called Maxis. It's usually full of security cops, sniffing
out deviants and such, but it's safe. I use it whenever I need
a fix without every keystroke being logged. Why?'

'No reason.' Harry noted the name for future use. He looked
across the street. 'Let's do this, shall we?'

Rik checked it was clear, then led the way to the kiosk.
Their approach was watched by a sharp-faced young man with
several days' growth of beard and a ponytail. Harry took it to
be local street-chic.

'Hey, Rudi,' Rik said, and bought a pack of cigarettes. He
turned to Harry and murmured. 'You need to buy some, too.
Shows goodwill.'

Harry pointed at a pack of Marlboro. The man flipped it
across the counter and took the money without speaking.

Rik signalled for a light. As he leaned over to suck in the
flame, he said, 'My friend needs a cell.'

'Uh-uh.' Rudi lit a cigarette, too, and gave Harry a quick
once over, squinting through the smoke. 'You calling local?'
His accent carried a faint American twang.

'No. Is that a problem?'

'For me, no. But some cells have limited range, you know?
For good signal you need top device. It cost more.' His eyes
had brightened with interest.

'How much?'

Rudi bent down, revealing a bald patch. He resurfaced and
slid an Ericsson T68 between two piles of magazines. 'Best
I got at the moment. You could ring the moon with that, no
problem.'

The phone looked new, except for a faint scratch on the
screen. It was either a clever copy or stolen from some luck-
less businessman. Either way, it was better than what he had.
'How much and how long will it last?' he said. 'And I don't
mean the battery.'

Rudi grinned good-naturedly. 'I get you, man. It last maybe
three days. For that I give you good price. One hundred dollars
US.'

Harry heard Rik give an intake of breath. 'What?'

'Don't touch it.' Rik gave Rudi a reproving look. 'A model that good but that cheap? It's probably got someone on its tail who wants it back. Three days means it was lifted locally.'

'Hey, what you saying?' Rudi protested mildly. 'You want to ruin my business?' He shrugged. 'Eighty dollars. Best price.'

'I'll take it.' A few days wouldn't matter; he was hardly going to be using it non-stop. He took out some dollars and slid them towards Rudi. The phone was good enough for his purposes, and instinct told him he wouldn't get a better deal anywhere else.

A dusty Volvo had turned into the street, heading towards them. One person inside. Square shoulders, short hair.

Rudi took the money and folded it into his pocket. 'Sure thing. But you know . . .'

'Yeah, I know. No keywords and we've never met before.' Harry picked up the Ericsson and walked away, tossing Rik the pack of Marlboro.

The Volvo rumbled by, spitting out gravel from beneath the tyres. Up close, the driver was in his fifties, with heavy jowls. He wore a thick jacket, ragged at the elbows, and was checking door numbers on the other side of the street.

Harry breathed out but kept his head down.

Rik seemed unaware of the car and fell into step alongside him.

'You want something?' said Harry. For what he was about to do, he didn't need an audience.

'Oh. Right. Sorry.' Rik's face fell but he peeled away obediently. 'Don't be too long, though,' he said. 'Mace likes to know where we are.'

Right, thought Harry. And why is that, I wonder? He hurried away, punching buttons until he found the SIM card directory. As he suspected, it contained a list of names and numbers, the former mostly Anglo, the latter with dialling codes he vaguely recognized. American.

Great. Knowing his luck, the mobile probably belonged to Carl bloody Higgins of the CIA.

He found a tiny basement bar beneath a small supermarket. It was grubby and workaday, of the type where the clientele looked as though they preferred minding their own business. He bought a coke and bagged a corner table, then switched on the mobile and waited while it searched for a signal. If it didn't work, he'd go back and cut off Rudi's ponytail.

He knew the number he had to dial by heart; he and Bill Maloney had spent a lot of time calling each other before, during and after operations. He thought over what he wanted to say. It had to be as lean as possible, as every second spent on the line increased the risk of discovery. Using a clean phone would avoid his name or number popping up on a monitor somewhere and sounding alarms all over London.

Need yr hlp. Rd 1. It wasn't elegant, not by the standards he'd seen kids texting each other, but he wanted brevity, not prizes. Hopefully, Maloney would recognize his call sign. He had a moment of doubt as he pressed the SEND button, but let it go. As long as Maloney received the message and didn't ignore it.

Or worse, call the dogs down on him.

TWENTY-EIGHT

I t was Jordan Conway's draw to fetch water. The day promised to be a long one. It wasn't fully light yet, but he knew the feel of the air enough now to be able to judge the conditions. They had picked up a satellite reading of the weather forecast in the last radio burst at midnight. It promised a brief spell of humidity before turning colder. This close to water, they would be at the mercy of the last of the midges, flies and mosquitoes, all vying for a final bite of human skin.

This time tomorrow, they'd probably be freezing their asses off.

He gently cleared a gummy throat and relished being down by the water, where it would be cooler. He edged forward until he drew level with Doug Rausing, who was on watch.

'OK, boss,' he breathed. 'We good to go?'

Rausing nodded without taking his eye away from the monocular's padded eyecup. 'We're clear. Nothing moving bigger than a fox, no change to the terrain. You set?'

'Yep. You want anything from the deli?'

'Some popcorn would be good,' replied Rausing, with a dark smile. 'If they don't have any, bring me some chips.'

'You got it. Pay me when I get back.' Conway secured the collapsible water container to his belt and slid away to the edge of their hide.

He studied the ground for a full five minutes before moving out, checking for wildlife. Animals were the best indicators of intruders; when someone alien moved in, the wildlife moved out or went quiet. Like they would when he began moving, although not, he hoped, at the same time. A few birds were skimming over the rough grass, and a couple of hares squatted a hundred yards off, heads down and munching. Some crows were in the trees by the lake, arguing the toss as usual. Apart from that, it looked good. He wondered whether Bronson and Capel, the other two Delta men, were watching. Maybe he'd see one of them down by the lake on water duty. They could have a chat, catch up on old times.

He looked up to where a few late stars showed between the clouds, and wondered briefly about the sky cover that was supposed to be up there, watching over them. They were probably brewing coffee and having breakfast about now, changing shift in their long hours spent patrolling while the cameras sent back images to base. And above them would be the satellites, forever circling, taking pictures of the aircraft taking pictures.

Seconds later he was moving, belly down and making his way carefully towards the lake. It was a 250-yard trip, mostly downhill, a gentle slope over undulating grass. There were a couple of gullies he could use, dead ground forged by decades of water coursing down to the lake, and some low scrub where he could take a look around without standing out. As long as he didn't run into trouble, it would take about an hour to complete the trip there and back. But there was no hurry.

TWENTY-NINE

To the west, the British Special Reconnaissance team was also on the move. But their objectives were different. 'Hunt' Wallis was scanning the ground in front of him through his glasses, fighting a rising sense of panic. He was desperate to see signs of Jocko Wardle, his colleague. Wardle had gone out on a recce after hearing noises in the trees. They had agreed it was better for Wardle, a former poacher, to do it, using the dark to move rather than waiting for daylight.

That had been an hour ago.

So far, there had been no sign of him coming back, no contact on the tiny radios they were each carrying. The sets had a short range of a few hundred yards, but were sufficient for communicating between OPs without disturbing the airwaves. Wardle should have been on by now, signalling the all-clear, or back in the basha, looking for something to eat.

'Anything?' Mike Wilson slid alongside Wallis, bringing an aroma of damp clothing and chocolate, and the familiar tang of oiled weapons.

'Fuck all. Something's up.'

Wilson nodded. 'He's run into trouble, daft bastard.'

'Unless he stopped for a crap. Or tripped over and broke his silly fuckin' neck.'

The dark humour hid a genuine concern for their colleague. But both men knew that if he hadn't come back by now, he probably wasn't going to.

He was either captive. Or dead.

Yet they had seen no sign of enemy forces.

Either way, he was beyond their reach. Their orders were not to engage with local forces under any circumstances unless their lives were at extreme risk. Agonizing over the rights and wrongs of leaving Wardle out there would only lead to negative thinking. And that was counter-productive. If there was an opportunity to take a look later, they would do it. For now, they could only watch and wait.

'Better call it in,' Wilson said soberly. 'I'll get on the net.'

Wallis nodded and continued scouring the darkness while Wilson went back to make the call. If Wardle turned up safe and well, they could cancel the alert. He'd get a beasting for causing them grief, but that was part of the job.

Until then, they had to figure out what kind of trouble had overtaken him . . . and whether they were next in line.

Wilson made his way carefully into deeper cover, wary of setting off the birds in the trees overhead. The comms equipment, a lightweight electronic pack which fired messages in split-second bursts, was concealed along with their rations and backpacks in a hollow beneath a fallen tree, and covered with camouflage netting spotted with leaves and twigs. Anyone coming through here would practically have to trip over it to see it.

He paused to gently brush aside a spider's web. Jocko's non-appearance was the worst kind of news; he wasn't the type to get lost, and would have found some way to contact them if he'd been compromised. A brilliant birdsong mimic, he'd have sent up a warning, to give them a heads up.

Wilson reached the hollow and checked the area. Just as they'd left it. No sign of intruders. He slipped under the camouflage netting and reached for the radio pack, mentally composing his message. It would have to be short, sharp and without embellishment. Ten seconds and London would know what had happened.

The radio was gone.

A bird flapped from the tree above his head, and he felt a momentary despair as the netting shifted behind him.

Then something cold and sharp pierced the back of his neck.

THIRTY

Doug Rausing felt his eyes closing and pinched his arm hard. Falling asleep right now wasn't good. He checked his watch. He was surprised to find that Conway had already been gone forty minutes. Still, that was OK; it took that long to get down to the water and start on the way back. He could take another forty if he had to – and some. Lack of sleep was something you got used to in Delta; that and being thirsty, uncomfortable and wishing you were in a nice bar somewhere, sucking down a cold beer.

He checked through the monocular. It was easier to carry than field glasses and lighter, too. He'd first used it in the Marine sniper section, and had grown to trust it.

The lake looked the same as before; lighter now, but no sign of anything that shouldn't be there. The surface of the

water carried the same glitter he'd noticed on previous morn-
ings, a ghostly sheen as if someone had lit it from underneath.
Must be some kind of optical flare, where the coming dawn
was feeding early rays across the land and into the tiny wind
ripples running from east to west.

A crow rose from the trees to the right, an untidy black
shape. He focussed the monocular, tracking the bird's progress
as it lifted into the sky. Must be the early bird he'd heard talk
about; keen to be up and out there, like Conway.

Another crow joined the first one, this time with a sound
of protest, wings clattering.

Something had disturbed it.

Rausing felt a flicker of alarm. He checked his watch, then
tracked along the route Conway should be taking back from
the lake. Down one way, back another; it was standard procedure. That way you didn't run into an ambush. He was tempted
to use the radio, but they were under silent conditions unless
open warfare broke out.

A third crow lifted out of the trees, and another, the protests
louder, and Rausing wonderer if Bronson and Capel had decided
to make a move. They were dug in at least three hundred yards
further on, and would have no reason to come this way; their
orders were to stay apart, to limit possible exposure.

Yet something wasn't right; he could sense it. Conway could
move like a ghost – they all could. But Conway was the best.

A snap echoed up the slope, like a twig breaking. Then
silence.

Rausing tracked across the terrain again, looking for the
slightest sign of movement. He knew the noise wasn't Conway;
the man didn't tread on twigs. Then a chilly feeling swept
right through him.

Jesus, he thought. *What twigs? There are no trees down
there!*

He swung left again. The lake was empty, same as the grass
leading down. Same with the edge of the trees.

Nothing. Not a damn thing.

He swore and toggled his radio. 'Conway. Come in. You
OK?' His voice was too loud, and he bit down on the temptation to move out. 'Dammit, Con, come in, man!' It wasn't
approved comms procedure, but who the hell was there to
hear him?

Silence.

He tried the other two again. 'Capel . . . Bronson. You there? Come in.' But they weren't listening . . . or couldn't. He went back to scouring the landscape. Another two sweeps and he'd bag up and move out.

Then he heard a rustle behind him. Fabric on grass. A faint shift in the air. He grinned with relief and turned his head. Conway, the sneaky bastard, had come round the long way just to freak him out—

It was the last thought he ever had.

THIRTY-ONE

Deep in the belly of the Naval Intelligence monitoring unit in Northwood, London, Lieutenant Commander David Brill was interrupted in the middle of a working desk break by a technician from Communications Support Group.

'Sir, there's something you should see.' The technician, named Tully, looked worried, and was already moving back down the corridor towards the main communications room.

Brill felt an unwelcome flip in his stomach. Tully wouldn't have interrupted him without good cause. He looked wistfully at the half-eaten cheese sandwich on his blotter and followed the technician out into the corridor.

Through two secure doors and past an array of ID scanners, they finally arrived in the main control centre, a circular room packed with electronic equipment, including large, wall-mounted plasma screens. One of these screens was currently 'live', showing a coloured map with two clusters of white lights. It was a pared-down version of a normal country map, devoid of unnecessary information unless called for, in which case it could be there at the press of a button.

The detail now on show was of a stretch of open country, with a large expanse of water representing an inland lake at bottom right. It was fed by a small river and, coming from the north, a run of high ground and further small streams and other lakes in the foothills of what Brill knew was the Caucasus

Mountains. Details of roads were sketchy, mostly because there were none.

Brill glanced at the other technicians. They were intent on the map, and he could feel the tension in the room.

Something was wrong.

He checked the bottom of the screen, where a constant loop display gave map coordinates and current local time, with temperature and weather data on the ground, and a group of six-figure numbers with alpha suffixes. Alongside was a small US flag.

Brill knew that the lights and alphanumeric references represented locator markers on the ground, and showed current strength of signals and position. What he wasn't privy to was why they were there. All he and his staff had to do was watch them. He scanned the map and data, but nothing sprang out at him.

'OK, Tully, what's the probl—' He stopped, a worm of apprehension taking hold in his gut.

One of the lights was blinking.

'Is that a malfunction?'

'No, sir.' Tully's voice was tight but controlled, professional. 'We checked it already.' He tapped at a keyboard and the map changed, along with the time and data read-out at the bottom. 'This was thirty minutes ago. Same place, same details.' The light clusters were the same, but firm and unblinking. 'The monitors pulled this up as usual, and we ran a check of the last fifteen hours. We noticed that the signal strength had changed overnight.'

'Changed how?'

'The lights are ground markers, sir, placed by an insert team.' He looked nervous.

'I know. So?'

'They're markers, all right, sir . . . but not ground-based. When we increased the magnification of the area around the lights, we noticed movement. Not great, but definitely movement – in one case by about three hundred metres. A single light. Then it returned to its original position.'

Brill didn't bother asking Tully if he was certain. The men and women in this room were a highly-trained team, their combined skills probably unrivalled anywhere in the world of electronic mapping and monitoring. And they all had experience of monitoring Special Operations.

'Maybe they were changing position . . . or one of them was carrying a marker.' Even as he said it, he knew that wasn't the reason. Ground markers or transponders of the type used in this situation were only switched on when in position. The moment they were planted, the man on the ground hit a button to activate the signal. Doing it while on the move was pointless . . . and could be fatally misleading for back-up forces. 'Go on.' He sensed there was more.

The technician brought up another screen, this one enhanced, and pointed to a light close to the lake. We got this read-out earlier . . . the mover. We think he went down to the lake – possibly for water. He could have been checking his perimeter. Impossible to tell.'

Brill suppressed a shiver. The use of the word 'he' suddenly made this much more personal. No longer were they merely lights on a screen, but people; living, breathing people.

'We think,' continued Tully, gathering confidence, 'that these markers are body locators. We thought they were sewn into the clothing. But I'm not so sure.' He tapped his keyboard and the screen changed again, this time displaying a read-out tag of numbers against each light.

'I don't see your point. What's the difference?'

Tully glanced at his colleagues, then said, 'I believe these numbers are body-activated. Thirty minutes ago, an alarm sounded. We weren't sure where it had come from – it wasn't part of the technical brief. Then we realized it must have come from the locator frequency. Watch this.' He changed the screen, and an electronic note echoed round the room. It lasted five seconds, then stopped. At the same time, one of the lights began blinking, then went out.

'What happened?' Brill felt panic blossom in his chest. Whatever the hell was going on, this didn't look good.

'It's possible these locators are matched to body temperature,' Tully replied softly. 'Life-sign readings. When we did a check after the first one down by the lake, we noticed that the numbers against some of the tags changed during the night. They were lower than the others, even those close by.' Before Brill could ask, he added, 'When the body is at rest, the pulse and heartbeat slow down and there are no spikes in body activity or life signs.' The screen changed. 'This is the first one.'

The light by the lake began blinking, and the electronic
alarm pinged.

The light went out.

Brill's throat went dry. 'What . . . ?'

'The locator has lost all life signs. Sir.' Tully's voice was
a whisper.

Brill reached for a phone. He felt sick. As a naval officer
he knew all about transponders. Some were water-activated,
for lifeboats and downed aircraft. But a whole new generation
of electronics had ushered in innovations for tracking and
locating which had less to do with boats or planes and more
to do with humans. 'You're sure? No chance of malfunction
or loss – a failed power source?'

'I'm sure, sir.' Tully coughed. 'Sir, the Yan— Americans
have started using small body trackers than can't be lost
or mislaid. They're powered by body heat and last for approx-
imately twenty-eight days before degrading. Some of our
Special Forces are trying them out, too . . . so I hear.'

'Go on.'

'There's only one reason for them to go offline before then.'

Brill didn't have to ask what that reason was. 'How do they
work?' He knew he was playing for time; he hadn't got the
slightest interest in how the tracking devices functioned, or what
stopped them working. But neither did he want to make this
particular phone call until he was absolutely certain of his facts.

'They're inserted beneath the skin, sir.' Tully pointed to his
upper arm. 'Here.' He held up a hand before Brill could use
the phone. 'There's more.' He turned back to his screen and
pointed. 'This came next.'

Brill waited, holding his breath.

One of the three remaining lights began blinking, followed
by the electronic alarm. Then another, this one of a pair slightly
separate from the first two. No sooner had it gone out than
the fourth light in the cluster went the same way.

The last alarm seemed to go on for ever, echoing with
haunting finality in the room. One of the operators swore
softly and turned down the volume.

Brill began to dial the number, his hand shaking, and
wondered about the men on the ground.

'Why the fuck didn't someone tell us?' he said
harshly, staring at the screen. But nobody answered.

THIRTY-TWO

M arcella Rudmann received the news and stared at the telephone before replacing it softly on its cradle. The call from Northwood had been routed through the MOD to all desks, and had already been confirmed by GCHQ and the National Security Agency watchers in Fort Meade, Maryland.

The Delta Force team had gone offline.

Across the desk from her, Lieutenant-Colonel Spake, the Deputy Director Special Forces, looked grim.

'Four undercover personnel disposed of in quick succession,' she said. 'How could that happen?'

Spake raised an eyebrow at the casual terminology, and she blushed, wishing she could retract it, but it was too late. 'Sorry.'

'It might have been a bomb-burst,' he said carefully. 'Although that's unlikely. Anything too powerful would show up on the monitors. It might have been a small piece of ordnance – an anti-personnel mine.'

'What do you think happened?' Rudmann asked. She knew nothing of battlefield tactics, but if anyone had a workable theory free of over-exaggeration, this man would.

'If they stumbled into a minefield, it's likely one or more would have survived, even if wounded – certainly long enough to keep the tracking devices going and call it in. That didn't happen. A larger explosion would have been captured on the watching satellites. Nobody has reported one. If they all went down in quick succession, with no time to call it in, there is only one explanation.'

Rudmann made a guess. 'They were taken out by ground forces.'

'Yes.'

'What about our own team?'

'There's no news.'

'That's good, isn't it?'

'It depends how you read it.' He stood up and moved to the door. 'They carried the same markers, but standing orders were to call in regularly. We use a different system to the

Americans. Harder to track.' He opened the door and looked
back at her with the steely look which Rudmann recognized
as the traditional soldier's face for politicians when importing
bad news. 'They failed to make the last two scheduled calls.'

Five hours later, an emergency meeting was convened in the
Cabinet Office at No. 10. Present were the Deputy PM, the
Secretary of State for Defence, Lieutenant-Colonel Spake and
Lieutenant Commander David Brill, rushed in by car from
Northwood.

'All of them?' The Deputy PM looked stunned by the news
Brill had delivered, and the confirmation email from the
National Security Agency's liaison officer in London which
was in his hand. He looked to Spake for a response which
might counter the information, and wondered how to tell the
PM.

'Yes, sir.' Spake's confirmation was enough for the Deputy
PM. The Special Forces man wasn't much liked in the corridors of Whitehall; his aura of quiet danger sat uncomfortably
alongside the well-fed civil servants and politicians. But his
credentials were beyond criticism. 'Both teams.'

'How?' the Deputy PM asked weakly. 'They were our top
men, weren't they?'

'My guess is, they were tracked from the moment they went
in.' Spake's voice was neutral. 'It was a risky operation anyway,
but if they were all spotted so quickly, it could have only been
because the Russians already had a detection shield in place.
They would have been tracked from the moment they went
in. Once they were down, they had nowhere to go.'

The Deputy blinked and glanced quickly at the Secretary
of State. He wondered whose signature was the most likely
to show up on the paperwork responsible for sending in the
Special Reconnaissance team. He was relieved it wasn't his.
That, thank God, had been something he had not been entrusted
with.

'The Prime Minister will be devastated,' he murmured
finally. 'Devastated.'

'I'm sure he will. Is that all, sir?' There was just
sufficient bite in his voice to make his feelings clear,
before he spun on his heel and made for the door.

The Secretary of State stopped him.

'Is there anything we can do? For the team, I mean?'

'What would you suggest?' Spake kept his back turned, his voice as bleak as Siberian snow. 'Send in another team to look for them?'

He strode from the room, leaving the two politicians and an embarrassed Lieutenant Commander Brill staring at each other in bewilderment.

THIRTY-THREE

'Rudmann's becoming a nuisance. She's asking too many questions.'

George Paulton eased his collar around his neck as he spoke. Either he was putting on weight or his shirts were shrinking. He crossed his ankles under the desk and tried to remain calm. *Sang froid* in the face of adversity was the way to play it, otherwise the hyenas would move in for the kill.

Hyenas like Marcella Rudmann.

'Ignore her.' The man standing near the window looked urbane and confident, at ease in a dazzling white shirt and light grey suit. Sir Anthony Bellingham – he rarely used the title – bore another, far more interesting designation: that of Deputy Director (Operations) of MI6 – Paulton's opposite number in the Secret Intelligence Service. He eyed Paulton with the intensity of an eagle looking at a morsel of food. 'You worry too much.'

'So you keep saying. But I don't have the same . . . resources that you enjoy.' It was Paulton's way of saying power and influence, without actually using those words. For two men on seemingly equal levels, the fact that Bellingham had more of both was a growing source of irritation, a reminder also reflected in the budgetary allocations poured into SIS.

'Be glad of it, George, be glad of it. It's working so far, isn't it, our little experiment? Keeps the dodgy ones out of the way until we know what to do with them. And all in the name of Her Majesty's security services.' He grinned comfortably. 'Reminds me, have you heard anything about your man Tate?'

'Nothing untoward. Why, have you?'

'Only that he arrived safely, and has been doing the rounds, getting the grand tour. No indication that he's planning to do a bunk, at least. Be a bad move if he tried it.' He scowled. 'You said he'd do as he was told, didn't you?'

'I said he would, as long as he believed it was a genuine posting. If he starts to think otherwise. . .' He left the rest unsaid, unwilling to provide guarantees he knew he couldn't keep. Men like Harry Tate were wild cards in the intelligence community, quiet and diligent most of the time, but apt to go off like a firecracker if something got under their skin.

'He'd better be a good boy.' The temperature in Bellingham's voice dropped several degrees. 'There's only one ending, otherwise.'

Paulton clamped his teeth together. He was beginning to wish he'd never agreed to this whole Red Station experiment. What had initially seemed a useful shared Five/Six exercise in budget allocation and a way of keeping potentially awkward intelligence officers under wraps until they were no longer a threat to themselves or anyone else, all under the guise of a live training facility, was beginning to look less and less attractive.

The truth was, he'd been bullied and flattered into it by Bellingham's smooth talk. But now there was no way out. Even worse was the knowledge that he had agreed to Bellingham's 'enhancement' of the Station scenario by the addition of a second team of watchers. Originally using one team to monitor the movements of the Station's members, he now knew there was another, far more proactive unit in place, with the unsubtle title of the Hit. They had been used twice so far. He prayed it didn't happen again.

'You got something on your mind, George?'

Bellingham was like bloody Merlin, reading his mind. Paulton wondered how much the man knew.

'I think Rudmann suspects something.' He paused, not sure how to broach the news about Whelan. 'Whelan was sniffing around after Tate,' he added. 'Rudmann seemed to think he ought to be dissuaded.' He shot his cuffs, wondering if it was too early for a stiff drink.

'Did she now?' Bellingham burst in before he could finish. 'Getting above herself, isn't she?' He scowled, then. 'Christ, don't tell me she had anything to do with his death. I'd agree to almost anything nasty happening to that little shite, but we can't go round knocking off the fourth estate, can we? Well, not yet.' He smirked and stood away from the window. 'Come on, George, buck up. Are you going to offer me a drink or what?'

'Of course.' Paulton felt faint. The solution had presented itself. Why not let Bellingham believe Rudmann was responsible? He'd never prove otherwise, so why not. He stood up and went to the drinks cabinet.

THIRTY-FOUR

H arry decided it was time to test the Clones. They had been notable by their absence the previous day when he was out with Rik, and he hadn't seen them when Clare Jardine took him out of town. They might have been assigned to other duties, or replaced by a different team. Yet Rik had said they were always around.

If so, it represented a break in continuity. And that made him uneasy.

'Why do you want to do that?' queried Mace, when he suggested a brief tag-and-tail exercise. It wouldn't take long, but to do it properly, he would need Jardine, Rik and Fitzgerald to act as decoys.

'It's a simple field test,' said Harry. 'It'll keep us on our toes, and we'll see if the Clones are out and about.'

Mace nodded reluctantly, brow crinkling. 'Not a bad idea, I suppose,' he conceded. 'But no confrontations. We don't need any grief from the local security police.'

Harry gave the other three a quick briefing, then let them go. Nobody argued – not even Jardine. He gave them a head start, and once Mace had gone back to his office, made sure both his mobiles were fully functional. He had no intention of using the Ericsson – that was for communicating with Maloney. But if one packed up, he wanted to be sure he had a stand-by.

Fitzgerald was the first to call in. Harry had given each of them instructions to walk to various points in the town, then to phone him with any news of tails. Fitzgerald's objective

was the central post office. He was carrying a large brown
envelope in plain sight. It would be enough to attract attention,
and easy enough to follow.

'Got a tail,' he reported succinctly. 'White male, late-
twenties, casual clothes. He knows what he's doing, although
he made a couple of minor errors.'

The next caller was Clare, from outside the station. She
said, 'I picked up one man a hundred yards from the office.
Looks military; young and fit. Reasonably good but no expert.
Should I lose him?'

'No. And don't stab him, either.' Harry rang off. It was
getting interesting.

Rik was last, calling from the town's museum. He also had
a follower, with a similar description to the men he had seen
before. He said he had performed a simple in-and-out
manoeuvre of a shop, and caught the man flat-footed in the
middle of the pavement.

Harry took the calls on the hoof while making his way in
a lengthy fashion to a local spa bath he'd picked out on the
map. His route crossed several streets, allowing him to spot
anyone who might be on his tail. He picked up a tail after
three blocks; another male, white and slim, with short hair
and dressed in jeans and a ski jacket.

He had instructed the others to return to the office after
calling him, and not to show they had seen their followers.
He continued walking, taking in the spa, the library, a café
where he enjoyed coffee and cake, and several statues of fallen
heroes. By the time he had seen enough sights for one day,
he had been out for two hours. He had not only retained his
original tail, but had picked up two more.

He hailed an unmarked cab and jumped in. He knew it was
a cab by the way the driver, a whiskery old man with a beret,
was drifting along hugging the kerb. He spoke no English,
but Harry had the address of the office written on a piece of
paper. The old man nodded and turned on his radio, drowning
the back of his battered Renault in the local brand of folk
music.

'So what did it prove?' Mace asked, when they assembled
back at the office. The other three had already told him what
they had accomplished, and were waiting for Harry to complete

the picture. 'And what the hell took you so long? You go to the border and back?'

'There are four of them,' said Harry, 'as Rik thought.' He caught a grin from the younger man out of the corner of his eye. 'We each got tagged, and when Clare, Fitz and Rik came in, their tails latched on to me.'

'Really?' Mace frowned. 'How?'

'By using mobiles,' said Clare. 'The moment they didn't need to follow us, they switched to Harry, to see where he was going.' Her expression was cool, but there was grudging approval in her voice at what Harry had accomplished.

'I still don't see what you've learned about them,' said Mace heavily. 'You don't know who they are or what they want. It's just another surveillance operation by local security cops. We should all be used to that.'

When they all dispersed, Harry sat at one of the desks, wondering what the hell was going on. So a group of unnamed men was following their every move. Not unusual in itself, given the territory and the in-built suspicion of foreigners. But there were inconsistencies in the Clones' individual skills. They operated well as a team, but at different levels. It still meant they were a team . . . but this wasn't their usual job.

Another thought occurred to him. He'd seen no sign of the Clones during his two trips out of town with Clare Jardine, nor when he'd gone to meet Mace. Neither had he seen a trace of them when he and Rik had gone shopping for the mobile phone. If they were as unskilled as he had witnessed today, he'd have seen at least one of them.

So why the uneven pattern?

There was only one answer: the Clones usually knew where their targets were going. Today, because he'd sprung the test on them, they'd scrambled all hands.

It meant someone was keeping the Clones informed of their movements. But who? Everyone was out and walking within minutes of his briefing.

Everyone except Mace.

'Why are you here, Harry?'

Clare Jardine stopped him as he was about to leave. Her expression was not unfriendly, but he detected a tone of puzzlement. He thought she looked tired.

'Because London sent me. I was a bad boy, remember?'

'I mean why did you agree to take this posting? You can't have wanted it – you must have known they only wanted rid of you until the fuss dies down.'

'Your point being?' He didn't feel inclined to discuss his decision to take the posting with Clare or anyone else. They were hardly friends, and there were people he knew better with whom he wouldn't ever talk about it.

'My point,' she said, with a flush of colour, 'is that I was finished when I came here – might still be for all I know. If they ever let me back inside Vauxhall Cross, it'll probably be in some lowly post where I'll die of boredom. I'm not sure I could take that.'

Harry wasn't sure what she was getting at. 'Rik Ferris is in the same boat. Same with me, same with Mace. So what?'

'Rik Ferris didn't know any better, did he? He was just grateful they didn't charge him under the anti-terrorism laws and throw him into prison for twenty years. They'll let him back sooner or later because they need his skills.' She paused, then said vaguely, 'I don't know about Mace.'

'Really?'

'Nobody does. He always played it dumb whenever we asked, so we stopped asking. Maybe there isn't anything; maybe he took the job because it was offered.' She shrugged. 'But you . . . you're different. You don't fit.'

Harry didn't say anything, content to let this go wherever she was taking it.

'You're not what we expected,' she continued. You see things. You question stuff. You faced up to those soldiers who stopped us the other day without turning a hair – I was watching you. If anything had kicked off, we'd have been dead. They'd have buried us in the hills and nobody would have known anything about it. But you had them laughing.'

'Kostova was there. He wouldn't have allowed anything to happen.'

Her eyes narrowed. 'You think?'

'What did you think he was doing – holding a political rally?'

'I don't know. As mayor, he has a wide remit.'

'So wide even local troops give way to him? Must be the only mayor in the world with that kind of power.'

She chewed her lip, digesting the fact. 'Perhaps. But what about today – you and that thing with the Clones?'

'It was a basic field test,' he said calmly. 'We conducted them all the time in London, tracking diplomats.'

'But we're not in London, are we?' Her eyes glittered. 'This is foreign soil, where I usually work. You took over like it was a second skin.'

'Are you just pissed because you should have organized it?'

'No. I'm saying it was well done.'

'For an MI5 officer.'

'For anybody. It makes me wonder all the more what made you agree to come here.'

Harry turned and walked out of the office. The truth was, he didn't know the real answer, either. At the time, it had seemed the only thing to do. There had been nothing special to keep him in the UK, no pressing reason to stay in London. He had no family, a few friends he was accustomed to seeing only occasionally because of his undercover work, and his divorce had been without hang-ups, a surgical separation with no backward looks – also a victim of his work. The few dates with Jean were irregular and casual, and now seemed beyond reach. He was surprised to realize that he didn't want them to be.

It made him wonder just how far they would go to stop him going back.

THIRTY-FIVE

Harry came to with a start, his throat dry. The room smelled of woodsmoke.

He was sprawled in the flat's one good armchair, shoes off, legs splayed out before him and head thrown back. Elegant. He peered at his watch. Gone midnight. The woodburner showed a faint glimmer of burnt embers. It took him a moment to work out what had woken him.

He'd been dreaming again; flashing images of the boat through the mist, Parrish running forward, the flare and crackle of gunfire. The two kids lying dead by the Land Rover.

But that wasn't it. Something else that had dragged him out of his sleep.

The mobile he'd bought from Rudi.

After leaving the office, he'd got back to the flat and opened a bottle of wine, stuck some logs with kindling in the wood-burner and ran his hands beneath the hot tap until he hissed with the pain. It was something he'd taken to doing without any conscious decision, and he knew why. Absolution. Pity it didn't work.

The wine was a cheap cooperative brand with a garish label and a harsh after-taste. But it did the trick, overriding the buzz going through his head and dulling his appetite.

It set him off thinking about Jean again, and their occasional dates. Sometimes they would stay in, content to share a bottle of wine and talk. He wondered what she was doing now.

They had met at a regimental reunion dinner. She was the widow of an officer killed in Iraq. Pretty, melancholy yet inter-esting; her throaty, irreverent laugh had drawn Harry to her. They had hit it off sufficiently to share a cab ride, and since then, an occasional drink or a meal whenever they felt the need.

She co-owned an upmarket flower shop in Fulham, a fact that she had not mentioned at first. When he had turned up with a meagre bunch of roses, the revelation had provoked much laughter and a halting explanation. The ice broken, he'd woken up in her bed the next morning surrounded by buckets of flowers.

Neither of them had mentioned taking the relationship to another level. It was an unspoken agreement which seemed to suit them both.

He thought about his message to Maloney, gauging the possibilities which might be unfolding back in London if he'd misjudged his colleague. In the end, he'd been spared further speculation when the combination of wine and tiredness had knocked him out.

The phone.

He scrambled to his feet and switched on the light. The floor was cold and rough through his socks and the air in the flat was like being in a fridge, in spite of the fire. He picked up the mobile and checked the screen. The sender's ID was blank.

It could only be one person. He brought up the message.
It was brief and to the point.

Fk!! U stl alive you bstrd???

Harry breathed a sigh of relief and instantly forgot the cold
and the tiredness. He scooted over to the door and found it
locked, grateful his security instincts hadn't fallen asleep, too.
Then he went through to the kitchen and put on the kettle.
The wine was tempting, but he needed to stay awake and
caffeine was a better bet.

He sat down to reply, all fingers and thumbs.

Just about. need info dq.

Double quick should make Maloney sit up. He didn't dare
use any official operational imperatives, in case they rang
alarm bells.

Ten minutes passed before the mobile beeped.

Ok. whre u?

Another good sign. Maloney didn't know his whereabouts.
If he had, Harry would have killed the connection immediately. Maybe his question about Harry still being alive hadn't
been a joke.

Outr space. Safe 2 talk?

No. Wlls & ears. Txt.

Harry gave it some thought while he made coffee. Texting
was safer than speech, but time-consuming. Talking would
have been easier, the huge boost of hearing a friendly voice
again immeasurable. Sod it – he'd just have to get quicker.
And avoid keywords like 'bombs', 'terrorist', 'Jihad' or, God
help him, 'Harry Tate'.

He sat down and began thumbing the keys.

Need 2 whrbouts urgnt. Sixer – man frm lilliput – init J.
Fiver – athlete started lndn mrthon – init G.

Silence. Had he been too convoluted? Maloney might not
pick up the reference to Lilliput straightaway. But he was no
dope; he'd be sure to catch on. The code for Brasher's name
was a gift; Maloney had once completed the London marathon
and talked about it non-stop for weeks.

The answer came back.

Gotcha. W8.

When he woke again, he was in bed and it was gone six in
the morning. He had a stale coffee-taste in his mouth and

gritty eyes, and a line of thin light was pushing through a
chink in the curtains. He checked the mobile, even though he
knew it was too soon for any response from Maloney. Finding
information about serving or former security officers didn't
exactly come off Wikipedia, and Maloney would have to tread
very carefully before even beginning his search.

He put on some tea and stood under the shower until the
water began to cool. When he was feeling half human, he got
dressed and set a password on the Ericsson, drank his tea and
walked to the office.

Mace was in, standing by a monitor. He nodded when Harry
walked in, but made no reference to their talk. Shortly afterwards, he went into his office and closed the door.

It was a long, frustrating day. Harry spent most of it working
with Clare to follow up on the report they had given to Mace
the previous day, checking all the international news channels
for any details on what was happening in the north. There
seemed precious little solid detail and he guessed the lid
was being held down deliberately while talks went on in the
background.

'London said good work,' Mace announced after lunch.
'Your report ties in with the latest satellite images. They're
building a picture of movements and distribution from both
sides and will let us know later what the state of play is. Pity
you didn't get unit IDs.'

'The fact that they weren't wearing any should tell us something,' said Clare. 'They're most likely local militia. They'll
be heading further north by now.'

'Can't you ask Kostova?' said Harry, looking at Mace. 'He
might tell you.'

Mace pursed his lips. 'He might . . . if there was something
in it for him.' He turned and went back into his office, leaving
them to monitor internet and radio reports for further news.

Rik Ferris drifted by and tapped a finger on Harry's desk.
'That, um . . . thing OK?' He was referring to the phone.

'Fine, thanks.' If Rik was hoping he would say who he'd
been calling, he was out of luck. But the comms man seemed
to have something else on his mind. He made a point of
hanging around, switching from foot to foot until Harry looked
up at him and nodded at the coffee table.

'Something bothering you?' he asked, when the kettle was

hissing loudly enough to shield his words. He threw a tea bag into a mug. If Rik was having a crisis of conscience about helping him get hold of a clean mobile, he needed to know now, before Mace found out.

Rik waited until Clare left the room, then jerked his head and walked back to his desk. Fitzgerald was downstairs doing an electronic sweep through the building.

'I got an email,' Rik explained. He spun his monitor round so that Harry could see the screen. 'Read it.'

The email was from someone called Isabelle in a company named SARFA. It had been sent at eleven a.m. It read: *You must leave. We are going tomorrow. Others are leaving, too. My boss says they are coming. I. xx*

'Isabelle?'

'She's a friend,' said Rik. 'French. She's with SARFA – supposedly a French non-governmental outfit, but everyone knows it's a cover for DGSE.'

The Direction Générale de la Sécurité Extérieure – French espionage service – was known to have agents operating world-wide. It was well-funded and resourced, and highly efficient. Harry hadn't expected to come across them here, although the proximity of the Med no doubt gave them a good enough reason to be monitoring the region.

He eyed Rik. 'Have you been sleeping with the enemy?'

'I wish.' The words came out with feeling, and the younger man blushed. 'Drinks only, so far. We meet up from time to time and talk shop.' He realized belatedly what that might imply, and added hastily, 'I don't mean we talk anything – you know. . . classified.'

'I should hope not. What does she do?'

'She's their comms officer.' He stared hard at Harry. 'Should I tell Mace, do you think? She's obviously referring to the Russians. I mean, if the French are bugging out, and others are going, too, that's bad news, right?'

'The only bad news,' Harry pointed out, 'is if you don't tell him about your contact and he finds out later.' The email from Isabelle hadn't been sent over a secure line, which meant anyone checking the files later might wonder why it had not been passed on.

Rik looked relieved. 'You're right. Thanks, Harry. I appreciate it.'

Harry left him to it and went in search of a meal. He was tired and hungry and still had no news from Maloney. He discovered a small family-style restaurant not far from the station, and ordered what a group at the next table were eating. It tasted like mutton stew.

It was late by the time he returned to his flat. Darkness was shrouding the town and the few people still about hurried along with their heads down. Even the military patrols had disappeared, no doubt hustled indoors by the cold winds scything between the buildings. As he turned the corner at the end of his street, Harry glanced instinctively towards his flat.

A glimmer of light flared briefly in one window.

THIRTY-SIX

Harry stepped into the shadow of the building and waited. He could see no obvious watchers at street level, and only one ancient Renault with a flat tyre thirty yards away. Even the local burglars weren't that desperate.

He retraced his steps, circling the block to approach the building from the rear. It meant making his way along a narrow back-alley with no lights and littered with rubbish, but it was safer than going through the front door. When he reached the rear entrance leading to his block, he stood and surveyed the area for a few minutes, waiting to see if anyone showed themselves.

Nobody did. He walked up the back path and eased open the door into the rear corridor.

The air here was heavy with the smell of dust and damp, and the sharper tang of cat's urine. The tinny sound of a radio seeped through the thin walls from the block next door. He closed the door softly behind him, wary of a lookout on the stairs.

He counted to thirty, then moved forward. Winced as his foot crunched on a piece of grit. He stopped, but nobody responded, then moved on, stepping carefully past a jumble of shadows which he knew from an earlier inspection was a collection of household goods abandoned by former tenants.

Nothing useful as a weapon, though – not unless he decided to threaten the intruder with a broken tumble dryer.

He took the stairs two at a time, moving slowly. The muscles in his calves and thighs protested at the effort, and he pushed down with his hands on his knees to give himself a boost. His shoes encountered more grit, but it was too late to stop now. Thirty seconds later, he was outside the door to his flat. He turned his head to listen, placing his ear against the grainy wood.

He counted to twenty. Not a sound. The intruder had either bugged out already or was very good at keeping quiet.

He reached out and tested the door. It wasn't locked. He nudged it further and it swung open to reveal a faint glow of a flashlight coming from the bathroom.

He stepped inside, flexing his hands. It had been too long since he'd engaged in any form of unarmed combat, and he hoped it didn't come to that. Being knocked on his arse by a local crackhead looking for a quick score would be too humiliating. But something told him this was no crackhead. As he moved away from the door, his foot nudged something solid. It was too late to remember a small footstool-cum-table standing against one wall.

It made a hollow clunking noise.

The flashlight snapped off.

Harry hit the wall switch. Sod what the training manual told you about using the dark; whatever was heading his way, he preferred to see it coming.

A blur of movement was all the warning he got as a tall figure burst out of the bathroom. The man was solidly built, dressed in dark clothing and holding a black torch in one hand. He wore a black ski cap on his head.

There was no time for finesse. Harry lashed out instinctively, turning his body to deliver a kick to the side of the advancing man's knee. His foot connected, drawing a grunt of pain from the intruder. But it wasn't enough to stop him. The man's momentum carried him forward, forcing Harry back. He threw up his arms to block the attack, but the man was too quick, slamming a fist into the side of his head. Harry felt the wall behind him and bunched his shoulders, launching a low, straight jab at the intruder's mid-section. It drew a satisfying whoosh of expelled breath, but the man kept coming, using his elbows and fists to jab at Harry's head in a series of rapid strikes and following up with a painful knee to the ribs.

Harry felt dizzy and breathless. The other man was younger, fitter and stronger, and if he kept this up, Harry would end the night in a hospital ward – or worse.

He slid sideways and felt his leg connecting with something which creaked and moved.

A basket of dried logs for the wood-burner.

Harry allowed himself to drop, scrambling for one of the logs. Each one was as thick as his arm and about a foot long. Grasping the first one he touched, he brought it up in a scything uppercut, smashing through the other man's defence. Before his attacker could react, Harry gripped the log with his other hand and swung it wildly straight at the man's head. There was a satisfying tingle as the wood connected and the man fell back, legs wobbling. Another swing and he crashed to the floor.

Harry dropped the makeshift weapon and leaned against the wall, trying not to throw up. The burst of exercise had taken more out of him than he'd thought. But there was no time to lose. Dragging the man into the bathroom, he went through to the kitchen and came back with a length of plastic-covered clothesline from one of the drawers. Tying the man's wrists together, he lashed him to the ornate cast-iron sink-support and finished by knotting his ankles where no amount of struggling would allow him to reach them.

The man was snuffling, his nose partially blocked by blood, and a large bruise was already forming across his chin, weeping blood where the skin had been scraped off by the log's rough bark. Harry wet a cloth and wiped the blood away from his nostrils. He didn't much care about the man's health, but having him choke to death before he could talk wasn't going to be much help.

He went through the man's pockets. Not surprisingly, he had no identification; no wallet, no papers, no scraps of information to reveal who he was. No clothing tags, either. That alone was unusual.

But he did have a mobile phone. Harry checked the directory. Three numbers in all. The man had called each of them, all within the past twelve hours, on or close to the hour.

Reporting in, thought Harry. With this one here making four, there were no prizes for guessing who they belonged to.

The other Clones.

He dropped the mobile in his pocket and slid to the floor, feeling the cold of the tiles seeping into his buttocks. He needed a rest. And he had time; after all, where was he going?

Eventually, the man stopped snuffling and stirred. His eyes flickered and rolled open, and he instantly shook his head and tried to stand. When he found that didn't work, he groaned and tugged at his bonds, head lolling forward to see what was holding him.

Operating by instinct, thought Harry, observing the bunching of muscle in his shoulders. This bloke has been trained; he knows he has to get free, no matter what.

He leaned forward and slapped the man across the face. It wasn't a brutal blow, but carried enough frustration and anger to rock his head back. His eyes opened and slowly focussed, finally settling on Harry with a start. He blinked twice and winced as pain began to register.

And at that moment, Harry saw something familiar in the man's face.

He felt a jolt of surprise. How could he know him? He'd only caught a glimpse of the Clones out on the street – hardly ideal conditions. Yet the feeling was overwhelming. Maybe he'd been on the plane in. Or at the airport. No. Christ, it was further back than that.

Then it began to filter through. The man was in his late thirties, with strong hands and an athletic build. He had short-cropped hair and the remains of a tan, faded to a dirty hue on the forehead and cheeks. He had the hard look of someone accustomed to regular exercise, and knew how to fight; the use of elbows and knee had proved that. Street thugs don't normally use their elbows.

Harry was well-acquainted with the kind of men who did.

'We've met before,' he said softly. The face was swimming up through a murky haze, from deep in his memory.

The man said nothing, struggling with his bonds.

'Give it up,' Harry told him. 'I learned from a master mariner.'

'Fuck you, bastard!'

The final piece of the puzzle fell into place. The oath was fluid, the accent familiar.

It came from somewhere in the Midlands.

The intruder was English.

THIRTY-SEVEN

'That was a mistake,' said Harry. 'I thought you were local. I was about to let you go. We've met before. Thing is, where?'

The man stopped struggling. If he recognized Harry, he was hiding it.

Harry finally got it. 'Stanbridge.' The man had been in Kosovo attached to the UN. Harry hadn't known him well; just another name and face in passing. They'd probably shared a truck, an APC or a canteen table. Maybe even a snow-filled shell hole. There had been lots of those.

Stanbridge said nothing. He stared at the floor and began working his wrists again. The skin around the bonds was beginning to turn dark red with the effort and the restricted blood flow, and Harry wondered whether he should ease up on them a bit. On the other hand, he still had no idea what the man was doing here.

'Tell me what's going on and I'll loosen those knots,' he said. 'Why are you here?'

'Screw you,' said Stanbridge.

'Hardly original, but suit yourself.' Harry stood up and went through to the kitchen, locking the front door on the way. If Stanbridge was one of the Clones, he didn't want to risk the other three piling all over him when they came to rescue their mate.

He made coffee, trying to figure out exactly what had brought the man here, to his flat. Why this godforsaken hole? If he was British, the others were, too. Unless he'd gone private.

He gave up and stared out of the narrow window overlooking the back alley. He could just make out the shape of a cat sitting on a crumbling section of wall, cleaning itself, relaxed. Better than a guard dog, he reflected. Quieter, too.

He took his coffee to the bathroom. There was nothing like the aroma of best roasted to make a man feel uncomfortable.

A classic softening-up technique, mostly recommended now to people selling houses.

He squatted in the doorway in case Stanbridge had somehow worked a miracle while he was out of sight, and waited. Stanbridge threw him a malevolent look. He had stopped working the bonds so maybe he'd realized he wasn't going anywhere.

'OK,' said Harry. He sipped his coffee, wincing as it touched a cut on the inside of his lip. 'Let's pretend you're not who we both know you are. We'll forget Kosovo, the UN mission, the crappy weather, the burial sites, the ethnic cleansing – all that. Let's just agree that I know who you are, and you know me. Right?'

Stanbridge cleared his throat and spat a bloody gobbet on the floor.

'Tough guy.' Another noisy sip. 'So what's your brief? You here to watch us – you and your mates? They call you the Clones, did you know that?'

'We know what they call us.' Stanbridge's voice was intense, pitched low.

'Really? How's that?' He didn't really need to ask, but it suited him to keep his prisoner talking. The Clones – if Stanbridge really was one of them – could have only discovered their nickname in one of two ways.

The first was by electronic eavesdropping.

The second was by talking to someone on the inside.

Stanbridge remained silent.

'What are you doing here?' Harry continued. 'Are you watching . . . or guarding? The former, I bet. There's no point in us having guardian angels because they're only assigned to diplomats and politicians . . . people of value. Last time I looked, I wasn't on anyone's preferred employees list.'

'I don't know what you mean.'

'Of course you don't. And I'm the ghost of Mahatma Gandhi.' He shifted his position. The cold from the tiles was making him stiff. 'It's a shitty assignment, this, whatever the purpose. I'm guessing you know who I am, right?'

No answer.

'If so, we've got the same employer. Unless you've gone over to the other side.' Stanbridge said nothing, but the way his eyes jumped told Harry that that wasn't the case. 'Well, good for you.'

He finished his coffee and dribbled the dregs on to the tiled floor. The smell lifted in the cold air, heavy and tantalizing. It would remain under Stanbridge's nose for a long time, an irritating reminder of the creature comforts he was missing.

'Problem is, what do I do about you? If I let you go, you'll come back. Probably with your mates.'

He stood up. He was wasting his time. Short of outright torture, he couldn't force the man to talk. And he wasn't about to get the contents of the cutlery drawer in here just to wind the man up. If you intend to bluff someone, you have to at least have the intention of carrying that bluff to reasonable lengths.

As he turned away, his mobile buzzed.

'Tate?' It was Clare Jardine. 'Have you got company?' Maybe she was calling to ask him round; vodka and olives between colleagues. Somehow he doubted it.

'I have, actually. Why?'

'Three of the Clones are parked in the street outside my place. I wondered if the fourth was on your place.'

'What are they doing?' Harry let out his breath slowly. They were sticking close. Was it a precursor to something else? If so, what?

'No. Just sitting there.'

Harry felt the pull of tension in his gut. They might be waiting to hear from Stanbridge. It wasn't a good sign.

Jardine said, 'If they're security police, they might be planning to pick us up – starting with me.'

Harry debated telling her about Stanbridge. If she was the Clones' inside source of information, she would already know if they were planning something. But if so, why would she be ringing him?

'They're not secret police,' he told her at last.

'How do you know that?'

'They're British.'

'That's absurd!' She was scornful, snappy. 'Are we talking about the same men?'

'Yes. I've got their number four in my bathroom. His name's Stanbridge, he's former British army and he comes from somewhere near Coventry.'

THIRTY-EIGHT

ilence. Bloody miracles do happen, thought Harry. 'You there?'

'I don't get it. Why would a Brit be watching us?'

'My guess?' Stanbridge was pretending not to listen, and Harry took a leap in the dark. 'London thinks we're a security risk. This is their way of making sure we don't jump the reservation. Unfortunately, the only way number four is going to tell me exactly what they're doing is when I start cutting off his fingers.'

'*What?*' Jardine's voice went off the scale, and Stanbridge's face went pale.

'Sure, why not? At least we'll find out what's going on. I'll tell you how it went in the morning—'

'Wait . . . *wait!*' Clare interrupted quickly. 'Don't. There's something else I didn't mention. The men outside . . . they're armed.'

That brought him up short. Stanbridge wasn't armed – he'd have found the weapon otherwise. So why were the others? Did they have another purpose other than watching?

Maybe it was time to discourage them. And to see how serious they were.

'Stay away from the windows,' he told her, 'and keep your door locked. Don't answer if anyone knocks.'

'Why, what are you going to do?'

'I want to take a look at the three on your place. What's your address?' He reckoned it would take ten to fifteen minutes to reach her place on foot. More if he had to avoid any armed patrols.

She gave him directions to an apartment block not far away. 'Don't come to my door, though. My neighbours are jumpy already. They've had trouble with drunken militia and call the police at the slightest noise.'

'OK. I'll see you later.'

'But what if you're wrong? What if—?'

He cut her off in midstream and took out Stanbridge's mobile. Then he left the flat and went downstairs.

Like the back passage, the stairs to the basement were covered with accumulated junk. He switched on the light and looked around. Most of it was a jumble of damaged furniture and discarded boxes, all beyond salvage and covered in mouse droppings. An ancient moped stood against one wall, the rubber grips perished with age. He shook it and heard liquid sloshing about in the pear-drop tank.

It was a start.

He searched through a pile of cardboard cartons and found a bathroom cabinet with broken mirrors. One side contained an empty toothpaste tin, several rusty razor blades, some dried soap and a half-empty tube of shower gel. Whoever had owned this was unlikely to be coming back for it. The other side held two shower caps and a box of foil-wrapped condoms. He opened one of the packs. The rubber looked in good condition; not that he'd chance using one of them as the makers intended, but for his purposes, they would do fine.

He emptied the petrol out of the moped's tank into a discarded wine bottle, then squirted the shower gel in after it and gently shook the contents for a few seconds before stuffing the neck of the bottle with a piece of rag. He placed the condoms and bottle in his pocket. If he got stopped carrying this lot, he might try claiming he was going round to warm up a girlfriend's flat and fuel her car, but he doubted anyone would believe him.

He turned off the light and left the building by the back door.

The walk to Jardine's flat took twelve minutes, using narrow alleys and back streets. He relied on his inner navigator to stay on the correct heading in the direction Rik had given him. Street lights were intermittent and weak, but provided enough ambient light for him to negotiate the route without incident. He saw neither military nor police patrols, but didn't argue with his luck. The further they stayed away, the better he liked it.

When he arrived at the end of Clare's street, he peered round the corner. A plain saloon was parked fifty yards away, facing the other way. The windows were misted over, but he could just make out a vague shape shifting on the passenger side.

He retreated and circled the block. He found an alleyway similar to the one behind his own flat, and counted doorways until he reached the building next to Clare's. The back door opened with a faint creak, and he made his way up the stairs to the roof. The muffled sound of voices and music came from behind the doors as he passed, but he encountered nobody.

At the top a small door opened on to a flat area littered with flowerpots and tubs. Doves or pigeons in a succession of wire cages cooed gently as he passed, and a web of clothes-lines and aerial wires brushed his head. He ducked beneath them and padded quietly to the front of the building.

He peered over the parapet. The car with the Clones inside was directly beneath him. The windows were up, but the angle prevented him seeing any detail of the men inside. Taking out the condoms, he opened three of them, unrolling the rubber to the fullest extent. Removing the rag stopper from the bottle, he fitted a condom over the neck of the bottle and tilted it, filling the sheath with the mix of petrol and gel. Then he knotted the condom and placed it carefully on the floor before repeating the exercise.

When he had his three devices ready, he looked over the edge of the roof and took out Stanbridge's mobile phone.

He pressed the re-dial button.

THIRTY-NINE

The atmosphere inside the car was foetid. Two of the men were snoring gently, the third was keeping watch and trying not to join his colleagues.

Nick Brockley was bored with this assignment. He'd been here too long and wanted to get out. Either home or Iraq. At least Basra offered some excitement. But they had been told to remain in their position until morning.

They called this gig a training exercise, but there was little variation and the training aspect offered nothing in the way of a challenge. Surveillance was an art learned best on hot targets, not these unsuspecting misfits. Brockley and his colleagues knew perfectly well what the people in Red Station were here for, and it wasn't for being top of their class.

The briefing files on each person had been cursory and

lacked specific detail other than the basics needed to help the
watchers identify their targets. But they'd heard enough from
the previous team to know that they had each screwed up in
some way. They had been consigned to this dump until they
got recalled or jumped ship. It was the jumping ship – and
every other movement they made – which had to be recorded
by the team of watchers, and noted for later evaluation.

So far, other than a couple of authorized trips out of town
and the daily journeys to work and back, there had been nothing
to get excited about.

He shifted his weight to ease an ache in his back, a hand-
me-down from too many days and nights on watch, and peered
upwards. He wondered what the Jardine woman was doing.
Having a bath, most likely, or lounging around in her jammies,
all soft and smelling of soap. He shifted in his seat, the image
burning in his brain. He wouldn't mind seeing some of that;
she was quite fit . . . for a spook. Small rack under that jacket,
but a nice arse to compensate. The others reckoned she was
butch but he could overlook that. She was still better than most
of the women he knew back home in Brighton.

His phone buzzed, making him jump.

He checked the screen. Stanbridge. He'd said he wanted to
check out Tate, the latest addition to the bunch of Security
Service losers, and Brockley had agreed. There was bugger
all else to do, so why not, if it kept him quiet. He'd told him
to stay off the phone until they met in the morning. So what
was he playing at?

'What?' He nudged Tucker with his other elbow. Time to
wake them up, anyway. Maybe send them off for a brisk stroll
round the block.

'This is your first warning.'

It was a voice Brockley didn't recognize. The hairs stirred
on the back of his neck.

'Stan? What the fuck are you playing at?'

There was no answer. Instead, he heard a soft thump on the
roof of the car. He looked up through the windscreen. A pigeon,
maybe? The place was full of the bloody things. Flying vermin.

A trickle of clear liquid ran down the side window.

'Stan? You daft git—'

'This is your second warning.' Another soft thump, this one
above the rear window.

'What's going on?' It was Rickard stirring in the back, his voice thick with sleep.

'How the fuck should I know? Stan playing silly bastards, probably.'

'What's that stink?' Tucker was watching a spray of liquid dribbling down the windscreen. It shimmered under the street light, colours showing like a rainbow waterfall.

'The next one comes with something extra,' said the voice in Brockley's ear, and for the first time he realized that the speaker was British.

'Who the fuck is this?' he demanded. He twisted in his seat and signalled frantically to the other two to eyeball all sides. For the first time on this poxy posting, he was wishing he had a gun. He'd soon see who was going to get something extra. 'Who are you – and where's Stan?'

Then it struck him. There was only one person it could be: the latest addition to the group. Tate. Harry Tate. Ex-army officer, according to the brief, transferred to MI5. But a screw-up, like the rest.

Something made him look up. He caught a glimpse of something pale at the edge of the roof, and an object sailed down through the air with a long, flickering tail.

Fire.

'Christ, get us out of here!' he yelled.

'What?' Tucker hadn't fully woken up yet. He sniffed and looked about him. 'Hey – I smell petrol.'

'Drive, you prick!' Brockley screamed. 'Before the bastard cooks us!'

Then the flash he'd seen was right upon them. There was a *whoosh* above their heads and the rivulets running down the windows flared into tongues of fire, the flickering light eating away at the shadows against the buildings on either side and singeing the rubber seals on the windows.

Tucker swore and turned the ignition, stamping on the accelerator. Seconds later, they hit the end of the street in a four-wheel drift, droplets of burning liquid falling from the car and laying a golden trail behind them.

Up on the roof, Harry watched them go. They'd probably be back, but at least he'd given them something to think about. He left the remnants of his fire-bombs where they were and

made his way down off the roof. He debated calling on Clare
Jardine but thought better of it. If she followed his advice,
she wouldn't answer anyway.

And he had a few more questions for Stanbridge.

He felt a buzzing at his hip. The Ericsson. He stepped into
a doorway and checked the screen.

Maloney. The message was brief.

Both files clsed. why?

Harry stared at the screen, felt a cold wind on his neck.

Even if Brasher and Gulliver had both left the service, their
personnel files would have been left open pending lengthy
debriefs, to make sure they weren't going elsewhere with any
information they might have stored up. Nobody got out of the
game that easily.

He texted back.

Why clsd?

Closed files could only mean one thing. He hoped he was
wrong.

He continued walking, and the answer came before he had
gone a hundred yards. Maloney must have been taking texting
lessons.

The text was clear and unequivocal.

Both dead. 5 – o'dose. 6 – climbng axdnt alps.

FORTY

Harry felt the air go out of him in a rush. After what
seemed an age, he tore his eyes away from the screen
and forced himself to continue walking. He was getting
careless; every second he stayed out here increased the risk
of discovery.

He tried to reason through the significance of Maloney's
message. There was no mistaking the words; dead was dead.
An overdose and a climbing accident. Maybe Brasher had been
depressed following his shock posting and the humiliation of
going back. It might have been enough to break anyone of a
cerebral nature, especially an analyst. But Gulliver? He recalled
what Clare had told him about the MI6 high-flyer. Thirty-two

was a young age for an exalted position in the Service. . . but an even younger one to die.

Two returns, both dead. What were the odds? But it answered another question that had been niggling at his subconscious: how was it he'd never heard of Red Station before? Secrecy may have been their game, but security services staff were notorious gossips when it came to internal rumours. And any staff member returning from a punishment posting in the back of beyond would have had colleagues buzzing around them like flies on an old steak, eager to hear every salacious titbit. News would have leaked out. It always did.

Unless the returnees were in no position to talk.

Stanbridge was exactly where Harry had left him, half prone and hanging off the sink support. In spite of the obvious discomfort, he was asleep, his eyes closed, breathing heavy and ragged.

Harry kicked him in the leg.

'Wake up, sunshine. Why are your mates tooled up and staking out Clare Jardine's place?'

Stanbridge came awake angry and resentful. He scrambled to sit up. His wrists were swollen and purplish in colour, and the skin had been scraped off in his struggles to get free.

'Armed? That's bollocks. When are you going to let me go?'

'When you answer some questions. Do you know Clare Jardine?' When the man nodded, Harry continued, 'Your mates were sitting outside her flat. They were armed.'

'Can't be.' Stanbridge looked confused, his eyes wide and red-rimmed.

'Really? Why is that?'

'Because we're not authorised, that's why. Jesus – we'd get shot if we were caught with guns in this place. We've got strict orders not to break cover . . . Who said they were armed?'

Now Harry was confused. The response sounded genuine, and he was certain Stanbridge was too dazed to concoct any lies. Or maybe he wasn't as dopey as he was pretending.

He squatted down next to him. Time to exert some pressure.

'Listen, son. I'm pretty pissed off at the moment. I was posted out here on a whim, I'm not allowed to leave and if our information is correct, there's a shit-storm heading this way in the shape of the Russian army. Now, I'd like to get

out in one piece and go home. But with you lot sitting on our
tails twenty-four hours a day, I doubt that's on the agenda.
Am I right?'

Stanbridge shook his head. 'I don't know what you mean.
Our orders are to monitor your movements. That's it. You
move, we follow. We log it and report in. But we don't carry
weapons.'

Harry sighed. It was no act; Stanbridge was telling the truth.
Clare Jardine must have imagined seeing weapons. Easy
enough to do in poor light under stressful conditions. He
changed tack.

'What's your cover story while you're here?'

'We're supposed to be doing a marketing study for inward
investment opportunities.'

Harry nearly laughed. 'You don't even look like marketing
people.' Still, as lame as it was, he'd heard worse. It wouldn't
take much to crack their cover if the local security police took
an interest. Still, that was the Clones' worry – them and the
people employing them. It provoked another thought.

'Where do you report to?'

'London via Frankfurt. It's a message link, outgoing only.
If they need to contact us, they do it by phone to our team
leader.'

'What happens when we leave town?' He was thinking
about his trips out with Clare; he was pretty certain they hadn't
been followed on either occasion.

Stanbridge looked blank. 'I don't have any instructions for
that. It would be handled by our team leader. He says follow,
we follow. Otherwise we stay on the office or stand down
until further orders.'

Again, it sounded genuine. Typical security services smoke
and mirrors; never let the left hand know what the right hand
was doing. So they hadn't been followed out of town. But
why not? Was it because the Clones hadn't been quick enough
to latch on to them? Or had they been told not to? Then he
had another thought.

'Do you know why you're doing this?'

An immediate nod. 'Yeah. It's a module in a training routine;
we have to complete it over a set period of time before going
on to something else. They don't tell us how long, though.
We wait until we're told to stand down.'

A *module*? They were being used as live targets for training newcomers? Christ, Harry thought bitterly, they'd be handing out MBA certificates in spying next.

'Bit late in the day to be doing this stuff, isn't it?'

Stanbridge shrugged with one shoulder. 'It's a job. I was leaving the army, they offered and I accepted.' He looked as if he was about to say something else, then stopped.

Harry leaned forward. 'What?'

'What did you do to the others?'

'Why are you bothered?' Harry knew the answer to that one.

'They're my mates.'

'I persuaded them to move on, that's all. Last thing I saw, they were driving like their pants were on fire.'

Stanbridge shifted his position and winced with cramp. 'You were right . . . about me in Kosovo, I mean. I was there for a couple of months, then rotated out.' He coughed. 'Could I have some water?'

Harry fetched a plastic mug and filled it from the tap. He held it to Stanbridge's lips at arm's length. If he tried anything, he'd get clipped. But the man drank greedily, gulping down the water.

When he was finished, he continued. 'There was another bloke in Kosovo at the same time, called Latham. He was part of a deep-cover team, Special Ops, spending weeks in the hills.'

'Doing what?' Harry thought he could guess.

'Hunting for war criminals. I knew him from years back. He was always looking to get transferred, hoping to pass selection for Special Forces. I never heard if he'd made it, but if he was in Kosovo doing that job, I guess he must have. He's not a bloke to cross, though. Bloody headcase.'

'What's this got to do with us?'

'Why I came here . . . to your flat; I told the lads I knew you, but I wanted to check you out, get some ID. I figured I might get some brownie points if I got background info that nobody else had.' He hesitated.

'Go on.'

'Soon as I clocked you first time, I was sure I knew you – and I was right.'

'How?'

'I was in the same convoy as you when we came to that Serb roadblock with the three kids. You were the one who jumped on that Serb APC and took out the gunner . . . rescued those kids.'

Harry nodded slowly.

'The lads didn't believe me. Said you wouldn't have pulled it off unless you were SAS or something, and why would you be out here now. I told them you'd got a round of applause from the guys in the convoy and free drinks all evening, so what did it matter?'

'I remember.' He'd got blind drunk with relief and the aftershock of what he'd done. He hadn't been a hero; he'd been stupid. One wrong move and half the convoy could have been blown away. He'd been moved out shortly afterwards following a complaint from the Serb Liaison Office. A diplomatic move was the official explanation. Later, he'd heard that a Serb hit squad had been looking for him.

'So the other lads . . . they're OK?' Stanbridge said.

'They're fine.' He knew why Stanbridge was asking; the answer might have an impact on his own future. 'I dropped some petrol condoms on their car, that's all. Singed the paintwork a bit.'

'Petrol *condoms*?' Stanbridge nearly laughed. 'Shit. Wish I'd seen that. What did they do?'

'They made a strategic withdrawal at speed. You mentioned this Latham. Why?'

Stanbridge licked his lips and Harry gave him another drink. 'This business is all messed up now, what with the Russian thing. We got orders to get ready to bug out in the morning and make tonight our last shift. Sounds like something big's going down.'

'Lucky you. We can all go home, then.'

Stanbridge shook his head again. 'We're being replaced. By another team.'

'What?'

'Latham's in charge.'

A Special Forces man-hunter. Coming here? His spirits sank. 'What does he look like?'

'From what I remember, tall, thin – skinny, actually. But fit. Hard. Lives like a monk. Extreme.'

The physical description fitted half the men in town. It wasn't much help.

'What's the new team's objective?'

Stanbridge shrugged. He was subdued, almost fearful. 'They didn't tell us. Just that the other team would take over. Same thing as us, I suppose. Only . . .'

'Only what?' Harry had a feeling he wasn't going to like what he heard next.

'Guys like Latham . . . they're way beyond our kind of exercise. We're still training, although we occasionally do other stuff, like Close Protection and that. But Latham . . .' He stopped.

'Spit it out, for Christ's sake.' Harry wasn't about to use force, but if something nasty was in the wind, he had to know what it was.

'Nick Brockley, our team leader, he said he'd heard whispers about Latham's team. They're not pleasant. Heavy duty.'

'What does that mean?'

'They're called the Hit. Word is, they kill people.'

FORTY-ONE

Harry left Stanbridge where he was, with a sandwich and water to keep him quiet. He promised to release him before morning when he'd checked something out. Then he made his way back to Clare Jardine's flat.

He was too wired up to contemplate sleep, but didn't fancy the idea of staying with Stanbridge. Neither could he turn him loose without knowing what the other Clones were doing. Stanbridge might be lying and bring the others here in force and armed. This way, at least one of them was neutralized and the others were getting over the shock of being under attack. It might keep them unsettled enough not to take offensive action.

There was no sign of the burned car. He toured the block twice, checking the side streets, gradually widening the search until he was satisfied. He glanced up at Clare's flat. It was in darkness. He considered going up to see if she was OK, then thought better of it.

Instead, he made his way to Rik's place, a few blocks over.

Novroni was a wide street close to the outskirts, a mix of family homes and one or two blocks which could have housed workers. There were very few cars in evidence, none of them new.

Number 24 was a single building squashed between two empty warehouses. The brickwork was crumbling, the front garden scrubby and abandoned to a litter of rusting metal and decaying packing crates. Originally part of the warehouses, he suspected, now leased by Red Station.

A light was on in one of the downstairs rooms, and he could see movement behind the net curtains. He made a tour of the area, checking cars and the dark spaces between buildings, until he was sure there were no watchers.

Stanbridge had been telling the truth.

He returned to his flat, stopping at an all-night workingmen's café for a mug of stewed coffee and a cold meat sandwich. He had to force the food down, but it could be a while before he got another opportunity. A few tired-looking men in dusty overalls and heavy boots were hunched over hot drinks or glasses of spirits, smoking and talking in low voices. They barely gave Harry a glance. Late shift or early? It was gone five and he wondered where the hell the time had gone.

He sensed something was wrong the moment he stepped off the street into the apartment building. It might have been in the quality of the grey light washing down the stairwell, or a shift in the atmosphere, as if the air inside had become charged with energy. He stopped and tilted his head to one side, listening. Something in the building had changed.

He waited for the telltale whisper of someone moving, the creak of shoe leather or the rustle of clothing. With no background noise, such sounds travelled easily at night.

Nothing.

He could have done with a weapon, but that was crying for the moon. Instead, he began the slow shift up the stairs, stepping carefully on to each tread.

He paused twice after hearing noises; one a scuffing sound, the other no more than a sigh. He decided it must be the building and continued on up. He stopped near the top to ease the aching muscles in his thighs. Jesus, he was getting far too old for this. If he made it out of here in one piece without getting shot, stabbed or having a bloody heart attack, he promised himself he'd start buying lottery tickets.

He arrived at his front door and stopped.

It was open.

Bugger. He breathed out in mild frustration. Stanbridge had managed to free himself and leg it. He pushed through the front door. Saw the bathroom light on. The door partly open.

Then came the smell.

Harry gagged. *Oh, Christ . . .*

He pushed the bathroom door back until it stopped with a bump. Stanbridge was lying in a foetal position against the wall. He had somehow managed to stretch the clothesline in his struggles to get free, but not enough to protect himself.

He'd been shot in the side of the head.

Harry didn't bother checking the body. There was a lot of blood and grey matter against the wall and across the floor, and signs of burn marks around the wound. Whoever had done this had stood very close to him before pulling the trigger.

Harry walked out of the bathroom and rang Clare Jardine.

'I don't have time to explain,' he said when she answered. 'Can you get over here right away?'

'What?' She sounded breathless and irritable, as if dragged from a deep sleep. 'Tate? Is this a joke?'

'Get over yourself,' he said brutally. 'This is a code red. I need help. Now.'

He switched off the phone, tired of her snarky attitude. Code red should get her moving. It meant the shit had hit the fan and there was no time to lose. He thought about calling Rik. No, he'd freak out; he wasn't trained for this. Fitzgerald, then. If Mace was right about him, he was used to making people disappear off the street. A third-floor bathroom should be right up his alley. Too late now – he'd wait for Clare.

He untied the body from the sink and disposed of the clothes line in a rubbish bag in the kitchen. Then he rolled the body flat, rearranging the clothes. He'd deal with the clean-up operation later.

Jardine was quick. Less than ten minutes later, Harry heard a footfall on the stair. He went to the window to check

the street. No cars, no watchers. The early morning light
filtering across the rooftops made the flat seem squalid and
depressing, and he suddenly wanted to get away from here.
He waited until he heard a soft knock before opening the door.

She gave him a cold look, a vein standing out on the side
of her face.

Harry was unimpressed. 'What did you do, take a bus?'

She ignored him and went on the offensive. 'What's your
problem, Tate? You didn't have to be so bloody insufferable
on the phone.' She pushed inside without waiting to be asked,
and he closed the door and led her to the bathroom. Stood
aside to let her see.

She froze when she saw the body, but that was all. No
histrionics, no panic.

Tough indeed, he decided, and a stomach to match. Most
people would have puked on sight.

'His name was Stanbridge,' he said.

She stared at him, eyes wide. 'Did you—?'

'Of course not. I caught him searching the place. He told
me he and his mates have been called off the job as of this
morning. I went out to see if the others were still around, and
when I got back he was like this.'

Clare bent to inspect the body. 'Who would have done
it?'

Harry decided to lie. They could worry later about what
Stanbridge had told him. 'I don't know. But we need to get
rid of the body. If whoever killed him makes a phone call,
we'll have the authorities all over us like a rash.'

'Or his mates.'

'I wouldn't bet on it.' He began looking round for something to wrap the body in. There were no plastic bags, which
would have made the task easier, so he took a blanket from
the bedroom.

He had already decided what to do with the body. The
further they moved it, the greater the risk of running into a
security patrol. It made sense, therefore, to move it somewhere close.

He placed the blanket on the floor, then grasped the dead
man's shoulders and looked up at Clare.

'You ready or not?'

FORTY-TWO

'We're discussing the evacuation of all British nationals.' Marcella Rudmann stared hard at George Paulton as if making a point.

They were in his office, where she had followed him from a crisis meeting between representatives of the Foreign Office, the MOD and the RAF. Paulton had been invited along even though Five had no relevant responsibility or input. He thought Rudmann looked ready for a fight and wondered what had provoked it. Doubtless he would soon find out.

'So I heard,' he said smoothly, sitting behind his desk. He indicated a chair, but she ignored him.

'*All* British nationals.'

'Sorry?'

'For heaven's sake, man, that place. . . the Red Station or whatever outlandish designation you've given it. What are you doing about the people there?' Rudmann looked white around the eyes, and he suspected it had less to do with her concern over the personnel in the station and more to do with his less-than-respectful response. Then he realized what she was saying.

She must know where Red Station was.

'I have no idea what you mean.' He fell back on the old civil service and Whitehall mantra: when in doubt, deny everything. But he felt a dizziness that threatened to knock him off his chair if he didn't control it. *How the hell could she know? Unless Bellingham . . .*

'Don't take me for an idiot, Paulton,' she hissed dangerously, barging in on his thoughts. 'I saw your reaction when Spake gave his briefing about the line the Russians were most likely to take across the border. It didn't take long to work out where you had put Tate and the others. Now, what are you doing about them?'

'Why, nothing,' he insisted. 'They will stay in place until we decide they can no longer do any good.'

'Are you *insane*? You send people like Tate out there – problem

people, you called them – and you think they can stay there
in the face of what might be about to happen? What if the
Russians scoop them up? It'll be their biggest intelligence coup
in years!'

'They are professional operatives and will be monitoring
the situation on the ground.' Paulton fought hard to keep his
tone level but realized he was sounding pompous. What
possible business did this *infernal* woman have questioning
how they carried out operations, he seethed quietly. But he
knew the answer: she had the ear of No. 10 and a *laissez-
aller* to the security agencies' innermost workings.

Fortunately, he had an answer to her meddling. 'Before you
start lecturing me about how far inside the PM's confidence
you are, you're wasting your time.'

'What do you mean?' She flushed crimson with anger.

'A decision was made less than thirty minutes ago, immediately after the crisis meeting. The station personnel have
been told to dig in and report as and when they can. They are
more use to us there than running for cover anywhere else.'

'But the evacuation—' she began.

'Will not apply to them,' Paulton broke in. 'If their cover
has already been compromised, like the Special Forces teams,
and they go near the airport, the Russians will be waiting for
them.' He smiled coldly, enjoying telling Rudmann that a decision had been taken without her being present – and that she
could never disprove what he was saying.

'I'll speak to the PM! This is unacceptable.'

'Maybe it is. But the Intelligence Committee has no say in
day-to-day operational matters such as this.' His eyes blazed
with fire. 'This is the sharp end of what we do, and it doesn't
always go according to plan. Not everyone ends their day
tucked up in bed with a warm cup of cocoa.'

'Who decided this?' she demanded, and Paulton could have
sworn she almost stamped her foot in frustration. 'Who advised
the PM?'

'That's something you don't need to know.' He checked his
watch. 'Now, you'll have to excuse me, but I have other matters
to deal with.'

When she had gone, the side door to Paulton's office opened,
and Sir Anthony Bellingham entered. He looked unperturbed
by what he had just heard.

'She doesn't sound happy,' the MI6 man commented.

'She isn't,' said Paulton. 'Let's hope she has too much on her plate to start digging around and making unnecessary noises.'

'Don't worry, George. We control what information comes out via Red Station. If we say they're blown, they're blown. Rudmann will be too busy fighting her corner to pursue it forever.'

'That was neat, sidestepping her. How did you manage it?'

'Simple. I checked her diary and arranged a meeting with the Cabinet Office while she was otherwise engaged. It took three minutes. So many meetings, so little time . . .' Bellingham smiled. 'It's amazingly simple to get a decision when the pressure's on. I didn't mention who the personnel were, of course. No sense in making problems for ourselves.'

'Any news from over there?' Paulton felt uneasy at having to ask Bellingham for information, but the MI6 man had the resources available without questions being asked.

'None. Either the lines are down or signals are being jammed. Can't say I'm surprised.'

'And Brockley's team?'

'Ah. Now that situation is not quite so good.'

Paulton paled. 'Why – what's happened?'

'One of them has disappeared. A man named Stanbridge. It seems he went to check on one of Red Station's personnel and never returned. The others were subsequently attacked with petrol bombs. They're on the way out as we speak.'

'*What?*' Paulton felt himself reeling. He tried to rationalize the situation. The man's disappearance might be down to the local militia or security forces. They would be especially jumpy with everything that was happening on their doorstep, and anyone acting strangely was probably being picked up as a matter of course. If Stanbridge had been in the wrong place at the wrong time with no useful explanation, it would account for his disappearance. No doubt he would surface sooner or later, none the worse for his experience.

The petrol bombs, however, were something else. Security forces wouldn't use them; they were hardly that ill-equipped, by all accounts, even the militia. That left civilians. But why?

Then another thought occurred to him.

Harry bloody Tate.

'What?' Bellingham had noticed his change of expression.

'Nothing.' He deflected the question with one of his own. 'How long are we going to leave them there?'

'Who?'

'*Them.* Mace . . . Ferris . . . the others.' He didn't dare mention Tate in case it betrayed what he was thinking.

'They can stay where they are. Why?' Bellingham was eyeing him with suspicion.

'Is that wise? There may not be much time left. Another couple of days and the borders could be locked tight. We should at least warn them.' Then a thought occurred to him and he stared at Bellingham. 'You haven't told them yet – about Delta and the Special Reconnaissance team.' Even as he said it, he knew he was right.

'There was no point.' Bellingham's tone was cool, his jaw flexing. It was the MI6 man's first real show of irritation over this issue that Paulton had seen. 'It wouldn't help their situation, would it? We leave them for now.'

'Why?' Paulton wondered what Bellingham was up to. As the only means of communicating with Red Station, the other man was in complete control of what information came out . . . and what went in.

'It's getting out of hand, George. Just as it did with Gulliver.' Bellingham's words were pitched low. 'I've already arranged for Brockley's team to be replaced.'

'I don't understand. To do what?' He immediately wished he hadn't asked, and realised with Bellingham's next words that he had lost any say in what was about to happen in the Red Station. And that with that, there was no going back.

'Don't ask, George. You really don't want to know.'

Back in her office, Marcella Rudmann was surprised to discover she had a visitor. Gareth Nolan, Deputy Commissioner for Operations in the Metropolitan Police, was waiting impatiently for her return.

'I'm sorry to drop in without an appointment,' he said smoothly, 'but I have some information which might be of interest.' He sat down without being asked and placed a folder on the desk in front of him.

Rudmann wondered who he was planning to undermine this time. She had no illusions about the senior policeman's ambition for favours and higher office, but he did have his uses. All she had to decide was whether the information he claimed to have was useful to her or not, and whether the knowledge might harm her in any way.

'What can I do for you?'

Nolan delved into his folder and produced a 10-inch by 8-inch black-and-white photograph. It was the sort that Rudmann had seen many times before, culled from security cameras. It had a row of numbers and letters printed in white across the bottom, and was grainy and lacking light. It was a profile shot of a man in jeans and a hooded top crossing a tiled floor.

'This was taken from a CCTV tape at Clapham South underground station,' Nolan explained importantly. 'It was timed, as you can see, at twenty-one thirty hours on the night Shaun Whelan was killed, and shows this man leaving the station.'

Whelan. Rudmann felt a chill across the back of her neck at the mention of the journalist's name.

'Go on.'

Nolan slid a second photo across the desk. Rudmann recognized the figure immediately.

'This shows Shaun Whelan leaving the station just before ten o'clock.' He paused for effect, then passed her a third photo. This showed a figure in a hooded top walking towards the camera. The time stamp was 22.20 hours. 'And this man was shown re-entering the station at twenty past.'

It was the same figure as in the original shot.

'Who is he?'

Nolan smiled and sat back. 'We're not sure. But we're running facial-recognition software to confirm it right now. I should have an answer for you by tomorrow morning at the latest.'

Rudmann was surprised. She was aware that the database of known 'faces' was very large, but it did not – could not – include everyone. 'You sound very sure of that. What do you mean by confirm?'

'One of my officers thinks he knows the man. It helps us narrow down the field considerably. Once we're certain, we'll pick him up.'

Rudmann tossed the last photograph on the desk. The senior policeman obviously wanted a pat on the head. 'It will be good work if you can get him, Deputy Commissioner. Very good work. But I'm not sure why you feel I should be interested in a murderous little mugger who preys on the unwary.'

Nolan gave a smug grin. 'Oh, he's no mugger. Far from it.'

Rudmann's stomach tightened. Nolan was looking too pleased with himself.

'What do you mean?'

'My officer thinks he met this man on an anti-terrorist training course.'

'What?' She sat forward.

'He works for the security services.'

FORTY-THREE

'**N**o sign of the Clones yet.' Rik sidled up to him at the coffee table next morning.

It was gone eleven. Harry had got in late, exhausted by lack of sleep. He had noticed the younger man staring out through the front windows, scanning the street, and guessed why. It was no surprise when he approached him the moment Harry walked through the door.

'Maybe they overslept.' Harry spooned in extra coffee and sugar; he needed a caffeine boost to keep his eyes open and his brain in full working order. He'd been extra careful coming in this morning, checking his route back and front for unusual faces. But other than a lot more military vehicles and soldiers standing around looking menacing, there had been no sign of watchers.

And that was a worry. If the Clones were already gone, abandoning their colleague in the process, did that mean the Hit was here? With Stanbridge's body lying in the flat below his, he could almost feel the increased threat in the air.

'Yeah, maybe.' Rik shifted his feet, then said, 'I told Mace about the email.'

'What did he say?'

'Not much. Just told me to pass it on. Said London would

know what to do. Do you reckon they'll pull us out if things get too hot?'

'I don't know,' Harry said honestly. 'If they do, it'll be to assign us somewhere else. Have you passed on the email?'

'Yes. First thing.' He wandered away to fiddle with one of the monitors.

Harry stretched his arms and felt his muscles complaining. With Clare a reluctant helper during the night, they had taken the body downstairs to Mario's flat. He had a feeling the Italian photographer wouldn't be needing it anytime soon. They had placed it in the bedroom, inside an old blanket box, with a jumble of clothes on top. It wasn't a pleasant task, but short of dumping the corpse out in the open countryside it was as good as they were going to manage.

He had been debating whether to tell the others about Stanbridge, and still hadn't made up his mind. Mace might blow a fuse and tell London, as he was officially required to do. If so, there was no saying what might happen. Knowing that a member of your own side, whatever their function, had been murdered, then hiding the body, wouldn't go down too well. It wouldn't matter what the likely motive might have been; a death was a death and would have to be investigated.

He waited for Clare to come in. When she put in an appearance, she looked even paler than usual, with dark rings around the eyes. She avoided catching Harry's eye and went straight to her desk.

No help there, then.

Mace came in and headed for the coffee pot, pouring himself a liberal dose. He looked a mess, as if he'd been on a bender. The others carefully avoided noticing and went about their business.

The Ericsson in Harry's pocket buzzed softly, and he stepped away from the others. He didn't think anyone else had heard it, although Rik was giving him an oblique look. Maybe the IT man had developed an especially acute ear for electronic noises over the years, and could identify a model by its tone.

Harry ignored him and went to the toilet on the ground floor. The phone was still buzzing and he realized it wasn't a text message.

Somebody was calling him.

The screen showed no caller ID. It had to be the former owner. He was surprised they hadn't tried already. They had probably blocked the phone automatically the moment it went missing, and were now trying to recover it any way they could.

'Huh?' he grunted.

'Who is this?' It was a man's voice; thin, reedy, American. Rudi sounded American. Maybe he was calling to offer an upgrade, although Harry doubted it.

'Why you call me?' he muttered gutturally. If he was lucky, the man might identify himself.

'I said, who is this? What the fuck are you doing with my fucking cell, you jerk?'

American. A very angry American. Harry cut the connection. Before he could switch it off, the text tone sounded.

Maloney.

Whre U?

Harry thought about it for a moment. It was just a name, for Christ's sake. And already all over the news and networks, filling the airwaves, making a trace less likely. He thumbed the name of the town and hit SEND.

The answer was swift and to the point.

Fk!! Gt out of there!!

FORTY-FOUR

He got back upstairs to find the others waiting for him. Mace stepped forward, a determined set to his jaw. 'Is there something you'd like to tell us, lad?' He had lost his hung-over expression but not his untidy appearance.

The others stood in the background, waiting. Clare refused to meet Harry's eye, concentrating on the contents of her mug.

'Like what?'

'Like what's going on. You've had a contact with the Clones.'

'They've been pulled out.' Harry didn't blame Clare; she would have had a duty to tell Mace eventually. She'd just done it sooner than he'd expected.

'How the hell do you know that?' Mace was bristling. 'What happened last night?'

He told them about finding Stanbridge in his flat, about recognizing the man from Kosovo; about Clare's call and how he had 'dissuaded' the other Clones from hanging around. When he looked at Clare for confirmation, she was staring down at the floor, her jaw clenched tight. Deniability, he thought angrily. It runs deep when your neck is on the block, even for colleagues.

'You took a bloody big risk,' Mace muttered. 'How did you know they wouldn't have back-up?'

'Because Stanbridge wasn't hiding anything. He had no reason to. All he knew was that he and his team had a simple assignment: to watch and follow. They wouldn't need back-up for that. Clearly our masters don't trust us very much.'

'What else?'

'He told me his team was being replaced this morning.'

'That would be standard procedure,' Fitzgerald mused thoughtfully. 'Rotate them on a regular basis and nobody gets to know their faces.' He chewed his lip. 'Are you sure they're a home team?'

'Yes,' Harry replied bluntly. 'But not friendly. The Clones were, but they've gone. The new team is a specialist unit called the Hit. And they're not coming to audit the books.'

'What sort of specialists?' Rik looked worried.

'With a title like that, what do you think? The leader's name is Latham. He tracks people for a living . . . and he's not always required to bring them back alive.'

There was a stunned silence in the room. Only Mace looked unsurprised, but that might have been because the idea was taking a while to sink through his alcohol-fuelled fog. He looked at Clare, but she didn't offer any helpful advice.

'You've been busy,' he said finally to Harry. It sounded like a condemnation.

'Well, it wasn't by choice.'

'It's nonsense, of course. I'll be putting that in my report to London.' Mace was finding comfort in bluster.

'You do that,' Harry replied. 'In the meantime, Latham and his buddies will be dropping by to say hi. They won't be asking anyone's permission, either.'

'You can't know that.' Fitzgerald was still frowning. 'This – Stanbridge? – could have been spinning you a load of tosh. Maybe somebody local showed up and did him in. It's not exactly law-abiding around here. There's a lot of poverty and not much in the way of jobs. People get desperate. Random killings happen all the time, mostly over small change and a mobile phone.'

Harry looked at him, trying to determine if that remark was meaningful in any way. He decided not. Fitzgerald wasn't the sort to make oblique comments. Blunt accusation was more his line.

'It wasn't random.' Clare Jardine finally spoke up. 'You didn't see the body. It was a professional hit. Harry had tied Stanbridge up with a clothes line. All the killer did was walk in and shoot him in the head. He had no chance.'

Nobody spoke for several seconds. Then Rik said, 'What do we do?' He looked anxious but determined, and Harry decided he would just need pointing in the right direction and he'd be all right.

'I don't know about you,' he said softly, allowing anger to fuel his own resolve, 'but I'm buggered if I'm going to sit here and wait for a bunch of Vauxhall Cross body snatchers to come and take me out.'

Fitzgerald nodded and went to the door. 'I'll get the lights.'

Nobody questioned what he meant.

Outside, someone shouted and a car door slammed, followed by a burst of laughter. Bottles rattled in a crate and somebody gave a wolf-whistle. Normal sounds. Echoes of life being lived.

The minutes crept by, each individual alone with their thoughts, until Harry turned to Mace. 'Something's wrong. Do you have any other weapons here?'

Mace shook his head. 'Never saw the need. Why?'

'I need an equalizer.' He moved over to the window and looked out. Nothing moved down there. Then he remembered the operations representative in London saying his sidearm would be sent out in a diplomatic pouch. 'Did a bag come for me?'

'A bag?' Mace was vague, his face pale.

'A secure pouch from London.'

Rik said, 'It arrived yesterday. Sorry, I forgot to tell you.'

'Where is it? Quick.'

Rik went to a metal cabinet on the wall and opened the door. Inside was a canvas bag the size of a small briefcase. It had a zipped front with a sturdy combination lock and seal.

Harry ripped off the seal with a pair of scissors and fed the last four digits of his field number into the combination dial. The lock sprang open.

'Now we've got an equalizer,' he explained, and withdrew his semi-automatic and two spare clips. He checked the action, the sounds loud in the quiet room.

'So now you're Action Man?' Rik looked stunned. 'I thought you were Five . . . and . . .' He stopped and blushed.

'Too old for this stuff?' Harry shrugged. 'I thought so, too. We'll soon find out.'

'Why would anyone come to take you out?' Clare Jardine looked calm but her voice trembled as she spoke.

'Does it matter?' he replied. 'Someone must have decided I'm a liability.' He nodded towards the north. 'Personally, with what's going on up there, I wouldn't bet on the rest of you being served tea and buns, either. Get used to it.'

He left them to digest that and went out on to the landing. The building was silent, with a buzz of traffic in the background. He walked slowly downstairs, the gun under his jacket. Noonday shadows filled the corners of the building, producing a variety of dark shapes.

He tried to recall how long it had been since he'd done the close-quarter combat course, where officers learnt the rudiments of sweeping a building. Five years at least. Too bloody long. But some things you never forgot – like the agony of letting off shots in a confined space.

He stopped at the halfway mark. A noise had disturbed the silence. Up or down? Difficult to tell. He waited. It came again: the scuff of shoe leather on tiles.

From above.

He looked up, sweeping the gun from under his jacket. Clare was looking down at him. Her eyes went wide when she saw the gun pointing at her.

He signalled for her to stay where she was, then turned and tossed a coin down the stairs. It bounced and rolled, the tinkling sound echoing off the walls like the ringing of a small bell. It finally came to a stop on the ground floor.

He followed it down, the gun held by his side. If anyone was waiting for him, being above them would give him a marginal element of surprise.

And margins were what counted in situations like this.

The foyer was empty.

He checked the front door, which was closed, then made his way to the basement. His breathing sounded unusually harsh in the enclosed space.

The storage rooms were undisturbed, the under-floor panel still in place.

There was no sign of Fitzgerald.

FORTY-FIVE

Harry left the guns where they were and went back upstairs to tell the others.

Mace looked stunned and reached for a phone. 'He's probably gone straight home,' he said. 'He was worried about his girlfriend and kid.'

'He lives with a local girl,' Rik explained to Harry. 'She's got a daughter and Fitz is nuts about them. The mother's been putting him under pressure to take her out of here. Can't say I blame her, with everything that's going on. I think he's scared she might dump him if he doesn't do something soon.'

'Why would that be bad?' said Harry.

Rik shrugged, his expression sombre. 'He's got nobody else. His wife and kids in the UK never speak to him, so this is a final posting for him.'

Harry understood. Fitzgerald wouldn't be the first security services employee to want to retire somewhere out of the way, where his old trade wouldn't keep coming back to haunt him. With nothing back home, it could be the only sense of belonging that he had left.

'No answer,' Mace announced. 'I'll try later.'

Harry left them to it and went back downstairs. He needed some fresh air. Being cooped up when danger threatened only increased a sense of paranoia. What he could see, he could deal with.

The streets were quiet. A few vehicles lumbered back and forth, mostly military, with smaller trucks and jeeps dotted at junctions and men in uniform standing in small groups. What civilians there were hurried along and avoided eye contact, apart from huddles of older men outside the basement shops where *chacha* was available.

The fabric of the town appeared to have suffered a change already. A truck had run off the road at one corner and ploughed into a grocery store, scattering a layer of broken glass, splintered wood, fruit and vegetables across the street. The shop-keeper was arguing heatedly with the driver, while an officer stood nearby, calmly ignoring them. Further on were signs of cracked paving stones where heavy trucks or APCs had parked, and other indicators of where the military presence was showing its impact on the civilian infrastructure in damaged street lamps and bent road signs. It all heightened the tension and gloom in the atmosphere, and Harry wondered how long this could continue before something broke.

He found a coffee shop and went inside. He ordered their version of liquefied mud and watched the world go by. Nobody paid him any attention. After thirty minutes, he got up and left. It was only as he stepped outside and felt the weight on his hip that he realized he was still carrying his gun. He cursed himself for being careless; he had to get off the street. If he ran into a patrol and they searched him, it would be the end of his freedom – or worse.

As he rounded the corner, he saw two men entering a basement bar across the street. They were deep in conversation and one of the men was in officer's uniform.

The other was Carl Higgins.

Harry checked the street both ways. If Higgins really was CIA, he might have outriders in place, watching his back – such as the three men he'd seen with him in the Palace Hotel bar. He couldn't see anyone matching their description, so he crossed the street and slowed to a dawdle as he passed the entrance to the basement.

The door was closed, but there was a gap between the numerous advertising stickers on the glass panel. He ducked his head to see inside, and saw Higgins and his companion sitting at a table. They were smiling like old friends.

The door opened and the sound of talking and laughter spilled out into the street. Harry kept walking, wondering what the CIA man was up to. Was he bolstering his cover as a journalist or working on something deeper?

He was so focussed on Higgins, he almost collided with the rear corner of a military jeep parked on the kerb. It had its bonnet raised and was covered in dust, testifying to a long journey between washes. Four men wearing local militia flashes were sitting in the back, facing each other in pairs. They were silent and watchful, and turned to eye Harry with open curiosity. One of them had his camouflage jacket opened, revealing a dark blue T-shirt stretched across a muscular chest. The garment bore the insignia of a black bat on a blue background.

Something about the men made him uneasy. They seemed different, less casual than the other soldiers he'd seen around town. More controlled. Professional.

And that insignia on the man's T-shirt.

As he drew level with the front of the vehicle, a soldier wearing the same flashes stepped on to the kerb. He was looking at a growing pool of oil on the ground beneath the jeep. When he saw Harry, he reached up and slammed the bonnet.

Harry felt the soldier's eyes on him all the way down the street.

Rik was alone in the office, standing by one of his monitors. Harry grabbed his arm.

'I need you to send a message to London, high priority,' he told him. 'Ask them if there are any Russians serving with the local militias.'

'What?' Rik looked sceptical. 'You kidding? We'd have heard, surely.'

'Ask them anyway. It's urgent.' He recalled what Mace had said about the Russians, and latterly the message from Rik's friend, Isabelle. It was possible that the soldier inside the jeep had been buying his underwear on the black market, but he doubted it. Trawling through his memory of lectures on foreign Military Intelligence unit insignia, he had recognized the black bat motif on the man's T-shirt. It was usually worn by *Glavnoye Razvedovatel'noye Upravlenie* (GRU) – Central Intelligence operatives. If he was right, then everyone's information was already out of date.

The Russians were already here.

'Harry,' Rik murmured to him ten minutes later. Harry was sitting at one of the monitors, checking out news channels on the internet. The situation had not changed much, but they were mostly reporting from the safety of news studios. 'Harry, you need to see this.' Rik was frowning at his screen and scrubbing at his hair.

Harry looked at Rik's monitor. A long table of alphanumeric codes was scrolling down the screen. It meant nothing to him but was clearly worrying Rik.

'What is it?'

'I sent the message you asked me to,' Rik replied and nodded at the screen. 'This is a log of outgoing message tags over the past three days, all of them to Clarion in London.'

'Clarion?'

'Our contact server at Thames House. At least, I thought it was at Thames House. It could be anywhere. Point is, it's an individual server set up to service this place.' He teased at a fingernail with his teeth. 'They probably didn't want to sully the other stations or networks with us bad boys, so they gave us our own robot. Anyway, it's where all our messages get processed and passed on. Housekeeping stuff, weekly data, intelligence reports, special requests like your message just now – Mace's report about Stanbridge – everything.'

'So?'

'I've had no reason to check before. I mean, what the hell happens here normally? And I wasn't sent here to do this kind of stuff, anyway. The opposite, in fact.'

'If you don't get to the point,' Harry told him, 'and in English, I'm going to shoot you in the leg.'

'Sorry. Just thinking it through. Thing is, it's usually Mace who deals with them through the secure terminal in his office, so I've never bothered querying it before.' He hit a key to scroll down the screen. The list showed a consistent number of characters without change. 'I just checked the log at our end, and there's a list of all outgoing messages, with the acknowledgement codes coming back.'

'Right. You send a message, you get an acknowledgement. So what?'

'That's the problem. I send messages, but I never see an open reply. Ever. The acknowledgement code is there, but that's the machine talking, not an operator. It's bugging the hell out of me. Surely at least *one* of the messages would initiate a human response?'

'Like you said, Mace deals with them.' Harry shrugged. 'He's the head of station; it's the way he's got it set up. With your record, are you surprised? They're hardly likely to want you anywhere in the system, are they?'

'Yeah. Fair enough.' Rik took a deep breath, as if about to confess to something awful. 'Only, yesterday I deliberately sent a rubbish message.'

'What the hell for?'

'To see what would happen. It was crap . . . gobbledygook. I wanted to see if anyone would ask for a re-send. That's what you'd expect, right? Some transmissions get screwed up, the line goes down, and if the guy on the other end is awake, he'll ask for a repeat. I mean, I would if I was on the end. It's really annoying me.'

'I can see that.' Harry wondered if paranoia was getting to Rik. He'd been out here too long.

'You don't get it. I could have sent a copy of *Das Kapital* in Hindustani and they wouldn't have noticed. Yet this morning, Mace comes in with a reply to a message he sent yesterday.'

'So his messages are rated a higher priority.' Harry began to move away before he also got infected by shadows and suspicions. He didn't need it, not on top of everything else.

Rik said, 'I think it's a blind drop.'

Harry stopped. 'Say again?'

'A blind drop. It's a server which allows files or messages to be dropped in and picked up remotely. It's dead simple. It's called a host, and gives out whatever automatic response they want it to – like these acknowledgement codes – and either sends on the messages automatically or holds them until the administrator or whoever wants to pick them up.'

'Where would this administrator be sitting?' Harry had no idea what Rik was saying but he guessed someone – a human body, at least – had to be located in an office with access to the server and incoming messages.

'They could be anywhere in the world. All they need to do is call up the host server, input the security code and retrieve the files.'

'And the host server isn't in Thames House?'

'That's the beauty of it – it doesn't have to be. It could be in an office in Mumbai or West Bromwich, just as long as it's got a web connection.'

'But someone must be reading the messages,' insisted Harry. He was getting a headache, of the kind brought on by too much techno-speak. 'You said yourself, Mace gets replies.'

'That's right. But nobody else does. I've never had one direct; I know Clare hasn't – she's bitched about it often enough. But I thought she was just being snooty about losing her place in the pecking order. All replies come through Mace. That means that whoever is monitoring our messages only responds to specifics. My rubbish message would have been dumped and wiped.'

'So anything we send, any data, any intelligence, any files – is seen only by one person?' Harry felt a shiver of unease. There could be only one reason for such a set up, and that was to avoid any odd-job administrative worker seeing the messages and forwarding them to the wrong person.

'Most likely. My bet is, he calls up from a remote terminal outside the network once a day, maybe less, and responds when he feels like it.'

'Which means?'

Rik shrugged. 'To anyone else outside Clarion and this office, we don't even exist.'

FORTY-SIX

Harry needed to find Mace. Whatever was going on wasn't going to be fixed by ignoring it. First Fitzgerald missing, now the discovery that they were isolated from all contact in London other than via Mace and his secure terminal. Rik didn't know where Mace was, so Harry looked in his office. There was nothing entered on his wall diary, but he found a menu card from the Odeon on the notice board and tried the number. There was no answer. He went back to the main office.

Rik looked up. 'You tried the Odeon?'

'Yes. Nothing.'

Rik raised his eyebrows. 'Must have felt like a change of scenery. You could try near the station. There's a workmen's place round the back he goes to. Next to a car-hire place. Serves strong coffee.' He grinned cynically. 'Chacha brand.'

Harry left him to it and made his way to the station, running checks to make sure he wasn't followed. He passed more military trucks and groups of soldiers huddled against the buildings, sharing cigarettes and bottles of coloured liquid. *Chacha* mixed with fruit juice, probably. The bloody country must run on the stuff.

On the way, he glanced down the street where Rudi's stall was located. There was a flurry of activity going on right in front of it, and someone was shouting. Several pedestrians were hurrying by on the other side without looking, although they looked the type to be among Rudi's regulars. Something in the atmosphere of the scene made Harry step into a doorway to watch.

It was a bad sign.

A man moved away from the kiosk and climbed into a big four-by-four at the kerb. He leaned out, holding the rear door open. It gave Harry a clear profile view.

It was Higgins. He was followed by three other men, one of them being dragged struggling across the pavement.

It was Rudi.

Harry left the doorway and walked away. If they merely suspected Rudi of handling a stolen phone, the most they could do was make a few threats. But if the Ericsson was theirs, and they had already traced its journey to the dealer, it wouldn't be long before they came calling on Rik. It depended on how much resistance Rudi offered up to safeguard his business.

Either way it was time to dump the phone.

He found a deserted building site away from curious eyes and took out the Ericsson. It was now a liability. If it belonged to Higgins or his colleagues, they would be able to put a trace on its signal and it wouldn't take long for them to follow it all the way into his pocket. He dropped it to the ground and stamped on it, reducing the plastic to a mash. Then he kicked the pieces into a muddy puddle. While he thought of it, he took out Stanbridge's mobile and rang Rik.

'Higgins and some of his pals have just taken Rudi for a ride,' he told him.

'What?'

'I've dumped the phone. If they come calling, play dumb.' He cut the connection and keyed a text message to Maloney.

New number, short life. Use w care.

He hit SEND and turned off the phone. He wouldn't need it for long and he doubted the Clones' handlers had the same ability to run a local trace that the Americans had. But he needed a means of contacting Maloney. Without it, he'd be left high and dry.

He reached the station and made his way round to the back. He found a café modelled on a Parisian bistro, jutting out aggressively from a corner plot like a sharp tooth. The wedge-shaped establishment was shiny with glass panels and copper screens, and small circular tables packed together with small, upright chairs. A few were occupied, some by men in uniform, sitting uneasily away from other men in work clothes and dusty boots.

Mace was sitting alone near a window, scanning the previous day's copy of *The Times*. A small glass of clear liquid and a coffee stood in the middle of the table.

He didn't look happy at the interruption

'You got a bloody tracking device on me?' he snarled, and threw the newspaper to one side. 'Can't get a moment's peace in this place since you arrived.'

'If I wasn't here,' Harry murmured, 'I wouldn't be bugging you. You could always send me back with a good review, or transfer me to somewhere civilized.'

'Forget it. Doesn't work like that.'

'Really? So how does it work?' Harry knew he wasn't going to get anywhere, but he felt like winding Mace up. He was feeling irritated by the whole place, but especially Mace's apparent acceptance of the situation.

'This is not like a career step in Shell Oil,' Mace replied.

'You don't go through here on a management trainee grant, collect your MBA and move on somewhere better. This is a proper posting and you only get a move-on card when London says you can. So I'm about as useful to you as tits on a fish.' His eyes flickered momentarily, and he wiped his face with a tired hand. 'Christ, listen to me. I sound like one of those self-righteous HR tits in Whitehall, hiding behind the rule book.' He raised a hand and signalled to the barman for a refill, then looked at Harry. 'You want one of these? Cleans your pipes like battery acid but you'll never get a cold again.'

'No. Coffee's fine,' said Harry. He pointed at the coffee machine and sat down. When the coffee arrived, he spooned in sugar and took a sip. It tasted like a sweeter brand of sump oil and had a greasy film on the surface. 'God help me, if I ever get out of this place, it'll be somewhere where they know what a coffee bean look like.'

'That would be Tbilisi, just down the road.' Mace smiled. 'Unfortunately, that's off-limits, so you're stuck in this shit-hole. What have you got?'

'What makes you think I've got anything?'

'Because you're a pit bull on the quiet, that's why. You see stuff others don't notice and you've got a nose for trouble. Now you've hunted me down to this place. You didn't do that just for the pleasure of my company.'

'Well, well, if it isn't my fellow passenger!' A familiar voice boomed across the café, cutting off what Harry was going to say about the server. He turned. Carl Higgins was ploughing his way between the tables like an ice-breaker, coat tails flapping around him. He dwarfed the room with his presence, and even the soldiers looked wary. On his way, he waved a beefy hand at the barman for refills. 'Time to dance, huh? Whaddya say? Cha-cha-cha!' He clapped Harry on the shoulder and eased himself alongside Mace, settling his buttocks on two chairs with a sigh. 'Man, this place is getting to me. I need to go home. I musta done something really wrong to get this shit assignment.'

'What do you want, Higgins?' Mace's voice was cool, his expression tight. Harry got the impression he was embarrassed at being seen here. Was that because of himself . . . or Higgins?

'Don't be like that, Mace.' The big American seemed unaffected by the chilly reception, but there was a tightness behind the smile. 'I need to speak to your buddy, here.' He looked at Harry. 'I hear you've been getting around a lot since you arrived.'

'It's my job,' said Harry, and resisted telling the American that he should mind his own business. Had Higgins spotted Harry lurking near Rudi's stall?

'Yeah, I figured. I should have known what you were when I saw who the driver was from the airport the other day. He fooled me good, that boy. Ferris, is that his name? Not bad for a computer geek. He's got some front.' He looked from Harry to Mace, daring them to deny their cover. 'But you know, you should be careful who else you mix with, Harry. There are people around here you really don't want to mess with, know what I mean?'

'No.'

'Well, you should.' Higgins picked up his glass as soon as the waiter set it down and drained the contents in one swallow. He winced as the liquid went down, shuddering like a huge dog. 'Man, this stuff's goddam lethal.' He looked at Harry. 'You've been making friends around town, I hear. Mr Mayor, Geordi Kostova for one. Nice guy but that Nikolai is a real creep. And Rudi's a real mover, isn't he? Thinks he's an entrepreneur, but he's just a street punk with some smarts. You should stay away from him – he squeals like a girl.'

Harry saw no sense in denying he knew Rudi. Whatever pressure Higgins had been able to apply to the dealer had clearly worked. But there was no mention of a phone. 'I'll keep it in mind.'

'You do that.' Higgins gave him a long, hard look, eyes like shards of flint. Then he turned to Mace and lowered his voice. 'You heard about the build-up long the border?'

Mace nodded. 'Bits and pieces.'

'You kidding me? It's more than bits and pieces. Don't they tell you anything from London? Any of you?' He lowered his voice even further. 'The Russians are right on the line, my friend. Any minute now, they'll come tripping over it and run right over this place.' He made a surfing gesture with one huge hand and frowned at Harry. 'But you guys know that, right? You haven't been sitting on your thumbs since you got here – you must have heard stuff.'

'What kind of stuff?' said Harry, his interest aroused. He wasn't sure if Higgins was trying to tell them something or merely showing off. Had he run into the same GRU men that Harry had seen?

'About the teams they sent in. The ones who disappeared.'

Mace lifted a hand. 'Higgins, what do you—'

'Let him speak.' Harry stared at the American, wondering why Mace had been about to stop him speaking. 'What teams?'

Higgins did a quick one-two, then shrugged, a sly curl edging his mouth as he speculated on the situation between them. He checked nobody was close enough to overhear, then leaned over the table, bringing an aroma of aftershave with him.

'A few days ago, London and Washington dropped in a couple of recon teams north of here. One Delta, the other a British recon unit. They had orders to eyeball the situation on the ground between here and the border. They had satellite images showing movements on this side, and some pictures further north, but they needed visual confirmation of unit strengths here and in the mountains, and signs of whoever else might be taking an interest.' He dropped the sly look, his face sombre. 'Both teams were taken out after just three days. There's been no word since.'

Mace muttered an oath and stood up, nearly upsetting the small table. Higgins didn't move, his eyes on Harry.

'How do you know this?' said Harry.

'How do you think?' Higgins' voice was soft, serious, no longer playing the gabby journalist role. 'It wasn't through CNN, that's for sure.' He clapped both hands together and stood up. 'Whatever, I'm outta here. Got my orders to light out. You'd best do the same, you know what's good for you.' He glanced at Mace and continued, 'Although from what I hear, getting out may be where your problems are just beginning.'

FORTY-SEVEN

Harry caught up with Mace as the older man walked unsteadily back towards the office. He looked badly shaken, and Harry didn't think it was entirely to do with the drink.

'What did he mean?' He grabbed Mace's arm, bringing him up short.

'About what?' Mace shook off Harry's grip and dug in his jacket pocket for a slim packet of cigars. He selected one and unpeeled the wrapper with shaky fingers, then jammed it in his mouth and found a lighter. It took five attempts before he got a steady flame.

'I didn't know you smoked,' said Harry.

'There's a lot you don't know.' He seemed to realize what that could imply and pulled a wry face. 'But you do know what Higgins is.'

'Yes.'

'Then you'll know he deals in misinformation.'

'Really? That stuff about teams – that was misinformation?'

Mace spat out a fragment of tobacco leaf. 'No. That was correct. They both went off the radar at about the same time. Must've been a coordinated strike.'

'Why didn't you tell us?' Harry fought to remain calm. Something of this magnitude should have been passed to all hands. It was too important, no, too *dangerous* not to have everyone made aware of. If the Russians had taken out the reconnaissance teams, then they were definitely closer than anyone thought, and probably *Spetznaz*, their Special Forces troops. He remembered the soldier in the jeep, wearing the GRU insignia. Same community, same abilities.

Same enemy.

It seemed a waste of time mentioning it now.

The strength of Mace's response came as a surprise. 'What the hell makes you think,' the head of station asked bitterly, kicking at a plastic bottle, 'that *I* knew?'

Harry couldn't believe it. He *had* to have known. Unless . . .

But Mace wasn't finished. 'I picked up on it through a contact in another agency. They thought it was common knowledge among the spook community.' He looked sour. 'So it was – everywhere but here. We're so fucking out on a limb they don't tell us anything.'

They walked on in silence. Harry was trying to decide whether Mace was lying or not, and if he was, why. But his whole demeanour seemed too angry to be faked.

'The server,' said Harry, as they arrived near the office. 'Clarion.'

'What about it?' Mace tossed his cigar aside and watched it bounce in a shower of sparks into the gutter, where it fizzed out in a stream of filthy water.

'Rik says it's a blind drop. It takes messages in but they don't get passed on.'

'Young Rik should mind his business.' The words were intended to be harsh, but Mace sounded half-hearted, as though he didn't have the stomach for a fight.

'What's going on?' Harry grabbed his shoulder and spun the older man round. 'This isn't a bona fide station, is it? It's a blind, like Clarion. We're here for no other reason than someone back in London wants us to be – and it has nothing to do with gathering intelligence. In fact, anything we do find is ignored.' He felt certainty grip his stomach and said acidly, 'What happens to us if the Russians arrive in force, Mace? Or haven't they given you a protocol for that?' When Mace didn't answer, he continued, 'You're still waiting to hear, aren't you? They must know by now, but they haven't told you. Well, I've got news for you: I've seen them already. They're here and waiting for the kick-off.'

Mace reached up and lifted Harry's hand off his shoulder. His expression was melancholy. 'I know, lad. I'm not blind – I've seen them, too.'

'So where does that leave us? If Higgins and his bunch are leaving, we should move, too. And what did he mean about getting out being the start of our problems?'

Mace sighed and stared up at the sky as if seeking inspiration. Then he said, 'It's complicated, lad. Let me give it some thought, eh? We'll talk again, I promise. I'll go tell the others.' He turned and walked away, his gait heavy.

Harry watched him go. Mace was like a man undergoing

a journey of self-discovery and not liking what he saw. It explained the drink, but in his frame of mind, he was no help to himself or anyone else.

He saw an internet bar down the street and went inside. He sat at one of the monitors. For a long moment he considered trying to get through to Thames House and demand some answers. Starting with Paulton, for example. But he knew the security barriers would present themselves, the mere mention of his name launching an automatic firewall.

Frustrated by indecision, he opened up the news channels and clicked on the BBC website, following the link to a fresh news item.

ARE SPOOKS PROTECTING THEIR OWN?

In a dramatic revelation today, a journalist working for a local London newspaper has revealed that just hours before his press colleague and friend, freelance inves- tigative reporter Shaun Whelan, was fatally stabbed in an alleged mugging on Clapham Common a week ago, he had claimed to have proof of an attempted cover-up of the fatal shooting in Essex two weeks ago, during which two civilians, a police officer and an alleged member of a drugs gang were killed. The unnamed journalist, who has asked for anonymity while his claims are being investigated, says he was in a local pub when Whelan, 58, revealed what he had discovered. He also claimed to know the name of the MI5 officer in charge of the attempted drugs intercept, and that the officer has been quietly spirited away by his superiors to avoid what is being described as their worst operational failure in years, certainly since the fatal shooting of Jean Charles de Menezes at Stockwell Tube station in 2005. Whelan did not reveal to his friend the name of this officer. 'Shaun,' said the man, 'always played his cards close to his chest. He was a thorough professional, and would not have made these claims without being able to substantiate them later.'

Asked if he thought Whelan might have become a target because of his determination to uncover the truth about the shootings and name those responsible, the journalist thought that it was possible. 'Shaun had

previously expressed concerns about his safety,' he said,
'and he once told me he thought he was being followed
by men who might be members of the security services
and "friends" of the disappeared MI5 officer.'

Both MI5 and the Metropolitan Police have declined
to comment pending the outcome of their investigation.

Harry was appalled. *This was him they were talking about!*
How the hell had it got this far? Was he now suspected of
orchestrating the death of a journalist?

He logged off and paid the bill. He had to get back to the
office.

As he stepped out of the internet bar, he glanced to one
side, his attention drawn to a line of pennants fluttering in
the wind. They were adorning a car-hire forecourt next to the
café where he had found Mace. Something about the place
tugged at his memory, but it took a few moments before it
registered.

He took out his mobile and rang Rik.

'Where's the best place to hire a car around here?' he said.
'If I wanted to go on a long trip.'

'What?' Rik sounded shocked, his voice dropping. 'Hey –
you're not thinking of bugging out, are you? If you are, I'll
go halves.'

'Relax,' said Harry. 'I need a name, that's all.'

'There's only one place worth trying. Are you at that café
I told you about, near the train station?'

'Yes.'

'Then you've found it. It's the place next door.'

Harry walked back up the street to the site with the pennants.
There were several vehicles on display, nearly all four-by-
fours, most showing signs of a hard and brutal life. But no
customers. He entered a small, bare office in one corner of
the yard, and hit a bell on the counter.

A fat, balding man in greasy overalls appeared through a
rear door, wiping his hands on a rag. 'American?' He clearly
had no problem identifying foreigners, and Harry assumed
that whatever the rental price had been, it had just taken a
hike upwards.

'You rented a car to an Englishman named Gulliver,' he
said, and spelled out the name. 'A few weeks ago. He was

supposed to take the car to your brother in Calais. Do you know when he arrived?'

'Why you ask?' The man's eyes flicked past Harry to the yard outside. He seemed relaxed, but wary.

'Because he never got home. His mother's worried about him.' He shrugged and smiled easily. 'The family asked me to look into it . . . before our government takes the matter up with your Interior Ministry.'

The man stared at him for a long moment, then tossed the rag to one side. He licked his lips. 'Why they do that? Is no concern to me what he does. Maybe he go for a holiday somewhere. Not my problem.'

'Actually, it is your problem. You were the last person to see him. Want the police coming here and asking questions?' He took out his wallet, counted out some US dollar notes. The man watched without expression. But his eyes stayed on the money.

'All I need,' said Harry quietly, 'is to know when and if he arrived at your brother's place in Calais.' He stopped counting and slid the notes halfway across the counter, but kept his hand on them. 'A phone call would do it. That's all. Then I'm gone.'

The man shrugged. 'Is easy. I don't need to make phone call. He never arrive. Car is missing.' He reached out and tugged the money from under Harry's hand. 'Maybe your friend is a thief.'

FORTY-EIGHT

'We got a problem, old son. Well, two, actually.' Bellingham was sprawled behind his desk when Paulton was ushered up to his third floor office. The MI6 Operations Director looked flushed, and had it not been too early in the day, Paulton would have sworn he'd been drinking.

After responding to Bellingham's call for an urgent meeting, it wasn't the best of openings. Paulton felt his spirits sink. 'What sort of problems?'

Bellingham flicked a sheet of paper across his desk. It was a photocopy of a press item. 'This is circulating faster than the pox,' he snarled. 'How the hell did Whelan get hold of your man's name?'

Paulton's stomach gave a lurch. He'd already seen the report. 'He hasn't – didn't,' he answered. His voice came out an octave above its normal pitch on hearing the journalist's name. 'This doesn't actually mention Tate's name. It's Whelan's friend making wild claims.'

'Don't act the arse, George. I don't care if he's got Tate's name sewn into his knicker elastic in gold thread. It's the idea that Whelan might have been knocked off by the establishment that worries me – and should be scaring the buggery out of you.' He sat back and clasped his hands over his belly. 'See, I know what you did, George. You were covering your backside, weren't you? You thought Whelan was getting too close so you decided to put him off. Permanently. Pity you didn't tell me first.'

'Why?'

'Because I'd have dealt with it a lot better, that's why.' He shifted in his chair. 'Still, as long as nobody left Tate's name lying around, we can deny it until the Second Coming and they'll never be able to prove otherwise.' He eyed Paulton carefully. 'I take it there's no chance of anything turning up, is there? No little clues that might drop you squarely in the kaka?'

'Of course there isn't!' Paulton's chest began pounding at a rate he was sure wasn't good for him. The way Bellingham was talking made him wonder if this conversation was being recorded. If so, he was cooked; he'd already said too much.

'Mmm. Good. Best forgotten, then.'

'What else was there?' Paulton asked him, anxious to get on and get out of here fast. There were things he needed to do.

'What? Oh, the other thing, yes. Y'know that server thing we set up for Red Station – Clarion? Bloody thing's worked well so far, absorbing useless messages from Mace's motley crew like a baby's nappy.'

'What about it?'

'I think somebody's rumbled us.'

'What?' Paulton jumped in his chair as if he'd been stung. 'Somebody here?'

'No, not here, you idiot. I'm the only one with access, remember? Over there, in the arse-end of beyond. Some smart-Alec – probably that communications twerp you sent out there – sent a couple of silly messages, one of them a load of nonsense which any fool could see was a deliberate draw. He was testing the response. The other was real, asking about Russian troops in militia uniform, initiated by your man Tate. I missed the rubbish one and didn't notice the second until it was too late. Other things on my plate.'

'Can't we explain away the situation – a communications malfunction or something, to keep them quiet?'

'Nix. We're too late.'

Paulton tried to think through the implications. His head suddenly felt inexplicably hot. It was one bloody thing on top of another. Ferris. Rik Ferris. A young IT graduate who'd got bored punching keys and saw things he shouldn't have. Nothing critical, but enough to cause a stink if he'd gone public. He wondered what had prodded him into action after all this time. There could only be one answer.

Harry Tate.

'Ferris – is that him?' Bellingham was still chuntering on, and came to the same conclusion. 'He's been getting very pally with your man Tate, I hear. Therein lies the real problem.'

Paulton stared at his opposite number and wondered just how many lines of communication he had into Red Station. The man was like a fat spider, tugging on his web. 'How do you know all this?'

Bellingham laid a finger alongside his fleshy nose. 'Got spies everywhere, that's how. Thing is, we overlooked one vital aspect of the people we were sending out there, you know that?'

'Did we?'

'They're professionals, that's what. Used to grubbing about in the muck and noticing stuff other people wouldn't see. Can't help themselves. See something and they have to report it. With all that's going on over there, they're starting to trip over raw intelligence they – and we – can't ignore. So far, Mace has been fielding it. But he's losing it, and now your man Tate has taken an interest in world events rather than his own sorry neck, and he's stirring up trouble.'

'What do we do?'

'Well, we can't just turn a blind eye. What would happen

if they found a way of by-passing the comms channel into Clarion? Worse, we have no way of explaining where this raw intel's coming from.'

'Don't you have any people on the ground?' Paulton was feeling desperate. 'You could attribute the source to them.' This entire business wasn't going the way Bellingham had said it would. In fact, it was beginning to unwind like a badly-knit jumper.

'Weren't you listening in that briefing the other day?' Bellingham replied irritably. 'They all got wiped out. The bloody forces of evil came along and nobbled them!' He looked morose for a moment, then continued, 'Apart from the embassy in Tbilisi, which is worse than useless, we haven't got anyone. Freedom bloody Square, that embassy address – did you know that, George? So free, they've got security spotters sitting on their shoulders every minute of the day. Probably on Putin's payroll, every damn one of them. As far as our lords and masters know, we've got bugger all over there, so we can hardly develop a new stream of intelligence chatter coming over official wires from the middle of nowhere, can we?'

'You've got access to satellite coverage.'

'We do. But it's open-channel. Might as well advertise it as Shareware, let everyone take a peek. They do, anyway, so I can't suddenly pop up with stuff nobody else can see. Might as well claim we're using a sodding medium.' He scowled. 'No, it's about time we recognized our limits, George. It was a nifty idea, but it's outlived its usefulness.'

Paulton felt a measure of relief. Maybe if they got everyone out of there, they could quietly let the whole affair fade into history. God knows what he was going to do with Tate, though. The shooting in Essex was still front-page news, with the parents of the dead girl raising hell about her murder and demanding names. And the family of the dead firearms officer was questioning why he was sent in to danger with insufficient back-up or training. Heaven alone knew how they had got that bit of information, but he was willing to bet Gareth Nolan, the Deputy Commissioner, had let it slip to a press buddy. Anything to cover his own feeble neck. Maybe another posting for Tate was the best, then they could all relax.

At which point Bellingham swept the rug from under his feet.

'I've sent in the Hit.'

'What?' the words kicked Paulton out of his reverie. Mention of the Hit brought the brutal realization that there would be no quiet and orderly retreat; no remote posting for Tate and no salve for his conscience over what had happened to Brasher and Jimmy Gulliver. That was gone the moment the Hit moved in, because they had one main function, and one only.

They killed people.

'Time to call it a day, George. We can't pull 'em out and we certainly can't have our rabbits turning up at Immigration with stories to tell. There's no way we could keep 'em all quiet. One flappy lip and they'd all be under the spotlight. With the fuss that's about to break anytime now, they'll simply have to disappear.'

'What – all of them?' Paulton's throat closed around the words. He knew his protests were futile, but a tiny vestige of self-respect made him try. 'You can't!'

'Can and will, George. Can and will.' Bellingham threw his head back and smiled with a ruthless absence of humour. 'It's a matter of expediency. Nasty word, expediency. But it was invented for a purpose. We can kill several birds with one stone. We're closing down Red Station. Permanently.'

FORTY-NINE

Paulton left Vauxhall Cross and made his way back towards his office. His cheeks were burning and he felt about as close to panic as he had ever been in his life. This had to be sorted out once and for all. What the bloody hell had Tate started? As for Bellingham, he'd completely lost the plot; suggesting wiping out an entire station was monstrous. Efficient, but monstrous.

Before reaching Thames House, he stopped and made a call from a secure mobile. 'That person you dealt with,' he said carefully, when a familiar male voice answered. 'Did you check his place thoroughly for paperwork?'

'Yeah, there was nothing, I told you. No names anywhere.'

'Right. So you did.' Paulton disconnected. He wasn't reassured. Whelan had been a professional, no matter what his strange proclivities; he'd have kept some sort of note – it was in the nature of the man. But if there had been no papers, what about electronic records? Surely his man would have thought to check?

He pocketed his phone and continued to Thames House, mounting swiftly to his office. He stayed long enough to delve in his desk drawer, then told his secretary he was going out for an hour.

This was too important to leave to chance.

Outside, he walked for five minutes before flagging down a taxi. 'Charing Cross,' he told the driver, and sat sideways on to check he wasn't being followed. At Charing Cross he left the cab and walked into the station, merging with the crowds. He entered the toilets, then came out again almost immediately and made his way back to the street, where he jumped on a bus heading east along the Strand. After five stops, when he was satisfied nobody was on his tail, he left the bus and took a cab heading west, avoiding conversation with the driver by hiding behind a discarded copy of *Metro*.

All the way, a barrage of questions jostled for attention: had his man made a thorough search of Whelan's home? What if he'd skimped on the job? What if he'd been disturbed in his search and hadn't got the nerve to admit it? If the police hadn't found anything – and so far they would have had no reason, if all they suspected was a mugging – then the latest reports in the news would soon have them scouring the place with every piece of technology at their disposal.

He knew Whelan lived in a small flat in a rundown block not far from Victoria Station. He told the driver to circle the area twice. Time was ticking away but rushing in when he didn't know the layout was a quick route to disaster.

Once he was satisfied there was no obvious police presence, he got the driver to drop him outside a pub and approached the block of flats on foot.

The foyer and stairwell were deserted, and smelled of damp paper and boiled milk. He hurried up the stairs and knocked lightly on Whelan's door, one ear cocked for sounds from the other residents. When he was sure nobody was going to answer, he spent thirty seconds on the lock before slipping inside.

The interior was sombre, a cluttered display of dark antique furniture, burgundy cushions and heavy curtains. Paulton winced at the overdone opulence. It supported what he'd heard about Whelan's lifestyle, which had led to the convenient method of his disposal. A tang of rich aftershave hung in the air, along with a slightly mildewed odour of trapped heat.

He did a quick walk-through first, to check there were no nasty surprises, then went through each room with the practised skill first learned in Belfast and perfected over several years operating in the field. It had been a long time since he'd needed to conduct a search, but it was something once learned, never forgotten.

It took him fifteen minutes to check all the obvious places, at the end of which he concluded that whatever Whelan's personal failings, he had not lacked professional discretion. Other than the usual household paperwork and some notes about contacts and future projects, there was no mention of any past, present or ongoing security investigations. He was also satisfied that there were no hiding places in the fabric of the building or under the floors.

He returned to the living room. The furnishings included a small desk and filing cabinet, and had served as Whelan's work place. He stared at them both, frustrated and relieved. Frustrated because the paperwork must exist and he hadn't found it; relieved because if he couldn't, it might mean nobody else would.

But that was a chance he couldn't afford to take.

A computer sat on the desk. He switched it on. He didn't have time for this, but he wasn't about to walk away and ignore the main tool in Whelan's working life. As soon as the machine was running, he took a small portable hard drive from his pocket and plugged it in. Then he copied the entire contents of the machine to the hard drive. As soon as that was done, he unplugged the drive and inserted a small memory stick in the USB port, and copied a file from the stick to the PC. Removing the stick, he switched off the screen and left the flat.

As he walked down the stairs to the street, the virus programme he'd left behind began eating its way into the belly of Whelan's computer. According to the techs who had devised it, in less than three minutes, everything would be gone for good.

By the time he reached the end of the street and began looking for a taxi, he was breathing a lot easier.

End of the PC. End of the source. End of his worries.

Back in his office, he checked the portable hard drive for viruses and scanned the contents. Most were everyday work files, correspondence, expense sheets and lists of names, addresses and contact numbers or emails. The ephemera of a working computer. Three documents contained notes about the Essex shooting. Two of these looked like drafts, with random notations in small print. There were lots of question marks dotted about, and he wondered whether they were expressing doubts or whether the author had been leaving indicators for later additions or corrections. The third was clean copy ready for submission.

It mentioned Harry Tate by name.

Paulton breathed softly and read through the document twice. It was speculation. The kind which managed to skate round the facts of what had happened at the inlet that night without actually getting it a hundred per cent right. But it was still close enough to have the conspiracy nuts wetting themselves if they got their hands on it, and it had a name they could feed on. The firestorm would be all-consuming.

He checked the email files. There was nothing to show where the journalist had got his information, and no sign that he had been in touch with anyone else about the detail of his discovery. Thank God, he thought, for journalistic paranoia. After forty minutes, satisfied that Whelan had not disseminated the information further, Paulton left his office and went for a brief walk.

By the time he returned, the portable hard drive with its incriminating files lay at the bottom of the Thames.

FIFTY

'Where does Fitz live?' Harry walked into the office and found Rik staring blindly at his computer screen. He didn't acknowledge Harry's presence. Mace must have told him the bad news. There was no sign of Clare Jardine.

'Fitz?'

'Just off the airport road, out of town. Why?' Rik turned from the screen and jerked a thumb towards Mace's office. 'Is it true what he said – the Russians have crossed the border?

'Apparently. We should check to see if Fitzgerald's all right. If they come this far, he'll be stranded. You still got the Merc?'

'Of course. But he won't leave his girlfriend and her kid. He told me a while back, he won't be going home again. He's got no reason to.' He jumped up, his face strained. 'Are we leaving? We can't stay here, can we? Mace wouldn't say.'

'He can't, that's why. He's had no orders.' Harry studied the younger man's face, and saw the beginnings of panic building in his eyes. He clapped him on the shoulder. Best give him something else to think about. 'I want to check on Fitzgerald.' He picked up Rik's leather jacket from the back of his chair and tossed it to him. 'You'll have to take me.'

He walked downstairs with Rik trailing behind. If Mace heard them leave, he made no attempt to stop them. Harry waited near the Mercedes until Rik caught up and unlocked it, then climbed in.

'What if we're followed?' said Rik, turning the key in the ignition and checking his mirrors.

'Just drive normally.' Harry had already checked the street; there was nobody in sight. 'If we pick up a tail, anyone who knows you will know Fitz and where he lives.'

Rik took a zigzag route through the back streets, bouncing over potholes and scattering rubbish. He held his hand on the horn at every small cross-section, his foot hovering above the brake pedal, creating a stop-go jerking motion which had Harry feeling nauseous after a few hundred yards. When he hit a straight stretch, he drove fast, but Harry thought his reactions were off. In a chase, they'd have been left behind or slammed into a corner by the first truck he failed to see.

There was less sign of military activity on the way, and Harry wondered if the army was being moved out of the town towards the north. If they were, he felt sorry for them; even a small Russian force would be more than a match for the kind of troops he'd been seeing over the past few days.

They arrived in a small outer suburb cut off from the town by a single-carriage ring road. Rik drove down a residential street with two-storey houses on either side. The gardens were small, but neat and free of rubbish. There were sounds of children playing behind the fences, a few toys scattered on steps and flashes of colour that the rest of the town lacked. An elderly woman in black watched without expression from a front door as they cruised by.

Rik pulled into the kerb and indicated the door of a house identical to its neighbours save for a wooden plaque cut from a cross-section of dried hardwood. A number had been scored by a hot iron into the surface. Fitzgerald, Harry thought, importing a touch of home.

'You want me to check?' Rik was ready to get out.

'No. I'll do it.' Harry climbed out and walked up the path. A woman along the street was watching him. He knocked on the door. The sound was hollow, reverberating through the building. He stepped over to the front window and peered through the glass. Evening shadows were lengthening across bare floors, and the sparse furniture was already showing a layer of dust. A sock lay on the floor alongside an old newspaper, and a child's shoe sat forgotten on a sideboard.

Fitzgerald had left in a hurry.

Harry returned to the car and got in.

'He's gone. Let's get back.'

This time, Rik stuck to the main streets. He was cruising along one of the boulevards when he said, 'Can we drop by and see Isabelle?'

'Why?' Harry's instinct was to say no; they didn't have time for romance.

'She might know more than Mace is telling us.'

'That wouldn't be hard, would it?' Harry mulled it over. Rik had a point. The French would have observers out on the ground, and they might be willing to share what they knew. 'OK. But make it quick.'

Rik took a series of turns and pulled up outside a three-storey office block in a broad, pleasant street lined with trees. A large truck was blocking the way, and several hard-looking men were standing around, watching the approaches. Two men in overalls were carrying boxes from the building and bundling them into the back of the truck. A third man was stacking them against the sides.

'They're moving out,' said Harry. He eyed one of the guards who was staring in their direction, one hand in his jacket pocket. A curl of wire ran up from the man's collar to behind his ear. He was talking, but standing too far away from the other guards to make himself heard, and Harry guessed he was using a throat microphone. 'Get out very slowly,' he warned Rik, 'and make sure your hands are in plain sight all the way.'

'What?' Rik looked at him. The guard had turned and was walking towards them as if he meant business. 'Oh. Christ.'

'Take it easy. They'll know we aren't here for trouble. Not in a Merc. Just don't make any sudden movements.'

Rik stepped out of the car holding his arms clear of his body. Harry waited a few beats, then did the same. When he was sure the guard wasn't going to produce a gun and start shooting, he turned and leaned on the roof of the car to show he wasn't a threat.

Rik approached the guard, a grizzled-looking man with tanned skin and bunched shoulders. French Special Forces, Harry guessed, capable and light on his feet and likely to be hostile at the first hint of danger. The man listened carefully to Rik, then looked past him and motioned for Harry to move closer.

Harry stayed where he was.

The guard motioned again, but Harry ignored him. Eventually, the man gave up and motioned for Rik to walk towards the building.

This time it was the guard who stayed where he was, eyes on Harry.

Rik emerged five minutes later. He was waved off by a

slim, studious-looking young woman in jeans and a cornflower-blue blouse. She stood and watched him walk away, a hand to her cheek.

'She looks nice,' said Harry with a wry smile. 'How come they've got her and we get stuffed with a geek like you?'

Rik wasn't amused. 'Why did you do that?' His expression was more puzzled than annoyed.

'Do what?'

'That thing with the guard. You might have pissed him off.'

'I doubt it. He's a professional; he was trying it on, to get us together away from the car. There was no need – he could see we weren't a threat.'

'Christ, you could have fooled me. I thought he was going to pull out a gun.' He started the car and pulled away from the kerb, did a three-point turn and took the main street into town. As he drove, he put his hand into his pocket and took out an envelope. He handed it over.

'What's this?' Harry opened the flap. Inside were three pieces of paper. They were in French and looked like vouchers. They were headed with an elaborate insignia and the French flag.

'Travel dockets,' said Rik. 'There's an Air France flight leaving at six thirty in the morning. Isabelle says we can get a seat if we show these. Other nationalities are being evac'd out, too. All except the Americans; they've got their own plane coming in.'

'There's a surprise. They wouldn't want Higgins and his mates rolled up by the Russians – they'd never get them back.' He handed the vouchers back. 'You're getting useful in a crisis, did I tell you?'

Rik smiled, then concentrated on his driving.

They passed a row of shops and small businesses behind steel shutters, mostly closing for the day. A supermarket was still open, with a delivery truck pulling away from the side doors. Harry told Rik to pull over.

'Why, what's up?'

'Nothing. We might need supplies in case we can't get out through the airport. There won't be time to get them later. Get water, chocolate, sandwiches if they have any and some fruit. And a large torch. We'll get coffee and tea at the office and make up some flasks.'

'Got you.' Rik stopped the car and disappeared inside the supermarket.

When he had gone, Harry texted Maloney on Stanbridge's mobile.

Cmng out. Stnd by 2 tlk 18tr.'

Rik returned with the supplies and placed them on the rear seat. He'd stocked up with biscuits as well, and fruit juice. They continued on their way, but hadn't gone two blocks before a shiny black Nissan Patrol pulled in hard alongside, forcing them to slow down.

The driver was Nikolai. Kostova was in the passenger seat.

Nikolai stabbed a finger at Rik to pull over.

FIFTY-ONE

'You'd better do as he says,' said Harry. 'He's got the army on his side; we don't want to piss them off.' He wondered what had prompted this. It was too much of a coincidence for the mayor and his bodyguard to turn up like this.

Rik pulled in to the kerb and went to turn off the engine. Harry stopped him.

'Leave it running.' If they had to leave in a hurry, he wanted to be ready.

He waited, eyes on the wing mirrors. Nikolai had pulled in behind them and Kostova was getting out. The mayor stopped to adjust his cuffs, waved to someone on the other side of the road, a professional politician's gesture, then walked towards the Mercedes.

'What do you think they want?' Rik asked nervously.

'It's a social call,' said Harry. 'Just sit tight and stay calm.'

Kostova came alongside and stopped by Harry's door. He smiled broadly as Harry got out to meet him. The mayor seemed in a genial mood, and was puffing on a black cheroot, a picture of relaxation. Although his suit was pressed, his shoes looked scuffed and covered in dust. He'd been travelling.

'Harry,' Kostova greeted him, and held out his hand.

Harry shook it, one eye on Nikolai. The bodyguard was
wandering along the inner edge of the pavement, eyeing the
front of an empty shop. He remembered what Mace had said
about the man and decided he wouldn't care to turn his back
on him.

'Mr Mayor. How are you today?'

'Please, call me Geordi. Everybody does.'

'OK, Geordi. What can I do for you?'

Kostova fanned away a cloud of cigar smoke and ducked
to look in the Mercedes, nodding at Rik and glancing at the
supplies on the back seat. 'Good car. Very strong – comfortable. You are going back to your Council office, yes?'

Harry nodded. The mayor was playing games; he knew
perfectly well that they were no more British Council than
Red Cross nuns. 'That's correct. I take it you know we intend
leaving shortly?'

Kostova grinned and flicked a piece of ash from his cheroot.
'I did not, but why should I? You are free to come and go as
you please. Of course, there are some restricted areas . . . to the
north, for example. But I doubt you will be going there, anyway.
Elsewhere?' He shrugged and pursed his lips, still smiling.

'The airport?'

'Airport no problem. Flights are unfortunately restricted, but
there are still seats available.' He paused and glanced at Nikolai,
who had walked past them and was watching the traffic. His
voice dropped slightly. 'If you are going, Harry, I think you
should do so as soon as possible. This is not a good time to be
here. I'm sure you know that.'

'I do, thank you. Is it true what they say?' He nodded
towards the north.

'I am afraid so, yes.' Kostova looked saddened. 'It is a pity,
but . . .' He looked towards the sky. 'Maybe it will be over
soon and we can all go back to the way things were before.'

'I hope so. You speak excellent English.'

'I was lucky. My mother was a teacher of English. She
believed it was the language we should all know for the future.
Although now,' he shrugged again, 'who knows? Chinese,
perhaps?' He dropped his cheroot and stood on it, adding with
almost studied deliberation, 'A fellow countryman of yours
arrived today. Did you know that?'

'No. I didn't. Why – does it concern me?'

'Who knows? It might. His name was . . .' Kostova pretended to search his memory, '. . . Phillips? Yes, Phillips.' He nodded. 'But I think that is not his real name.'

Latham. It had to be. 'Are you taking an interest?'

'We have no reason for doing so. Unless, of course, you know something about him which means we should detain him?' He lifted his eyebrows, inviting confirmation.

It was tempting, but Harry didn't bite. 'I don't think so. The name means nothing to me.'

'Very well.' Kostova appeared to dismiss the subject. 'Your colleague, Clare Jardine. She is unhappy with her employment, I think. Did you know she has been trying to acquire new papers?'

Harry wondered what stroke this was meant to be. Disinformation or mischief-making? He had no doubts that Kostova was an expert at both.

'What sort of papers?'

'Passport . . . visa . . . driving licence.' He smiled thinly. 'What the Americans call the whole nine yards. She has been meeting with people who are involved in such things. But they cannot help her. They tell me instead. I wonder why would she need these things?' His eyes twinkled to show that he knew her cover was false.

Harry decided to go with care. Act dumb and Kostova might think he was being played for a fool. Too much outrage and he would see through it. If it were true, what the hell was Clare Jardine doing looking for new documents? Unless she was planning to make a run for it. New papers, new life. If anyone could disappear forever into the woodwork, it would be a member of MI6.

But why would she?

'Did she ask you?'

'Only once, and couched – is that it, couched? – in careful words. But definitely a shopping trip, I think you would call it.' He smiled. 'You English are so playful with your language. But amusing, too. I like English.'

'Why are you telling me this?'

Nikolai was walking towards them, eyes on the car and the two men. He seemed to float over the ground, detached. Like a bloody ninja, Harry reflected.

'Simple,' said Kostova quickly. 'We have a lot of trouble

coming this way. What we do not need is for you or your colleagues to be – engaged? – in a private internal war. We have enough of that already. Neither do we need the eyes of the world on us should something befall any foreign nationals within our borders. You understand?'

'I think so.'

Kostova flexed the fingers of one hand and studied his nails. 'Believe me, it would be better for us all if you left.'

Orders from Moscow, Harry wondered? Perhaps they had reasoned that invading a small state like Georgia was one thing. That would be weathered in time, like so many things Moscow did which aroused the ire of the western world. But being suspected of 'disappearing' a number of British nationals working for a seemingly legitimate organization – no matter what their true function – would hardly go unnoticed. The media would love it.

'You didn't say whether you had given Miss Jardine the papers she asked for.'

'I gave her nothing. If she were to disappear, I am sure a person of her . . . status . . . would attract some unnecessary attention. Besides, we are not in the business of supplying members of your security services with false documentation.' He raised an eyebrow, daring Harry to deny it. 'You do that quite adequately yourselves. Although,' he smiled and added, 'I know you yourself would not be guilty of such misleading activities.'

'Thank you for the warning.'

Kostova nodded and put out his hand, which Harry took. It was a firm grip, and warm. 'Watch your back, Harry,' he said softly. 'You have enemies here and at home, I think. I wish you well when you return. I, too, know what it is like to experience the . . . fallout of failure. Fallout – is that a good word?'

'It's a very good word.'

'Then I wish you good luck.'

Kostova turned and walked back to the Nissan and climbed aboard, Nikolai following closely behind. Seconds later, they were gone.

'What the hell was that about?' asked Rik. He was staring at Harry with something approaching respect. 'I didn't know you were mates with him.'

'I'm not. We were being warned off; get out of town before we become an embarrassment he could do without.'

'Suits me. Was that all?'

'Pretty much. Oh, and Latham's arrived.'

'What?' Rik looked startled, but Harry pointed to the road ahead.

'Drive.' He settled back as the Mercedes pulled away from the kerb, and frowned at the passing street scene, thinking about timing. If what Stanbridge had said was true, the Clones weren't employed for heavy work. They were here for training purposes and to keep basic surveillance on the members of Red Station.

Their duties had ceased on the night Stanbridge had died.

But if Kostova was telling the truth, Latham had only just arrived – *after* the Clones had gone.

So if it wasn't Latham who killed Stanbridge two nights ago, who had?

Back at the office, the message light on the answering machine was green. Rik hit the button and a woman's voice gave a name and number.

Rik turned to look at Harry. 'That was Fitz's wife, Amina.'

'Call her,' said Harry.

Rik dialled the number and waited. 'Fitz?' he said, and beckoned Harry over. 'Where are you, man? We're ready to roll out of here.' He listened some more then said, 'No, just me and Harry. OK, sure.' He hit a button on the console and Fitzgerald's voice filled the room.

'Listen, I'm sorry about running out like that.' Fitzgerald sounded tired. 'I checked downstairs, and when I saw it was clear, I decided to keep going. I should have told you but . . . you know, I've got a daughter here . . . and something special, which is more than I've got back home. I don't want to lose that, you know? We're out in the woods . . . staying with Amina's family. We're safe here. We've got money to last us. I heard you'd been round to the house – the neighbour recognized the Merc, Rik. I thought I should at least let you know the score.'

'If the Russians come through here,' said Harry, 'they'll scoop you up, you know that.'

'No chance.' Fitzgerald's voice was flat, confident. 'They'll have to find me first. I won't let that happen. Take care, you two. Watch your backs.'

There was a click and Fitzgerald was gone.

FIFTY-TWO

'I thought I might find you here.' The Odeon was dark, but not merely with the gloomy decor of previous days; there were no lights, no sounds from the kitchen and a chill in the air signalling a lack of heating. It had the air of a building being allowed to die slowly, like a terminal patient cut off from life-saving drugs.

Harry closed the front door behind him, shutting out the colder air. Mace was alone in shadow at his usual table. A bottle stood on the table in front of him and his glass was nearly empty. There were no other customers.

'Where else would I be?' He sounded drunk, and Harry guessed he'd been hammering the booze since they'd parted. The man must be working his way through every drinking joint in town. He looked exhausted and grey, his hair limp and no longer swept back elegantly over his ears.

'We should leave,' said Harry. 'They could be rolling down the street any minute.'

'They? You mean the Russians? Or the Hit?'

'Same difference. I'd rather not meet any of them if I can help it.' He explained about the flight vouchers Rik had got from the French.

Mace spun the glass on the table top. 'Good idea. Well done, Rik, eh? Either way, I'm staying.' He waved a tired hand in the air around him. 'After all, how can I leave this? It's the only investment I've got left.'

'You *own* this place?'

'Sure. Have done for a while. It was going to close, so I put some money on the table.' He grinned crookedly. 'Seemed a good idea at the time, even if it does break every Service rule in the book.'

'Where's the old woman?'

'My business partner, you mean? Up-country somewhere.

Said she had to see her niece, make sure she was OK. She'll be back – she's keen to pro . . . protect her share of the assets.' He swallowed and blinked at the verbal stumble. 'Christ, think I've had too much.'

Harry sat down. He wasn't sure he wanted to do this. Confrontations rarely went well in his experience, even less so when alcohol was part of the mix. But if Mace was staying put, it might be the last opportunity he had of getting him to talk.

'You knew all along what was happening here, didn't you? What Red Station was for . . . what might happen to anyone sent here. Especially if they tried to leave.'

Mace's silence was enough.

'Did you volunteer for this?' Harry pressed him. He could hear people running in the street, and someone banged on the door as they passed. A car horn sounded, impatient and tinny, and distant shouts echoed off the buildings. The early sounds of panic; the prelude to forced flight. Close by, a man's voice shouted something at length. He didn't understand a word of it and cared less. Not right now. 'Or did they offer you the top desk to keep you quiet?' He suddenly wanted a drink. This wasn't like interrogating terrorists or drug smugglers. This was working on your own people. It felt . . . unclean. 'They'd have needed someone here, on the inside,' he continued. 'Someone they could trust . . . someone who would agree to working here rather than being pensioned off early. Isn't that right? The Clones could only do so much . . . hear so much. What better than having a man on the inside to keep London in the loop?'

Still no reply. No shouting now from outside. Just a distant drone of a car engine. If it turned into something heavier, he was out of here. Mace would have to fend for himself.

'Did you allow the Clones inside to set up their bugs? Drop them the nod when a team member was away from home so they could run a quick check of their phones and correspondence? Tell them in advance when we were going on a pointless errand so they didn't have to follow?'

'It wasn't like that.' Mace's voice was sticky and dull, like congealing treacle.

'Of course it was. They couldn't have run it all the way from London. Someone had to be the eyes and ears on the inside, to make sure the boys ands girls behaved themselves and didn't get restless.' He pressed on, feeling like a heel but desperate to know. 'You were ideal; no further chance of advancement in the Service; your best years were behind you. It must have been a life-saver.' He reached out and picked up the bottle. Read the label. Felt disgusted by what he was doing, but more so with the man across the table. 'Pity Jimmy Gulliver didn't get the same deal.' He put the bottle down.

Mace blinked heavily. 'What d'you mean?'

'You told them Gulliver was going home, didn't you? That he'd had enough. That he was going to make noises.' He breathed in, fighting the nausea. 'You gave them his travel details so they could arrange for an intercept. It had to be you – you were the only one who knew him well enough. The only one he trusted enough to talk to.'

'I told them he'd left,' Mace growled. 'That was all.'

'I don't believe you. You could have left it . . . let it slip out quietly later that he'd skipped town without warning. It would have given him, what – twenty-four hours head start? Time to lose himself *en route.*'

'But I did.' Mace's skin was mottled and a flick of spit dropped on to the table. He stared at Harry, eyes watering and red. 'I knew he wouldn't do anything stupid . . . I've known him since he was a kid. That stuff about making noises . . . that was just anger talking.'

'Say again?' Harry sat forward. 'You knew him *before?*'

Mace hesitated, then gave a long sigh of capitulation. 'Jimmy was my nephew – my younger brother's kid. His parents were killed on a farm they ran in Zimbabwe . . . part of Mugabe's land grab. Jimmy came back and started over, brought up by an aunt – my sister. Did well, won a place at Cambridge, got picked out by an agency talent-spotter and offered a fast-track through Six.'

'But they must have known you were related.'

'The vetting didn't pick it up. I didn't know he was back until I bumped into him in Vauxhall Cross one day. Knew him immediately, of course, even though I'd last seen him as a boy.' He shrugged. 'Bloody shock, I can tell you, finding him in the same grubby line of business. He slipped through the net. It happens.'

'And you never said anything?'

'Why should I?' Mace looked sullen and defensive. 'They'd have tossed him out. What was the point?'

'Fat lot of good it did him.' Harry wondered if he was telling the truth. After his whole life working in the deception game, setting up a smokescreen would be second nature to a man like Mace. Yet he sounded convincing.

'What d'you mean?' Mace demanded.

The reality of the situation hit Harry like a thunderbolt. He could see it in Mace's eyes. He'd asked him not long after arriving here if he'd ever heard from Gulliver. The answer had been no.

It had been the truth.

'You don't know, do you?' Harry said, and wondered how to tell him.

'Know what?'

He took a deep breath. 'Jimmy Gulliver died in a climbing accident in the Alps not long after leaving here.' He waited while the news sank in to Mace's fuddled brain, then continued before he lost his nerve, 'I had a friend check it out. He never made it back to London.'

'I don't understand.' Mace sounded utterly confused. 'That can't be right – he went home. They never told me.'

'They didn't intend to,' said Harry brutally. 'He was marked down from the moment he came out here. We all were – you know that. Only some of us are graded a bigger risk than others. Gulliver was fast-track, and good. He'd have been pitched right in at the deep end, fed high-grade intelligence normal trainees never see . . . the pressure-cooker approach to see if he could stand it.'

'A climbing accident?' The awful realization was slowly making an impact on Mace's brain.

'Yes. He must have chosen to take some time off. Sort himself out.' Harry was speaking to fill the silence, embarrassed by Mace's expression of loss. Whatever the man's previous failings, this was a lot for him to take in. 'Clare Jardine told me he hired a car and planned to drive back overland. It would have taken him a while. He obviously decided to stop off for some climbing.'

'He couldn't.'

'Sorry?'

'He couldn't. Jimmy couldn't climb. He wasn't equipped for it.'

'Clearly. But it doesn't seem to have stopped him trying.'

'You don't understand what I'm saying, man.' Mace looked angry. 'He couldn't have gone climbing – it was his one weakness, same as his father. They both suffered from chronic vertigo.' He hit the table with his fist for emphasis. 'You'd have no more got Jimmy climbing the Alps than walking up the Eiffel fucking Tower!'

Shit.

FIFTY-THREE

H alf an hour later, Mace was about as sober as he would ever be this side of tomorrow. It was pitch black outside and there was no traffic noise. Harry had hunted down the mains fuse-box and got the electricity fired up, turning on the kettle and making a pot of industrial strength coffee. The decor hadn't improved with the lights on; it looked sad and neglected, out of date like a subject in a sepia photograph.

He'd so far poured a pint of the coffee down Mace's throat, and the powerful brew seemed finally to be working. From initial unwillingness to see that the death of his nephew had been anything other than a mistake, Mace had finally reached some kind of plateau; he was beginning to realize that it must have been deliberate, to keep Gulliver permanently silenced.

'Who set up Red Station?' said Harry, refilling Mace's mug. He was determined to keep going until the chief's liquid level read 'full'. 'It must have been someone with clout; arranging the building and the funding, the Clones – all that. You don't set up something like this using cash from the milk money.' He sipped his own coffee. 'Was it Paulton?'

'He's one of them.' The answers seemed to be coming easier, the effects of increasing sobriety and the beginnings of cold reasoning. 'But he wasn't the one who really got it working. He wouldn't have had the clout to get it past all the Whitehall watchdogs.'

'So who? MI6? They'd have to be in on it, with their staff involved.'

Mace nodded, his breath whistling through his nose. His skin had taken on a greasy pallor, as though he was leaking *chacha* through his pores. 'Bellingham. Try Sir Anthony Bellingham.'

Harry had heard the name before. One of the ghosts, usually spoken of in whispers. Bellingham was high up the tree in Vauxhall Cross. 'What does he do?'

'He's one of their ODs – Operational Directors. Access to funds, an organizer, a strategist. He can get whatever manpower he needs, no questions asked. He's strictly old-school ruthless, all posh vowels and a black heart. You want to watch yourself with him, lad. He's toxic. Cut your heart out and smile doing it.'

Harry breathed out. It was starting to gel. 'And the Hit? Are they Bellingham's people?'

'Yes. The Clones are Paulton's. The two groups stay compartmentalized. Never meet. Different jobs, you see. Different skill sets.'

He made them sound like corporate departments. 'How do you mean?'

'The Clones are a training wing. They ship 'em in, teach 'em how to track and monitor, give them a taste of a foreign turf, then move them on. It's what the original idea was all about . . . what the explanation is if anyone starts asking too many questions.'

'But you had direct contact with them.'

'Yes. As far as the Clones were concerned, it was all part of the course. I fed them information about our movements, but only to save wasted trips.'

'Really? But that day I ran the field test, they followed everyone.'

'I didn't tell them, that's why.'

'Why not? All it would have taken was a phone call.'

'I . . .' He stopped and pawed at the table top. 'I never wanted this . . . this sell-out. Not particularly proud of myself, either. That day . . . I pretended to be sceptical when you suggested the test but I wanted to see if you could get one over on them.' He shrugged miserably. 'It was a small victory.'

'What about the Hit? You have contact with them?'

'No!' Mace's voice held the ring of truth. 'Never. Nor would I want to. The Hit have . . . other uses.'

'Go on.'

'Black Ops. Wet work.'

Stanbridge had been telling the truth.

'Who are their targets?' Apart from Brasher and Jimmy Gulliver, he wanted to add. But he didn't. He'd exhausted that route already.

'Whoever they're pointed at. Gang bosses, terrorists, assassins . . . whoever looks like jumping the fence and getting away with the chickens.' He grunted. 'I told you Bellingham's old-school. He's a solutions man . . . gets things done and doesn't ask permission. He doesn't like untidy ends – you'd do well to remember that.'

Harry accepted the warning with a nod. There had always been rumours about teams operating on the grey fringes of the security community; shadowy groups of individuals apparently moving in the half-light of black operations, trained to kill when the call came, when all else had failed. It was canteen gossip wherever you went, mostly romantic chit-chat, a spawn of the Bond movies where licences to kill were dished out to hardened veterans when the need arose and deniability was paramount.

'An alternative justice, is that what you're saying? A bullet is cheaper and quieter than a trial – and more guaranteed?'

'You got it.' Mace sounded almost his old self. He didn't look proud of it. But neither was he looking as if shame or guilt were going to overcome him any time soon. Too late for that. Angry, though; he looked that and more.

'Risky, wasn't it?' Harry was referring to Red Station.

'Maybe. Bellingham got involved because he got tired of having to answer Joint Intelligence Committee enquiries every time an operation went wrong or an agent turned bad. He wanted cleaner solutions.' Mace sighed, shook his head. 'You still think I dobbed in Jimmy?'

'No.' Harry couldn't see it, not now. But if not Mace, then who – and how? They were supposed to be isolated, out of touch, Mace's the only terminal linked to London.

It was Mace who provided the answer. 'I knew Jimmy was driving back. Thought he was insane, personally. But I didn't tell London immediately. Should have . . . but I didn't. He needed time to think. I hoped he'd see sense on the way back and get out for good.'

'What did you tell the others?'

'That he'd been recalled. I had to tell London eventually, but I waited until I was sure he was on his way. Then I gave the job to someone else, using my terminal.' His face took on a look of self-loathing. 'I wasn't feeling well. No excuse, but I couldn't face going through all the palaver. I told them to send it among a whole load of useless chaff, saying he was on his way back. Big mistake, as it turns out. The worst.'

'Who did you tell?'

'The way I planned it, London might have missed it for a while, giving Jimmy more time to sort himself out. But it went by itself, didn't it? A message like that stood out like tits on a duck.'

'*Who?*' Harry repeated.

'The only other person who got close enough to find out what he was doing. Bloody Sixer.' His face twisted with bitterness.

Suddenly Harry knew.

Clare Jardine.

'You're too late, you know,' Mace continued, reading his expression. 'She's probably long gone. She's a bright girl, I told you. She'll have seen the writing on the wall days ago. She knew that even if she helped London by keeping an eye on the rest of you, they'd never trust her – not fully. She'll be halfway to Timbuktu by now.' His eyes went cold. 'You'll never find her. Why do you think she got close to thugs like Kostova and Nikolai? She needed help so she could disappear. Like I said, bright. A survivor.'

So Kostova had been telling the truth. But how had Mace found out? Maybe that was *his* passport to staying here when everyone else was baling out: feeding Kostova bits of information.

Christ on a bicycle, Harry thought tiredly, they're all as bad as each other.

But he wasn't interested in Jardine or Mace; not now.

He was after a bigger fish.

'Where do I find Bellingham?' he said quietly. 'How can I get to him?'

Mace didn't answer straight away. He picked up the bottle and went to fill his glass. His hand shook as he upended it. The bottle was empty. He tossed it across the room, where it shattered on the floor.

Then he told Harry what to do.

FIFTY-FOUR

Clare Jardine's block was in darkness. Harry checked his watch. It was just after midnight.

He called Rik at the office. 'Follow the destruct sequence,' he told him.

'What about Mace? He's supposed to authorize that.'

'Mace isn't in a fit state to authorize his own name. Do it.'

'OK. Everything?'

'Records, files, hard drives, the lot. Don't worry about the BC stuff – just everything else. Can you do it?'

'Bloody right I can. It'll be fun. What I don't wipe forever, I'll burn or hit with a hammer.'

Harry cut the call and climbed the stairs. The air smelled clean, of flowers. Different to his place. The stair treads were lined with rubber, and were clean. Somebody must sweep it regularly, although he couldn't quite picture Clare Jardine behind a broom.

Standing over someone with a whip was more her style.

He knocked gently on her door and stepped back so she could see him through the peephole.

'What do you want?' she demanded, flinging open the door. She was wearing jeans and a T-shirt, and looked rumpled. She clearly hadn't slept.

'Nice to see you, too,' he muttered. 'Care to invite me in or shall we have a slanging match out here?'

She stood aside. He stepped past her into a comfortable, if minimally furnished flat. It was not unlike his own in size, although there were a few feminine touches. Not many, but enough to be noticed. He concluded that she either didn't have the nesting gene or had placed it on hold.

'We're leaving,' he said. 'You coming?'

'We?'

'Rik and me. Mace is staying and Fitzgerald's gone native. They'll have to take their chances.'

She shook her head, eyes blank. 'I'm staying.'

'Why? You think Kostova will look after you? Or Bellingham?'

Her face tightened. 'What do you mean?'

'You've been cosying up to Kostova and Nikolai. And you've been feeding information back to Bellingham in London.'

'That's rubbish. Who the hell do you think you are—'

'Save the wounded outrage,' he said. 'I don't have the time. You've been working on Kostova to get you some papers. Bellingham's made you some promises in return for your help, but you don't believe him. Frankly, I don't blame you. But you thought you'd set up an alternative escape plan by getting a new passport from Geordi Kostova. He hasn't delivered, has he?'

'You're insane.'

'Maybe. But I've met people like him before. He found out what you are and he'll promise anything to get what he wants. But his demands will never stop. You know that as well as I do. What did he ask you for in return – the keys to Vauxhall Cross?' He shook his head, hating this line of attack. But he had to shock her into seeing reason. 'What he doesn't know is that you're not an active agent in the real sense. Which puts you out of the loop. You haven't told him that, have you? What did you tell him – that you could get him something to take to Moscow and get himself some promotion?'

'I've been working him, you fool!' she snapped, her voice was low and trembling with anger. 'Finding out exactly why he's here. Him and his creepy friend, Nikolai. It's what I was trained for . . . what we were all trained for – even you. The rest of you may have resigned yourselves to your fate, but I haven't!' She turned away from him. 'I'm not going to stay in this shithole for ever. I'll do whatever it takes to get back.'

'Whatever it takes? Including tapping up the only Russian intelligence officer for a hundred miles? You thought you'd do that for the good of Queen and country?' He stopped; he didn't want to alienate her entirely. 'Did Bellingham put you up to it?'

By the way she looked at him, he knew he'd hit the button.

'What did he promise you?' he asked gently. 'Home and absolution? A welcome back into the fold?'

'Why not?' she said hotly. 'Anything's better than staying here.' She clutched her arms around her. 'He said I could have my old desk back if I got close to Kostova.' She looked at him. 'I don't mean that close – I know what you're thinking.'

It sounded convincing, reasonable, all that passion. But Harry wasn't taken in. Clare had been trained in the art of deception, of feeding people what they expected to hear. She could be doing it to him right now.

He changed tack. 'So why is he here?' He was aware that time was running out. They had to be moving before everything hit the fan. But information was power, and the more he knew now, the better he was prepared for what lay ahead.

'He's a plant. He's Georgian originally, but he's lived in Russia most of his life. They sent him back here with a cover story to get himself in with the locals.'

'Why would they do that?' Harry wasn't up on current Russian thinking, but he knew they hadn't changed their methodology much. And the Russians of old had always taken the long view. If Kostova had been sent here, it had to be with some strategy in mind, and not a short-term view.

'Because Vladimir Putin wants everything back the way it was. He wants all the satellites back, all the breakaway states, all the power that will bring. A politician here, a mayor there . . . it's takeover by stealth. Why do you think they're so eagerly massing to the north – just for the sake of the separatists?'

'And Nikolai? What's his place in all this?'

'He's FSB. Originally KGB. Sent to make sure Kostova stays loyal and to protect their investment. If the locals found out what Kostova was really doing here they'd string him up on his own front gate. Nikolai plays on that fear to get him to do what Moscow wants.'

He could see that working. But it still didn't explain the relationship between Clare and Kostova. 'Did he get you the papers you wanted?' He was interested to see whether their answers would be the same.

She didn't say anything for a moment. Then, 'No. He didn't.'

So she was stuck. Unless she came out with them.

'It's us or nothing,' he told her. 'It's all the same to me.

But you really don't want to stay here. They'll roll right over you. Rik's destroying all the records right now.'

She shook her head, suddenly looking very vulnerable. But she hadn't lost any of her steel. 'Good for Rik. Why should you care about me?'

'Because I need to get to Paulton. And through him to Bellingham. You can help me do that.'

She frowned. 'Why do you want to get to them?'

'To set things right.'

Her face twisted. 'Christ, Tate, what are you – a boy scout? Set things right? That's positively archaic. Are you on some kind of revenge trip?'

'Maybe. But *you* owe it to Jimmy Gulliver.'

Her frown deepened. 'What the hell is that supposed to mean? What's Jimmy got to do with it? He's lucky – he's out of this, safely back home.'

He didn't think twice; she had to know. 'Actually, you're wrong. Jimmy Gulliver's dead.'

The words were like a slap to the face. Clare staggered, her eyes registering a rush of emotions. Harry saw doubt followed by denial, then anger.

'Rubbish. He's back in London.'

'Is that what they told you? Your open message back to Bellingham put Gulliver under the spotlight. He died not long after leaving here. A climbing accident. That's the official explanation, anyway. Odd that, because Jimmy suffered from chronic vertigo. He wouldn't go near a set of stepladders, much less a mountain.'

'Wha— how can you know that? Who told you?'

'Mace. Jimmy Gulliver was his nephew. He'd known him as a kid, but they'd lost touch.'

She said nothing, her expression dissolving inwards.

Harry moved towards the door. It was now or never. But he couldn't force her to do anything. 'Are you coming? We don't have long. Kostova and Nikolai, the Russian army . . . or Latham. He's already here, by the way. Or we make a try for the airport, morning flight. Take your pick.'

She turned away, her face pale. 'Can you give me five minutes?' She sounded desolate.

'Make it four. Pack light.'

FIFTY-FIVE

Fifteen minutes later, they entered the rear door to Red Station and walked up the stairs. Clare was carrying a dark green rucksack, which she'd said was all she needed.

Harry led the way. He had seen no signs of watchers lurking in the shadows, but he felt the hairs rise on the back of his neck as they reached the second floor. There was a steady pounding noise coming from the main office.

He took out his gun and slipped off the safety. Clare stepped quickly to one side, giving him a clear run.

Harry input the security code. As soon as it beeped, he shouldered the door open and stepped inside, covering the room. Rik was there, calmly smashing up a hard drive with a heavy length of piping. He had a dreamy smile on his face and was surrounded by fragments of plastic and computer components. He stopped when he saw the gun and went pale.

'Have you done playing?' Harry asked him. He slipped the weapon into his pocket and beckoned Clare inside.

'Almost.' Rik swallowed and looked surprised to see her. 'The link to the server's gone forever, so even if we wanted to send a final message, we can't. That OK?'

'It'll have to be.' Harry did a walk-through, making a final check and leaving Clare to do a sweep of her own workplace. There were a few files in Mace's desk, but nothing of benefit to anyone. The PC was a wreck, smashed beyond recognition. He dropped the paper files into a metal waste bin and doused them with the contents of a bottle of *chacha*. Found a box of matches in Mace's desk drawer and lit one, dropped it in and stepped back as the fumes went up with a *whoomph*.

He went down to the basement and lifted the panel in the floor. Lifted out the three handguns and spare ammunition. He hoped they weren't going to need them, but leaving them behind with Latham out there was unthinkable.

When he got back upstairs, the other two were waiting by the outer door.

He handed Clare one of the guns and a spare clip. 'This could be hairy.'

'Where are we going?' She gave the gun a quick check, hands moving with easy skill.

'The airport,' Rik replied. 'First plane out tomorrow morning.'

'Isn't that the obvious place to go?'

'That's why we'll make it,' said Harry. 'The only people trying to stop us leaving are Latham and his team. Nobody else gives a damn – certainly not the locals; they've got bigger things to worry about. If we head out in any other direction, we've got mountains to cross or miles of empty road where we'll stick out like clowns at a funeral. Heading west takes us to the Black Sea, which is hopeless – and I doubt we'd make it, anyway. That whole area will be blocked. Going east is as bad. If we make it to the airport, we'll be fine.'

'Sounds good to me,' said Rik. 'The sooner I get on that flight, the better. Won't we be noticed, though, driving at this time of night?' He held up his watch. It had gone one o'clock.

Harry shrugged. Time had slipped by quicker than he'd planned. 'We'll get out of town and find somewhere to lie low, in case Latham comes looking.' It was a risk either way, leaving at any time. But years of operating in the open had left him with a familiarity for the dark; it was where he felt safest, especially when faced by dangers he couldn't see. Staying here would soon turn into a trap, because Latham would know where to find them.

He turned and led the way out.

Clare joined him by the Land Cruiser and held out her hand. 'I'll drive.' She took the keys and he didn't argue. He was no wheelman and was pretty certain Rik had never taken the evasive driving course. Clare, however, undoubtedly knew the roads better than either of them and could drive accordingly. He climbed into the front passenger seat and left Rik to occupy the back with the bags.

Clare stamped on the accelerator and took them away like a rocket, narrowly missing an old BMW parked at the corner. Harry said nothing; she was reacting to the rush of adrenalin and leaning on her to take it easy wouldn't help. Besides, she could do with the practice; if things went belly-up and Latham found them, they would need all the hard driving skills she could muster.

He told her to head west at first, away from the airport. Deflecting attention away from their intended route might give them an edge. Clare took them through a series of back streets and rat runs, avoiding the main boulevards where the military patrols were concentrated. There were few other vehicles, and only an occasional pedestrian showing as a fleeting shadow between the buildings. From residential areas they sped through a series of small commercial zones housing light engineering works, leather workshops and trading depots. There were no lights in any of the buildings and the town already appeared to be shut up for the night.

Nobody spoke. The Toyota's heavy springs protested as they bounced across open gullies, potholes and fissures in the tarmac, and the noise of the fat tyres and the well-worn engine combined to make any kind of chat difficult.

Harry took out the second semi-automatic and handed it to Rik, and placed the third one under his seat. He kept his own in his pocket. The approved place to keep a handgun when travelling by car in a high-risk area was under one thigh for easy access. But with the way the Toyota was bouncing around, he didn't dare risk it for fear of shooting himself by mistake.

He kept a weather eye on their rear, even though he knew Clare would be doing the same. So far, he had seen no sign of pursuit.

'Trucks.' Clare pointed ahead. They were just emerging on to an open beltway which curved round towards the south-west in the general direction of the airport. The road was wider here, designed to carry heavier traffic. Now, it seemed, from the long line of lights, it was given over to military trucks in convoys. And one of them was coming their way.

'Blast on through,' said Harry. 'They won't have orders to stop us.'

The lights grew larger. The drivers hogged the middle of the road but Clare refused to back down until the last second, when she was forced to use a flat section of verge to avoid being pulped by the oncoming vehicles. Then suddenly the trucks were upon them, fanning past in a blare of horns and the roar of heavy diesel engines. Seconds later, they were through and the trucks were vanishing into the night, leaving the interior of the car thick with diesel fumes and dust.

Ten miles out of town they came to a small village, a huddle of houses and farms clinging to the side of a hill. Clare slowed as they approached the first buildings, where the road narrowed and bent away out of sight. It was the classic situation for a road block or ambush.

'Keep going,' Harry instructed her. He placed a hand on the gun in his pocket. If they were stopped here, there would be no easy way out. Behind him Rik tossed the bags into the rear compartment to leave the rear seat clear and lowered the windows.

They reached the bend and Clare flicked the headlights to full beam. The road beyond was empty. She stamped on the accelerator and took them past the remaining houses at speed, the engine's roar echoing off the walls like thunder.

A few miles later, as they bounced along a secondary road leading through open fields, Harry glanced in the wing mirror.

Twin headlights had appeared out of nowhere. They were some way back, but closing fast.

Latham.

FIFTY-SIX

'Harry.' Clare had seen them, too.

'What's up?' Rik twisted in his seat and looked back. 'Who is that?'

'Could be anybody,' said Harry calmly. But his heart was thumping. He took out his gun and checked the clip.

Clare increased speed, the engine howling in competition with the furious drumming of the tyres over the roughened surface and the machine-gun clatter of stones hitting the underneath of the chassis.

Harry checked the petrol gauge. They had plenty of fuel as long as they weren't forced to abandon the airport idea and drive for miles through the night. At this demanding rate, that could become a problem and he suspected petrol stations were few and far between . . . and not all likely to be operating.

'Slow down,' he suggested to Clare. 'Fake a burst tyre. See what they do.'

'OK. Hold tight.' Clare took her foot off the accelerator, allowing their speed to drop sharply as if they were experiencing problems. She dabbed the brakes a few times, the red glow flashing in the dark behind them, and hauled on the steering wheel causing the car to fishtail across the road.

Harry looked back. The other car hadn't slowed. In fact it was approaching way too fast to be anything but a threat. Any normal driver on seeing their brake lights would have backed off immediately. But the lights were growing at a frightening rate, and when the other driver flicked on his full beams, Harry knew they were in trouble.

'Go!' he shouted. But Clare had already floored the pedal, the Land Cruiser's engine roaring in response.

He glanced at Rik, who was sitting upright in his seat, holding his gun in his lap. The younger man was staring through the side window with no expression, but he seemed calm enough.

'You OK?' said Harry, and received a terse nod in return.

'We should take him,' Clare said. 'There's nothing ahead; we're in the open.'

Harry considered it. Their options were limited. If the car behind them contained Latham and his team, stopping to argue in this relative wilderness would be a short form of suicide. The Hit would be trained for this kind of terrain and this scenario, and spoiling for a fight. The odds of three comparative amateurs gaining superiority over them was therefore minimal. But staying on the road at this rate was merely prolonging the inevitable. And if Clare lost control of the car because of a burst tyre or a mechanical fault, the end would come just as quickly and with less chance of fighting back.

He signalled ahead. He would have to trust Clare to know what she was doing. 'Choose your spot.'

'What are we doing?' Rik leaned forward between the seats to make himself heard over the noise.

'Get ready to bale out,' Harry warned him. 'The moment we stop, go left and find cover off the road. *Don't* stay with the car.'

Rik nodded and sat back, swallowing hard.

Moments later, Clare shouted, 'Now!' Then she stamped hard on the brakes, bracing herself on the wheel.

For a moment nothing happened. Not even the engine noise

diminished. The car's velocity continued unabated, the tyres drumming on the gravelled road and dust billowing around their tail, glowing red in the aura of the brake lights. Then the tyre treads began to grip and they were thrown forward against their seat belts. Another release as the vehicle skidded and lost traction, but Clare adjusted smoothly with a spin of the wheel and pointed the nose of the car at the side of the road. They thumped against the grass verge and over, taking them in a crazy slide, the headlights throwing up a whirl-wind kaleidoscope of bushes, saplings and rocks, and a family of skinny goats leaping out of their way.

Harry thumbed his seat belt release and leapt out of the car as it came to a stop, vaguely aware of Clare doing the same. He stumbled as his shoes skidded on damp grass, then pitched forward, his momentum overtaking him. He rolled instinc-tively, one shoulder crunching against a series of small stones and one hand scraping across the rough ground. His head brushed a large, solid object and he closed his eyes, tucking himself into a tight ball.

He came up the right way and threw himself to one side, away, he hoped, from the car and the glare of lights. If he stayed too close, he would be backlit for anyone to take a shot at him. He hoped Clare and Rik had done the same.

The Toyota's lights went out.

He turned away and stared into the night, eyes still holding the echo of the glare. Loss of night vision was the last thing he needed.

There was no sign of the other vehicle.

'Clare?' He peered towards the Toyota. She was either close enough to it to have leaned in and doused the lights, or was now keeping very still nearby.

He heard a scrape from further along the gully they had just come down. He froze. He felt vulnerable not knowing what his cover was like, and braced himself. For all he knew, he could be lying out in the open; and if Latham and his men had night-vision equipment, they were done for. Yet instinct told him that the Hit had been expecting to take them in town, where the need for specialist tools wouldn't be needed. He hoped he was right.

A rock rolled against his leg, and he spun round, finger on the trigger.

'*Harry – it's me!*' Clare's whisper was close by, and it took a deliberate effort of will to stop himself pulling the trigger. He relaxed his finger, breathing out in a long, slow sigh.

'Did you see where they went?' he whispered.

'No.' She moved, her foot brushing against his. He could tell by the scuff of cloth that she was moving, twisting her body and scanning the area immediately around them. 'They stopped about a hundred yards back.'

Too close. If the opposition had decamped from their vehicle, they could already be moving in for the kill. He wondered how many were in the team. Not that it mattered; more than two of Latham's kind and they were well and truly stuffed.

Then he recalled something Mace had said about Kostova. '*He likes to keep close tabs on everyone who drops by his little bailiwick. He doesn't miss a trick.*'

And Kostova had said that a man had arrived. One man.

'*A fellow countryman of yours . . . a man named Phillips.*'

Harry hadn't given it much thought at the time, his mind too focussed on Latham. The precise size and make-up of his team hadn't been a burning issue.

Had Kostova missed other arrivals, slipping in under separate cover? Or did it mean there was no team at all?

He thought it over, his brain in a spin. The idea of efficient, fast-moving four-man teams was long built into military thinking, his own included. That number had filtered automatically through to many quasi-military operations. Four worked well, and had become an acceptable fact. But did it have to be true? And why would assassins need to travel in teams of four?

Assassins.

'See if you can locate Rik,' he said softly, and slid away before Clare could argue. The sound of voices out here would travel too easily, and he didn't want to run the risk of Latham zeroing in on them. He made his way off to the side, probing the dark, stopping every few feet to listen. He heard only the drumming of his heart and the sigh of the wind fanning the bushes and the grass. Then a goat bleated softly, and he hugged the ground tight.

Was it reacting to his presence . . . or someone else?

Then he was blinded as the world was lit up by a twin array

of headlights and two huge spotlights not fifty yards away. It was the other car, and he'd wandered right in front of it!

He cursed and rolled away, sucking himself closer to the earth and rocks. A volley of shots rang out from behind the lights, three double-taps in quick succession. The sounds were flat and soon lost over the open countryside, and he caught a glimpse of the red-hot muzzle flash from near the car. He winced as something tugged at his sleeve and he felt the brush of heat against his skin. He continued rolling, desperately trying to keep his legs from windmilling and giving away his position. He bumped over a series of rocks, feeling jabs of pain in his ribs and hips, and wondered where he would end up.

Then the ground disappeared beneath him and he dropped into a void.

FIFTY-SEVEN

Harry landed without warning. The breath was dashed from his lungs and his gun fell from his hand. As he scrambled to find it, he heard another burst of shooting and the car lights went out.

He retrieved the gun and checked it over, then did a quick touch-recce of his surroundings. Rocks and grass, but how dense?

He hugged the ground. As far as he could tell, he was lying in a hollow. He must have rolled into a ditch or a depression of some kind – he could feel moisture and soft earth beneath him. At least, he hoped it was earth. It reminded him too readily of the Essex inlet where all his troubles had begun.

It all seemed a long time ago.

He waited, regaining his breath. The lights and the burst of gunfire had been intended to confuse and kill. Latham had succeeded in the former, and Harry prayed Rik and Clare hadn't fallen victim to any of the shots.

A thin scrape of metal sounded in the dark. Someone brushing against a car body. Not Rik and not Clare; it was the wrong direction. Latham, then . . . or one of his team.

He was coming for them.

Harry took a deep breath, fighting a rising sense of panic. Time wasn't on their side. He had to do something. Waiting here for Latham to hunt them down wasn't an option; the killer had far too many advantages. He braced himself and hoped he was clear of whatever hollow he was in, and not facing a wall of earth or rocks. A ricochet here could be messy. And fatal.

Holding the gun two-handed, he lunged upwards and fired three times in rapid succession towards the other car. He heard the tinkle of breaking glass and the hollow ping of a round hitting metal. A volley of answering shots came back over his head and he crabbed to one side, a snapshot of the area in front of him captured by the flare of gunfire.

The terrain was a mix of dry bushes, scrubby grass and rocks. A nightmare for anyone to move across in a hurry, yet, unwittingly, it might prove to be their salvation. A car – a heavy four-by-four – was parked at the edge of the road, facing down at him.

And a man standing by the front wing.

The image remained clear. He had his legs slightly bent, arms held out before him, the dark shape of a weapon in his hand. Tall, slim, face unclear, he could have been any age. But there was no mistaking his stance.

Harry crabbed sideways, threading among the rocks and scrub. If he had seen Latham in the muzzle flash, then Latham would have seen him, too. And fixed his position.

Another burst of gunfire opened up the night from his left, with more sounds of shots hitting metal. Clare or Rik? He couldn't tell. The echoes were distorted by the dead ground, their points of origin muted and difficult to pin down.

He risked another try and stood up, letting off another double-tap before dropping to the ground. Too far right and off-target. But close enough when it was three against one.

Then an engine burst into life, followed by the high-pitched whine of reverse gear and the furious scrape of tyres on loose shale.

Latham moving out? They'd surprised him; scared him off.

But for how long?

Ditching caution in favour of speed, Harry scrambled

towards the Toyota, stubbing knees and toes on rocks. They'd been given – had taken – one chance to get away from their pursuer, and he wasn't going to waste it. Cuts and bruises were an acceptable trade-off compared with the alternatives.

'Clare! Rik!' he yelled. 'Back to the car!'

He got there just as the driver's door opened and Clare reached up to smash the interior light with the butt of her pistol. Rik dived in from the other side, and once Harry was aboard, they took off again.

The headlights revealed a continuation of the gully which took them back on to the road, past a ramshackle wooden pen which a local farmer must have used for housing the goats. Clare pushed the Toyota out on to the tarmac without waiting to see if the other car was coming up behind them.

'You OK?' Harry asked. Clare nodded, focussing on the road ahead. She looked determined in the glow of the instrument panel, with a gleam of excitement in her eyes and smudges of dirt showing on her face and shoulders where she had hit the ground after abandoning the car.

He turned to look at Rik, who was watching the rear. 'How about you?'

Rik shook his head and held up his gun. He didn't meet Harry's eye. 'I'm fine. I didn't . . . I couldn't do it.' He cleared his throat and looked at the back of Clare's head. 'I tried, but . . . I fucked up the safety catch and it wouldn't fire. My hands were greasy . . . I was nervous. Sorry.'

'Forget it,' said Harry. Rik was feeling ashamed at not having been able to use his gun. It took guts to admit that in front of a colleague. 'Let me see.'

He took the gun and checked it over. The safety was on, and a knob of dirt was stuck to the slide. He cleaned it off and ejected the clip, then worked the mechanism. There was nothing wrong with it. Rik had suffered a simple attack of nerves. It happened. He handed the gun back.

'The safety was jammed with muck. Must have picked it up when you hit the ground.' He added, 'Strip out the magazine, make sure you haven't got a round up the spout and put it back together again.'

He knew the breech was empty, but it wouldn't do Rik any harm to go through the process. It would give him confidence to know that he could do it when it mattered.

Rik nodded and did as Harry had said. When he straightened up, he looked and sounded calmer. 'It's good.'

'Right,' said Harry, not looking at him. 'Next time, you'll be fine, too. Is the safety on?'

There was a pause, a click, and Rik said, 'Yes.'

An hour later, they swung sharply left and bounced down a muddy track.

Harry looked questioningly at Clare. She pointed towards a dark mass in the distance showing a single point of light. A farm. It was too remote to be anything else.

'If you've got some of that chocolate handy,' she added, 'I could use it to bribe the farmer into letting us stay in his barn.'

Harry nodded and checked the track behind them. There had been no sign of pursuit, and he doubted if even Latham was capable of driving through the dark without lights. They had been pushing hard and were all desperate to stop; it made sense to lay up while they could.

He had debated the wisdom of arriving at the airport in the middle of the night, and dismissed it. The place was likely to be locked up tight until just before the first flight in the morning, which would leave them with nowhere but the terminal and surrounding shadows to hide when Latham arrived. And he was sure to turn up sooner or later.

At least in the morning, with airport security and army patrols, the killer would find it difficult to go on the offensive.

Rik passed Clare two chocolate bars from their supplies. She drew up a hundred yards short of the nearest building, a wooden cowshed with weatherworn slats and a sunken roof. Taking the chocolate, she got out and disappeared into the dark.

The single light had gone out.

Five minutes later, she was back, minus the chocolate. She pointed to the cowshed. 'There's a small barn behind that. He says we can stay there, but wants us gone before five. He's already had two military patrols go through the place.'

Once the Toyota was safely out of sight, they went inside and found a place to settle down. The air was surprisingly warm, and smelled of hay and animals. Movement in a stall at the rear was followed by the snuffle of a horse and a bleat from a goat. Dried rabbit skins hung from the wall and a chicken poked its head out from a pile of sacking.

'It's Noah's bloody ark,' said Rik, and threw himself down on a pile of hay.

Harry instinctively checked the barn for a rear exit. He found a single door in one corner. Then he did a tour of the outside and stood listening to the night. No sounds. No movement.

He stood for a while, enjoying the solitude and allowing the kinks from the car ride and the rolling around in the dirt to ease themselves from his body. His thoughts turned to Jean, and he wondered what she was doing. He realized with surprise that he'd been doing that quite a bit lately.

The idea of making her smile sounded promising.

Now all he had to do was get back.

He went back inside. The other two were in separate corners, fast asleep.

FIFTY-EIGHT

Five o'clock brought a thin dawn and a cold snap to the air. An easterly wind was curling round the barn and the temperature inside dropped sharply as the warmth of the previous night seeped out into the dark.

Harry rolled himself out of the natural hammock he'd created in a pile of hay. He looked for Clare and found her already up and watching the track through a small gap in the wooden slats. She looked composed and resolute, in spite of the strands of hay sticking to her jacket.

'A car went by fifteen minutes ago,' she announced. 'Four-wheel drive, one occupant. Couldn't see any detail but it might have been Latham. Two military-style convoys, too. Couldn't see if they were army or militia.'

'Good thing none of them stopped,' said Rik, pulling his gun out from under him. He winced. He'd been lying on it. His face was dirty and his spiky hair looked unkempt, but he sounded calm, as if he'd found some reserves of inner resilience.

'We'll eat first,' said Harry. 'If he's ahead of us, there's no point rushing off.'

'He'll be waiting, then.' Clare looked at him. 'We won't know he's there until he hits us.'

Harry nodded and rubbed at the bristles on his chin. He needed a shave and a shower. 'I know. But if it was him you saw, he'll be there whether we eat or not. I'd rather make him wait.' He checked his watch and calculated their probable travel time to the airport. Three quarters of an hour should do it, if he'd got his sums right and they were given a clear run.

'So we just drive straight at him?' Clare looked ready for a fight – although not just with Latham.

'Not exactly. I've got a cunning plan.'

'Have you used it before?' said Rik anxiously.

'Yes.' Harry preferred not to think about it. It had been a long time ago, with different enemies. Then, he'd been lucky. Time to see if it still worked.

His main worry was Latham would probably also have seen what he was planning to do.

A phone buzzed in the silence.

It was Rik's mobile. He snatched it out of his pocket and checked the screen. 'It's Fitz!' he said, then answered. 'What's up, man? We're on the road. Oh, OK.' He looked at Harry and handed him the mobile. 'He wants to talk to you.'

Harry took the phone. 'You all right?'

'Yeah, I'm fine. You clear yet?' Fitzgerald's voice was tinny, and occasionally dogged by static. A child was crying in the background, and a woman's voice murmured something. The sound of normality.

'We're working on it.'

'Anyone with you apart from the lad?'

'Yes.' Fitzgerald was deliberately avoiding the use of names, he noticed. Probably because he knew more about the local intercept capabilities than he had let on. 'The big club wouldn't come.'

'The big cl— Oh, right . . . got you. Is the girl with you?'

'Yes. Problem?'

'You could say that. The uh . . . club; he won't be going anywhere. That's why I rang.'

An icy feeling settled in Harry's stomach. 'What do you mean?'

'He's dead.'

'How?'

'Hit and run. Might be genuine, but I doubt it. I got a call from a friend at the hospital. You ask me, you've got trouble close to home, Harry.'

'Thanks for telling me. Any ideas?'

'Sorry. Can't help you there. I'd watch the girl, though; I think she's bad. This call's over . . . I'm bricking the mobile and we're moving to another location. And before you ask, I won't be coming in.'

'You sure?'

'Dead sure. Watch your back.'

Twenty minutes later, they drove away from the farm, their mood further subdued by the news of Mace's death. The light was still low but getting better with very passing minute. Leaving it any longer would improve visibility, but that would be the same for Latham. And they'd be cutting it too fine to make their flight if they ran into him.

Before leaving, Harry placed some money inside a plastic food container by the horse stall where the farmer would be sure to find it. As long as the goat didn't get to it first.

They reached the end of the farm track and stopped. The road was empty in both directions, save for an ancient tractor towing a trailer loaded with wood. A curtain of dust hung in the air, legacy of the earlier truck convoys.

Clare was driving again, while Harry and Rik concentrated on the terrain around them. He'd told them to keep an eye out for high ground with trees or large outcroppings of rock – anywhere a gunman might position himself. It would be where Latham was waiting.

'You think it was him?' said Rik. 'Killed Mace, I mean.'

'Yes.' He'd never be able to prove it, but he was sure Latham was responsible. He considered Fitzgerald's warning about Clare, but dismissed her as the killer. She wouldn't have been able to accomplish it in the time frame available. Anyway, Fitz had said bad. Bad in his book would have meant untrustworthy.

Latham, on the other hand, was something else.

Mace would have made an easy target; predictable, slow-moving and unlikely to have been sober, he wouldn't have seen the danger coming. Or maybe hadn't cared. 'He's doing what he's good at: clearing up the evidence.'

And now he was out here, looking for the rest of them.

'How do we reduce the odds?' Clare asked. It was the first time she had spoken since leaving the barn. She seemed to have gotten rid of her earlier irritation, settling instead for a plan to survive.

'We stop here and wait.' Harry pointed to a section of clear ground coming up, just off the road. The ruts in the earth and a scattering of litter showed that it was in regular use as a pull-in for other vehicles. He took out a map and checked their position.

Clare stopped the car. 'What exactly are we waiting for?'

'That lot.' Harry jerked a thumb over his shoulder. A line of dots was approaching a mile away. Another military convoy, kicking up a swirl of dust behind them.

He'd noticed them earlier. They were moving fast and hadn't taken long to catch up. Wherever they were going must be important. He hoped it was the airport.

'With a bit of luck,' he said, 'they're going our way.'

'We tag along behind?' said Clare. She looked unsure.

'Not behind. Wait until you see a gap, then get in among them.'

'Hey, neat,' said Rik. 'If Latham can't get a bead on us, he can't shoot.'

'Maybe.' Harry looked at Clare. 'Just make sure we're nowhere near a fuel or ammo truck.'

At that, Rik's face fell.

Harry didn't mention what might happen if Latham decided to take them out regardless of the risk. They would have the cover of the trucks to keep them from a direct confrontation, but amid the noise and dust of the convoy, a rifle shot from five hundred yards away wouldn't even register – apart from the person it hit.

The thought made his forehead itch.

The first truck drew level and pounded by, the driver and his mate leaning over to stare down at them. Five seconds later another one roared past. Both were full of troops in camouflage combats, automatic rifles held between their knees. The ones nearest the tailgate grinned and made faces when they saw Clare. Ten seconds later came another truck, this one heavily-laden and double-wheeled, the ground vibrating under its weight. Fifteen seconds and a fuel tanker, another ten and a box-shape communications truck with a fold-down antennae array. The noise was deafening and the smell of diesel fuel hung in the air like a cloak, seeping into the Toyota. The convoy was travelling fast and efficiently, plainly part of a battle group with full supplies.

'It's too tight,' said Clare, her voice cracking above the din. She was blipping the throttle, handbrake off and ready to go. 'If I mistime it, we'll get crushed.'

'You'll do it.' Harry kept his voice calm and checked his wing mirror. The biggest gaps were between the fuel and ammo trucks; nobody wanted to be close to them if they blew. The end of the convoy was in sight, with another half-dozen vehicles to go. If they missed their chance, they were on their own.

Exposed.

Suddenly Clare floored the pedal. The Toyota's engine howled as she spun the wheel and pulled on to the road right on the tail of a water tanker spraying a fine mist in the air from a bad seal. Seconds later their rear-view mirror was filled with the radiator of the truck behind, bouncing wildly over the surface of the road as it bore down on them with its lights full on. In spite of the proximity, the driver leaned on his horn at the uninvited intrusion and kept coming.

'Bastard! Back off!' muttered Clare, fighting to control the wheel. She flicked on the wipers to counter the water spraying across the windscreen. With no view to speak of around the tanker's fat, swaying rear end, and not enough room to go round it, she was having to drive blind and trust the convoy didn't stop without warning.

'Ease back gradually,' advised Harry. 'He won't argue.'

She did so, gradually fighting to regain some space between them and the tanker. It was a risky undertaking but Harry was gambling on the driver behind not wanting to cause a pile-up. The manoeuvre worked; the driver suddenly gave up and dropped back, giving them room.

Clare dropped her window and gave a friendly wave. The other driver didn't respond at first, then he grinned and waved back.

Ten minutes later the convoy came to a fork in the road.

The trucks in front were all bearing right, heading towards high ground.

The hills.

'Which way?' said Clare. 'Left? It must be left.'

Harry checked the map. Damn. She was right. If they stayed with the cover of the convoy, they would end up in the hills, miles from the airport and with no obvious way back other than down this same road. If there were other routes, this map didn't include them.

The road to the left looked very empty.

'Left or right – come on!'

'Left,' he confirmed, and held on as she swung the wheel and shot out from the line of trucks. She let the Toyota run on for a hundred yards to make sure they were clear, then halted at the side of the road. The rest of the convoy roared on by, horns tooting and men weaving at this minor break in their day, leaving behind a heavy cloud of dust settling on the damp windscreen.

At Harry's insistence, they checked their weapons and took a drink. He estimated from the map that they had just over ten miles to go before they reached the main airport road. From that point, the perimeter fence would be in sight, as would the army patrolling its length.

But that ten miles consisted mostly of deserted countryside through low hills and wooded areas. Ripe terrain for an ambush.

'Let's go,' he said, and wound down the window, signalling for the others to do the same. Closed windows gave a false sense of invulnerability and flying splinters from a gunshot would only add to their problems.

The first three miles took them along a looping, dusty switchback, mostly single-track with poor verges and a scattering of straggly bushes on either side. Nowhere looked good for an ambush. An occasional farm showed far back in the fields, but they saw nobody, passed no other vehicles. It was like being on the moon.

'*Shit!*' They were rounding a gradual curve with a dip in the road when Clare swore and stamped hard on the brakes, the rear of the car fishtailing wildly.

A white horse was lying in the road, the broken arms of a

hay cart half under its body. Nearby lay the crumpled form of an elderly man, eyes turned sightlessly at the sky.

'Keep going!' Harry shouted, hand braced against the dashboard. There was a widening pool of blood beneath the man's head and the horse had a bright a smear of red down its muzzle.

'But he might be alive!' Clare protested. She lifted her foot off the pedal and the car began to slow.

As it did so, the first bullet struck.

FIFTY-NINE

The shot tore through the windscreen, leaving a ragged hole, and blew out Clare's head-rest in an explosion of foam and fabric. She cried shrilly with shock but retained her grip on the wheel.

Latham.

'Go, *go!*' Harry tried to see where the shot had come from. There were two clumps of trees in front of them, and an outcropping of rocks. Both had been hidden by the bend in the road. Latham was clever; any of them would have been good firing points, invisible until it was too late to turn back. Shooting the horse and farmer merely helped finalize the set-up. But Latham would have gone for the best cover available; cover to allow him to blend in so he could wait patiently until he took his shot; surroundings that would also allow a safe evacuation afterwards. Rocks were good, but too consistent in shape and colour. They didn't provide a camouflaged background the way trees did.

A loud clang and another bullet struck, this time ripping a hole in the bonnet and kicking off flecks of paint and a chunk of bodywork.

The clump of trees to their right was high, and well away from the road. But there didn't appear to be any direct access that Harry could see. He dismissed it; the position was too high. From up there, the shot would have hit the seat at a sharper angle and would have killed Clare instead.

Latham was playing with them.

A loud bang followed by an explosion of glass, this time through the upper corner of the windscreen close to Harry's head. He ducked instinctively and felt ridiculous. Too bloody late for that!

Another bullet buried itself directly into the radiator, and this time they felt the impact go all the way through the vehicle.

The engine stuttered; kicked in again as Clare stamped on the accelerator; ran for a few seconds, then died. Steam began billowing out from under the bonnet, cloaking the windscreen and clouding their view.

'Out!' Harry shouted, and reached for the door catch as Clare braked hard. He hit the ground running and aimed two fast shots at the clump of trees, then rolled into a depression at the side of the road. He landed in a heap, half-winded, and looked up at the sky, regaining his breath. Then he rolled over and faced forward.

The tops of the trees where the shooter was firing from were just visible, the thinner branches waving in the breeze. Unless the man was a monkey and wanted to risk climbing to the top, they were protected. But for how long?

'Clare? Rik? You OK?' He kept his voice low.

Two responses, both lively, and accompanied by oaths. A good sign.

He checked his gun and considered what to do. Their options didn't look good. Either Latham would come looking to finish them off before anyone else happened along, or he'd play safe after last night's exchange of gunfire and wait for them to show their heads.

And take them out one by one.

A shot hit the road surface ten feet to Harry's right, kicking up chunks of gravel and tarmac. It ricocheted off into the distance like an angry hornet, mashed out of shape by the impact.

A warning shot.

Harry checked his watch. Time was running out. If they managed to slip away but missed the French flight, they might be lucky enough to get another. But Latham would be right behind them.

And right now, their only means of transport was sitting uselessly in the road, leaking fluids.

Footsteps.

Harry froze. He was coming for them.

He peered out over the rise in the ground in front of him. A tall, thin figure was walking casually along the road towards them. He wore a dark combat jacket and blue jeans, and carried an assault rifle in one hand, the barrel pointing forward. For a man who knew they were armed, he seemed absurdly relaxed and unconcerned about any possible retaliation.

Harry studied the man's face. Felt a glimmer of recognition. Was it the man he recognized or was it the type he'd seen too often before?

Whatever. The rifle said it all.

Harry rolled sideways, aiming to reach dead ground away from the road and Latham's direct line of sight. If he could get on his flank unseen, he'd be able to—

A shot rang out and kicked up earth a foot to his left.

He froze. Latham could see him; probably not completely, but enough to know when he moved.

'Stand up!' It was a voice accustomed to giving orders. Cold, unemotional.

Harry got to his feet, the gun concealed behind his leg.

Latham had stopped thirty yards away, the rifle barrel lifting. Too far away for a handgun, Harry thought distractedly. But easy meat for a rifle.

Latham knew it, too. He had a trace of a smile on his face.

Harry flicked his eyes sideways to see if he could spot Rik or Clare. But they were nowhere to be seen.

It was a tight situation, and not merely for them. If Latham opened fire on Harry, he'd be exposing his side for the brief seconds it took to aim and pull the trigger. It would be long enough to allow Clare and Rik to take him out and Latham would know that.

Harry watched the rifle barrel lifting towards him, and got ready to throw himself sideways. He wondered how much time Clare had put in on the combat course with a hand-gun.

Nothing like enough, if Latham was all he was supposed to be.

SIXTY

'It's not going well, I grant you. But it will.' Sir Anthony Bellingham stared out over the river towards Westminster and lit a cigar. The dawn was slow in rising, and a cold wind was scything across the water, chopping the tops of the waves into droplets of spray. He puffed on the cigar until it was burning satisfactorily and glanced sideways at George Paulton. The MI5 man was chewing on a fingernail and looked miserable with worry and cold.

They were alone apart from Sir Anthony's bodyguard standing thirty yards away. It was too soon in the day for the area to be populated by anyone other than those with secrets on their minds, so there was little chance of anyone coming too close.

'So you said.' Paulton didn't sound comforted.

'Come on, George, for Christ's sake!' Bellingham spat out a mouthful of smoke. 'You knew this venture was risky, same as I did. It's what we do, isn't it? It's what gets the blood racing. Is for me, anyway.'

'I could do without it, thank you.' Paulton's voice was barely registering. 'You said this was controllable; that you had them watched twenty-four-seven, over and above my watch team. So how is it they've all disappeared into the woodwork apart from Mace? Is your man going to find them or not?'

'He's not bloody Superman, George. There's the added problem of the Russians to cope with . . . and Tate's not helping. Where in God's name did you pick him up, by the way? The man's a frigging menace.'

'Does it matter now?' Paulton resented the accusatory tone, implying that this was, by implication of who he employed, entirely down to him.

'I suppose not.' Bellingham spat out a fragment of tobacco. 'Do you know what the people in Red Station call your watch team, George? Did I ever tell you?'

'Is it relevant?'

'Very. They refer to them as the Clones. Shows how seriously they're taken, doesn't it? Clones. They were supposed to be invisible; unidentifiable. But guess who went out of his way to identify the current batch by drawing them out? Harry Tate, that's who. Drew them out and painted them with a giant bloody cross.'

Paulton said nothing, but stared down at the grey water. He felt sick.

'Did you hear, by the way,' Bellingham continued, his voice like poisoned silk, 'that one of your Clones ran into trouble?'

'Yes. He got dragged into a local argument. He'll be back as soon as he can get a flight out.' Paulton's tone was flat, resentful.

'Is that what the team leader told you – that he'd be coming back? I wouldn't bet your braces on it.'

Paulton's head snapped round. 'What do you mean?'

Bellingham tapped ash from his cigar on to the wall, where the wind picked it up and rolled it over the edge into the water. 'Seems your man – name of Stanbridge, by the way – got bounced while searching Tate's flat. Bit careless of him, I thought.' He smiled. 'Not that he lived to regret it.'

'*What?*'

'He's dead, George. As cold mutton. Last seen in a flat rented out to an Italian David Bailey who's been taken into custody for spying . . . or something close to it. Tate moved the body down there after it'd been turned over by the local security police. Clever chap; quick on his feet for an old 'un. Should have recruited him myself, then maybe we wouldn't be in this God-awful mess.'

'How do you know all this – and why wasn't I told?' Paulton was quivering with a mixture of rage, fear and the chill coming off the river. 'I don't believe it – Tate's not a killer.'

'Bollocks.' Bellingham had had enough. He tossed his cigar into the water and turned up his coat collar. 'Everyone's a killer if you press the right buttons. Stanbridge didn't top himself, did he? Don't worry about it, George. It's all in hand. Latham has his orders. If he doesn't get them in town, he'll do it before they leave the country. One, two, three, out.'

He turned and walked away, leaving George Paulton fuming impotently.

SIXTY-ONE

atham's eyes were blank; plain dark flints in an unemotional face. He was gaunt, with bony cheeks and a scrub of mousy brown hair over a wide forehead. Standing there, relaxed and in control, he could have been an athlete waiting for his next event.

Except for the assault rifle.

'They don't come out,' Latham said easily, loud enough for the others to hear, 'I shoot you. Then I go looking for them.'

'Is that your assignment?' Harry asked. 'To terminate us?' He blinked hard. He was sure he'd seen something moving in the background, some way behind Latham. Wishful thinking, maybe? Or a hallucination?

'Something like that.' Latham glanced away and lifted his voice. 'Come on – I don't have much patience! Out here, both of you!'

Harry watched the barrel of the assault rifle. He was trying not to focus on the flicker of movement he'd seen by the side of the road. It had come from the same point where Latham must have emerged from the trees. Had he got help after all?

If it was Clare or Rik, what could they do? They'd have to be quick.

'Orders from Bellingham, is it?' Harry forced Latham to look at him, to draw his attention away. 'Or was it Paulton? Has to be one of them, although I can't see Paulton authorizing someone like you.'

Latham lifted one eyebrow and the rifle moved an inch. 'Careful, Tate. You really shouldn't be rude, not in your position. Getting gut-shot can be very painful, so I'm told.' He feigned a yawn. 'But you're right: Paulton hasn't got the balls.'

Harry tensed his body and gripped the semi-automatic even tighter. It occurred to him that Latham must know he was still armed. So why hadn't he ordered him to drop his weapon? A random shot from a handgun could still kill you, even over thirty yards. Or was the man so arrogant that he was beyond all caution?

The muzzle of the assault rifle flashed briefly, and the sound of the shot rolled away into the open countryside. Harry felt a sharp tug at his left arm, then he was spinning away, a mixture of messages relayed to his brain and informing him that he'd been hit and that pain was sure to follow.

He dropped to one knee, a stone gouging sharply against the bone, and felt the first wave of agony stitch across his upper body. A flesh wound, he told himself, and felt an impulse to giggle. A Monty Python movie. *Only a flesh wound.* Bloody hell, it was still flesh – and it hurt!

'One thing I've always been good at,' said Latham chattily, 'is weaponry. I was a sniper for a bit, in the first Gulf job. Got bored, though. Like shooting ducks off a plank. No real challenge. This is much better.'

There was a movement to Harry's right, and Clare Jardine climbed to her feet. Six feet further on, Rik did the same. They both held their guns pointed at Latham.

Shit! Harry wished they'd stayed down. They were too far off for accurate shooting, and if they were hoping Latham would freak out, they were wrong. He eased the gun in his palm and got ready to move. He'd get one chance and one chance only.

There was another movement, this time behind Latham. And much closer. A figure loomed up, seeming to float above the ground. It closed in on the killer, as silent as smoke. Then came a faint scuff of sound, of leather on tarmac.

Latham sensed the threat like the hunter he was. He began to turn his head, mouth opening in surprise. The rifle barrel wavered.

He was alone after all.

The figure behind him suddenly became clear.

Nikolai.

The Russian moved with the precision of a dancer, weaving slightly to stay out of Latham's line of sight. He covered the last few feet in a rush, then he was on the killer like a wraith, one arm wrapping around his head, clamping him rigidly in place, the other swinging round and up beneath the ribs with a deadly flash of silver.

He's a cutter, if ever I saw one. Mace's words came back to Harry.

Latham's mouth opened wide, his eyes stared uncomprehendingly at Harry as the improbable happened.

A grunt from both men and another thrust of the knife. A muffled thump as it was driven home. Latham reared up on his toes, chest thrust outward in pain, a brief, almost balletic move that was over even as it began. He coughed once.

Then his eyes fluttered. And closed.

He was dead before his body hit the ground.

'You should go. Now.' Nikolai kicked some brushwood over Latham's body. Under his instructions they had dragged it in among the trees, to a small depression in the ground. Moments before, he had wiped his blade on the dead man's combat jacket, then searched the body for anything that might identify him.

'These should not be left here.' He handed a wallet and a passport to Harry. Nikolai's accent was noticeable, but the English was fluent, confident.

Harry passed his gun to Clare, took the documents and put them in his pocket.

'Why did you do this?' he asked. He wondered how the Russian had got here. He must have followed them . . . or Latham.

'Because it would not be helpful if you or your colleagues came to harm here.' The eyes were without expression, cold. . Then he said, echoing Kostova's words, 'We have enough problems without your Foreign Office asking questions about missing . . . tourists.' There was no humour in the deliberate euphemism.

Harry nodded. 'Thank you. What now?'

'His car is behind the trees. Take it and go. I will take care of the rest.'

'How did you know about him?'

Nikolai shrugged. 'It is not important. Go.' He turned and walked away, and was soon lost behind the trees.

Harry took a deep breath as a wave of nausea overtook him. The wound in his arm was beginning to throb. He signalled to the others to collect everything from the Toyota, then led them through the trees and out the other side to where a battered Hyundai off-road vehicle stood waiting. It had a smashed headlamp and side window, with bullet holes in the bonnet and wing. Not bad shooting, he reflected. Especially in the dark and under pressure. Pickering, his first weapons instructor, would have been proud.

'We need to get rid of the guns,' he said, and leaned against the car, sucking in air. Nikolai was a hundred yards away by some bushes, shrugging on a camouflage jacket. A crash helmet lay at his feet and a glint of metal showed through the leaves.

He'd come by trail bike.

Clare stared at Harry. 'Are you OK?'

'Yes. Just tired, that's all.' He checked the rear of the vehicle in case it contained anything incriminating. *As if*, he thought wryly, *anything could be more incriminating than a car riddled with bullets*. He wanted to throw up but decided it would be very uncool right now. Concentrating on something mundane would take his mind off it.

He found a small holdall tucked away under a waterproof sheet. Inside was a change of clothes, a wash-kit and a plastic Ziploc bag. Just as he'd hoped: Latham believed in travelling prepared for emergencies. The Ziploc contained a miniature trauma pack, with enough bandages and dressings to keep his injured arm protected until he got back to England. Or fell over trying.

He joined Rik in the back seat and dumped the Ziploc in his lap. 'Read the instructions and play nurse, and I'll promise not to scream.' He pulled back his sleeve and revealed the blood on his arm.

'What? *Christ, man* . . .!' Rik looked horrified, but took the bag and found a pair of scissors. He cut away Harry's sleeve and exposed the wound, and Harry saw he was missing a small chunk of flesh. But no broken bones.

That was OK, he decided. It was a flesh wound after all.

Then he fainted clean away.

SIXTY-TWO

Six hours later, they were in a hire car heading north on the A1 to Calais.

Getting on board the Air France evacuation flight had been without incident. Anxious to get all foreign nationals away as quickly as possible, the authorities had ensured that passport control had been brief. Isabelle was waiting, checking people in against a list. At Rik's request, she had vouched for Clare as an extra passenger, and allowed them to consign their rucksacks to cargo baggage.

The wait in the departure lounge had been short, during which all eyes were fixed on the military vehicles patrolling the perimeter. Then they were ushered on to the plane surrounded by French security personnel and accompanied by a variety of other nationals, all keen to get out of the way of impending trouble. One of them, a Swiss doctor, had seen blood on Harry's sleeve, and insisted on bandaging his wound.

'You were fortunate,' he said with great cheerfulness. 'Another two centimetres and you would have maybe lost the arm. The concussive effect on bone can be like an amputation.'

'Thanks for that,' Harry replied, wincing. 'You don't do house calls, do you?'

'For you, I am afraid not. But you must have this checked . . . wherever you are going next. Each day, you understand?'

Harry nodded gratefully and sank back in his seat, closing his eyes. He was bewildered by the narrowness of their escape, thanks to Nikolai, and their safe arrival at the airport.

Latham's battered Hyundai was now concealed behind a large skip at one end of the airport car park, where it would hopefully remain undetected for several days. The guns had been disposed of in a silage pit barely a mile along the road from where they had buried Latham's body.

After arriving in Paris and retrieving their bags, they had dodged the inevitable press scramble and hired a car. Harry decided that an unobtrusive entry via the channel ports was safer than Heathrow or Eurostar. Clare elected to drive and they headed towards Calais.

As they passed the Amiens–Compiegne intersection, Harry took out Stanbridge's mobile. He dialled Maloney's number and wondered if his colleague's phone was on the watch list.

'Yes?' Maloney answered against a background buzz of traffic. He was on foot in the open. He sounded cautious.

'Can you talk?' said Harry.

'Bloody hell! I was getting worried. Where are you?'

'France, heading for the next available ferry. Can you meet us in Dover?'

'Sure can. Ring me when you know the time.' He paused and Harry could tell he was choosing his words carefully. 'All hell's breaking loose here. Word got out that some British nationals got caught up in the stampede across the border, and we're all wondering who. Funny thing is, in-house, your name's top of the pile.'

'How did that get out?'

'Don't know. Could be someone laying a trail in case it goes public. Is there anyone with you?'

'Two. One stayed behind to look after things. Another went native.' Harry decided to leave the news about Mace until later.

'Right. You sound like you had a bad time. You all right?' Maloney had clearly picked up something in Harry's tone of voice.

'Fine. Got a graze on the arm, that's all.'

'The opposition playing rough?'

'Not theirs. One of ours. I'll tell you more when I see you. Can you look out a name for me?'

'Sure. Go ahead.'

'Latham. Not sure of other names. He worked for Legoland.' The nickname for MI6.

There was a longer pause. 'Did you say *worked*?'

'He resigned.'

'Ouch. That'll cause a rumpus.'

'He was trying to resign us at the time.'

'Oh. Well, that's different. What happened?'

'He ran into an unfriendly Russian.'

'I hear there are some about. Well, take care and see you soon.'

Harry switched off the phone and sat back. His arm was throbbing fiercely, a relentless ache which reached down to his fingertips and burned across his shoulders. He nudged Rik and handed him the trauma pack, gritting his teeth while the young man removed his soiled bandage and cleaned the wound.

'We need to get this looked at,' said Rik. He applied a fresh dressing and wrapped the arm firmly to avoid excess movement, then folded the dirty bandages into a plastic bag. He passed Harry two tablets and a bottle of water. 'Swallow these. You're going to have a bit of a hole there now.'

'Damn.' Harry downed the tablets and leaned his head against the seat rest. 'Bang go my chances of being a male model.'

He closed his eyes and let sleep take him.

'Harry! Wake up!'

'Wha—? What's the matter?' Harry scrambled to sit up, shocked out of a heavy sleep by Rik's voice and a hand pounding on his good arm. He felt awful; his mouth was dry and his head was spinning. He peered through the side window. They were on the *autoroute*, with the flat, muddy fields of northern France rolling by outside. It looked grey, cold and unwelcoming. Foreign.

'We've got company.' It was Clare Jardine's hand on his arm. She was in the front passenger seat, looking past him at the road behind. They had clearly managed to make a changeover without waking him.

'OK . . . I'm with it. Who?'

'Three men in a big Renault. They've been there for about five miles now. They've been hanging back most of the time – we thought it was just a coincidence. But now they've started moving closer.'

Harry turned and peered over the back of his seat. A dark blue Renault was a hundred yards behind on the inside lane. He counted the outlines of three figures inside. Other traffic was sporadic, a few trucks but mostly cars and the odd motorbike. Only the Renault was keeping station with them.

He drank some water, hoping to dull the growing nausea. He was dehydrated and suffering shock; hardly best conditions for dealing with another threat.

So who were they?

'Could be DST,' said Clare, reading his mind. 'Making sure we leave.' The *Direction de la Surveillance du Territoire* – France's counter-espionage department – were responsible along with the police for their country's internal security. It was a job they took very seriously.

'Could be Latham's mates.' Rik was gripping the wheel tightly, eyes fixed on the road ahead.

'Let's not get ahead of ourselves. It could be anybody.' Harry

rubbed his face with his good hand, trying to coax some life
into the skin and get his brain in gear. He was also playing
for time and inspiration. If the men were French Intelligence,
they might be following them because of their presence on the
Air France evacuation flight. Orders would almost certainly
have gone ahead prior to take-off as a matter of normal security, alerting Paris to the identities and backgrounds of all
foreign nationals on board. And Rik's young friend Isabelle
would have been duty bound to pass on what she knew about
them.

If the people in the car weren't DST, but were part of the
Hit, they were in trouble. With no weapons and little chance
of avoiding a direct attack, the odds were heavily against
them.

He took another look. The Renault had crept closer. The
front-seat passenger was heavy-set, with a shaved scalp and
black eyebrows. He was holding a mobile to his ear and
nodding, leaning forward with his face close to the windscreen.
He took the phone away from his ear and said something to
the driver.

The Renault accelerated and began to pull out.

Harry watched the move and felt his gut contract. 'They're
coming alongside.' He kept his voice casual and reached
forward to touch Rik's shoulder, hoping to instil in him a
sense of calm. 'Hold your speed steady but get ready to brake
hard when I say.'

'Brake?' Rik's voice wobbled. 'Wouldn't it be better to
outrun them?'

'No. This is their turf and we don't have the punch.' Harry
didn't know how powerful the other vehicle was, but instinct
told him that it would be an unequal contest. Besides, if they
were French law enforcement or Intelligence officers, it would
provide just the reason they needed to pull them over.

The other car drew alongside and remained level. The
two passengers turned their heads to stare. Harry glanced
across. Bullet Head in the front was replicated by the other
passenger in the rear, a perfect pair, while the driver was a
skinnier version with a bony forehead. None of them looked
friendly, and they all reminded Harry of the security guards
he had seen outside the SARFA building where Isabelle
worked.

He caught the eye of one of the men and smiled. *Bonjour*, he thought. *Now piss off, mes amis.*

He realized he was holding his breath and tried to relax. Just as long as the side windows stayed up. That was all he asked. Windows up meant everything was normal; windows down meant they were about to go on the offensive.

The man in the front passenger seat lifted his chin at Harry in a mute query. *What are you looking at?*

Harry lifted his water bottle in a silent salute. If the three men weren't interested in them it would mean nothing. If they were . . . well, it wouldn't matter much.

The Renault surged away. Two hundred yards ahead, as they approached a junction, the driver began signalling.

Moments later, they were gone.

Harry slumped back and closed his eyes. He could have done without that. His head was pounding and he felt like shit.

In the front, Rik gave a soft whoop and Clare muttered in relief.

'Bloody kids,' he murmured. 'Scaredy-cats.' Then he went back to sleep.

SIXTY-THREE

It was mid-afternoon before they boarded the first ferry and watched through the window of the forward bar as the grey French coast slipped away. The boat was busy, with the aisles and bars full of foot passengers on day trips and vehicle passengers looking weary after long drives across France.

Clare had been getting more and more restless the closer they got to home, and was drumming her fingers on the table. She had changed into fresh black cargo pants and a dark T-shirt, and apart from an increasing look of unease, could have been a student on vacation.

'So what's the plan?' she queried shortly, eyeing Harry. 'I take it you've got one?'

Harry shrugged. The movement was a painful reminder of his injury and he adjusted his position before replying.

'Nothing specific. Haven't figured it all out yet. I want to get back on home soil first. Then we'll see.'

'We?'

'Why not? We can hardly just walk back into work and clock on. It'll need all of us to put up a front. Someone's got some explaining to do.'

'They won't listen. Why should they?'

'Someone has to.' Rik sounded unconvinced, but seemed happy to lean on hope against despair. 'Maybe we should hook up with the press as a guarantee.' He looked at Harry. 'What do you think?'

'It might be an option. But I think we'll need more than that. We need to go to someone with enough clout to take positive action. Mace gave me a name – a woman on the Joint Security Committee.' Harry looked at him. 'She'll have influence and she's accountable. Get to her and it'll go higher. Leave it to Bellingham and Paulton, and they'll stamp on it – and us. Red Station will be airbrushed out of existence and we'll have no protection.'

'This is mad, what you're suggesting.' Clare interrupted harshly. She was staring balefully at a small girl wailing at the next table. 'Once they have us, we won't see the light of day. They can't afford to let Red Station become public knowledge; they've already had too much mud slung at them over de Menezes and the terrorist arrests. Can't you see that?'

Harry studied her, wondering whether she had only just come to this conclusion or if she had been aware right from the start that going back might not be as easy as she hoped. He still wasn't convinced about her reasons for allegedly trying to get documents from Kostova. Had she really been working him and Nikolai, and hoping to get back in favour with MI6 or did she suspect what might really happen if they strolled back into town?

Rik let out a deep sigh. 'I'm for trying to sort it out. I don't want to be on the run forever.' He toyed with a button before continuing. 'Having guys like Latham on my back.' He shook his head in wonder. 'What kind of bloke sets out to waste his own side? And what kind of people employ guys like him? He was going to drop us. If Nikolai hadn't come along, we'd be—'

'Don't worry about it.' Harry cut him off before he could get going. 'Forget Latham. Forget Nikolai. They're history, done. Just concentrate on the days ahead. Maloney will help us.'

But the mention of Latham had struck a chord in Harry's head. It was a good question. How was a man able to turn and kill his own, with no more hesitation than it took to swat a fly? Did soldiering do that to you if you stuck at it long enough? But he knew that wasn't it. He'd known hundreds of soldiers who had served long and dangerous careers, and they would have no more done what Latham did than flown to the moon. So what, then?

His brain was spinning from the accumulated effects of exhaustion, shock from the bullet wound and their enforced flight. Even so, some thoughts kept slipping through, like fragments of hard matter dropping through holes in a net. And the more that happened, the more they began to coagulate into something concrete.

Rik had been at home the night Stanbridge had died; Harry had seen movement through the window, of that he was certain. He glanced at Clare, who was still staring at the noisy child, her face set. When he'd returned to check on the area around her flat, the place had been in darkness, and he'd assumed she was tucked up in bed.

But was she?

Would an experienced MI6 officer calmly climb into bed after seeing armed men outside her flat? Would she have done so knowing that a colleague was in the vicinity and might drop by to check she was all right?

Except that she had deliberately asked him not to because of the neighbours. Was that the only reason?

And then there was Latham. If the MI6 assassin had been in town that night, why did he leave it for another three days to do something about the people he'd been sent to eliminate? He knew who they were, where they lived and worked. Making a surgical hit, with no footprints left behind, would have been a priority. Waiting three days made no sense.

Unless Kostova had lied about Latham's arrival.

He reached in his pocket and took out Latham's passport and wallet. Everything in it was in the name of Graham John Phillips, with an address in Walthamstow. Driver's licence,

two credit cards, paper money, a couple of petrol receipts –
even a lender's card for the local library. There was a photo
of Latham with a woman and a child. Harry suspected they
were fakes, part of Latham's cover or legend. Attention to
detail; it was something MI6 was good at.

No return air ticket, though. Nothing to show how or when
he was moving on. Maybe it was the way Latham preferred
to operate, taking whatever means of travel came to hand
according to circumstances.

He sensed he was under scrutiny. He looked up. Clare was
watching him. She glanced at the wallet and papers on the
table, but said nothing and looked away.

'Excuse me.' She stood up and grabbed her rucksack, then
walked out of the bar.

Harry watched her go. Her body was rigid with tension,
but she was light on her feet, like an athlete about to face a
tough challenge. He noticed a length of cord hanging from
one of the side pockets of her rucksack. He wondered what
she used it for. A make-do washing line, probably. He'd done
the same many times when staying in fleapit hotels with no
facilities—

He sat bolt upright, the movement jarring his arm. The
washing line.

It was Clare who had told the others in the office about
Stanbridge's death; how Harry had tied him to the bathroom
sink . . . with a clothesline. It hadn't registered at the time, his
mind too focussed on the man's death. Now it had come back
and was staring him in the face.

He had untied Stanbridge's body and disposed of the clothesline *before* Clare arrived. How could she have known about
the clothesline?

He stared after her, a leaden feeling growing in his stomach.
He recalled Fitzgerald's words on the phone. *Watch the girl,
though; I think she's bad.*

There was only one way she could have known.

Clare had been inside his flat. Seen Stanbridge.

Killed him.

He ran through the sequence of events, his tiredness gone.
The moment he had rung her and told her about capturing the
Clone, she must have been desperate to find out whether

the man knew her real role in Red Station: that she was the inside source of information.

It explained something else: when she heard Harry was planning to question him, she'd told him that the men outside her flat were armed – a guarantee that he would take it seriously enough to go and see for himself. Yet Stanbridge had been adamant that they did not carry weapons. It also explained why Clare hadn't wanted Harry to call on her. Trained to think on her feet, she'd already been planning to leave her flat and go to Harry's. With him out of the way watching the other men, she had a clear field to quiz Stanbridge and find out what he knew . . . and how much he'd told Harry.

Then she had silenced him.

Something else slipped into place. When he'd called her after finding Stanbridge's body, she had sounded breathless. Why breathless if she had been sleeping?

Because she wasn't at home. He'd called her on her mobile. No wonder she had arrived so quickly – she was already out and on the move!

He waited for her to return, chewing it over and coming to the same conclusion every time. He would have to face her with it. It wouldn't be pretty right here – there were too many people about. They'd have to go up on deck, somewhere quiet. But it had to be done before they got to London.

Thirty minutes later, there was still no sign of her.

Rik said, 'She's been gone a long time.'

'Too long,' Harry agreed. He added, 'That bag that arrived for me from London.'

Rik nodded. 'What about it?'

'Did Clare ever get one?'

Rik thought about it. 'I never saw one.' He paused. 'But she had some ammo. One dropped out of her bag once.' He shrugged. 'I put it back. Figured it was above my pay grade, stuff like that.'

Harry stood up. 'You take the sharp end, I'll do the rest. Check everywhere, including the washrooms.'

'I'll get arrested.'

'So improvise.'

They split up. Harry found the nearest washrooms and asked

a female member of staff to check on his lady colleague. He gave her a description. Black cargo pants, dark T-shirt, athletic build, no make-up.

The woman came back out shaking her head.

'There's only a few kids in there,' she told him. 'Are you sure she came to this one?'

'No, not really. Maybe I got it wrong.'

'You could try the ones on D deck. They're not so busy.'

Harry was about to leave when he glanced down at the woman's hand. She was holding a flat plastic case in one hand. It looked new. 'What's that?'

She glanced down. 'Oh, I found this by the sinks. Someone's going to be kicking themselves; they're new on sale in the shop today. It's a travel make-up kit . . . hardly used.'

Harry took it off her and opened it. She was right – it was barely touched and the mirror was clean. Every woman's compact he'd ever seen had been a mess.

Make-up. Appearance. *Disguise*.

Harry thanked the woman and handed back the compact, then toured the rear half of the boat on all decks. He scoured the bars, the cafeteria, the cinema and the restaurant, and went out on the open deck, checking the club-style chairs and the plastic deck seats. He was looking for a new face.

Still Clare Jardine's face, but no longer plain.

He eventually returned to where they had been sitting. Rik was back, looking worried. 'I checked everywhere. Can't find her.'

Harry nodded. 'Me too.' There was no doubt about it.

Clare Jardine had done a runner.

SIXTY-FOUR

Bill Maloney was waiting at Dover in a mud-spattered Volvo. The former Royal Marine was wrapped in a waterproof jacket, with heavy rain clouds milling overhead like horses in a corral. The ground around the vehicle was awash with puddles, but he seemed immune to the conditions.

Where the hell, thought Harry, trudging to meet him, are the blue clouds everyone raves about?

Maloney gave a sketchy wave, then looked around quizzically. 'I thought there were three of you.'

'There were. One pulled out,' said Harry. He told him about Clare's disappearing act.

'Why would she do that?'

'I don't know. Could be she knows she'll never get back in. She even tried to get a set of false papers. I think she's been planning this for a while. Either way, she's cooked.'

If Clare was still on board, she had found somewhere secure to hide. With a change of clothes and make-up, it wouldn't be difficult for someone with her training to latch on to a friendly face and hitch a ride.

Unless she had jumped. But he didn't believe that.

'Gone native, you think?' Maloney meant had she gone over to the opposition.

'No. I think she decided to get lost for good.'

Maloney shrugged and got in. He drove them towards London, one eye on the speed limit and waiting for them to talk.

'You got somewhere to stay?' he asked Harry, as they took the M20 towards Swanley and Lewisham.

'I know a hotel. It's good for now.'

Maloney looked at Rik. 'How about you?'

Rik shook his head. 'I'll stay with my mum. She's moved twice since I got tabbed, so she should be OK.'

'Fair enough.' He glanced at Harry. 'Listen, there's stuff I have to tell you about the Essex thing.'

'Go on.'

'I did some digging. There's been a lot of chaff thrown out about the shooting, how it all went shit-shaped. It bugged me how those two kids managed to penetrate the cordon.'

'Me too. There was a hole.' It was the only explanation. But what sort of hole?

'That's the thing. I know a guy whose brother is in the local armed response unit. He was on the team supposed to be covering that track. He says they were told to stand down about two hours before the ETA.'

Harry breathed a lengthy sigh. There was the answer. 'Why?'

'Same old thing: budgets. Someone decided it didn't need

that number of bodies to intercept one small boat.' He shrugged. 'There was also a PM's visit at Stansted Airport the following morning. They needed a show of strength because of protests against expansion plans. It left Red Three short of men. No way could he keep it secure.'

Fuck. Harry felt sick with anger. Budgets and political face.

'There's something else.' Maloney sounded sombre. 'Colin Parrish – the dead copper? He was new. That gig was his first ever. They sicked us with a newbie. Can you believe it?'

Harry shook his head. After what he'd been through, he was ready to believe anything. Another screw-up to be swept clean and sanitized. And for what?

'Have they found out how the dead kids got there?'

'Not so far. But with the team cut back it left holes all over. I reckon the pick-up team got out the same way.'

Harry thought about the two dead civilians. Killed because they had stumbled into the wrong place at the wrong time. Someone had to pay for that. And Parrish; a young copper who had more vim than sense. He re-ran the scene though his mind. Parrish had run out probably counting on using the arrival of the Land Rover as a distraction, or to draw fire from the boat. They would never know which. All he'd done was make the men on the boat think the kids in the Land Rover were part of the intercept.

And therefore a target.

Unless . . .

'Who was Red Three?'

'Bloke called Doyle? Why?'

'I tried to raise him when the Land Rover turned up. There was no reply.'

'Could have been a comms breakdown. He was covering a lot of ground that night.'

'Is he any good?'

'Yeah, I'd say so. What do you want him to do?'

'The Met were taking regular aerial shots of the area the day before the bust, right up to the closure of the cordon. I saw a couple during the briefing, when we were going over the approaches. Can you get a look at other copies through Doyle?'

'I suppose so. Not sure what I'd tell him, though. Like you, I'm out of it.'

'Not quite. You can still walk in the building without being

arrested. This is important. Tell him something's been bugging
you about the Land Rover and you can't let go of it. Professional
pride and all that. You don't have to mention me, though.'

'What about it? He's bound to ask.'

Harry shrugged. 'Like how did it get there? A noisy great
Land Rover out of *nowhere*?' He shook his head.

Maloney thought about, then did a double take, nearly slamming into the rear of a truck pulling out with a signal. 'Shit!
You're right. Even with the holes in the cordon, *someone*
would have seen it. But if they didn't drive through the cordon
right then . . .'

'. . . they must have been inside already,' Harry finished. 'Get
the aerials of the track and anywhere that could have housed a
Land Rover. And look at the background on the two kids.'

'I can tell you that now. The girl was Estelle McGuiness,
the daughter of a local chief superintendent.'

'You're kidding!'

'I know. It gets worse. He admitted he'd talked about the
operation at home. His daughter was into birdwatching and
the Wetland Trust activities in a big way, and worried a drugs
bust would upset the birds.'

'So she'd have known when it was going to be shut down.'

'Exactly.' He looked grim. 'Her father's been suspended.'

'And the boyfriend?'

'Nothing. Friends say she'd only recently met him in a local
club and she was besotted. He showed particular interest in
her birdwatching. Apart from that, he's a mystery.'

'Meaning bent – he's got to be.'

'But how do we prove it?'

'There's only one way. We find where that bloody Land
Rover was stashed. After that, it's up to the Met to trace the
boyfriend.' Harry's mind went back to the way the young man
had held up a hand towards the incoming boat. Was it the
gesture of an innocent man seeing the gun – and making a
vain attempt to ward off the shot that followed?

Or a not so innocent man finding himself in the middle of
a police trap and trying to tell his friends on the boat that he
hadn't betrayed them?

It was nearly dark by the time they reached the river in central
London. Rik had already jumped out at New Cross, saying

he would be in touch. Shoulders bunched against the cold and damp, he had merged swiftly with the crowd near the station.

'He doesn't say much,' said Maloney, pulling into the traffic.

'He's in IT. He's been through a steep learning curve. Good, though. Steady under pressure. I trust him.'

'That's enough for me.' Maloney smiled. 'You haven't exactly had a lot of that, have you? Trust.'

Harry didn't say anything. He'd filled Maloney in about Red Station, its members, the Clones, their narrow escape from Latham. Nikolai. With the telling, he was once more feeling drained. And now, with Rik gone, it was as if a string had been broken.

He thought about trust, and those who knew him. 'What's the chatter?' he asked. The security industry was secret, but people still gossiped. The nuts and bolts of the shooting would have got out eventually.

'You were handed a shitty deal,' said Maloney. 'Everyone knows it, too. If you were spotted right now, there's not many would go out of their way to turn you in.'

'Thanks. But it's not them I have to worry about.'

'No, I suppose not.' He started to say something else, then stopped.

'What?' said Harry.

Maloney picked at the steering wheel. 'Whoever's behind all this . . . they'll be seriously worried about you, Harry. You and your mate. You're the bogey who should have stayed in the cupboard.'

'Are you saying I'm on *another* hit list?'

Maloney smiled at the irony in his voice. 'Yeah . . . I suppose you wouldn't be too bothered – not after what you've been through.'

Harry got Maloney to drop him off in Southwark. He knew a small hotel where he could hide for a few days and acclimatize himself once more to the noise and pace of London. With Waterloo station nearby, it provided him with an invaluable melting pot of humanity in which to lose himself should the need arise. All those entrances and exits, crammed with people; he actually felt safer when it was within reach.

Maloney handed him a mobile phone and a slip of paper.

'Pay As You Go disposable,' he said. 'Same as mine. Ring if you need to. And the address of a doctor so you can get your arm looked at. He's five minutes from here and knows not to talk. Mind your back.'

'You, too. Thanks for your help. But stay clear from now on . . . it could be bad for your career.'

SIXTY-FIVE

H arry met Rik the following morning in a burger bar near Waterloo station. He wanted to discuss tactics. He had already visited Maloney's friendly doctor for a change of bandages and a pronouncement that the wound was free of infection.

They found a table against the back wall. Harry had checked the rear and found a fire exit leading down to a narrow side street.

'Is this what it's going to be like?' said Rik, twirling a tall mug of Cola. He sounded depressed. 'Eyes in the back of our heads and frightened to go out anywhere?'

'It doesn't have to be.' Harry tried not to scratch at his arm. It was driving him nuts. 'Not if I can help it.'

'Hope not. My mother's already asking when am I going back to work. She's not used to me being at home like this.'

'It won't be much longer.' Harry sipped his coffee. It was worse than the stuff he'd been drinking in Georgia. At least that brew had a kick to it.

'What are we going to do?'

'Before we left, Mace gave me two names. One is Sir Anthony Bellingham.'

Rik nodded. 'MI6. Something to do with operations.'

'Right. He's the one who set up Red Station . . . also the one who set Latham on us.'

Rik stared down at the table. 'You do pick them, don't you? Who's the other one – the PM?'

'Marcella Rudmann.'

'Oh. Yeah. The one on the Joint Intelligence Committee.'
To Harry's surprise, Rik began to look shifty.

'You've heard of her.'

'Sort of.'

'How sort of?'

Rik shifted awkwardly in his seat. 'She was one of the names I was looking at when I got caught and tabbed.'

Harry chuckled. 'You're kidding.'

'No. I was looking through some operation files to do with Afghanistan and saw her name attached to a JIC note. I wondered who she was, that was all.' He picked at the table with his thumbnail. 'I . . . uh, took a look around her computer files.' He looked abashed. 'She's got a secret boyfriend.'

'So what? It happens, you know – even among politicians. Especially politicians. It's called sex.'

'I know. But she's already in a long-term relationship.'

'I think you need to get out more.'

'With a woman.'

'Ah. Really? That's different.' Harry lifted an eyebrow. Information was power. The only question was, if push came to shove, would he use it? 'Anyone I'd know?'

'Her partner's in politics – a second secretary or something like that. The boyfriend's in pharmaceuticals. Very big.' He shrugged. 'I got out of there quick.'

Harry breathed deeply, his mind working. 'Did you leave a trace?'

'No!' Rik looked affronted.

'Could you get into the files again – if you had to?'

'Of course.'

'Good. For now, get me her home address and phone number.'

'No problem. I'll access the Civil Service Directory.'

Harry nearly laughed. 'It's as simple as that?'

'Well, not quite. There's a gateway to a sub-level directory for specialist contacts; I'll have to go through that first. But it's doable. Why do you need her stuff?'

'Because she's in the right job, powerful, connected and I want to unsettle her. If I just ring her at the office and say "Hi, honey, I'm home" she'll have the Rottweilers on our backs before I put the phone down. I have to get to her in a way that won't get me arrested.'

'Oh. OK.'

'Then there's Bellingham.'

'I was afraid you'd get round to him. He's bad news. His address won't be on file.'

'Probably not. But he's the main mover behind this, along with Paulton. And any time I want him, he'll be in Vauxhall Cross.'

'But you can't go in there.'

'I don't intend to.'

'What, then?'

'I want you to access Clarion.'

'*What?*' Rik nearly overturned his drink and scrambled to rescue it, attracting a scowl from the woman behind the counter. Probably thinks we're discussing a drugs deal, thought Harry.

He handed Rik a tissue. 'Take it easy. We can do this.'

'No way, man – you're nuts!'

'Well, if it's beyond you.' Harry shrugged and began to get up.

'No. Wait . . . I can. I will. Just . . . give me a second.' Rik finished mopping the table and tossed the sodden tissue aside. 'That was a low blow.' He looked genuinely hurt.

'I know.' Harry smiled. 'That's why I said it. You in or not?'

Rik relaxed, mollified. 'OK. I suppose.' He chewed his lip for a few seconds, then said, 'I'll need a laptop – a good netbook would be better – and a list of places where we can hook into the wireless network and move on. When we hit the directory and then Clarion, it'll have to be in short bursts in case they've got a watch on them – and I bet they do.'

Harry took an envelope from his inside pocket and handed it to Rik. If the woman hadn't suspected they were conducting a drugs deal before, she certainly would now. 'There's five hundred in there. Do what you have to and we'll meet up again tomorrow. Can you do it?'

'Easy. I'll pick up a machine and check out some places where we can work.'

'Even better.' Harry was impressed. Rik evidently worked best when he was challenged on his own turf. 'Call me when you're set.'

After Rik had gone, Harry took out a new Pay As You Go mobile and dialled a number from memory. When it was answered, he asked for George Paulton. Time to set the ball rolling.

'Which department is that?' said the operator smoothly.

'Operations.' Harry quoted a six-digit code, part of which was Paulton's extension. He doubted it would still work because the codes were changed on a regular basis. But it might get him past the watchdog on reception.

'I'm sorry, sir, I don't recognize that number. Could I ask who's calling, please?'

'Tell him it's Harry Tate. I'd like to meet.'

'Mr Tate? Just a moment, sir.'

Harry counted to ten, then twenty. Paulton was playing hard to get. Nobody should be faster at answering his phone when a 'hot' name was mentioned. And right now, the name Harry Tate should be melting the wires around the building.

He switched off the mobile and walked outside. An entire system committed to tracing and analysing calls would now be trying to find where the call had originated, triggered by his use of an out-of-date code. He dumped the mobile in a rubbish skip. He had others and would try again.

Next he called Maloney.

'I can't get to Paulton. You heard anything?'

'I was about to call you.' Maloney sounded worried. In the background Harry could hear voices and the shrill ring of telephones.

'What's up?'

'First the good news. I got the aerials. You were right: they show a Land Rover parked all afternoon next to an old boat. It was left in such a way it looked like a write-off . . . doors open and a damaged roof. But in a sweep the following morning, it was gone.'

'Surprise, surprise. It was down by the landing stage. Good vehicle for driving through mud and picking up a load of drugs.'

'Right. Anyway, I spoke to Doyle; he's making noises and they're turning over the area right now, especially the old boat. That's probably where they were hiding.'

'Anything on the boyfriend?'

'Nothing yet. They're still processing his prints. They think he might be foreign – maybe Romanian.'

Harry waited, then said, 'OK. So what's the bad news?'

'Paulton's gone missing.'

SIXTY-SIX

Harry disconnected with Maloney and called Rik Ferris. Whatever he did now, he had to act fast. Without Paulton to lean on, they were at a disadvantage.

'I need Rudmann's direct number,' he said when Rik answered.

'What, now?' Rik sounded unimpressed. 'Christ, what's the rush?'

In the background, Harry heard a woman's voice asking if Rik wanted the printer bundle. Rik's voice faded and said no.

'Our main player in Five has done a runner. I need to shake the tree.' He gave Rik a quick rundown of what Maloney had said.

'You think he's ducked out?'

'I don't know. He either jumped or Bellingham got to him. It means we've lost one of our chances to prove what Red Station was all about. If Paulton chose to go missing, he's gone for good.'

'Give me a few minutes. I'll find a network and call you back.'

Harry waited fifteen minutes. He took the opportunity to find a quiet stretch of pavement where he could walk and talk undisturbed. Any conversations he was about to have would be best conducted privately.

His phone rang. It was Rik.

He read out a number followed by an address. 'The number's her direct line. After you call her, dump the phone; they'll probably have an automatic trace on it.'

'Right. How long will it take to access the server?' He didn't want to use the name Clarion over the phone.

'That'll take a bit longer, and I'll need your help.'

'Me? What do I know about computers?'

'I need you to act as a spotter. Once we start, we might trip over a Guardian – that's an automatic alarm-and-trace system, set up to monitor unauthorized access. If Bellingham's being really clever, he'll have a team on standby ready to jump all over us.'

Harry was in a quandary. He had to speak to Rudmann. According to Mace, she was the only person with the clout who could help him. Anyone else would merely pass the ball. If it reached Bellingham, it was likely to be fatal. But without proof of Bellingham's use of Clarion, and any messages it contained, he would have nothing to convince her that he was telling the truth.

'Where are you now?' He decided to go for Clarion before Bellingham shut it down. 'You ready to do this?'

'Yes. I'm near Piccadilly. Can you head for Maddox Street?'

'Maddox— Jesus, why there?' Maddox Street was a stone's throw from Grosvenor Square, home of the fortress known as the US Embassy. After Thames House, Vauxhall Cross and the headquarters of the Met, it probably housed more police and security officials than anywhere in London.

Rik's voice held a chuckle. 'Traffic. Electronic and people. We can get lost if anyone gets on our tracks. There's a place called Café Risoux. See you there.'

Thirty minutes later, Harry entered the Café Risoux. It was long and narrow, given the illusion of space by large wall mirrors at strategic points. It wasn't yet lunchtime, and held a mixed clientele of young women shoppers, elderly tourists and a few suits, and two men with American accents who were collecting bagged snacks to go. Rik was hunched over a table at the rear, close by the fire exit and staring at the screen of a tiny laptop.

'All set.' Rik waved him to sit. 'I've done some tracking already; he's not as clever as he thinks. I'll be two ticks. Can you get coffee? Americano – four sugars.'

'You'll get nervous and fat.' Harry went to the counter. While his order was being prepared, he checked the street outside. He'd been careful on his way here. The likelihood of being spotted by someone from MI5 was remote, but fate had a habit of turning and biting you when you least expected it.

When he got back to the table, Rik was looking pleased with himself.

'I'm in,' he breathed, and checked the nearest customer, a student type using a laptop two tables away. He pulled a chair round and nodded for Harry to sit, blocking the man's view. Then he bent back to his keyboard.

'What I'm doing,' he explained softly, 'is accessing Clarion, then checking all the outgoing lines to see if I can spot a pattern or a name which looks good. It might take some time.'

'Time we have,' said Harry, and hoped he was right. 'But is it safe?'

'Sure. Unless I trip any of the numbers.'

'How will you know when you've got the right one?'

'By a process of elimination. I reckon he'll have been using the same number all along. It's his set-up, and I bet he didn't share it with anyone else or change his settings.'

Harry drank his coffee while Rik worked, and kept an eye on the room via the wall mirrors. No sign of anyone who didn't look natural.

'Got it.' Rik sounded quietly triumphant. He'd been scribbling numbers and codes on a notepad, and underlined one of them.

'You sure?' Harry read the number. It was an alphanumeric string and made no sense to him at all. 'What the hell is that?'

'It's our way in. But we need to take a chance.'

'Great.'

'Have you got a spare throwaway?'

'Yes.' Harry took it out of his pocket. It was unused.

'Cool. We need to ring the number in the middle of this string.' Rik jabbed the digits he'd noted down. 'It looks like a mobile number, but it's the only one that stands out among the regular callers. I think it's the mobile Bellingham calls from to access Clarion and pick up messages from Red Station.'

Harry glanced sideways. The student sitting two tables away was looking at them. He must have picked up the air of excitement emanating from Rik. When he saw Harry looking, he ducked his head.

'What if this doesn't work?'

'Then we go the other way, into Clarion. That's when we might need to be quick on our feet.'

'Why not do that first?'

'Belt and braces. If we get confirmation it's Bellingham, we know we're on to it. He won't know my voice, and I doubt they'll have it on the voice recognition database. I'll call and pretend to be a misdial, and you listen in case he speaks.'

'But I don't know what his voice sounds like. If he doesn't say his name, we're no further forward.'

'Shit.' Rik looked crestfallen. 'I didn't think of that.'

'Doesn't matter.' Harry handed him the mobile. 'Do it, anyway. We can't sit around here all day.' He checked the mirrors again. The customer turnover was regular, with no-one staying for long. The student was just getting up and leaving.

Rik finished dialling, then plugged in a small pair of earbuds and handed them to Harry.

The number began to ring.

Harry checked the mirrors and adjusted the earbuds. The student was at the counter, talking animatedly to the manager.

They turned and looked at Harry and Rik.

The number kept ringing.

The student scurried out of the door with a backwards glance. The manager picked up a mobile and dialled.

'We've got to go—'

'*Bellingham.*'

SIXTY-SEVEN

'This will do.' Rik stopped in front of a doorway and motioned for Harry to follow. It was a small independent coffee bar in a side street. It carried a notice advertising wireless facility. They were both breathless after leaving the Risoux Café, hurrying past the manager who was shouting into his phone. Harry had heard enough to realize that the man had called the police.

Grabbing a passing cab, they had jumped out near Charing Cross Road, amid a tangle of cafes, restaurants and bookshops.

Rik set up his laptop at a spare table at the rear and dialled the access to Clarion. 'OK, this is where it gets touchy,' he said, flexing his fingers. 'Can you time me for five minutes?'

'OK.' Harry glanced at his watch and kept one eye on the door. He turned and saw a fire escape notice above a narrow stairway in one corner. It would be their escape route if they suddenly got company.

'I'll go in as far as I can,' said Rik. 'But I might trip an alarm. If I do, depending on the level, we'll have anything up to twenty minutes before they come and kick the door in.'

'Do it.'

Harry didn't bother watching the screen as Rik worked; it would mean little to him until Rik accessed the message files – if they still existed – and he didn't need to clog his brain with unwanted information. If they got the messages, it would prove a link between Bellingham and Clarion. What it wouldn't prove was that he had sent Latham to Red Station with instructions to kill. But it was better than nothing. At the very least, it would be enough to put a scare into Bellingham and start an internal enquiry.

'Got it,' Rik hissed. His fingers flew across the keyboard. He was breathing like an athlete, eyes fixed on the screen, and Harry could feel his excitement. It was a small insight into what made hackers tick. 'How are we for time?'

'Edging on four minutes.' He was amazed by the passage of time.

Rik muttered to himself and carried on tapping away before taking out a data stick and plugging it into the side of the laptop. He hit a series of keys then sat back.

He was smiling.

'What are you so happy about?'

'I recognize some of these messages. Mostly from Mace.' He tapped the keyboard. 'Here's one I sent last week. Seems weird being back here now.'

The front door of the café rattled open and two office workers strode in. The sound of a police siren drifted in behind them, distant and fading.

'Christ!' Rik sat forward, jerked out of his bubble of concentration, and reached for the data stick.

'Easy,' cautioned Harry. 'It's moving away.'

Rik relaxed and breathed out. 'If you say so. How much shall I copy?'

'As much as you can . . . names, dates, subjects, whatever proves we were there and that Bellingham was running the operation.' He had a thought. 'Does it include Mace's report about Stanbridge?'

'Yeah, I just saw it. How are we doing for time?'

Harry checked his watch. 'Six minutes gone.'

'We're pushing it.' Rik looked annoyed with himself and explained, 'I may have tripped an alarm on the way in. It's not easy to tell.'

Outside, a car blew by with a roar of a powerful engine. There was a squeal of brakes and someone shouted. The crackle of a radio voice echoed along the street.

'Let's go.' Harry didn't want to push their luck. They had enough to use and he knew they were on borrowed time.

Once they were clear of the area, they stopped off for Rik to copy the files to a second data stick, and for Harry to buy a small jiffy bag and scribble an address on the front. He placed the stick inside with a note, then sealed it and stopped to speak to a motorcycle courier perched on his bike and eating a sandwich. A quick exchange of notes and the courier nodded and dumped his sandwich.

They walked away as the bike took off down the street.

'Right,' said Harry, as they reached Oxford Circus station. 'Go home and get lost. Take your mum out for dinner or something and meet me at the National Gallery at nine tomorrow morning.'

Rik nodded. 'Fine by me. What did you say in that note?'

'I said I'd call her tomorrow at ten with information about a rogue operation involving MI5 and MI6, and a government hit squad.' He smiled. 'A slight exaggeration, that last bit, but it should get her attention.'

SIXTY-EIGHT

'What's the plan?' They were in the cafeteria of the National Gallery at the top of Trafalgar Square, and Rik was restless.

Harry had deliberately chosen the cafeteria as a start point. It was busy, it was anonymous and a short walk from Whitehall. With the usual crowds of tourists and workers in the area, it would make surveillance and pursuit difficult if they had to move quickly.

He checked his watch. Nearly nine. He took out another mobile. 'If this all goes wrong, you know what to do with that other data stick.'

'Yes. Hit the media with the full story, then disappear until the dust settles.' He looked confused. 'You said you'd call her at ten.'

'I lied. Don't worry – she's already there.'

He hit dial and waited for Marcella Rudmann to answer.

'Does he have to be here?' Harry nodded at the security guard standing inside the door. They were in Rudmann's office off Whitehall, and he had been kept waiting no more than thirty seconds before being ushered upstairs. Instead of leaving, the man had stationed himself by the door, six feet from Harry's right shoulder.

'I don't know. You tell me.' Rudmann seemed very calm, he thought, with no obvious signs of concern at having a man she probably looked on as a renegade in her office.

'You think I mean you harm?'

She said nothing, but he thought he saw a faint flicker beneath the skin of one cheek.

'If you think like that,' he said finally, 'you should try changing your routine.'

She frowned. 'What do you mean?'

'You left your flat in Dolphin Square at seven thirty this morning, carrying a burgundy briefcase. Your front door hinges need oiling, by the way. You turned left out of the entrance and left again down St George's Square, accompanied by your minder. He's sloppy; he thinks anyone carrying a cardboard box and waving a delivery note is a driver and therefore to be ignored.'

'You followed me.' She looked shocked. 'How did you know where I lived?'

'I'm in the game, remember? He allowed traffic to get between you when you crossed Bessborough Street. I was close behind you when you got into your cab on Vauxhall Bridge Road, and could see the tiny run in your right leg. You might want to check that when you get a moment.'

Her face went red. Harry wasn't sure if it was through the obvious lapses in security, or because of the fault in her tights. One thing he would lay money on was that her minder would shortly be joining the ranks of the jobless. But he was past caring how she felt; she, like Paulton and Bellingham, had been arrogant enough to believe themselves fireproof, to the degree that they thought men like Harry Tate were toothless.

'I think I get the picture,' she said quietly, and looked at the security guard behind Harry. A toss of her head and he left.

Harry doubted he would be very far away, though. Rudmann and her kind did not lose their badges of office too easily, and a minder was one of the most visible and potent imaginable.

'All right,' she said when the door had closed. 'What do you want?'

'You know what I want. If you looked at the files on the stick and checked my personnel records, you'll know.'

'I looked at them, Mr Tate.' Rudmann smoothed her skirt over her knee. 'What I don't know is why you have come to me . . . or what you claim to have found.'

'I've just returned from a foreign station set up by Sir Anthony Bellingham of MI6 and George Paulton of MI5. It was conceived as a hole-in-the-wall base to use as a training area. At least, that's their story. In fact, it was where they sent employees who had defaulted in some way; employees who might prove an embarrassment if their mistakes ever went public.'

'I see.'

'If you do, you're quick off the mark. I was the most recent posting, and I was sent out there while the dust died down after the shooting of the two kids and the armed copper in Essex. They did it to keep me away from the press.'

'I'm sure you're mistaken.' By the way Rudmann avoided meeting his eye, Harry knew she was lying. 'Setting up a training base is hardly a criminal offence, is it?'

'Maybe not. But queuing up security service defaulters to act as bait for trainee operatives is one thing; quietly disposing of anyone they saw as a threat, or any officers who threatened to blow the lid on underground or black operations is something else.'

Rudmann blinked. 'That's an outrageous suggestion.'

Harry ignored her. 'The first posting was an MI5 analyst named Gordon Brasher. He was sent home after a while and died of a drugs overdose.'

Rudmann's expression suggested scepticism. He ploughed on. 'The next was a fast-track MI6 recruit named Jimmy Gulliver. He decided he didn't want to stay in the middle of nowhere, shovelling forms and leaflets, so he left and came back under his own steam. I believe Gulliver was dangerous because he knew far more than anyone in his position had a right to know. Someone overestimated his capabilities, promoted him up the chain until he cracked, then panicked and sent him somewhere where he couldn't do any harm. He decided to jump ship and head for home, which made him a loose cannon. He knew things and there was a danger he might talk about Red Station. I mean, it hardly looks good, does it, squirrelling people away in the middle of nowhere on the public budget just to keep them quiet?'

'Can you substantiate these claims?' Rudmann's look was wary.

'Only one. Apart from a conscience, Gulliver suffered from chronic vertigo. I'm sure if you check his training record, you'll find he was graded unfit for active work; he got dizzy standing on tiptoe. But someone decided his brain could be useful as long as they didn't ask him to climb anything higher than a career ladder.'

'You've lost me. What has his condition got to do with this?'

'Gulliver disappeared on his way back. He never made an agreed rendezvous. Yet his file was closed and he was reported killed in a climbing accident. Question one: with his fear of heights and after months of being posted to Red Station, when all he wanted to do was get back to Vauxhall Cross, would he have really gone climbing? I doubt it. Question two: how did they know to close his file? Files only get closed on death.'

'I see.' Rudmann looked at a point above his head for a moment, then said, 'How do you know about his medical background?'

'Stuart Mace told me. Mace knew of his problem, had done so since he was a kid.'

'How?'

'Jimmy Gulliver was his nephew.'

Her mouth opened but she said nothing.

Harry waited, trying to gauge how much was play-acting, how much was genuine.

'Carry on.'

'Mace told me that Gulliver also had a morbid fear of flying, so he chose to drive back to the UK. He hired a car locally

with an agreement to drop it off in Calais. Neither Gulliver
nor the car ever arrived.'

She tapped a glossy fingernail on the desk. 'You mentioned
trainees were used. What was their function?'

'They were rotating four-man teams Paulton had in place
watching the members of Red Station around the clock, to
see that nobody took off or misbehaved. They were nicknamed
the Clones by Red Station staff and their job was strictly
watch-and-report.'

'That's good security, surely, given the circumstances?'

'Says you. The Clones were changed every few weeks as
part of a training schedule. That way they didn't get close to
Red Station and none of the staff knew they were British,
much less part of an official operation.' He shifted in his chair,
and wondered what activity was going on in the corridor
outside Rudmann's door. Too late now, whatever it was. 'But
Sir Anthony Bellingham also had a team,' he continued. 'They
were called the Hit. They had a different agenda. I should say
have, because I don't know if they still exist.'

'What do they do?'

'They kill people.'

SIXTY-NINE

Marcella Rudmann's face went pale beneath her make-up.
'That's rubbish—!'

'No. It's not. They deal with terrorists and war criminals and people who talk too much . . . like journalists and
disenchanted security officers. Do you know what wet work is?'

'Yes, but our government—'

'Doesn't employ such people? That's bullshit and you know
it. Anyway, as soon as the Russians marched across the border,
the Clones were ordered to leave.'

Rudmann said nothing, but he could tell by her stillness
that he had finally got her full attention. She hadn't even
queried the mention of Russians.

Because she knew where Red Station was.

He told her, anyway, just for the record. 'Red Station is in

Georgia, just south of the border with Ossetia. Remote and off the beaten track; ideal for keeping people out of the public eye. It's now in what we call a hot zone.'

By Rudmann's expression, Harry guessed she was reviewing recent events and coming to grips with what he had told her. She shook her head. 'I'll need verification of the location later. Please continue.'

'Not all of the Clones made it out. One of them got left behind.'

'What happened?'

'He was murdered. Shot in the head. Then the Hit came in. Bellingham and Paulton must have decided that with the Russians on the way, it would be an ideal moment to get rid of all links to Red Station and forget we ever existed. If anyone had asked questions, they'd have blamed Russian forces or the local militia.'

'This is speculation,' said Rudmann quietly. 'Do you have a grain of proof to substantiate these claims?'

'Proof that there was such a place as Red Station? Of course. And proof of the personnel. You've already seen the copy files off the data stick; they came directly from a remote server here in London. One of those messages is from Mace, reporting the Clone's murder.'

'I see.'

'It's not a direct link to Vauxhall Cross or Thames House; they were too clever for that. But it will be to Bellingham. He was the only one with access. The server's code-name is Clarion. Bellingham's mistake was checking it on a regular basis to monitor messages. We've got his trail mapped out for every call he made; times, dates and names.'

'We? Who else is involved?'

Harry shook his head. 'Sorry. That's confidential.'

She considered that for a moment. 'You say a member of the observation team – these Clones? – was killed. I need his name.'

'Stanbridge. Ex-army. I don't know his first name. You can cross-check with service records for Kosovo; he served there with the UN.'

Rudmann made a brief note, although Harry was sure their conversation was being recorded.

'If I read between the lines, you seem to think it was this

second team – the Hit – which was responsible. Why would they do that . . . kill one of their own?'

They had finally reached the tricky part. Did he tell Rudmann that it was most likely Clare Jardine who had killed Stanbridge, or allow the blame to settle on a dead killer? He couldn't prove it either way with absolute certainty, so what did it matter?

'If it was the Hit who killed him, there were only two reasons I can think of: they found out that Stanbridge had talked to me, or Stanbridge recognized Latham and knew what his function was. In actual fact, Latham *was* the Hit. This was a job they couldn't trust to more than one man. In Latham's narrow world, Stanbridge was a liability to get rid of.'

'And you're suggesting that Latham was after you?'

'Not just me; all of us. We were lucky to get away.' Those of us who did, he thought. She could find out about Mace's death herself, if she wanted.

'I see. Where is Latham now?'

'He ran into some trouble.'

'That doesn't answer my question.'

'So sue me.'

'You killed him.' It was a statement.

'Don't be silly.'

'Very well.' She brushed at her hair, a small charm bracelet tingling on her wrist. 'I'll have to verify what you've told me, of course. It might take some time.'

He stared at her. 'Is that all? You'll look into it?'

'Is there something else?' For a second, she looked faintly alarmed, and Harry wondered how closely aware she had been of the decisions made by Bellingham and Paulton over the past few months. The civil service and government was a notoriously small community and as incestuous as a bunch of alley cats. It was inconceivable that she or some of her colleagues hadn't been at least partly aware that something was going on in the woodpile. But suspicions didn't amount to definite knowledge. And he couldn't go down the route of divisive thinking, he reminded himself. He had to trust someone, at least part of the way, otherwise he'd go quietly mad.

'Is something going to be done about them?' he demanded

quietly. 'About what happened . . . setting up Red Station . . . the
murder of Brasher and Gulliver?' He suddenly found an impulse
to shout this bloody woman out of her immaculately coiffed and
manicured air of control. Instead he kept his voice even.

She nodded slowly. 'It's in hand. That's all you need to
know.' She reached out and pressed a button on the telephone
console. The door opened and the security guard stepped in.

Harry stayed where he was. 'There's also the shooting,' he
said, 'for which I was sent out there.'

Rudmann nodded at the security guard, and he retreated
and closed the door.

'That is still under investigation. What of it?'

Harry told her what Maloney had discovered about the over-
flight photos and the Land Rover; how the shooting of the
man, at least, might not be as innocent or as accidental as it
had seemed. Rudmann made more notes on a pad.

'I'm not saying it wasn't a disaster,' he finished quietly. 'It
shouldn't have happened and those people shouldn't have died.
But neither was it the simple lash-up that everyone assumes.
Cuts were made to manpower on economic grounds and
because the Prime Minister was due to visit Stansted.'

'I'm not sure that has any relevance.' She dropped into
denial mode, the government's default position.

'But the PM was at Stansted the next day?'

Hesitation. 'Yes.'

'You know that? Or you checked?' She wouldn't know all
his engagements.

'I checked.'

'Why?'

Rudmann looked uncomfortable at the probing, but couldn't
avoid the question.

'You had doubts,' said Harry. 'Didn't you?'

'Some, yes.'

'Pity you didn't ask more questions, then,' Harry retorted
bluntly. 'You should have asked about Red Station, too. It
might have saved some lives.'

She showed no emotion, but said, 'We will be reviewing
all the facts, I promise.'

It seemed to be the best answer he was going to get, and
he decided not to outstay his welcome. He reached the door
and turned to look at Rudmann. She was watching him, hands

folded on the desk before her, a perfect mandarin, unemotional, impassive.

He wondered if coming here had been a mistake.

'This won't go away,' he told her. 'It will come out . . . who set it up, who knew about it. People like Bellingham, they'll talk. You can't sweep it under the carpet.'

Rudmann returned his stare. 'What do you want, Mr Tate?'

'Me? I want my life back. Simple as that. Not too much to ask, is it?'

SEVENTY

M arcella Rudmann sat and waited for confirmation from the front desk that Harry Tate had left the building. When the call came, the security man asked if she wanted Tate followed.

'Don't bother,' she said. 'He'll spot whoever you send after him.'

She cut the connection and made two calls, then walked along the corridor to a small office at the end. It was windowless, drab and overheated, and contained a single desk holding an array of audio equipment. A man in shirtsleeves sat waiting.

He stood up when she entered. His name was Everett and he was a senior officer in Home Office Security and had Rudmann's full confidence.

'Did you get all that?' she asked.

Everett nodded. 'Nice and clear.' He picked up his jacket from the back of the chair. 'I'll get it transcribed right away.' He paused. 'Tate's a bit of a time-bomb, isn't he? Is it true what he said – about your front door?'

'Yes.' She shook her head. 'I'll arrange it today. I'm more concerned about what he claims about Red Station. If it's true, it's appalling.' She looked at her hands as if wanting to wash them clean, and paced across the office and back. Everett waited for her to speak. 'I've just had confirmation that George Paulton has disappeared,' she said finally. 'I always had my doubts about that man. And the police have now identified the man they believe was responsible for Shaun Whelan's death. It wasn't a mugging. The killer is a subcontractor for the security services.'

'Ouch.' Everett pulled a face. 'And Paulton was involved.'

'I'm certain of it.'

Everett's eyebrows rose. 'I'll talk to the Met. Not that I expect they'll find anything; if Paulton's gone, he'll have covered his tracks.' He hesitated. 'It leaves Sir Anthony Bellingham rather exposed, doesn't it?'

Rudmann nodded. She had reached the same conclusion. Which was why the other call she had made before leaving her office had been to the deputy PM.

His question had been simple and to the point. Two very senior security officers had gone stratospherically beyond their brief. What was she going to do about it?

SEVENTY-ONE

Harry leaned on the wall overlooking the Thames and watched a plank floating downriver. It swirled almost majestically, flashing bright against the grey wash, then was gone, consumed by the fierce undercurrent.

A bit like me, he reflected, that plank. Thick, weather-worn and likely to be dragged under when not expecting it.

He looked to his left and saw a familiar face strolling along the riverside walkway. He cut a smart figure, an unhurried, well-fed man in an expensive suit; an anachronism compared with the fleeting, toned and anxious office workers hurrying by elsewhere.

Sir Anthony Bellingham. It had to be.

Behind Bellingham, a tall man in a dark suit wandered along at the same pace, eyes on the road, the walkway and the river. Bellingham's bodyguard.

Harry waited. There was plenty of time. He'd come a long way for this. He glanced at the nearest camera focussed on the length of the riverside walkway. It would have a clear view of everyone passing by; of their faces, clothes, what they

carried and even their conversation if the operators had a good
lip-reader handy.

Across the river were more cameras. Most would be concentrated on the several hundred square metres surrounding the
stone building of the MI5 complex, known as Thames House.
One or two might be temporarily offline; according to Rik
Ferris, the number of cameras inoperative in London at any
one time was staggering. Maintenance cuts, mostly, aided by
the occasional brick lobbed by a disgruntled resident or an
aggrieved motorist.

As if on cue, Rik Ferris appeared in the background
beyond Bellingham. He was dressed in a tracksuit and
trainers, and holding a drinks bottle. He jogged easily, a
spring in his step, covering the ground with ease. He looked
fit and Harry was surprised; a few good nights' sleep had
worked wonders.

Bellingham paused to stare across the river and took a cigar
from his top pocket. He carefully unwrapped it, placing the
cellophane film in his pocket, then reached for a lighter. It
flashed as he stroked it with his thumb.

Probably gold and heavy, thought Harry. Not designed to
impress, though; just the way the man was. The flame flared,
followed by a puff of grey smoke which hung momentarily
around the spy chief's head before swirling and disappearing
on the river breeze.

Harry had rehearsed this moment in his head several times.
With Paulton gone, Bellingham must have considered himself
safe. He could go about his daily business until it was time for
him to go, a faithful and loyal servant of her majesty's civil
service. Then he could slide into a comfortable, index-linked
retirement and disappear off the face of a planet he had only
ever served beneath the surface.

All would be well with the world.

Not a chance, Harry had decided. Not a bloody chance. He
had weighed the pros and cons, looked at what kind of a life
awaited him if he did what was expected of him. He, too,
could move back into the fold, all sins forgiven, the records
expunged. Say no more, all done and dusted. He could see
out his service until retirement called.

Only it wouldn't be quite as comfortable as anyone imagined. It would carry, for a start, the images of that night in

Essex, when bad decisions had left three people dead – one of them a good policeman, one an innocent girl.

Not all the bad decisions were his, he knew that; cutting the manpower at a crucial moment was the most damaging, leaving him badly outgunned. But he still hadn't forgotten his own moment of inaction, that split-second of hesitation just before the gunman on the boat had opened fire. Even though Maloney had confirmed a few days ago in a pub off the Charing Cross Road that a few seconds would have made no difference whatsoever, it was still with him.

He took a deep breath and felt the weight of the gun in his pocket. He'd sliced a hole in the fabric and fitted a special holster – more of a sack, really – so that the gun barrel, with its suppressor, wouldn't snag.

Pulling it out would take half a second. Levelling it would take even less, and less still to pull the trigger. A spit of sound, the explosion of gasses muffled to little more than a cough by the suppressor, and even that would be lost in the noise from the traffic and the rush of the river. Then he'd be gone, walking away as casually as he could manage. In minutes he could be in Waterloo Station, shrouded by crowds of commuters.

But Bellingham wouldn't be going anywhere.

He had tried to argue Rik Ferris out of his part in what was to follow, but to no avail. Bill Maloney had insisted on running interference, too. If anyone saw what happened, and attempted to interfere, they would be mugged by a hooded figure in a tracksuit or a heavily-built lout in jeans and a donkey jacket. Neither would be recognizable and neither would hang around afterwards to answer questions.

The worst of it was, in a way that made him wonder and smile, he knew both of them were relishing their part in it.

He walked towards Bellingham, keeping an eye on the bodyguard. The man was looking down at the water. Harry took a deep breath, trying to walk softly, taking the weight off his heels, the way they'd trained him. Trouble was, he sounded like one of the guardsman outside Buckingham Palace, his footsteps echoing off the walls like gunshots.

Bellingham looked up as Harry approached, a dribble of smoke coming from his lips. If he had concerns about his personal security, he was careful not to show it, eyes steady.

'You want something?' He sounded belligerent, a fact reflected in his stance. Up close, he smelled of soap and cigar smoke.

'You know who I am?' Harry knew he'd been recognized. The MI6 director must have a good memory. Or maybe he'd been checking through MI5 personnel records to see who else he could despatch to the back of beyond for 'training' purposes.

Then it hit him: he had met Bellingham before.

He was the man with Paulton when he'd had his debrief prior to leaving for Red Station. At the time, he had said nothing, remaining in the background, a suited figure with a bland face. Paulton had done all the talking.

The MI6 man nodded. 'Tate, isn't it? What are you doing here?'

Harry paused, surprised by Bellingham's easy reaction, his apparent self-control. He'd expected to have to introduce himself at least. But maybe this proved just how hands-on Bellingham was in the Red Station set-up, and how well he knew its personnel.

'Where did you expect me to be? In a Russian lock-up? Or disposed of in a quiet gully by the Hit?'

'The what? Hit? No idea what you're talking about.' Bellingham glanced at his cigar, flicked some ash off the end. Harry noted that he also took the opportunity to check for his bodyguard.

'You should know. You sent them after us. His name was Latham.'

'Really? Why would I do that?'

'You know why.' Harry breathed easily. Bellingham was playing it just the way he'd expected: deny and counter-attack. 'They were supposed to kill us; Mace, Ferris, Clare Jardine, Fitzgerald and me. The members of Red Station. With the Russians coming over the border, you and Paulton decided it would be a good idea to clear the decks. After all, who else would anyone blame?' He waited, but there was no reaction. He added, 'Did Latham arrange for Gordon Brasher to take an overdose? And for Jimmy Gulliver to have a climbing accident?'

'You're talking rubbish, man. Who the hell are – Brasher, was it? – and Gulliver? I suggest you get help. In fact, I'll get Paulton to arrange it.' Bellingham began to turn away. 'Now, if you'll excuse me—'

'Don't you want to know about Latham?'

Bellingham's face barely registered a flicker. But it was enough to betray him.

'He's dead.'

SEVENTY-TWO

Bellingham's mouth dropped open. He recovered quickly, but Harry knew he'd finally hit home.

'We buried him face down in a ditch. It seemed a fitting end.'

Bellingham stepped back. 'I don't know what you mean. I don't know anyone called Latham. What do you want from me?' A slight tic had started up under his left eye.

'You. We want you. And Paulton. Although somehow I doubt we'll get to him. He seems to have done a runner. But you'll do for starters.'

'We?' The cigar was forgotten now. Bellingham was beginning to look trapped. He looked beyond Harry, sweeping the area with a practised eye.

'Enough of us to bury you.' Harry felt the response was over-dramatic, but it seemed appropriate. Bellingham and Paulton had buried him and the others in Red Station; it seemed right to think of retribution in the same terms.

'Don't flatter yourselves – any of you.' Bellingham tossed the cigar into the river and thrust his hand in his pocket. 'Who the hell would believe you?'

For a second, Harry thought he might be going for a weapon, and got ready to draw the gun in his pocket. It would probably be the last thing he ever did, but he was damned if this man was going to take him down. Then he realized Bellingham would be carrying a panic button. Press once in case of threats from foreign agents or pissed-off security officers. Bellingham wasn't the gun type; he employed others to do his shooting for him.

He reckoned on having just a few minutes before the summons brought a response. 'I've spoken to Marcella

Rudmann,' Harry said. 'I think she'll be looking to have a chat sometime. She's particularly interested in Clarion.'

'Don't be pathetic.' Bellingham's voice dripped contempt, his mouth contorted, but he looked haunted at the mention of his server link. 'You think you can come back here and take *me* on? You're deluded, all of you, like that pathetic drunk, Mace. I suppose he's hiding somewhere, afraid to come out and face the world without a stiff drink inside him?'

'He's alive, if that's what you mean.' The lie came easily. 'And ready to talk.'

'Then he'll be arrested,' Bellingham replied. 'As will you. Your friends too. Is Jardine one of them?'

Another name, another point of reference. It confirmed that Bellingham knew who was in Red Station. By itself it might not be enough, but it added background colour for any subsequent enquiry.

'Yes, she's out there,' he said. 'I'd watch your back, if I were you. You made her some promises then let her down. She's unlikely to forgive you for that.'

Bellingham's eye gave a twitch, and he struggled to hold his gaze on Harry's face. He said acidly, 'We'll see. You'll all serve time in the darkest hole I can find. Believe me, you have no idea what being buried really means!'

A touch of spittle from Bellingham's mouth landed on Harry's cheek. He gripped the gun harder and wondered what it would be like to take it out and deliver his own brand of justice on behalf of those Bellingham had consigned to oblivion. The man didn't have the slightest sense of remorse or fear, even when faced by someone who could bring him down.

Bellingham turned and walked away, his coat tails flapping around him, his head swivelling as he looked for his bodyguard.

But the tall man had disappeared.

SEVENTY-THREE

Harry checked the walkway in both directions. *What the hell was happening?*

The nearest figure ahead of Bellingham was an old

lady with a dog, its nose buried in a discarded fast-food carton. Bellingham *always* walked down here, Maloney had told him, and always accompanied by his minder. Two hundred yards from the bridge down and two hundred back, without fail. Such a predictable pattern was almost suicidal for a man in his position, but nobody had seen fit to get him to change it.

On the other hand, nobody had tried to kill him, either.

So far.

Judging by his stance and the urgency with which he was moving, Bellingham had only just realized that he was without protection. And he didn't like it.

Harry set off after him.

He didn't understand the inconsistency with the bodyguard. It was standard procedure that the principal was never out of his protection officer's sight. A decent distance might be observed for confidential discussions, but that was all.

Now the game had changed completely.

As he increased his pace, he sensed another figure moving up into his field of vision. He relaxed. It was a woman in a running suit and hooded top, jogging easily along by the inner wall, head down. She had an MP3 player strapped to her upper arm, the wire curling up under the hood, and was fiddling with the player's retaining strap while keeping up a steady pace. She was thirty yards away from Bellingham and posed no threat.

Harry concentrated on walking as fast as he dared without attracting attention. Maybe he should have got himself a running suit. Now that *would* have raised a few eyebrows.

The woman runner passed Bellingham without a glance. Bellingham turned his head, eyeing the woman's trim buttocks. She was twenty yards ahead of him and close to a concrete bench when she appeared to stumble. She threw out one arm, her pace broken, and something fell to the ground. Small, rectangular and white: the MP3 player. There was a faint clatter as it hit the ground and shattered, bits of plastic pinging into the air. Harry heard her cry of dismay as she stooped too late to catch it.

Bellingham was closer than anyone. His body language betrayed hesitation, then he stepped forward to help, his proximity overriding any concern at the disappearance of his bodyguard. He raised a hand to touch the woman's arm, his rich voice floating back to Harry's ears, solicitous and soothing.

It was all done very smoothly. One second they were standing alongside the bench, then the woman sat down, the pieces of her player on the ground around her feet, her hand to her face.

Bellingham sat alongside her, one hand reaching out to pat her arm, then dropping to pat her knee. *Never mind*, the gesture implied. *It could have happened to anyone.*

The woman didn't look up, didn't object to the hand on her leg. Instead, she rubbed her arm where the MP3's retaining strap was still in place. When she brought her hand away, she was holding something.

She reached down to Bellingham's thigh, and daylight flashed on shiny metal.

'*No!*' Harry swore and broke into a run.

In a continuous movement, the woman reached up and drew her hand across Bellingham's front, just beneath his chin. It might have been a caress, the intimate touch of a lover, almost smooth and gentle. But the way Bellingham's head went back indicated it was anything but.

By the time Harry reached the bench, breathing hard, the woman was eighty yards away and covering the ground in a floating, easy run. Bellingham was still sitting as if stunned.

'Jesus, what happened?' Rik Ferris raced up to join Harry, and they stood and stared at the MI6 director. He was bleeding profusely, his body slumped and held in place only by its own downward weight. His thighs and chest were a mess of red, and spurts of blood were pulsating past the layers of fat around his collar and dripping on to the paving slabs beneath.

Clare Jardine happened, thought Harry. Her and her evil bloody powder compact, the blade curved and razor sharp, like a pruning knife. Lethal in the hands of an expert. But he didn't say anything. He had no proof. In any case, there was no point. Not now.

Instead, he said, 'Femoral artery and throat. A professional kill.' He pulled out his mobile – actually, Stanbridge's mobile, which he'd never got rid of – and looked at the screen. The signal was strong down here; he'd get a 999, no problem. They'd be here in seconds, all bells and whistles. Hell, St Thomas's hospital was a spit away; they'd almost be able to see the body from the front door.

He turned and threw the mobile over the wall into the river. 'Bloody things. Never work when you need them.'

'What?' Rik, who knew about communications and signals, especially in London, looked towards the river in confusion. 'But that—'

'Wasn't working.' Harry looked at him, daring him to argue. It was better than looking at Bellingham. 'Trust me. By the time the medics get here, he'll be dead. He's nearly gone already.'

'I've got a phone.' Rik started to reach for it.

'Great. Phone them. And while you're about it, you can explain what you were doing here while a senior MI6 officer was getting his throat cut. A man who, just a couple of days ago, ordered your execution.' Harry walked away without looking back. A gaggle of early sightseers was approaching a hundred yards away, festooned with cameras and curiosity. 'Don't take too long to decide,' he called back. 'The heavies will be along soon and looking for anyone with a grudge.'

SEVENTY-FOUR

'You were right,' said Rik, staring out across Hyde Park. It was a week later and they had met at Harry's suggestion. Somewhere open and public, he'd said. They had been keeping their heads down ever since Bellingham's death.

'How so?' said Harry. He peered into a bag of peanuts and flexed his fingers before selecting one. His injury was now down to a dull ache, and lifting much easier than a few days ago.

'Down by the river. After you left, a couple of blokes turned up in a black car. Some sort of security, I reckon. They took a look, called an ambulance and carted Bellingham away. He must have been dead – they covered his face.' Rik rubbed his fingers across a leather satchel on his knee.

'Well, that suits everyone, doesn't it? He'll get an honourable mention in despatches, good and faithful servant, blah, blah, blah. End of story.'

'That's a bit cold, isn't it?'

'It's reality. He went too far, stepped over the line; him and Paulton, both. If it ever got out, it would have gone international. Thing like that, the Russians and Georgians would have had no choice but to raise hell. We were on their turf, along with the Clones and a government hit-man.'

Rik looked surprised. 'You make it sound like his death was . . . sanctioned.'

'I doubt that. I think the bodyguard disappearing was a signal to Bellingham that he was isolated. On his own. He'd have been picked up – that's probably what the two men you saw were there for – and made to resign. Only he didn't get the opportunity.'

A woman jogger was running under a line of trees. She moved confidently, flowing in an easy gait across the grass towards them. Harry felt a jolt in his gut. She reminded him of someone.

'It was her, wasn't it, who did Bellingham?' said Rik sombrely, also watching the woman. 'Clare, I mean.'

'Forget it. If it was, she's gone. It's done and dusted.'

'Do you think we'll see her again?'

'Jesus, I hope not.' Harry had certain views on the kind of psyche it took to use a knife on someone, especially the way it had been done on Bellingham. If he ever did see her again, he hoped he was armed and ready to shoot. He changed the subject. 'Did you get your clearance?' He was referring to the official security clearance they had both been granted in the wake of Bellingham's death and the investigation into Red Station. It was a token forgiveness only, and did not include re-employment. But it was better than nothing. It offered a severance payment in lieu of all claims, which was government-speak for going away and developing total amnesia. He'd also had a call from Bill Maloney. The man killed with the girl in Essex had been identified as Romanian, with known drugs trafficking connections across Europe. And the Land Rover had contained a handgun, two false passports and a secret compartment under the floor panels.

'Yeah. You?'

'Yes. How's your mum?'

'She's fine. Pleased I'm back, even if I haven't got a job.' He grinned, and for the first time since Harry had known him, looked thoroughly relaxed.

Harry knew how he felt. Jean had expressed similar delight, albeit thankfully of a far less motherly nature, when he'd called the previous evening. Learning that he wasn't going to be hung out to dry and consigned to hard labour for thirty years had clearly pleased her. The pleasure had lasted into the small hours, and he had left her flat just two hours ago with a smile on his face and a spring in his step.

They sat in silence for a few minutes, enjoying the freedom. Then Harry said, 'I've been offered some private security work. Good pay and conditions. Freelance. It's in the area of internet fraud.'

It hadn't sounded quite his thing, but he was too young to retire and too old to sign on for Iraq as a 'consultant' – even if he'd wanted to. And it would do to keep him going. He had some ghosts to lay along the way, and that would take time, after everything that had happened. One ghost in particular.

Then Rik surprised him. 'You're going after Paulton,' he murmured. 'Don't deny it.'

'Maybe.' He had little to go on, save some knowledge of the man. But knowledge was power and eventually, people who ran usually surfaced somewhere they knew well; somewhere they felt secure.

All he had to do was unpick Paulton's past life and find that place.

'Hey, that's good,' said Rik enthusiastically. He shrugged. 'I wish I could help. I've got a few job feelers out myself. Something will turn up.'

Harry looked at Rik, nudging him with his elbow. 'I just offered you a job, you geek. I need someone I can trust. You do the IT, I'll do the legwork. You in?'

Rik looked stunned. 'Me?'

'You. Don't take too long or I'll go elsewhere.' He stood

up and looked at his watch. 'I know quite a few ex-security bods who'd jump at the chance—'

'I'm in!' Rik leapt to his feet and threw his satchel over his shoulder. 'When do I start?'

Harry was walking away. 'You already have,' he called back. 'I'll buy the coffee, you fire up the laptop.'